Welcome to THE WHEEL OF TIME

Praise for:

From the Two Rivers and *To the Blight*
Parts One and Two of
The Eye of the World

VOYA Outstanding Books of the Year

American Library Association
Best Book for Young Adults

"A major piece of fantasy."   *—Chicago Sun-Times*

"This richly detailed fantasy presents a fully realized complex adventure which will appeal to fans of classic quests. Recommended."   *—Library Journal*

"This exciting fantasy adventure tale chronicles the coming of age of Rand. Jordan's fantasy world is well presented, the characterizations are precise, and the action is fast paced with a great many hairbreadth escapes."   *—KLIATT*

"An excitiing story. The reader is drawn in early and kept there until the last page. There is adventure and mystery and dark things that move in the night—a combination of Robin Hood and Stephen King that is hard to resist."
—Milwaukee Sentinel

"A powerful novel. A fantasy epic. As the novel progresses, the young heros develop new talents, a different one for each."   *—Locus*

THE WHEEL OF TIME
by Robert Jordan

From the Two Rivers

Part One of
The Eye of the World

The Beginning of
The
Wheel
of Time

Robert Jordan

STARSCAPE

A TOM DOHERTY ASSOCIATES BOOK
NEW YORK

This is a work of fiction. All the characters and events portrayed in this novel are either fictitious or are used fictitiously.

FROM THE TWO RIVERS: The Eye of the World, Part 1

Copyright © 1990 by Robert Jordan
Introductory material and Glossary Copyright © 2002 by Bandersnatch Group, Inc.

Maps by Elissa Mitchell
Interior illustrations used with permission by Wizards of the Coast, Inc.
Copyright © 2001 Wizards of the Coast
Additional interior illustrations by Sally Wern Comport
Interior ornament art by Matthew C. Nielson
Cover art by Charles Keegan

A Starscape Book
Published by Tom Doherty Associates, LLC
175 Fifth Avenue
New York, NY 10010

www.starscapebooks.com

First edition: January 2002

ISBN 0-765-34184-0

Printed in the United States of America

0 9 8 7 6 5 4 3 2 1

To Harriet
Heart of my heart,
Light of my life,
Forever.

Contents

x   *Contents*

EARLIER

Ravens

This far below Emond's Field, halfway to the Waterwood, trees lined the banks of the Winespring Water. Mostly willows, their leafy branches made a shady canopy over the water near the bank. Summer was not far off, and the sun was climbing toward midday, yet here in the shadows a soft breeze made Egwene's sweat feel cool on her skin. Tying the skirts of her brown wool dress up above her knees, she waded a little way into the river to fill her wooden bucket. The boys just waded in, not caring whether their snug breeches got wet. Some of the girls and boys filling buckets laughed and used their wooden dippers to fling water at one another, but Egwene settled for enjoying the stir of the current on her bare legs, and her toes wriggling on the sandy bottom as she climbed back out. She was not here to play. At nine, she was carrying water for the first time, but she was going to be the best water-carrier ever.

Pausing on the bank, she set down her bucket to unfasten her skirts and let them fall to her ankles. And to retie the dark green kerchief that gathered her hair at the nape of her neck. She wished she could cut it at her shoulders, or even shorter, like the boys. She would not need to have long hair for years yet, after all. Why did you have to keep doing something just because it had always been done that way? But she knew her mother, and she knew her hair was going to stay long.

Close to a hundred paces further down the river, men stood knee-deep in the water, washing the black-faced sheep that would later be sheared. They took great care getting the bleating animals into the river and back out safely. The Winespring Water did not flow as swiftly here as it did in Emond's Field, yet it was not slow. A sheep that got swept away might drown before it could struggle ashore.

A large raven flew across the river to perch high in the branches of a whitewood near where the men were washing sheep. Almost immediately a redcrest began diving at the raven, a flash of scarlet that chattered noisily. The redcrest must have a nest nearby. Instead of taking flight and maybe attacking the smaller bird, though, the raven just shuffled sideways on the limb to where a few smaller branches sheltered it a little. It peered down toward the working men.

Ravens sometimes bothered the sheep, but ignoring the redcrest's attempts to frighten it away was more than unusual. More than that, she had the strange feeling that the black bird was watching the men, not the sheep. Which was silly, except . . . . She had heard people say that ravens and crows were the Dark One's eyes. That thought made goosebumps break out all down her arms and even on her back. It *was* a silly idea. What would the Dark One want to see in the Two Rivers? Nothing ever happened in the Two Rivers.

"What are you up to, Egwene?" Kenley Ahan demanded, stopping beside her. "You can't play with the children today." Two years older than she, he carried himself very straight, stretching to seem taller than he was. This was his last year carrying water at the shearing, and he behaved as if that cloaked him with some sort of authority.

She gave him a level look, but it did not work as well as she hoped.

His square face twisted up in a frown. "If you're turning sick, go see the Wisdom. If not . . . well . . . get on about your work." With a quick nod, as if he had solved a problem, he hurried off making a great show of holding his bucket with one hand, well away from his side. *He won't keep that up long once he's out of my sight,* she thought sourly. She was going to have to work on that look. She had seen it work for older girls.

The dipper's handle slid on the rim of her bucket as she picked it up with both hands. It was heavy, and she was not big for her age, but she followed Kenley as quickly as she could. Not because of anything he had said, certainly. She *did* have work to do, and she *was* going to be the best water-carrier ever. Her face set with determination. The mulch of last year's leaves rustled under her feet as she walked through the river's shadowy fringe of trees, out into the sunlight. The heat was not too bad, but a few small white clouds high in the sky seemed to emphasize the brightness of the morning.

Widow Aynal's Meadow—it had been called that as long as anyone could remember, though no one knew which Aynal widow it had been named after—the tree-ringed meadow stood empty most of the year, but now people and sheep crowded the whole long length of it, a good many more sheep than people. Large stones stuck out of the ground here and there, a few almost as tall as a man, but they did not interfere with the activity in the meadow. Farmers came from all around Emond's Field for this, and village folk came out to help relatives. Everyone in the village had kith or kin of some sort on the farms. Shearing would be going on all across the Two Rivers, down at Deven Ride and up to Watch Hill. Not at Taren Ferry, of course. Many of the women wore shawls draped loosely over their arms and flowers in their hair, for the formality, and so did some of the older girls, though their hair was not in the long braid the women had. A few even wore dresses with embroidery around the neck, as if this really were a feastday. In contrast, most of the men and boys went coatless, and some even had their shirts unlaced. Egwene did not understand why they were allowed to do that. The women's work was no cooler than the men's.

Big, wooden-railed pens at the far end of the meadow held sheep already sheared, and others held those waiting to be washed, all watched by boys of twelve and up. The sheepdogs sprawled around the pens were no good for this work. Groups of those older boys were using wooden staffs to herd sheep to the river for washing, then to keep them from lying down and getting dirty again until they were dry for the men at this end of the meadow who were doing the shearing. Once the sheep were shorn, the boys herded them back to the pens while men carried the fleece to the slatted tables where women sorted the wool and folded it for baling. They kept a tally, and had to be careful that no one's wool was mixed with anyone else's. Along the trees to Egwene's left, other women were beginning to set out food for the midday meal on long trestle tables. If she was good enough at carrying water, maybe they would let her help with the food or the wool next year, instead of two years later. If she did the best job ever, no one would ever be able to call her a baby again.

She began making her way through the crowd, sometimes carrying the bucket in both hands, sometimes shifting it from one to the other, pausing whenever someone motioned for a dipper of water. Soon she began to perspire again, sweating dark patches on her woolen dress. Maybe the boys with their shirts unlaced were not just being foolish. She ignored the younger children, running around rolling hoops and tossing balls and playing keep-away.

There were only five times each year when so many gathered: at Bel Tine, which was past; at shearing; when the merchants came to buy the wool, still a month or more off; when the merchants came for the cured tabac, after Sunday; and at Foolday, in the fall. There were other feastdays, of course, but none where *everyone* got together. Her eyes kept moving, searching the crowd. Among all these people, it would be all too easy to walk up on one of her four sisters. She always avoided them as much as possible. Berowyn, the eldest, was worst. She had been widowed by the breakbone fever last fall and moved back home in the spring. It was hard not to feel for Berowyn, but she *fussed* so, wanting to dress Egwene and brush her hair. Sometimes she wept and told Egwene how lucky she felt that the fever had not taken her *baby* sister, too. Feeling for Berowyn would have been easier if Egwene could stop thinking that sometimes Berowyn saw her as the infant she had lost along with her husband. Maybe all the time. She was just watching for Berowyn. Or one of the other three. That was all.

Near the sheep-pens, she stopped to wipe the sweat from her forehead. Her bucket was lighter, now, and no trouble to hold with one hand. She eyed the nearest dog cautiously. Standing in front of one of the pens, it was a large animal with a close, curly gray coat and intelligent eyes that seemed to know she was no danger to the sheep. Still, it was very big, almost waist-high to a grown man. Mainly the dogs helped protect the flocks when they were in pasture, guarding against wolves and bears and the big mountain cats. She edged away from the dog. Three boys passed her, herding a few dozen sheep toward the river. All five or six years older than she, the boys barely gave her a glance, their full attention on the animals. The herding was easy enough—she could have done it, she was sure—but they had to make sure none of the sheep had a chance to crop grass. A sheep that ate before being sheared could get the gasping and die. A quick look around told her that none of the other boys in sight was anyone she wanted to speak to. Not that she was looking for a particular boy to speak to, of course. She was just looking. Anyway, her bucket would need refilling soon. It was time to start back toward the Winespring Water.

This time she decided to go by way of the row of trestle tables. The smells were tantalizing, as good as any feastday, everything from roast goose to honeycakes. The spicy aroma of the honeycakes filled her nose more than all the rest. Every woman who cooked would have done her very best for the shearing. As she made her way down the tables, she offered water to the women setting out food, but they just smiled at her and shook their heads. She kept on, though, and not just because of the smells. They had tea water boiling on fires behind the tables, but some of them might want cool water from the river. Well, not so cool, now, but still . . . .

Ahead of her Kenley was slouching along beside the tables, no longer trying for every inch of height. If anything, he seemed to be trying for shorter. He still carried his bucket in one hand, but from the way it swung, it must have been empty, so he could not be offering water to anyone. Egwene frowned. Furtive was the only word to describe him. Now, what was he . . . ? Abruptly his hand darted out and snatched a honeycake from the table. Egwene's mouth fell open indignantly. And he had the nerve to talk to her about children? He was as bad as Ewin Finngar!

Before Kenley could take a second step, Mistress Ayellin descended on him like a stooping falcon, seizing his ear with one hand and the honeycake with the other. They were her honeycakes. A slim woman with a thick gray braid that hung below her hips, Corin Ayellin baked the best sweets in Emond's Field. *Except for mother,* Egwene added loyally. But even her mother said Mistress Ayellin was better. With sweets, anyway. Mistress Ayellin handed out crusty cakes and slices of pie with a free hand, so long as it was not near mealtime or your mother had not asked her not to, but she could deal heavily with boys who tried to filch behind her back. Or with anyone else. Stealing, she called it, and Mistress Ayellin did not abide stealing. She still had Kenley by his ear and was shaking a finger at him, talking in a low voice. Kenley's face was all twisted up as if he was about cry, and he shrank in on himself till he appeared shorter than Egwene. She gave a satisfied nod. She did not think he would try to give orders to anyone any time soon.

She moved further from the tables as she walked on by Mistress Ayellin and Kenley, so no one would suspect *her* of trying to filch sweets. The thought had never entered her head. Not really, anyway, not so it counted.

Suddenly she leaned forward, peering between the people moving back and forth in front of her. Yes. That was Perrin Aybara, a stocky boy taller than most his age. And he was a friend of Rand. She darted through the crowd without noticing whether anyone motioned for water and did not stop until she was only a few paces from Perrin.

He was with his parents, and his mother had the baby, Paetram, on her hip, and little Deselle clinging to her skirt with one hand, though Perrin's little sister was looking around with interest at all the people and even sheep being herded past. Adora, his other sister, stood with her arms folded across her chest and a sullen expression that she was trying to hide from her mother. Adora would not have to carry water until next year, and she probably was anxious to be off playing with her friends. The last person in the little group was Master Luhhan. The tallest man in Emond's Field, with arms like treetrunks and a chest that strained his white shirt, he made Master Aybara look slight instead of just slender. He was talking with Mistress Aybara and Master Aybara both. That puzzled Egwene. Master Luhhan was the blacksmith in Emond's Field, but neither Master Aybara nor Mistress Aybara would bring the whole family to ask after smithing. He was on the Village Council, too, but the same thing applied. Besides, Mistress Aybara would no sooner open her mouth about Council business than Master Aybara would about Women's Circle business. Egwene might only be nine, but she knew that much. Whatever they were talking about, they were almost done, and that was good. She did not *care* what they were talking about.

"He's a good lad, Joslyn," Master Luhhan said. "A good lad, Con. He'll do just fine."

Mistress Aybara smiled fondly. Joslyn Aybara was a pretty woman, and when she smiled, it seemed the sun might hide its head in defeat. Perrin's father laughed softly and ruffled Perrin's curly hair. Perrin blushed very red and said nothing. But then, he was shy, and he seldom said very much.

"Make me fly, Perrin," Deselle said, lifting up her hands to him. "Make me fly."

Perrin barely waited to sketch a polite bow to the grownups before turning to take his sister's hands. They moved a few steps from the others, and then Perrin begin to spin around and around, faster and faster, until Deselle's feet left the ground. Round and round he spun her, higher and higher in great swoops, while she laughed and laughed in delight.

After a few minutes, Mistress Aybara said, "That's enough, Perrin. Put her down before she sicks up." But she said it kindly, with a smile.

Once Deselle's feet were back on the ground, she clung to one of Perrin's hands with both hers, staggering a little, and maybe not too far from sicking up. But she kept laughing and demanding he make her fly some more. Shaking his head, he bent to talk to her. He was always so serious. He did not laugh very often.

Abruptly Egwene realized that someone else was watching Perrin. Cilia Cole, a pink-cheeked girl a couple of years older than she, stood only a few feet away with a silly smile on her face, making calf eyes at him. All he needed to do was turn his head to *see* her! Egwene grimaced in disgust. *She* would never be fool enough to make big eyes at a boy like some kind of woolhead. Anyway, Perrin was not even a whole year older than Cilia. Three or four years older was best. Egwene's sisters might have no time to talk to her, but she listened to other girls old enough to know. Some said more, but most thought three or four. Perrin glanced toward Egwene and Cilia and went back to talking quietly to Deselle. Egwene shook her head. Maybe Cilia was a ninny, but he ought to at least *notice*.

Movement in the limbs of a big wateroak beyond Cilia caught her eye, and she gave a start. The raven was up there, and it still seemed to be watching. And there was a raven in that tall pine tree, too, and one in the next, and in that hickory, and . . . . Nine or ten ravens that she could see, and they all seemed to be watching. It had to be her imagination. Just her—.

"Why were you staring at him?"

Startled, Egwene jumped and spun around so fast that she banged herself on the knee with her bucket. A good thing it was nearly empty, or she could have hurt herself. She shifted her feet, wishing she could rub her knee. Adora stood looking up at her with a perplexed expression on her face, but she could not be more puzzled than Egwene.

"What are you talking about, Adora?"

"Perrin, of course. Why were you staring at him? Everybody says you'll marry Rand al'Thor. When you're older, I mean, and have your hair in a braid."

"What do you mean, *everybody* says?" Egwene said dangerously, but Adora just giggled. It was exasperating. Nothing was working the way it should today.

"Perrin *is* pretty, of course. At least, I've heard lots of girls say so. And lots of girls look at him, just like you and Cilia."

Egwene blinked and managed to put that last out of her head. She had not been looking at him anything at *all* the way Cilia had! But, Perrin, pretty? Perrin? She looked over her shoulder to see whether she could find pretty in him. He was gone! His father was still there, and his mother, with Paetram and Deselle, but Perrin was nowhere to be seen. Drat! She had meant to follow him.

"Aren't you lonely without your dolls, Adora?" she said sweetly. "I didn't think you ever left your house without at least two."

Adora's open-mouth stare of outrage was quite satisfying.

"Excuse me," Egwene said, brushing past her. "Some of us are old enough to have work to do." She managed not to limp as she made her way back to the river.

This time she did not pause to look at the men washing sheep, and she very carefully did not look for a raven. She did examine her knee, but it was not even bruised. Carrying her filled bucket back out to the meadow, she refused to limp. It had just been a little bump.

She kept watching cautiously for her sisters as she carried water, pausing only to let someone take the dipper. And for Perrin. Mat would be as good as Perrin, but she did not see him, either. Drat Adora! She had no right to say things like that!

Walking in among the tables where women were sorting the wool, Egwene came to a dead stop, staring at her youngest sister.

She froze, hoping Loise would look the other way, just for an instant. That was what she got for trying to watch for Perrin and Mat as well as her sisters. Loise was only fifteen, but she had a sour expression on her face and her hands on her hips as she confronted Dag Coplin. Egwene could never make herself call him Master Coplin except aloud, to be polite; her mother said you had to be polite, even to someone like Dag Coplin.

Dag was a wrinkled old man with gray hair that he did not wash very often. Or maybe not at all. The tag hanging from the table by a string was inked to match the ear-notches on his sheep. "That's good wool you're setting aside," he growled at Loise. "I won't be cheated on my clip, girl. Step aside and I'll show you what goes where my own self."

Loise did not move an inch. "Wool from bellies, hindquarters and tails has to be washed again, Master Coplin." She put just a bit of emphasis on 'Master.' She *was* feeling snippish. "You know as well as I, if the merchants find twice-washed wool in just one bale, everyone will get less for their clip. Maybe my father can explain it to you better than I can."

Dag drew in his chin and grumbled something under his breath. He knew better than to try this with Egwene's father.

"I'm sure my mother could explain it so you'd understand," Loise said relentlessly.

Dag's cheek twitched, and he put on a sickly grin. Muttering that he trusted Loise to do what was right, he backed away, then hurried off little short of running. He was not foolish enough to bring himself to the attention of the Women's Circle if he could help it. Loise watched him go with a definite look of satisfaction.

Egwene took the opportunity to dart away, breathing a sigh of relief when Loise did not shout after her. Loise might prefer sorting wool to helping with the cooking, but she would much rather be climbing trees or swimming in the Waterwood, even if most girls had abandoned that sort of thing by her age. And she would take her chore out on Egwene, given half a chance. Egwene would have liked to go swimming with her, but Loise plainly considered her company a nuisance, and Egwene was too proud to ask. She scowled. All of her sisters treated her like a baby. Even Alene, when Alene noticed her at all. Most of the time, Alene had her nose in a book, reading and re-reading their father's library. He had almost *forty* books! Egwene's favorite was *The*

Travels of Jain Farstrider. She dreamed of seeing all those strange lands he wrote about. But if she was reading a book and Alene wanted it, she always said it was much too 'complex' for Egwene and just took it! Drat all *four* of them!

She saw some of the water-carriers taking breaks to sit in the shade or trade jokes, but she kept moving, although her arms did ache. Egwene al'Vere was not going to slack off. She kept watching for her sisters, too. And for Perrin. And Mat. Drat Adora, anyway! Drat *all* of them!

She did pause when she neared the Wisdom. Doral Barran was the oldest woman in Emond's Field, maybe in the whole Two Rivers, white-haired and frail, but still clear-eyed and not stooped at all. The Wisdom's apprentice, Nynaeve, was on her knees with her back to Egwene, tending Bili Congar, wrapping a bandage around his leg. His breeches had been cut away short. Bili, sitting on a log, was another grownup who Egwene found it hard to show the proper respect. He was always doing silly things and getting himself hurt. He was the same age as Master Luhhan, but he looked at least ten years older, his face hollow-cheeked and his eyes sunken.

"You've played the fool often enough in the past, Bili Congar," Mistress Barran said sternly, "but drinking while handling wool shears is worse than playing the fool." Oddly, she was not looking down at him, but at Nynaeve.

"I only had a little ale, Wisdom," he whined. "Because of the heat. Just a swallow."

The Wisdom sniffed in disbelief, but she continued to watch Nynaeve like a hawk. That was surprising. Mistress Barran often praised Nynaeve publicly for being such a quick learner. She had apprenticed Nynaeve three years earlier, after her then-apprentice died of some sickness even Mistress Barran could not cure. Nynaeve had been a recent orphan, and a lot of people said the Wisdom should have sent her to her relatives in the country after her mother died, and taken on someone years older. Egwene's mother did not say so, but Egwene knew she thought it.

Nynaeve straightened on her knees, done with fastening the bandage, and gave a satisfied nod. And to Egwene's surprise, Mistress Barran knelt down and undid it again, even lifting the bread-poultice to peer at the gash in Bili's thigh before beginning to wrap the cloth back around his leg. She actually looked . . .

disappointed. But why? Nynaeve began fiddling with her braid, tugging at it the way she did when she was nervous, or trying to bring attention to the fact that she was a grown woman, now.

When is *she going to outgrow that?* Egwene thought. It was nearly a year since the Women's Circle had let Nynaeve braid her hair.

A flutter of motion in the air caught Egwene's eye, and she stared. More ravens dotted the trees around the meadow now. Dozens and dozens of them, and all watching. She knew they were. Not one made a try to steal anything from the tables of food. That was just unnatural. Come to think of it, the birds were not looking at the trestle tables at all. Or at the tables where women were working with the wool. They were watching the boys herding sheep. And the men shearing sheep and carrying wool. And the boys carrying water, too. Not the girls, or the women, just the men and boys. She would have bet on it, even if her mother did say she should not bet. She opened her mouth to ask the Wisdom what it meant.

"Don't you have work to do, Egwene?" Nynaeve said without turning around.

Egwene jumped in spite of herself. Nynaeve had been doing that ever since last fall, knowing that Egwene was there without looking, and Egwene wished she would stop.

Nynaeve turned her head then, and looked at her over one shoulder. It was a level look, the sort Egwene had been trying on Kenley. She did not have to hop for Nynaeve the way she would for the Wisdom. Nynaeve was just trying to make up for Mistress Barran doubting her work. Egwene thought about telling her that Mistress Ayellin wanted to talk to her about a pie. Studying Nynaeve's face, she decided that might not be a good notion. Anyway, she had been doing what she had vowed not to, slacking off, standing around watching Nynaeve and the Wisdom. Making as much of a curtsey as she could while holding her bucket—to the Wisdom, not Nynaeve—she turned away. She was not hopping, and not because Nynaeve looked at her. Certainly not. And not hurrying, either. Just walking—quickly—to get back to her work.

Still, she walked quickly enough that before she realized it, she was back among the tables where the women were working wool. And face to face across one of the tables with her sister Elisa.

Elisa was folding fleece for baling, and making a bad job of it. She seemed distracted, barely even noticing Egwene, and Egwene knew why. Elisa was eighteen, but her waist-length hair was still tied with a blue kerchief. Not that was she was thinking about getting married—most girls waited at least a few years—but she was a year older than Nynaeve. Elisa often worried aloud about why the Women's Circle still thought she was too young. It was hard not to feel sympathy. Especially since Egwene had been thinking about Elisa's predicament for weeks, now. Well, not about Elisa's problem, exactly, but it had set her thinking.

Off to one side of the tables, Calle Coplin was talking with some young men from the farms, giggling and twisting her skirts. She was always talking to some man or other, but she was *supposed* to be folding fleece. That was not why she caught Egwene's eye, though.

"Elisa, you shouldn't worry so," she said gently. "Maybe Berowyn and Alene got their hair braided at sixteen . . ." *Most girls did,* she thought. She was not *all* sympathy. Elisa had a habit of offering sayings. "The hour wasted won't be found again," or "A smile makes the work lighter," till your teeth started to ache from them. Egwene knew for a fact that a smile would not make her bucket lighter by one dipper-full. ". . . but Calle's twenty, with her nameday coming in a few months now. Her hair's not braided, and you don't see her moping."

Elisa's hands went still on the fleece on the table in front of her. For some reason, the women on either side of her put their hands over their mouths, trying to hide laughter. For some reason, Elisa's face turned bright red. Very bright red.

"Children should not . . ." Elisa spluttered. Her face might be burning like the sun, but for all her spluttering her voice was cold as mid-winter snow. "A child who talks when . . . . Children who . . . ." Jillie Lewin, a year younger than Elisa and her black hair in a thick braid that hung below her waist, sank to her knees, she was laughing into her hand so hard. "Go away, child!" Elisa snapped. "Grownups are trying to work here!"

With an indignant glare, Egwene turned and stalked away from the folding tables, the bucket thumping her leg at every step. Try to help someone, try to buck up her spirits, and see what you got? *I should have told her she* isn't *a grownup,* she thought

fiercely. *Not until the Circle lets her braid her hair, she isn't.*
That's what I should have said.

The fierce mood stayed with her until her bucket was empty
again, and when she filled it once more, she squared her shoulders. If you were going to do a thing, then you had to *do* it.
Heading straight for the sheep-pens, she walked as fast as she
could and ignored anyone who motioned for water. It was not
slacking off. The boys would need water, too.

At the pens, the dozen or so boys waiting to move sheep gave
her surprised looks when she offered the dipper, and some said
they could get water when they went to the river, but she kept
on. And she always asked the same question. "Have you seen
Perrin? Or Mat? Where can I find them?"

Some told her Perrin and Mat were herding sheep to the river,
and others that they had seen the pair of them watching sheep
that had already been shorn, but she did not mean to go chasing
off just to find them already gone. Finally, a big-eyed boy named
Wil al'Seen, from one of the farms south of Emond's Field, gave
her a suspicious look and said, "Why do you want them?" Some
girls said Wil was pretty, but Egwene thought his ears looked
funny.

She started to give him a level look, then thought better of it.
"I . . . need to ask them something," she said. It was only a small
lie. She really did hope one of them would lead her to some
answers. He said nothing for a long time, studying her, and she
waited. *Patience is always repaid,* Elisa often said. Too often.
She wished she could forget Elisa's sayings. She tried to forget.
But kicking Wil's shins would not get what she wanted from him.
Even if he did deserve it.

"They're over behind that far pen," he said finally, jerking his
head toward the east side of the meadow. "The one with the sheep
that have Paet al'Caar's ear-marks." The boys herding sheep had
to talk that way, even if it was not really proper, or no one would
know whether they were talking about Paet al'Caar's sheep or
Jac al'Caar's or sheep belonging to one of a dozen other al'Caars.
"They're just taking a rest, mind. Now, don't you go getting them
in hot water by telling anybody different."

"Thank you, Wil," she said, just to show that she could be
polite even to a woolhead. As if she would run carrying tales! He
looked startled, and she thought about kicking his shins anyway.

The large pen holding Paet al'Caar's shorn sheep was almost to the trees on the Waterwood side of the meadow. Master al'Caar's big black sheep-dog raised her head from where she was lying in front of the pen and watched Egwene approach for a moment before settling back down. Egwene eyed the sheep-dog warily. She did not like dogs very much, and they did not seem to care for her, either. The dog went out of her head completely, though, once she was close enough to see clearly. The split wooden railings of the pen gave little concealment, and she could see a group of boys behind the pen. She could not really make out who they were, though.

Setting her bucket down carefully, she walked along the side of the sheep-pen. Not sneaking. She just did not want to make too much noise, in case . . . . In case noise might startle the sheep; that was it. At the corner of the pen, she peeked around the cornerpost.

Perrin was there, and Mat Cauthon, just as Wil had said, and some other boys about the same age, all with their shirts unlaced and sweaty. There was Dav Ayellin and Lem Thane, Ban Crawe and Elam Dowtry. And Rand, a skinny boy, almost as tall as Perrin, with hands and feet that were too big for his size. He could always be found with Mat or Perrin sooner or later. Rand, who everybody said she would marry one day. They were talking and laughing and punching one another on the shoulder. Why did boys do that?

Glowering, she pulled back from the cornerpost and leaned back against the railings. One of the sheep inside the pen snuffled at her back, but she ignored it. She had heard women say that about her and Rand, but she had not known that *everybody* said it. Drat Elisa! If Elisa had not started sighing and moaning over her hair, Egwene would never have started thinking about husbands. She expected she would marry one day—most women in the Two Rivers did—but she was not like those scatterbrains she heard going on about how they could hardly wait. Most women waited at least a few years after their hair was braided, and she . . . She wanted to see those lands that Jain Farstrider had written about. How would a husband feel about that? About his wife going off to see strange lands. Nobody ever left the Two Rivers, as far as she knew.

I *will*, she vowed silently.

Even if she did marry, would Rand make a good husband? She was not sure what made a good husband. Someone like her father, brave and kind and wise. She thought Rand was kind. He had carved her a whistle once, and a horse, and he had given her an eagle's black-tipped feather when she said it was pretty, though she still suspected he had wanted to keep it for himself. And he watched his father's sheep in pasture, so he had to be brave. The sheep-dog would help, if wolves came, or a bear, but the boy watching had to be ready with his sling, or a bow if he was old enough. Only . . . . She saw him every time he and his father came in from their farm, but she did not really know him. She hardly knew anything *about* him. Now was as good a time as any to start learning. She eased back to the cornerpost and peeked around it again.

"I'd like to a be a king," Rand was saying. "That's what I'd like to be." He flourished his arm and made an awkward bow, laughing to show that he was joking. A good thing, too. Egwene grimaced. A king! She studied his face. No, he was not pretty. Well, perhaps he was. Maybe it did not matter. But it might be nice to have a husband she liked to look at. His eyes were blue. No, gray. They seemed to change while you watched. Nobody else in the Two Rivers had blue eyes. Sometimes his eyes looked sad. His mother had died when he was little, and Egwene thought he envied boys who had mothers. She could not imagine losing her mother. She did not even want to try.

"A king of sheep!" Mat hooted. He was smaller than the others, always bouncing on his toes. One glance at his face, and you knew he was looking for mischief. He *always* looked for mischief. And usually found it. "Rand al'Thor, King of the Sheep." Lem snickered. Ban punched him on the shoulder, and Lem punched Ban back, and then they both snickered. Egwene shook her head.

"It's better than saying you want to run off and never have to work," Rand said mildly. He never seemed to get angry. Not that she had seen, anyway. "How could you live without working, Mat?"

"Sheep aren't so bad," Elam said, rubbing at his long nose. His hair was cut short, and he had a cowlick that stood up at the back. He looked a little like a sheep.

"I'll rescue an Aes Sedai, and she'll reward me," Mat shot back. "Anyway, I don't go around looking for work when there's more than work enough without looking." He grinned and poked Perrin's shoulder.

Perrin rubbed his nose, abashed. "Sometimes you have to be sensible, Mat," he said slowly. "Sometimes you have to think ahead." Perrin always talked slowly, when he talked at all. And he moved carefully, as if he was afraid he might break something. Rand spoke before he thought, sometimes, and he always looked as though he was ready to start haring off and not stop until he caught the horizon.

"'Sensible' says I'll work in my da's mill," Lem sighed. "Inherit it one day, I expect. Not too soon, I hope. I'd like to have an adventure first, though, wouldn't you, Rand?"

"Of course." Rand laughed. "But where do I find an adventure in the Two Rivers?"

"There has to be a way," Ban muttered. "Maybe there's gold up in the mountains. Or Trollocs?" He suddenly sounded as if he was not so certain about going up in the mountains. Did he really believe in *Trollocs*?

"I want to have more sheep than anybody in the whole Two Rivers," Elam said stoutly. Mat rolled his eyes in exasperation.

Dav had been sitting back on his heels listening, and now he shook his head. "You *look* like a sheep, Elam," he muttered. At least *she* had not said it aloud. Dav was taller than Mat, and stockier, but his eyes had that same light. His clothes were always rumpled from something he should not have been doing. "Listen, I just got a great idea."

"I just got a better one," Mat put in quickly. "Come on. I'll show you." He and Dav glared at one another.

Elam and Ban and Lem looked ready to follow either one, or both, if they could figure out how. Rand put a hand on Mat's shoulder, though. "Hold on. Let's hear these great ideas, first." Perrin nodded thoughtfully.

Egwene sighed. Dav and Mat seemed to *compete* to see who could get into the most trouble. And Rand might sound sensible, but when he was around the village, they often managed to pull him along, too. And Perrin, as well. The other three would fall in with anything at all Mat or Dav suggested.

It seemed time for her to leave. She would not be able to follow them to see what they were getting up to, not without them seeing her. She would die before she let Rand suspect that she had been watching him like some goosebrain. *And I didn't even learn any-thing.*

As she walked back along the sheep-pen to where she had left her bucket, Dannil Lewin passed her, heading toward the back of the pen. At thirteen, he was even skinnier than Rand, with a thrusting nose. She hesitated over the bucket, listening. At first, she heard nothing but murmurs. Then . . . .

"The Mayor wants me?" Mat exclaimed. "He can't want me! I haven't done anything!"

"He wants *all* of you, and double quick," Dannil said. "I'd get over to him now, if it was me."

Quickly picking up the bucket, Egwene walked slowly away from the sheep-pen, back toward the river. Rand and the others soon passed her, trotting in the same direction. Egwene smiled, a small smile. When her father sent for people, they came. Even the Women's Circle knew Brandelwyn al'Vere was no man to trifle with. Egwene was not supposed to know that, but she had overheard Mistress Luhhan and Mistress Ayellin and some of the others talking to her mother about her father being stubborn and how her mother had to do something about it. She let the boys get a little ahead—just a little—then increased her pace to keep up.

"I don't understand it," Mat grumbled as they came near the line of men shearing. "Sometimes the Mayor knows what I'm doing as soon as I do it. My mother does it, too. But how?"

"The Women's Circle probably tells your mother," Dav muttered. "They see everything. And the Mayor's the Mayor." The other boys nodded glumly.

Ahead of them Egwene saw her father, a round man with thinning gray hair, his shirtsleeves rolled up past his elbows, a pipe in his teeth, and a set of shears in his hand. And ten paces off from the sheep shearers, watching the boys approach, stood Mistress Cauthon, Mat's mother, flanked by her two daughters, Bodewhin and Eldrin. Natti Cauthon was a calm, collected woman, as she would have to be with a son like Mat, and at the moment she wore a contented smile. Bodewhin and Eldrin wore almost identical smiles, and they watched Mat twice as hard as his mother did. Bode was not quite old enough to carry water, yet, and it would be two years before Eldrin could. *Rand and the others must be blind!* Egwene thought. Anyone with eyes could see how Mistress Cauthon always knew.

Mistress Cauthon and her daughters slipped away into the crowd as the boys approached Egwene's father. None of the boys appeared to notice her. They all had eyes for no one but Egwene's father. All but Mat looked wary; he wore a big grin that made him look guilty of something, for sure. Rand's father glanced up from the sheep he was bent over, and caught Rand's eye with a smile that made Rand, at least, seem less like a heron ready to take flight.

Egwene began offering water to the men shearing with her father, all of them on the Village Council. Well, Master Cole appeared to be taking a nap with his back against a waist-high stone thrusting out of the ground. He was as old as the Wisdom, maybe older, though he still had all of his hair, white as it was. But the others were shearing, the fleece falling away from the sheep in thick white sheets. Master Buie, the thatcher, a gnarled man but spry, muttered under his breath as he worked, and the others did two sheep to his one, but everyone else seemed caught up in the work. When a man was done, he let the sheep go to be gathered up by waiting boys and herded away while another was brought to him. Egwene went slowly, to have an excuse to linger. She was not really slacking; she just wanted to know what was going to happen.

Her father studied the boys for a moment, pursing his lips, then said, "Well, lads, I know you've been working hard." Mat gave Rand a startled look, and Perrin shrugged his shoulders uncomfortably. Rand just nodded, but uncertainly. "So I thought it might be time for that story I promised you," her father finished. Egwene grinned. Her father told the *best* stories.

Mat straightened up. "I want a story with adventures." The look he shot at Rand this time was defiant.

"I want Aes Sedai and Warders," Dav said hurriedly.

"I want Trollocs," Mat added, "and . . . and . . . and a false Dragon!"

Dav opened his mouth, and closed it again without saying anything. He glared at Mat, though. There was no way for him to top a false Dragon, and he knew it.

Egwene's father chuckled. "I'm no gleeman, lads. I don't know any stories like that. Tam? Would you like to give it a try?"

Egwene blinked. Why would Rand's father know stories like that if her father did not? Master al'Thor had been chosen to the Council to speak for the farmers around Emond's Field, but as far she knew, all he had ever done was farm sheep and tabac like anyone else.

Master al'Thor looked troubled, and Egwene began to hope he did not know any stories like that. She did not want anyone to show up her father. Of course, she liked Rand's father, so she did not want him embarrassed, either. He was a sturdy man with gray flecks in his hair, a quiet man, and just about everybody liked him.

Master al'Thor finished shearing his sheep, and as he was brought another, he exchanged smiles with Rand. "As it happens," he said, "I do know a story something like that. I'll tell you about the real Dragon, not a false one."

Master Buie straightened from his half-shorn sheep so fast that the animal nearly got away from him. His eyes narrowed, though they were always pretty narrow. "We'll have none of that, Tam al'Thor," he growled in his scratchy voice. "That's nothing fit for decent ears to hear."

"Be easy, Cenn," Egwene's father said soothingly. "It's only a story." But he glanced toward Rand's father, and plainly he was not quite as certain as he sounded.

"Some stories shouldn't be told," Master Buie insisted. "Some stories shouldn't be known! It isn't decent, I say. I don't like it. If they need to hear about wars, give them something about the War of the Hundred Years, or Trolloc Wars. That'll give them Aes Sedai and Trollocs, if you have to talk about such things. Or the Aiel War." For a moment, Egwene thought Master al'Thor's face changed. For an instant he seemed harder. Hard enough to make the merchants' guards look soft. She was imagining a lot of things, today. She did not usually allow her imagination to run away with her this way.

Master Cole's eyes popped open. "It's just a *story* he'll be telling them, Cenn. Just a story, man." His eyes drifted shut again. You could never tell when Master Cole was really napping.

"You never heard, smelled or saw anything you did like, Cenn," Master al'Dai said. He was Bili's grandfather, a lean man with wispy white hair, and as old as Master Cole, if not older. He had to walk with a stick most of the time, but his eyes were clear and sharp, and so was his mind. He was almost as quick with the wool-shears as Master al'Thor. "My advice to you, Cenn, is chew on your liver in silence and let Tam get on with it."

Master Buie subsided with a bad grace, muttering under his breath. Scowling at Rand's father, he bent back to his sheep. Egwene shook her head in surprise. She had often heard Master Buie telling people how important he was on the Council, and how all the other men always listened to him.

The boys moved closer to Master al'Thor and squatted on their heels in a semi-circle. Any story that caused an argument on the Council was sure to be of interest. Master al'Thor carried on with his shearing, but at a slower pace. He would not want to risk cutting the sheep with his attention divided.

"This is just a story," he said, ignoring Master Buie's scowls, "because no one knows everything that happened. But it really did happen. You've heard of the Age of Legends?"

Some of the boys nodded, doubtfully. Egwene nodded, too, in spite of herself. She had heard grownups say, "Maybe in the Age of Legends," when they did not believe something had really happened or doubted a thing could be done. It was just another way saying, "When pigs had wings," though. At least, she had thought it was.

"Three thousand years ago and more, it was," Rand's father went on. "There were great cities full of buildings taller that the White Tower, and that's taller than anything but a mountain. Machines that used the One Power carried people across the ground faster than a horse can run, and some say machines carried people through the air, too. There was no sickness anywhere. No hunger. No war. And then the Dark One touched the World."

The boys jumped, and Elam actually fell over. He scrambled back up, blushing and trying to pretend he had not toppled at all. Egwene held her breath. The Dark One. Maybe it was because she had been thinking about him earlier, but he seemed particularly frightening now. She hoped that Master al'Thor would not actually name him. *He wouldn't* name *the Dark One*, she thought, but that did not stop her being afraid that he might.

Master al'Thor smiled at the boys to soften the shock of what he had said, but he went on. "The Age of Legends hadn't so much as the memory of war, so they say, but once the Dark One touched the world, they learned fast enough. This wasn't a war

like those you hear about when the merchants come for wool and
tabac, between two nations. This war covered the whole world.
The War of the Shadow, it came be called. Those who stood for
the Light faced as many who stood for the Shadow, and besides
Darkfriends beyond counting, there were armies of Myrddraal and
Trollocs greater than anything the Blight spewed up during the
Trolloc Wars. Aes Sedai went over to the Shadow, too. They were
called the Forsaken."

Egwene shivered, and was glad to see some of the boys wrapping their arms around themselves. Mothers used the Forsaken to
frighten their children when they were bad. If you keep lying,
Semirhage will come and get you. Lanfear waits for children who
steal. Egwene was glad her mother did not do that. Wait. The
Forsaken had been Aes Sedai? She hoped Master al'Thor did not
say that too freely, or the Women's Circle would come calling
on him. Anyway, some of the Forsaken were men, so he had to
be wrong.

"You'll be expecting me to tell you about the glories of battle,
but I won't." For a moment, he sounded grim, but only for a
moment. "No one knows anything about those battles, except that
they were huge. Maybe the Aes Sedai have some records, but if
they do, they don't let anyone see them except other Aes Sedai.
You've heard about the great battles during Artur Hawkwing's
rise, and during the War of the Hundred Years? A hundred thousand men on each side?" Eager nods answered him. From Egwene, too, though hers was not eager. All those men trying to
kill one another did not excite her the way it did the boys. "Well,"
Master al'Thor went on, "those battles would have been counted
small in the War of the Shadow. Whole cities were destroyed,
razed to the ground. The countryside outside the cities fared as
badly. Wherever a battle was fought, it left only devastation and
ruin behind. The war went on for years and years, all over the
world. And slowly the Shadow began to win. The Light was
pushed back and back, until it appeared certain the Shadow would
conquer everything. Hope faded away like mist in the sun. But
the Light had a leader who would never give up, a man called
Lews Therin Telamon. The Dragon."

One of the boys gasped in surprise. Egwene was too busy goggling to see who. She forgot even to pretend that she was offering
water. The Dragon was the man who had destroyed everything!

She did not know much about the Breaking of the World—well, almost nothing, in truth—but everybody knew that much. Surely he had fought for the Shadow!

"Lews Therin gathered men around him, the Hundred Companions, and a small army. Small as they counted such things then. Ten thousand men. Not a small army now, would you say?" The words seemed an invitation to laugh, but there was no laughter in Master al'Thor's quiet voice. He sounded almost as though he had been there. Egwene certainly did not laugh, and none of the boys did, either. She listened, and tried to remember to breathe. "With only a forlorn hope, Lews Therin attacked the valley of Thakan'dar, the heart of the Shadow itself. Trollocs in the hundreds of thousands fell on them, Trollocs and Myrddraal. Trollocs live to kill. A Trolloc can rip a man to pieces with its bare hands. Myrddraal *are* death. Aes Sedai fighting for the Shadow rained fire and lightning on Lews Therin and his men. The men following the Dragon did not die one by one, but ten at a time, or twenty, or fifty. Beneath a twisted sky, in a place where nothing grew or ever would again, they fought and died. But they did not retreat or give up. All the way to Shayol Ghul they fought, and if Thakan'dar is the heart of the Shadow, then Shayol Ghul is the heart of the heart. Every man in that army died, and most of the Hundred Companions, but at Shayol Ghul they sealed the Dark One back into the prison the Creator made for him, and the Forsaken with him. And the world was saved from the Dark One."

Silence fell. The boys stared at Master al'Thor with wide eyes. Shining eyes, as if they could see it all, the Trollocs and the Myrddraal and Shayol Ghul. Egwene shivered again. *The Dark One and all the Forsaken are bound at Shayol Ghul, bound away from the world of men,* she recited to herself. She could not remember the rest, but it helped. Only, if the Dragon had saved the world, how had he destroyed it?

Cenn Buie spat. He spat! Just like some merchant's smelly guard! She did not believe she would think of him as Master Buie again after today.

That broke the boys out of their reverie, of course. They tried to look anywhere but at the gnarled man.

Perrin scatched at his head. "Master al'Thor," he said slowly, "what does 'the Dragon' mean? If somebody's called the Lion, it means he's supposed to be like a lion. But what's a dragon?"

Egwene stared at him. She had never thought of that. Maybe Perrin was not as slow as he appeared.

"I don't know," Rand's father answered simply. "I don't think anyone does. Maybe not even the Aes Sedai." He let the sheep go that he been shearing, and motioned for another to be brought. Egwene realized that he had been done with it for some time. He must not have wanted to interupt his story.

Master Cole opened his eyes and grinned. "The Dragon. It surely sounds fierce, though, now doesn't it?" he said before letting his eyes drift shut again.

"I suppose it does at that," her father said. "But it all happened long ago and far away, and it doesn't have anything to do with us. Well, you've had your break and your story, lads. Back to work with you." As the boys began standing up reluctantly, he added, "There are plenty of lads here from the farms I don't think any of you know, yet. It's always good to know your neighbors, so you should acquaint yourselves with them. I don't want any of you working together today; you already know one another. Now, off with you."

The boys exchanged startled glances. Had they really thought he would let them go back to whatever mischief they had been planning? Mat and Dav looked especially glum as they walked away exchanging glances. She thought about following, but they were already splitting up, and she would have to trail after Rand to learn anything more. She grimaced. If he noticed, he might think she was goosebrained like Cilia Cole. Besides, there were those far-off lands. She did intend to see them.

Abruptly she became aware of ravens, many more than there had been before, flapping out of the trees, flying away west, toward the Mountains of Mist. She shifted her shoulders. She felt as if someone were staring at her back. Someone, or . . . .

She did not want to turn around, but she did, raising her eyes to the trees behind the men shearing. Midway up a tall pine, a solitary raven stood on a branch. Staring at her. Right at her! She felt cold right down to her middle. The only thing she wanted to do was run. Instead, she made herself stare back, trying to copy Nynaeve's level look. After a moment the raven gave a harsh cry and threw itself off the branch, black wings carrying it west after the others.

Maybe I'm starting to get that look right, she thought, and then felt silly. She had to stop letting her imagination get the better of her. It was just a bird. And she had important things to do, like being the best water-carrier ever. The best water-carrier ever would not be frightened of birds or anything else. Squaring her shoulders, she set out through the crowd again, watching for Berowyn. But this time, it was so she could offer Berowyn the dipper. If she could face down a raven, she could face down her sister. She hoped.

Egwene had to carry water again the next year, which was a great disappointment to her, but once again she tried to be the best. If you were going to do a thing, you might as well do the best you could. It must have worked, because the year after that she was allowed to help with the food, a year early! She set herself a new goal, then: to be allowed to braid her hair younger than anybody ever. She did not really think the Women's Circle would allow it, but a goal that was easy was no goal at all.

She stopped wanting to hear stories from the grownups, though she would have liked to hear a gleeman, but she still liked to read of distant lands with strange ways, and dreamed of seeing them. The boys stopped wanting stories, too. She did not think they even read very much. They all grew older, thinking their world would never change, and many of those stories faded to fond memories while others were forgotten, or half so. And if they learned that some of those stories really had been more than stories, well . . . . The War of the Shadow? The Breaking of the World? Lews Therin Telamon? How could it matter now? And what *had* really happened back then, anyway?

PROLOGUE

Dragonmount

The palace still shook occasionally as the earth rumbled in memory, groaned as if it would deny what had happened. Bars of sunlight cast through rents in the walls made motes of dust glitter where they yet hung in the air. Scorch-marks marred the walls, the floors, the ceilings. Broad black smears crossed the blistered paints and gilt of once-bright murals, soot overlaying crumbling friezes of men and animals which seemed to have attempted to walk before the madness grew quiet. The dead lay everywhere, men and women and children, struck down in attempted flight by the lightnings that had flashed down every corridor, or seized by the fires that had stalked them, or sunken into stone of the palace, the stones that had flowed and sought, almost alive, before stillness came again. In odd counterpoint, colorful tapestries and paintings, masterworks all, hung undisturbed except where bulging walls had pushed them awry. Finely carved furnishings, inlaid with ivory and gold, stood untouched except where rippling floors had toppled them. The mind-twisting had struck at the core, ignoring peripheral things.

Lews Therin Telamon wandered the palace, deftly keeping his balance when the earth heaved. "Ilyena! My love, where are you?" The edge of his pale gray cloak trailed through blood as he stepped across the body of a woman, her golden-haired beauty marred by the horror of her last moments, her still-open eyes frozen in disbelief. "Where are you, my wife? Where is everyone hiding?"

His eyes caught his own reflection in a mirror hanging askew

from bubbled marble. His clothes had been regal once, in gray
and scarlet and gold; now the finely-woven cloth, brought by
merchants from across the World Sea, was torn and dirty, thick
with the same dust that covered his hair and skin. For a moment he fingered the symbol on his cloak, a circle half white
and half black, the colors separated by a sinuous line. It meant
something, that symbol. But the embroidered circle could not
hold his attention long. He gazed at his own image with as
much wonder. A tall man just into his middle years, handsome
once, but now with hair already more white than brown and a
face lined by strain and worry, dark eyes that had seen too
much. Lews Therin began to chuckle, then threw back his
head; his laughter echoed down the lifeless halls.

"Ilyena, my love! Come to me, my wife. You must see this."

Behind him the air rippled, shimmered, solidified into a man
who looked around, his mouth twisting briefly with distaste.
Not so tall as Lews Therin, he was clothed all in black, save for
the snow-white lace at his throat and the silverwork on the
turned-down tops of his thigh-high boots. He stepped carefully,
handling his cloak fastidiously to avoid brushing the dead. The
floor trembled with aftershocks, but his attention was fixed on
the man staring into the mirror and laughing.

"Lord of the Morning," he said, "I have come for you."

The laughter cut off as if it had never been, and Lews Therin
turned, seeming unsurprised. "Ah, a guest. Have you the
Voice, stranger? It will soon be time for the Singing, and here
all are welcome to take part. Ilyena, my love, we have a guest.
Ilyena, where are you?"

The black-clad man's eyes widened, darted to the body of the
golden-haired woman, then back to Lews Therin. "Shai'tan
take you, does the taint already have you so far in its grip?"

"That name. Shai—" Lews Therin shuddered and raised a
hand as though to ward off something. "You mustn't say that
name. It is dangerous."

"So you remember that much, at least. Dangerous for you,
fool, not for me. What else do you remember? Remember, you
Light-blinded idiot! I will not let it end with you swaddled in
unawareness! Remember!"

For a moment Lews Therin stared at his raised hand, fascinated by the patterns of grime. Then he wiped his hand on his
even dirtier coat and turned his attention back to the other
man. "Who are you? What do you want?"

The black-clad man drew himself up arrogantly. "Once I was called Elan.Morin Tedronai, but now—"

"Betrayer of Hope." It was a whisper from Lews Therin. Memory stirred, but he turned his head, shying away from it.

"So you do remember some things. Yes, Betrayer of Hope. So have men named me, just as they named you Dragon, but unlike you I embrace the name. They gave me the name to revile me, but I will yet make them kneel and worship it. What will you do with your name? After this day, men will call you Kinslayer. What will you do with that?"

Lews Therin frowned down the ruined hall. "Ilyena should be here to offer a guest welcome," he murmured absently, then raised his voice. "Ilyena, where are you?" The floor shook; the golden-haired woman's body shifted as if in answer to his call. His eyes did not see her.

Elan Morin grimaced. "Look at you," he said scornfully. "Once you stood first among the Servants. Once you wore the Ring of Tamyrlin, and sat in the High Seat. Once you summoned the Nine Rods of Dominion. Now look at you! A pitiful, shattered wretch. But it is not enough. You humbled me in the Hall of Servants. You defeated me at the Gates of Paaran Disen. But I am the greater, now. I will not let you die without knowing that. When you die, your last thought will be the full knowledge of your defeat, of how complete and utter it is. If I let you die at all."

"I cannot imagine what is keeping Ilyena. She will give me the rough side of her tongue if she thinks I have been hiding a guest from her. I hope you enjoy conversation, for she surely does. Be forewarned. Ilyena will ask you so many questions you may end up telling her everything you know."

Tossing back his black cloak, Elan Morin flexed his hands. "A pity for you," he mused, "that one of your Sisters is not here. I was never very skilled at Healing, and I follow a different power now. But even one of them could only give you a few lucid minutes, if you did not destroy her first. What I can do will serve as well, for my purposes." His sudden smile was cruel. "But I fear Shai'tan's healing is different from the sort you know. Be healed, Lews Therin!" He extended his hands, and the light dimmed as if a shadow had been laid across the sun.

Pain blazed in Lews Therin, and he screamed, a scream that came from his depths, a scream he could not stop. Fire seared his marrow; acid rushed along his veins. He toppled backwards, crashing to the marble floor; his head struck the stone and rebounded. His heart pounded, trying to beat its way out of his chest, and every pulse gushed new flame through him. Helplessly he convulsed, thrashing, his skull a sphere of purest agony on the point of bursting. His hoarse screams reverberated through the palace.

Slowly, ever so slowly, the pain receded. The outflowing seemed to take a thousand years and left him twitching weakly, sucking breath through a raw throat. Another thousand years seemed to pass before he could manage to heave himself over, muscles like jellyfish, and shakily push himself up on hands and knees. His eyes fell on the golden-haired woman, and the scream that was ripped out of him dwarfed every sound he had made before. Tottering, almost falling, he scrabbled brokenly across the floor to her. It took every bit of his strength to pull her up into his arms. His hands shook as he smoothed her hair back from her staring face.

"Ilyena! Light help me, Ilyena!" His body curved around hers protectively, his sobs the full-throated cries of a man who had nothing left to live for. "Ilyena, no! *No!*"

"You can have her back, Kinslayer. The Great Lord of the Dark can make her live again, if you will serve him. If you will serve me."

Lews Therin raised his head, and the black-clad man took an involuntary step back from that gaze. "Ten years, Betrayer," Lews Therin said softly, the soft sound of steel being bared. "Ten years your foul master has wracked the world. And now this. I will. . . ."

"Ten years! You pitiful fool! This war has not lasted ten years, but since the beginning of time. You and I have fought a thousand battles with the turning of the Wheel, a thousand times a thousand, and we will fight until time dies and the Shadow is triumphant!" He finished in a shout, with a raised fist, and it was Lews Therin's turn to pull back, breath catching at the glow in the Betrayer's eyes.

Carefully Lews Therin laid Ilyena down, fingers gently brushing her hair. Tears blurred his vision as he stood, but his voice was iced iron. "For what else you have done, there can be no forgiveness, Betrayer, but for Ilyena's death I will destroy you beyond anything your master can repair. Prepare to—"

"Remember, you fool! Remember your futile attack on the

Great Lord of the Dark! Remember his counterstroke! Remember! Even now the Hundred Companions are tearing the world apart, and every day a hundred men more join them. What hand slew Ilyena Sunhair, Kinslayer? Not mine. Not mine. What hand struck down every life that bore a drop of your blood, everyone who loved you, everyone you loved? Not mine, Kinslayer. Not mine. Remember, and know the price of opposing Shai'tan!"

Sudden sweat made tracks down Lews Therin's face through the dust and dirt. He remembered, a cloudy memory like a dream of a dream, but he knew it true.

His howl beat at the walls, the howl of a man who had discovered his soul damned by his own hand, and he clawed at his face as if to tear away the sight of what he had done. Everywhere he looked his eyes found the dead. Torn they were, or broken or burned, or half-consumed by stone. Everywhere lay lifeless faces he knew, faces he loved. Old servants and friends of his childhood, faithful companions through the long years of battle. And his children. His own sons and daughters, sprawled like broken dolls, play stilled forever. All slain by his hand. His children's faces accused him, blank eyes asking why, and his tears were no answer. The Betrayer's laughter flogged him, drowned out his howls. He could not bear the faces, the pain. He could not bear to remain any longer. Desperately he reached out to the True Source, to tainted *saidin,* and he Traveled.

The land around him was flat and empty. A ·river flowed nearby, straight and broad, but he could sense there were no people within a hundred leagues. He was alone, as alone as a man could be while still alive, yet he could not escape memory. The eyes pursued him through the endless caverns of his mind. He could not hide from them. His children's eyes. Ilyena's eyes. Tears glistened on his cheeks as he turned his face to the sky.

"Light, forgive me!" He did not believe it could come, forgiveness. Not for what he had done. But he shouted to the sky anyway, begged for what he could not believe he could receive. "Light, forgive me!"

He was still touching *saidin,* the male half of the power that drove the universe, that turned the Wheel of Time, and he could feel the oily taint fouling its surface, the taint of the Shadow's counterstroke, the taint that doomed the world. Because of him. Because in his pride he had believed that men could match the Creator, could mend what the Creator had made and they had broken. In his pride he had believed.

He drew on the True Source deeply, and still more deeply, like a man dying of thirst. Quickly he had drawn more of the One Power than he could channel unaided; his skin felt as if it were aflame. Straining, he forced himself to draw more, tried to draw it all.

"Light, forgive me! Ilyena!"

The air turned to fire, the fire to light liquefied. The bolt that struck from the heavens would have seared and blinded any eye that glimpsed it, even for an instant. From the heavens it came, blazed through Lews Therin Telamon, bored into the bowels of the earth. Stone turned to vapor at its touch. The earth thrashed and quivered like a living thing in agony. Only a heartbeat did the shining bar exist, connecting ground and sky, but even after it vanished the earth yet heaved like the sea in a storm. Molten rock fountained five hundred feet into the air, and the groaning ground rose, thrusting the burning spray ever upward, ever higher. From north and south, from east and west, the wind howled in, snapping trees like twigs, shrieking and blowing as if to aid the growing mountain ever skyward. Ever skyward.

At last the wind died, the earth stilled to trembling mutters. Of Lews Therin Telamon, no sign remained. Where he had stood a mountain now rose miles into the sky, molten lava still gushing from its broken peak. The broad, straight river had been pushed into a curve away from the mountain, and there it split to form a long island in its midst. The shadow of the mountain almost reached the island; it lay dark across the land like the ominous hand of prophecy. For a time the dull, protesting rumbles of the earth were the only sound.

On the island, the air shimmered and coalesced. The black-clad man stood staring at the fiery mountain rising out of the plain. His face twisted in rage and contempt. "You cannot escape so easily, Dragon. It is not done between us. It will not be done until the end of time."

Then he was gone, and the mountain and the island stood alone. Waiting.

And the Shadow fell upon the Land, and the World was riven stone from stone. The oceans fled, and the mountains were swallowed up, and the nations were scattered to the eight corners of the World. The moon was as blood, and the sun was as ashes. The seas boiled, and the living envied the dead. All was shattered, and all but memory lost, and one memory above all others, of him who brought the Shadow and the Breaking of the World. And him they named Dragon.

> (from *Aleth nin Taerin alta Camora,*
> *The Breaking of the World.*
> Author unknown, the Fourth Age)

And it came to pass in those days, as it had come before and would come again, that the Dark lay heavy on the land and weighed down the hearts of men, and the green things failed, and hope died. And men cried out to the Creator, saying, O Light of the Heavens, Light of the World, let the Promised One be born of the mountain, according to the prophecies, as he was in ages past and will be in ages to come. Let the Prince of the Morning sing to the land that green things will grow and the valleys give forth lambs. Let the arm of the Lord of the Dawn shelter us from the Dark, and the great sword of justice defend us. Let the Dragon ride again on the winds of time.

> (from *Charal Drianaan te Calamon,*
> *The Cycle of the Dragon.*
> Author unknown, the Fourth Age)

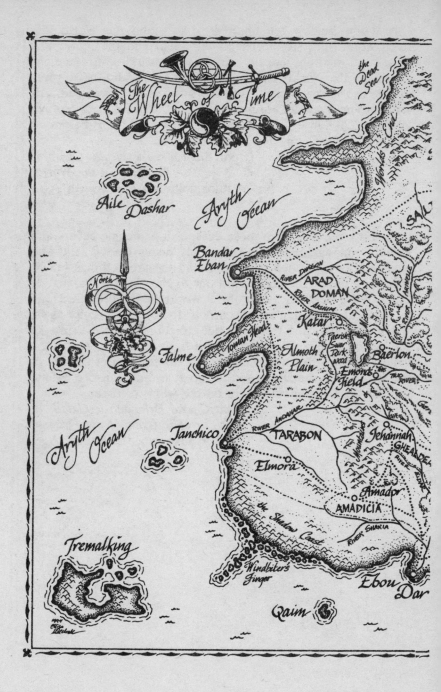

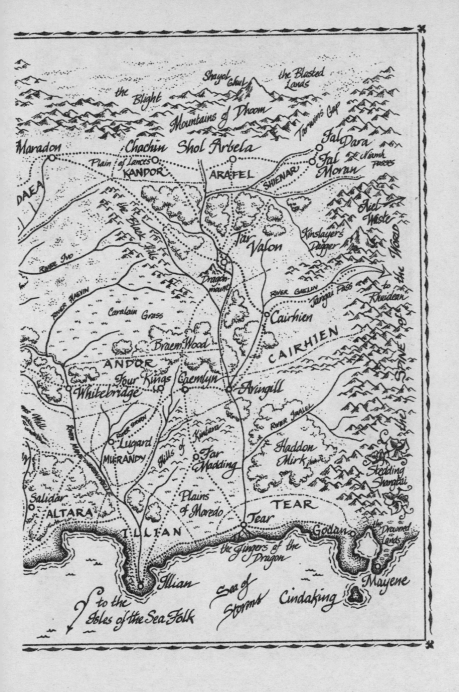

CHAPTER
1

An Empty Road

The Wheel of Time turns, and Ages come and pass, leaving memories that become legend. Legend fades to myth, and even myth is long forgotten when the Age that gave it birth comes again. In one Age, called the Third Age by some, an Age yet to come, an Age long past, a wind rose in the Mountains of Mist. The wind was not the beginning. There are neither beginnings nor endings to the turning of the Wheel of Time. But it was *a* beginning.

Born below the ever cloud-capped peaks that gave the mountains their name, the wind blew east, out across the Sand Hills, once the shore of a great ocean, before the Breaking of the World. Down it flailed into the Two Rivers, into the tangled forest called the Westwood, and beat at two men walking with a cart and horse down the rock-strewn track called the Quarry Road. For all that spring should have come a good month since, the wind carried an icy chill as if it would rather bear snow.

Gusts plastered Rand al'Thor's cloak to his back, whipped the earth-colored wool around his legs, then streamed it out behind him. He wished his coat were heavier, or that he had worn an extra shirt. Half the time when he tried to tug the cloak back around him it caught on the quiver swinging at his hip. Trying to hold the cloak one-handed did not do much good anyway; he had his bow in the other, an arrow nocked and ready to draw.

As a particularly strong blast tugged the cloak out of his hand, he glanced at his father over the back of the shaggy brown mare. He felt a little foolish about wanting to reassure himself that Tam was still there, but it was that kind of day. The wind howled when it rose, but aside from that, quiet lay heavy on the land. The soft creak of the axle sounded loud by comparison. No birds sang in the forest, no squirrels chittered from a branch. Not that he expected them, really; not this spring.

Only trees that kept leaf or needle through the winter had any green about them. Snarls of last year's bramble spread brown webs over stone outcrops under the trees. Nettles numbered most among the few weeds; the rest were the sorts with sharp burrs or thorns, or stinkweed, which left a rank smell on the unwary boot that crushed it. Scattered white patches of snow still dotted the ground where tight clumps of trees kept deep shade. Where sunlight did reach, it held neither strength nor warmth. The pale sun sat above the trees to the east, but its light was crisply dark, as if mixed with shadow. It was an awkward morning, made for unpleasant thoughts.

Without thinking he touched the nock of the arrow; it was ready to draw to his cheek in one smooth movement, the way Tam had taught him. Winter had been bad enough on the farms, worse than even the oldest folk remembered, but it must have been harsher still in the mountains, if the number of wolves driven down into the Two Rivers was any guide. Wolves raided the sheep pens and chewed their way into barns to get the cattle and horses. Bears had been after the sheep, too, where a bear had not been seen in years. It was no longer safe to be out after dark. Men were the prey as often as sheep, and the sun did not always have to be down.

Tam was taking steady strides on the other side of Bela, using his spear as a walking staff, ignoring the wind that made his brown cloak flap like a banner. Now and again he touched the mare's flank lightly, to remind her to keep moving. With his thick chest and broad face, he was a pillar of reality in that morning, like a stone in the middle of a drifting dream. His sun-roughened cheeks might be lined and his hair have only a sprinkling of black among the gray, but there was a solidness to him, as though a flood could wash around him without uprooting his feet. He stumped down the road now impassively. Wolves and bears were all very well, his manner said, things that any man who kept sheep must be aware of, but they had best not try to stop Tam al'Thor getting to Emond's Field.

With a guilty start Rand returned to watching his side of the road, Tam's matter-of-factness reminding him of his task. He was a head taller than his father, taller than anyone else in the district, and had little of Tam in him physically, except perhaps for a breadth of shoulder. Gray eyes and the reddish tinge to his hair came from his mother, so Tam said. She had been an outlander, and Rand remembered little of her aside from a smiling face, though he did put flowers on her grave every year, at Bel Tine, in the spring, and at Sunday, in the summer.

Two small casks of Tam's apple brandy rested in the lurching cart, and eight larger barrels of apple cider, only slightly hard after a winter's curing. Tam delivered the same every year to the Winespring Inn for use during Bel Tine, and he had declared that it would take more than wolves or a cold wind to stop him this spring. Even so they had not been to the village for weeks. Not even Tam traveled much these days. But Tam had given his word about the brandy and cider, even if he had waited to make delivery until the day before Festival. Keeping his word was important to Tam. Rand was just glad to get away from the farm, almost as glad as about the coming of Bel Tine.

As Rand watched his side of the road, the feeling grew in him that he was being watched. For a while he tried to shrug it off. Nothing moved or made a sound among the trees, except the wind. But the feeling not only persisted, it grew stronger. The hairs on his arms stirred; his skin prickled as if it itched on the inside.

He shifted his bow irritably to rub at his arms, and told himself to stop letting fancies take him. There was nothing in the woods on his side of the road, and Tam would have spoken if there had been anything on the other. He glanced over his shoulder . . . and blinked. Not more than twenty spans back down the road a cloaked figure on horseback followed them, horse and rider alike black, dull and ungleaming.

It was more habit than anything else that kept him walking backward alongside the cart even while he looked.

The rider's cloak covered him to his boot tops, the cowl

tugged well forward so no part of him showed. Vaguely Rand thought there was something odd about the horseman, but it was the shadowed opening of the hood that fascinated him. He could see only the vaguest outlines of a face, but he had the feeling he was looking right into the rider's eyes. And he could not look away. Queasiness settled in his stomach. There was only shadow to see in the hood, but he felt hatred as sharply as if he could see a snarling face, hatred for everything that lived. Hatred for him most of all, for him above all things.

Abruptly a stone caught his heel and he stumbled, breaking his eyes away from the dark horseman. His bow dropped to the road, and only an outthrust hand grabbing Bela's harness saved him from falling flat on his back. With a startled snort the mare stopped, twisting her head to see what had caught her.

Tam frowned over Bela's back at him. "Are you all right, lad?"

"A rider," Rand said breathlessly, pulling himself upright. "A stranger, following us."

"Where?" The older man lifted his broad-bladed spear and peered back warily.

"There, down the. . . ." Rand's words trailed off as he turned to point. The road behind was empty. Disbelieving, he stared into the forest on both sides of the road. Bare-branched trees offered no hiding place, but there was not a glimmer of horse or horseman. He met his father's questioning gaze. "He was there. A man in a black cloak, on a black horse."

"I wouldn't doubt your word, lad, but where has he gone?"

"I don't know. But he was there." He snatched up the fallen bow and arrow, hastily checked the fletching before renocking, and half drew before letting the bowstring relax. There was nothing to aim at. "He was."

Tam shook his grizzled head. "If you say so, lad. Come on, then. A horse leaves hoofprints, even on this ground." He started toward the rear of the cart, his cloak whipping in the wind. "If we find them, we'll know for a fact he was there. If not . . . well, these are days to make a man think he's seeing things."

Abruptly Rand realized what had been odd about the horseman, aside from his being there at all. The wind that beat at Tam and him had not so much as shifted a fold of that black cloak. His mouth was suddenly dry. He must have imagined it. His father was right; this was a morning to prickle a man's imagination. But he did not believe it. Only, how did he tell his father that the man who had apparently vanished into air wore a cloak the wind did not touch?

With a worried frown he peered into the woods around them; it looked different than it ever had before. Almost since he was old enough to walk, he had run loose in the forest. The ponds and streams of the Waterwood, beyond the last farms east of Emond's Field, were where he had learned to swim. He had explored into the Sand Hills—which many in the Two Rivers said was bad luck—and once he had even gone to the very foot of the Mountains of Mist, him and his closest friends, Mat Cauthon and Perrin Aybara. That was a lot further afield than most people in Emond's Field ever went; to them a journey to the next village, up to Watch Hill or down to Deven Ride, was a big event. Nowhere in all of that had he found a place that made him afraid. Today, though, the Westwood was not the place he remembered. A man who could disappear so suddenly could reappear just as suddenly, maybe even right beside them.

"No, father, there's no need." When Tam stopped in surprise, Rand covered his flush by tugging at the hood of his cloak. "You're probably right. No point looking for what isn't there, not when we can use the time getting on to the village and out of this wind."

"I could do with a pipe," Tam said slowly, "and a mug of ale where it's warm." Abruptly he gave a broad grin. "And I expect you're eager to see Egwene."

Rand managed a weak smile. Of all things he might want to think about right then, the Mayor's daughter was far down the list. He did not need any more confusion. For the past year she had been making him increasingly jittery whenever they were together. Worse, she did not even seem to be aware of it. No, he certainly did not want to add Egwene to his thoughts.

He was hoping his father had not noticed he was afraid when Tam said, "Remember the flame, lad, and the void."

It was an odd thing Tam had taught him. Concentrate on a single flame and feed all you passions into it—fear, hate, anger—until your mind became empty. Become one with the void, Tam said, and you could do anything. Nobody else in Emond's Field talked that way. But Tam won the archery competition at Bel Tine every year with his flame and his void. Rand though he might have a chance at placing this year himself, if he could manage to hold onto the void. For Tam to bring it up now meant he *had* noticed, but he said nothing more about it.

Tam clucked Bela into motion once more, and they resumed their journey, the older man striding along as if nothing untoward had happened and nothing untoward could. Rand wished he could imitate him. He tried forming the emptiness in his mind, but it kept slipping away into images of the black-cloaked horseman.

He wanted to believe that Tam was right, that the rider had just been his imagination, but he could remember that feeling of hatred too well. There *had* been someone. And that someone had meant him harm. He did not stop looking back until the high-peaked, thatched roofs of Emond's Field surrounded him.

The village lay close onto the Westwood, the forest gradually thinning until the last few trees stood actually among the stout frame houses. The land sloped gently down to the east. Though not without patches of woods, farms and hedge-bordered fields and pastures quilted the land beyond the village all the way to the Waterwood and its tangle of streams and ponds. The land to the west was just as fertile, and the pastures there lush in most years, but only a handful of farms could be found in the Westwood. Even those few dwindled to none miles short of the Sand Hills, not to mention the Mountains of Mist, which rose above the Westwood treetops, distant but in plain sight from Emond's Field. Some said the land was too rocky, as if there were not rocks everywhere in the Two Rivers, and others said it was hard-luck land. A few muttered that there was no point getting any closer to the mountains than needs be. Whatever the reasons, only the hardiest men farmed in the Westwood.

Small children and dogs dodged around the cart in whooping swarms once it passed the first row of houses. Bela plodded on patiently, ignoring the yelling youngsters who tumbled under her nose, playing tag and rolling hoops. In the last months there had been little of play or laughter from the children; even

when the weather had slackened enough to let children out,
fear of wolves kept them in. It seemed the approach of Bel
Tine had taught them how to play again.

Festival had affected the adults as well. Broad shutters were
thrown back, and in almost every house the goodwife stood in a
window, apron tied about her and long-braided hair done up in
a kerchief, shaking sheets or hanging mattresses over the win-
dowsills. Whether or not leaves had appeared on the trees, no
woman would let Bel Tine come before her spring cleaning was
done. In every yard rugs hung from stretched lines, and children who had not been quick enough to run free in the streets
instead vented their frustration on the carpets with wicker beat-
ers. On roof after roof the goodman of the house clambered
about, checking the thatch to see if the winter's damage meant
calling on old Cenn Buie, the thatcher.

Several times Tam paused to engage one man or another in
brief conversation. Since he and Rand had not been off the
farm for weeks, everyone wanted to catch up on how things
were out that way. Few Westwood men had been in. Tam
spoke of damage from winter storms, each one worse than the
one before, and stillborn lambs, of brown fields where crops
should be sprouting and pastures greening, of ravens flocking in
where songbirds had come in years before. Grim talk, with
preparations for Bel Tine going on all around them, and much
shaking of heads. It was the same on all sides.

Most of the men rolled their shoulders and said, "Well, we'll
survive, the Light willing." Some grinned and added, "And if
the Light doesn't will, we'll still survive."

That was the way of most Two Rivers people. People who
had to watch the hail beat their crops or the wolves take their
lambs, and start over, no matter how many years it happened,
did not give up easily. Most of those who did were long since
gone.

Tam would not have stopped for Wit Congar if the man had
not come out into the street so they had to halt or let Bela run
over him. The Congars—and the Coplins; the two families
were so intermarried no one really knew where one family let
off and the other began—were known from Watch Hill to Deven Ride, and maybe as far as Taren Ferry, as complainers and
troublemakers.

"I have to get this to Bran al'Vere, Wit," Tam said, nodding to the barrels in the cart, but the scrawny man held his ground with a sour expression on his face. He had been sprawled on his front steps, not up on his roof, though the thatch looked as if it badly needed Master Buie's attention. He never seemed ready to start over, or to finish what he started the first time. Most of the Coplins and Congars were like that, those who were not worse.

"What are we going to do about Nynaeve, al'Thor?" Congar demanded. "We can't have a Wisdom like that for Emond's Field."

Tam sighed heavily. "It's not our place, Wit. The Wisdom is women's business."

"Well, we'd better do something, al'Thor. She said we'd have a mild winter. And a good harvest. Now you ask her what she hears on the wind, and she just scowls at you and stomps off."

"If you asked her the way you usually do, Wit," Tam said patiently, "you're lucky she didn't thump you with that stick she carries. Now if you don't mind, this brandy—"

"Nynaeve al'Meara is just too young to be Wisdom, al'Thor. If the Women's Circle won't do something, then the Village Council has to."

"What business of yours is the Wisdom, Wit Congar?" roared a woman's voice. Wit flinched as his wife marched out of the house. Daise Congar was twice as wide as Wit, a hard-faced woman without an ounce of fat on her. She glared at him with her fists on her hips. "You try meddling in Women's Circle business, and see how you like eating your own cooking. Which you won't do in my kitchen. And washing your own clothes and making your own bed. Which won't be under my roof."

"But, Daise," Wit whined, "I was just. . . ."

"If you'll pardon me, Daise," Tam said. "Wit. The Light shine on you both." He got Bela moving again, leading her around the scrawny fellow. Daise was concentrating on her husband now, but any minute she could realize whom it was Wit had been talking to.

That was why they had not accepted any of the invitations to stop for a bite to eat or something hot to drink. When they saw Tam, the goodwives of Emond's Field went on point like hounds spotting a rabbit. There was not a one of them who did not know just the perfect wife for a widower with a good farm, even if it was in the Westwood.

Rand stepped along just as quickly as Tam, perhaps even more so. He was sometimes cornered when Tam was not around, with no way to escape outside of rudeness. Herded onto a stool by the kitchen fire, he would be fed pastries or honeycakes or meatpies. And always the goodwife's eyes weighed and measured him as neatly as any merchant's scales and tapes while she told him that what he was eating was not nearly so good as her widowed sister's cooking, or her next-to-eldest cousin's. Tam was certainly not getting any younger, she would say. It was good that he had loved his wife so—it boded well for the next woman in his life—but he had mourned long enough. Tam needed a good woman. It was a simple fact, she would say, or something very close, that a man just could not do without a woman to take care of him and keep him out of trouble. Worst of all were those who paused thoughtfully at about that point, then asked with elaborate casualness exactly how old *he* was now.

Like most Two Rivers folk, Rand had a strong stubborn streak. Outsiders sometimes said it was the prime trait of people in the Two Rivers, that they could give mules lessons and teach stones. The goodwives were fine and kindly women for the most part, but he hated being pushed into anything, and they made him feel as if he were being prodded with sticks. So he walked fast, and wished Tam would hurry Bela along.

Soon the street opened onto the Green, a broad expanse in the middle of the village. Usually covered with thick grass, the Green this spring showed only a few fresh patches among the yellowish brown of dead grass and the black of bare earth. A double handful of geese waddled about, beadily eyeing the ground but not finding anything worth pecking, and someone had tethered a milkcow to crop the sparse growth.

Toward the west end of the Green, the Winespring itself gushed out of a low stone outcrop in a flow that never failed, a flow strong enough to knock a man down and sweet enough to justify its name a dozen times over. From the spring the rapidly widening Winespring Water ran swiftly off to the east, willows dotting its banks all the way to Master Thane's mill and beyond, until it split into dozens of streams in the swampy

depths of the Waterwood. Two low, railed footbridges crossed
the clear stream at the Green, and one bridge wider than the
others and stout enough to bear wagons. The Wagon Bridge
marked where the North Road, coming down from Taren Ferry
and Watch Hill, became the Old Road, leading to Deven Ride.
Outsiders sometimes found it funny that the road had one
name to the north and another to the south, but that was the
way it had always been, as far as anyone in Emond's Field
knew, and that was that. It was a good enough reason for Two
Rivers people.

On the far side of the bridges, the mounds were already
building for the Bel Tine fires, three careful stacks of logs almost as big as houses. They had to be on cleared dirt, of
course, not on the Green, even sparse as it was. What of Festival did not take place around the fires would happen on the
Green.

Near the Winespring a score of older women sang softly as
they erected the Spring Pole. Shorn of its branches, the
straight, slender trunk of a fir tree stood ten feet high even in
the hole they had dug for it. A knot of girls too young to wear
their hair braided sat cross-legged and watched enviously, occasionally singing snatches of the song the women sang.

Tam clucked at Bela as if to make her speed her pace,
though she ignored it, and Rand studiously kept his eyes from
what the women were doing. In the morning the men would
pretend to be surprised to find the Pole, then at noon the unmarried women would dance the Pole, entwining it with long,
colored ribbons while the unmarried men sang. No one knew
when the custom began or why—it was another thing that was
the way it had always been—but it was an excuse to sing and
dance, and nobody in the Two Rivers needed much excuse for
that.

The whole day of Bel Tine would be taken up with singing
and dancing and feasting, with time out for footraces, and contests in almost everything. Prizes would be given not only in
archery, but for the best with the sling, and the quarterstaff.
There would be contests at solving riddles and puzzles, at the
rope tug, and lifting and tossing weights, prizes for the best
singer, the best dancer and the best fiddle player, for the quickest to shear a sheep, even the best at bowls, and at darts.

Bel Tine was supposed to come when spring had well and truly arrived, the first lambs born and the first crop up. Even with the cold hanging on, though, no one had any idea of putting it off. Everyone could use a little singing and dancing. And to top everything, if the rumors could be believed, a grand display of fireworks was planned for the Green—if the first peddler of the year appeared in time, of course. That had been causing considerable talk; it was ten years since the last such display, and that was still talked about.

The Winespring Inn stood at the east end of the Green, hard beside the Wagon Bridge. The first floor of the inn was river rock, though the foundation was of older stone some said came from the mountains. The whitewashed second story—where Brandelwyn al'Vere, the innkeeper and Mayor of Emond's Field for the past twenty years, lived in the back with his wife and daughters—jutted out over the lower floor all the way around. Red roof tile, the only such roof in the village, glittered in the weak sunlight, and smoke drifted from three of the inn's dozen tall chimneys.

At the south end of the inn, away from the stream, stretched the remains of a much larger stone foundation, once part of the inn—or so it was said. A huge oak grew in the middle of it now, with a bole thirty paces around and spreading branches as thick as a man. In the summer, Bran al'Vere set tables and benches under those branches, shady with leaves then, where people could enjoy a cup and a cooling breeze while they talked or perhaps set out a board for a game of stones.

"Here we are, lad." Tam reached for Bela's harness, but she stopped in front of the inn before his hand touched leather. "Knows the way better than I do," he chuckled.

As the last creak of the axle faded, Bran al'Vere appeared from the inn, seeming as always to step too lightly for a man of his girth, nearly double that of anyone else in the village. A smile split his round face, which was topped by a sparse fringe of gray hair. The innkeeper was in his shirtsleeves despite the chill, with a spotless white apron wrapped around him. A silver medallion in the form of a set of balance scales hung on his chest.

The medallion, along with the full-size set of scales used to weigh the coins of the merchants who came down from Baerlon for wool or tabac, was the symbol of the Mayor's office. Bran only wore it for dealing with the merchants and for festivals, feastdays, and weddings. He had it on a day early now, but that night was Winternight, the night before Bel Tine, when everyone would visit back and forth almost the whole night long, exchanging small gifts, having a bite to eat and a touch to drink at every house. *After the winter,* Rand thought, *he probably considers Winternight excuse enough not to wait until tomorrow.*

"Tam," the Mayor shouted as he hurried toward them. "The Light shine on me, it's good to see you at last. And you, Rand. How are you, my boy?"

"Fine, Master al'Vere," Rand said. "And you, sir?" But Bran's attention was already back on Tam.

"I was almost beginning to think you wouldn't be bringing your brandy this year. You've never waited so late before."

"I've no liking for leaving the farm these days, Bran," Tam replied. "Not with the wolves the way they are. And the weather."

Bran harrumphed. "I could wish somebody wanted to talk about something besides the weather. Everyone complains about it, and folk who should know better expect me to set it right. I've just spent twenty minutes explaining to Mistress al'Donel that I can do nothing about the storks. Though what she expected me to do. . . ." He shook his head.

"An ill omen," a scratchy voice announced, "no storks nesting on the rooftops at Bel Tine." Cenn Buie, as gnarled and dark as an old root, marched up to Tam and Bran and leaned on his walking staff, near as tall as he was and just as gnarled. He tried to fix both men at once with a beady eye. "There's worse to come, you mark my words."

"Have you become a soothsayer, then, interpreting omens?" Tam asked dryly. "Or do you listen to the wind, like a Wisdom? There's certainly enough of it. Some originating not far from here."

"Mock if you will," Cenn muttered, "but if it doesn't warm enough for crops to sprout soon, more than one root cellar will come up empty before there's a harvest. By next winter there may be nothing left alive in the Two Rivers but wolves and ravens. If it is next winter at all. Maybe it will still be this winter."

"Now what is that supposed to mean?" Bran said sharply.

Cenn gave them a sour look. "I've not much good to say about Nynaeve al'Meara. You know that. For one thing, she's too young to— No matter. The Women's Circle seems to object to the Village Council even talking about their business, though they interfere in ours whenever they want to, which is most of the time, or so it seems to—"

"Cenn," Tam broke in, "is there a point to this?"

"This is the point, al'Thor. Ask the Wisdom when the winter will end, and she walks away. Maybe she doesn't want to tell us what she hears on the wind. Maybe what she hears is that the winter won't end. Maybe it's just going to go on being winter until the Wheel turns and the Age ends. There's your point."

"Maybe sheep will fly," Tam retorted, and Bran threw up his hands.

"The Light protect me from fools. You sitting on the Village Council, Cenn, and now you're spreading that Coplin talk. Well, you listen to me. We have enough problems without. . . ."

A quick tug at Rand's sleeve and a voice pitched low, for his ear alone, distracted him from the older men's talk. "Come on, Rand, while they're arguing. Before they put you to work."

Rand glanced down, and had to grin. Mat Cauthon crouched beside the cart so Tam and Bran and Cenn could not see him, his wiry body contorted like a stork trying to bend itself double.

Mat's brown eyes twinkled with mischief, as usual. "Dav and I caught a big old badger, all grouchy at being pulled out of his den. We're going to let it loose on the Green and watch the girls run."

Rand's smile broadened; it did not sound as much like fun to him as it would have a year or two back, but Mat never seemed to grow up. He took a quick look at his father—the men had their heads together still, all three talking at once—then lowered his own voice. "I promised to unload the cider. I can meet you later, though."

Mat rolled his eyes skyward. "Toting barrels! Burn me, I'd rather play stones with my baby sister. Well, I know of better things than a badger. We have strangers in the Two Rivers. Last evening—"

For an instant Rand stopped breathing. "A man on horseback?" he asked intently. "A man in a black cloak, on a black horse? And his cloak doesn't move in the wind?"

Mat swallowed his grin, and his voice dropped to an even hoarser whisper. "You saw him, too? I thought I was the only one. Don't laugh, Rand, but he scared me."

"I'm not laughing. He scared me, too. I could swear he hated me, that he wanted to kill me." Rand shivered. Until that day he had never thought of anyone wanting to kill him, really wanting to kill him. That sort of thing just did not happen in the Two Rivers. A fistfight, maybe, or a wrestling match, but not killing.

"I don't know about hating, Rand, but he was scary enough anyway. All he did was sit on his horse looking at me, just outside the village, but I've never been so frightened in my life. Well, I looked away, just for a moment—it wasn't easy, mind you—then when I looked back he'd vanished. Blood and ashes! Three days, it's been, and I can hardly stop thinking about him. I keep looking over my shoulder." Mat attempted a laugh that came out as a croak. "Funny how being scared takes you. You think strange things. I actually thought—just for a minute, mind—it might be the Dark One." He tried another laugh, but no sound at all came out this time.

Rand took a deep breath. As much to remind himself as for any other reason, he said by rote, "The Dark One and all of the Forsaken are bound in Shayol Ghul, beyond the Great Blight, bound by the Creator at the moment of Creation, bound until the end of time. The hand of the Creator shelters the world, and the Light shines on us all." He drew another breath and went on. "Besides, if he was free, what would the Shepherd of the Night be doing in the Two Rivers watching farmboys?"

"I don't know. But I do know that rider was . . . evil. Don't laugh. I'll take oath on it. Maybe it was the Dragon."

"You're just full of cheerful thoughts, aren't you?" Rand muttered. "You sound worse than Cenn."

"My mother always said the Forsaken would come for me if I didn't mend my ways. If I ever saw anybody who looked like Ishamael, or Aginor, it was him."

"Everybody's mother scared them with the Forsaken," Rand

said dryly, "but most grow out of it. Why not the Shadowman, while you're about it?"

Mat glared at him. "I haven't been so scared since. . . . No, I've never been that scared, and I don't mind admitting it."

"Me, either. My father thinks I was jumping at shadows under the trees."

Mat nodded glumly and leaned back against the cart wheel. "So does my da. I told Dav, and Elam Dowtry. They've been watching like hawks ever since, but they haven't seen anything. Now Elam thinks I was trying to trick him. Dav thinks he's down from Taren Ferry—a sheepstealer, or a chickenthief. A chickenthief!" He lapsed into affronted silence.

"It's probably all foolishness anyway," Rand said finally. "Maybe he is just a sheepstealer." He tried to picture it, but it was like picturing a wolf taking the cat's place in front of a mouse hole.

"Well, I didn't like the way he looked at me. And neither did you, not if how you jumped at me is any guide. We ought to tell someone."

"We already have, Mat, both of us, and we weren't believed. Can you imagine trying to convince Master al'Vere about this fellow, without him seeing him? He'd send us off to Nynaeve to see if we were sick."

"There are two of us, now. Nobody could believe we both imagined it."

Rand rubbed the top of his head briskly, wondering what to say. Mat was something of a byword around the village. Few people had escaped his pranks. Now his name came up whenever a washline dropped the laundry in the dirt or a loose saddle girth deposited a farmer in the road. Mat did not even have to be anywhere around. His support might be worse than none.

After a moment Rand said, "Your father would believe you put me up to it, and mine. . . ." He looked over the cart to where Tam and Bran and Cenn had been talking, and found himself staring his father in the eyes. The Mayor was still lecturing Cenn, who took it now in sullen silence.

"Good morning, Matrim," Tam said brightly, hefting one of the brandy casks up onto the side of the cart. "I see you've come to help Rand unload the cider. Good lad."

Mat leaped to his feet at the first word and began backing away. "Good morning to you, Master al'Thor. And to you, Master al'Vere. Master Buie. May the Light shine on you. My da sent me to—"

"No doubt he did," Tam said. "And no doubt, since you are a lad who does his chores right off, you've finished the task already. Well, the quicker you lads get the cider into Master al'Vere's cellar, the quicker you can see the gleeman."

"Gleeman!" Mat exclaimed, stopping dead in his footsteps, at the same instant that Rand asked, "When will he get here?"

Rand could remember only two gleemen coming into the Two Rivers in his whole life, and for one of those he had been young enough to sit on Tam's shoulders to watch. To have one there actually during Bel Tine, with his harp and his flute and his stories and all. . . . Emond's Field would still be talking about this Festival ten years off, even if there were not any fireworks.

"Foolishness," Cenn grumbled, but fell silent at a look from Bran that had all the weight of the Mayor's office in it.

Tam leaned against the side of the cart, using the brandy cask as a prop for his arm. "Yes, a gleeman, and already here. According to Master al'Vere, he's in a room in the inn right now."

"Arrived in the dead of night, he did." The innkeeper shook his head in disapproval. "Pounded on the front door till he woke the whole family. If not for Festival, I'd have told him to stable his own horse and sleep in the stall with it, gleeman or not. Imagine coming in the dark like that."

Rand stared wonderingly. No one traveled beyond the village by night, not these days, certainly not alone. The thatcher grumbled under his breath again, too low this time for Rand to understand more than a word or two. "Madman" and "unnatural."

"He doesn't wear a black cloak, does he?" Mat asked suddenly.

Bran's belly shook with his chuckle. "Black! His cloak is like every gleeman's cloak I've ever seen. More patches than cloak, and more colors than you can think of."

Rand startled himself by laughing out loud, a laugh of pure relief. The menacing black-clad rider as a gleeman was a ridiculous notion, but. . . . He clapped a hand over his mouth in embarrassment.

"You see, Tam," Bran said. "There's been little enough laughter in this village since winter came. Now even the gleeman's cloak brings a laugh. That alone is worth the expense of bringing him down from Baerlon."

"Say what you will," Cenn spoke up suddenly. "I still say it's a foolish waste of money. And those fireworks you all insisted on sending off for."

"So there are fireworks," Mat said, but Cenn went right on.

"They should have been here a month ago with the first peddler of the year, but there hasn't been a peddler, has there? If he doesn't come by tomorrow, what are we going to do with them? Hold another Festival just to set them off? That's if he even brings them, of course."

"Cenn"—Tam sighed—"you've as much trust as a Taren Ferry man."

"Where is he, then? Tell me that, al'Thor."

"Why didn't you tell us?" Mat demanded in an aggrieved voice. "The whole village would have had as much fun with the waiting as with the gleeman. Or almost, anyway. You can see how everybody's been over just a rumor of fireworks."

"I can see," Bran replied with a sidelong look at the thatcher. "And if I knew for sure how that rumor started . . . if I thought, for instance, that somebody had been complaining about how much things cost where people could hear him when the things are supposed to be secret. . . ."

Cenn cleared his throat. "My bones are too old for this wind. If you don't mind, I'll just see if Mistress al'Vere won't fix me some mulled wine to take the chill off. Mayor. Al'Thor." He was headed for the inn before he finished, and as the door swung shut behind him, Bran sighed.

"Sometimes I think Nynaeve is right about. . . . Well, that's not important now. You young fellows think for a minute. Everyone's excited about the fireworks, true, and that's only at a rumor. Think how they'll be if the peddler doesn't get here in time, after all their anticipating. And with the weather the way it is, who knows when he will come. They'd be fifty times as excited about a gleeman."

"And feel fifty times as bad if he hadn't come," Rand said slowly. "Even Bel Tine might not do much for people's spirits after that."

"You have a head on your shoulders when you choose to use it," Bran said. "He'll follow you on the Village Council one day, Tam. Mark my words. He couldn't do much worse right now than someone I could name."

"None of this is unloading the cart," Tam said briskly, handing the first cask of brandy to the Mayor. "I want a warm fire, my pipe, and a mug of your good ale." He hoisted the second brandy cask onto his shoulder. "I'm sure Rand will thank you for your help, Matrim. Remember, the sooner the cider is in the cellar. . . ."

As Tam and Bran disappeared into the inn, Rand looked at his friend. "You don't have to help. Dav won't keep that badger long."

"Oh, why not?" Mat said resignedly. "Like your da said, the quicker it's in the cellar. . . ." Picking up one of the casks of cider in both arms, he hurried toward the inn in a half trot. "Maybe Egwene is around. Watching you stare at her like a poleaxed ox will be as good as a badger any day."

Rand paused in the act of putting his bow and quiver in the back of the cart. He really had managed to put Egwene out of his mind. That was unusual in itself. But she would likely be around the inn somewhere. There was not much chance he could avoid her. Of course, it had been weeks since he saw her last.

"Well?" Mat called from the front of the inn. "I didn't say I would do it by myself. You aren't on the Village Council yet."

With a start, Rand took up a cask and followed. Perhaps she would not be there after all. Oddly, that possibility did not make him feel any better.

CHAPTER
2

Strangers

When Rand and Mat carried the first barrels through the common room, Master al'Vere was already filling a pair of mugs with his best brown ale, his own make, from one of the casks racked against one wall. Scratch, the inn's yellow cat, crouched atop it with his eyes closed and his tail wrapped around his feet. Tam stood in front of the big fireplace of river rock, thumbing a long-stemmed pipe full of tabac from a polished canister the innkeeper always kept on the plain stone mantel. The fireplace stretched half the length of the big, square room, with a lintel as high as a man's shoulder, and the crackling blaze on the hearth vanquished the chill outside.

At that time of the busy day before Festival, Rand expected to find the common room empty except for Bran and his father and the cat, but four more members of the Village Council, including Cenn, sat in high-backed chairs in front of the fire, mugs in hand and blue-gray pipesmoke wreathing their heads. For once none of the stones boards were in use, and all of Bran's books stood idle on the shelf opposite the fireplace. The men did not even talk, peering silently into their ale or tapping pipestems against their teeth in impatience, as they waited for Tam and Bran to join them.

Worry was not uncommon for the Village Council these days, not in Emond's Field, and likely not in Watch Hill, or Deven

Ride. Or even Taren Ferry, though who knew what Taren Ferry folk really thought about anything?

Only two of the men before the fire, Haral Luhhan, the blacksmith, and Jon Thane, the miller, so much as glanced at the boys as they entered. Master Luhhan, though, made it more than a glance. The blacksmith's arms were as big as most men's legs, roped with heavy muscle, and he still wore his long leather apron as if he had hurried to the meeting straight from the forge. His frown took them both in, then he straightened around in his chair deliberately, turning his attention back to an over-studious tamping of his pipe with a thick thumb.

Curious, Rand slowed, then barely bit back a yelp as Mat kicked his ankle. His friend nodded insistently toward the doorway at the back of the common room and hurried on without waiting. Limping slightly, Rand followed less quickly.

"What was that about?" he demanded as soon as he was in the hall that led to the kitchen. "You almost broke my—"

"It's old Luhhan," Mat said, peering past Rand's shoulder into the common room. "I think he suspects I was the one who—" He cut off abruptly as Mistress al'Vere bustled out of the kitchen, the aroma of fresh-baked bread wafting ahead of her.

The tray in her hands carried some of the crusty loaves for which she was famous around Emond's Field, as well as plates of pickles and cheese. The food reminded Rand abruptly that he had eaten only an end of bread before leaving the farm that morning. His stomach gave an embarrassing rumble.

A slender woman, with her thick braid of graying hair pulled over one shoulder, Mistress al'Vere smiled in a motherly fashion that took in both of them. "There is more of this in the kitchen, if you two are hungry, and I never knew boys your age who weren't. Or any other age, for that matter. If you prefer, I'm baking honeycakes this morning."

She was one of the few married women in the area who never tried to play matchmaker with Tam. Toward Rand her motherliness extended to warm smiles and a quick snack whenever he came by the inn, but she did as much for every young man in the area. If she occasionally looked at him as if she wanted to do more, at least she took it no further than looks, for which he was deeply grateful.

Without waiting for a reply she swept on into the common room. Immediately there was the sound of chairs scraping on the floor as the men got to their feet, and exclaimings over the smell of the bread. She was easily the best cook in Emond's Field, and not a man for miles around but eagerly leaped at a chance to put his feet under her table.

"Honeycakes," Mat said, smacking his lips.

"After," Rand told him firmly, "or we'll never get done."

A lamp hung over the cellar stairs, just beside the kitchen door, and another made a bright pool in the stone-walled room beneath the inn, banishing all but a little dimness in the furthest corners. Wooden racks along the walls and across the floor held casks of brandy and cider, and larger barrels of ale and wine, some with taps driven in. Many of the wine barrels were marked with chalk in Bran al'Vere's hand, giving the year they had been bought, what peddler had brought them, and in which city they had been made, but all of the ale and brandy was the make of Two Rivers farmers or of Bran himself. Peddlers, and even merchants, sometimes brought brandy or ale from outside, but it was never as good and cost the earth, besides, and nobody ever drank it more than once.

"Now," Rand said, as they set their casks in the racks, "what did you do that you have to avoid Master Luhhan?"

Mat shrugged. "Nothing, really. I told Adan al'Caar and some of his snot-nosed friends—Ewin Finngar and Dag Coplin—that some farmers had seen ghost hounds, breathing fire and running through the woods. They ate it up like clotted cream."

"And Master Luhhan is mad at you for that?" Rand said doubtfully.

"Not exactly." Mat paused, then shook his head. "You see, I covered two of his dogs with flour, so they were all white. Then I let them loose near Dag's house. How was I to know they'd run straight home? It really isn't my fault. If Mistress Luhhan hadn't left the door open they couldn't have gotten inside. It isn't like I intended to get flour all over her house." He gave a bark of laughter. "I hear she chased old Luhhan and the dogs, all three, out of the house with a broom."

Rand winced and laughed at the same time. "If I were you, I'd worry more about Alsbet Luhhan than about the blacksmith. She's almost as strong, and her temper is a lot worse. No matter, though. If you walk fast, maybe he won't notice you." Mat's expression said he did not think Rand was funny.

When they went back through the common room, though, there was no need for Mat to hurry. The six men had their chairs in a tight knot before the fireplace. With his back to the fire, Tam was speaking in a low voice, and the others were leaning forward to listen, so intent on his words they would likely not have noticed if a flock of sheep had been driven through. Rand wanted to move closer, to hear what they were talking about, but Mat plucked at his sleeve and gave him an agonized look. With a sigh he followed Mat out to the cart.

On their return to the hallway they found a tray by the top of the steps, and hot honeycakes filling the hall with their sweet aroma. There were two mugs, as well, and a pitcher of steaming mulled cider. Despite his own admonition about waiting until later Rand found himself making the last two trips between cart and cellar while trying to juggle a cask and a piping honeycake.

Setting his final cask in the racks, he wiped crumbs from his mouth while Mat was unburdening himself, then said, "Now for the glee—"

Feet clattered on the stairs, and Ewin Finngar half fell into the cellar in his haste, his pudgy face shining with eagerness to impart his news. "There are strangers in the village." He caught his breath and gave Mat a wry look. "I haven't seen any ghost hounds, but I hear somebody floured Master Luhhan's dogs. I hear Mistress Luhhan has ideas who to look for, too."

The years separating Rand and Mat from Ewin, only fourteen, were usually more than enough for them to give short shrift to anything he had to say. This time they exchanged one startled glance, then both were talking at once.

"In the village?" Rand asked. "Not in the woods?"

Right on top of him Mat added, "Was his cloak black? Could you see his face?"

Ewin looked uncertainly from one of them to the other, then spoke quickly when Mat took a threatening step. "Of course I could see his face. And his cloak is green. Or maybe gray. It changes. It seems to fade into wherever he's standing. Sometimes you don't see him even when you look right at him, not unless he moves. And hers is blue, like the sky, and ten times fancier than any feastday clothes I ever saw. She's ten times prettier than anybody I ever saw, too. She's a high-born lady, like in the stories. She must be."

"Her?" Rand said. "Who are you talking about?" He stared at Mat, who had put both hands on top of his head and squeezed his eyes shut.

"They're the ones I meant to tell you about," Mat muttered, "before you got me off onto—" He cut off, opening his eyes for a sharp glance at Ewin. "They arrived last evening," Mat went on after a moment, "and took rooms here at the inn. I saw them ride in. Their horses, Rand. I never saw horses so tall, or so sleek. They look like they could run forever. I think he works for her."

"In service," Ewin broke in. "They call it being in service, in the stories."

Mat continued as if Ewin had not spoken. "Anyway, he defers to her, does what she says. Only he isn't like a hired man. A soldier, maybe. The way he wears his sword, it's part of him, like his hand or his foot. He makes the merchants' guards look like cur dogs. And her, Rand. I never even imagined anyone like her. She's out of a gleeman's story. She's like . . . like. . . ." He paused to give Ewin a sour look. ". . . Like a high-born lady," he finished with a sigh.

"But who are they?" Rand asked. Except for merchants, once a year to buy tabac and wool, and the peddlers, outsiders never came into the Two Rivers, or as good as never. Maybe at Taren Ferry, but not this far south. Most of the merchants and peddlers had been coming for years, too, so they did not really count as strangers. Just outsiders. It was a good five years since the last time a real stranger appeared in Emond's Field, and he had been trying to hide from some sort of trouble up in Baerlon that nobody in the village understood. He had not stayed long. "What do they want?"

"What do they want?" Mat exclaimed. "I don't care what they want. Strangers, Rand, and strangers like you never even dreamed of. Think of it!"

Rand opened his mouth, then closed it without speaking. The black-cloaked rider had him as nervous as a cat in a dog run. It just seemed like an awful coincidence, three strangers around the village at the same time. Three if this fellow's cloak that changed colors never changed to black.

"Her name is Moiraine," Ewin said into the momentary silence. "I heard him say it. Moiraine, he called her. The Lady Moiraine. His name is Lan. The Wisdom may not like her, but I do."

"What makes you think Nynaeve dislikes her?" Rand said.

"She asked the Wisdom for directions this morning," Ewin said, "and called her 'child.'" Rand and Mat both whistled softly through their teeth, and Ewin tripped over his tongue in his haste to explain. "The Lady Moiraine didn't know she was the Wisdom. She apologized when she found out. She did. And asked some questions about herbs, and about who is who around Emond's Field, just as respectfully as any woman in the village—more so than some. She's always asking questions, about how old people are, and how long they've lived where they live, and . . . oh, I don't know what all. Anyway, Nynaeve answered like she'd bitten a green sweetberry. Then, when the Lady Moiraine walked away, Nynaeve stared after her like, like . . . well, it wasn't friendly, I can tell you that."

"Is that all?" Rand said. "You know Nynaeve's temper. When Cenn Buie called her a child last year, she thumped him on the head with her stick, and he's on the Village Council, and old enough to be her grandfather, besides. She flares up at anything, and never stays angry past turning around."

"That's too long for me," Ewin muttered.

"I don't care who Nynaeve thumps"—Mat chortled—"so long as it isn't me. This is going to be the best Bel Tine ever. A gleeman, a lady—who could ask for more? Who needs fireworks?"

"A gleeman?" Ewin said, his voice rising sharply.

"Come on, Rand," Mat went on, ignoring the younger boy. "We're done here. You have to see this fellow."

He bounded up the stairs, with Ewin scrambling behind him calling, "Is there really a gleeman, Mat? This isn't like the ghost hounds, is it? Or the frogs?"

Rand paused long enough to turn down the lamp, then hurried after them.

In the common room Rowan Hurn and Samel Crawe had joined the others in front of the fire, so that the entire Village

Council was there. Bran al'Vere spoke now, his normally bluff voice pitched so low that only a rumbling murmur traveled beyond the close-gathered chairs. The Mayor emphasized his words by tapping a thick forefinger into the palm of his other hand, and eyed each man in turn. They all nodded in agreement with whatever he was saying, though Cenn more reluctantly than the rest.

The way the men all but huddled together spoke more plainly than a painted sign. Whatever they were talking about, it was for the Village Council alone, at least for now. They would not appreciate Rand trying to listen in. Reluctantly he pulled himself away. There was still the gleeman. And these strangers.

Outside, Bela and the cart were gone, taken away by Hu or Tad, the inn's stablemen. Mat and Ewin stood glaring at one another a few paces from the front door of the inn, their cloaks whipping in the wind.

"For the last time," Mat barked, "I am *not* playing a trick on you. There *is* a gleeman. Now go away. Rand, will you tell this woolhead I am telling the truth so he'll leave me alone?"

Pulling his cloak together, Rand stepped forward to support Mat, but words died as the hairs stirred on the back of his neck. He was being watched again. It was far from the feeling the hooded rider had given him, but neither was it pleasant, especially so soon after that encounter.

A quick look about the Green showed him only what he had seen before—children playing, people preparing for Festival, and no one more than glancing in his direction. The Spring Pole stood alone, now, waiting. Bustle and childish shouts filled the side streets. All was as it should be. Except that he was being watched.

Then something led him to turn around, to raise his eyes. On the edge of the inn's tile roof perched a large raven, swaying a little in the gusting wind from the mountains. Its head was cocked to one side, and one beady, black eye was focused . . . on him, he thought. He swallowed, and suddenly anger flickered in him, hot and sharp.

"Filthy carrion eater," he muttered.

"I am tired of being stared at," Mat growled, and Rand real-

ized his friend had stepped up beside him and was frowning at
the raven, too.

They exchanged a glance, then as one their hands darted for
rocks.

The two stones flew true . . . and the raven stepped aside;
the stones whistled through the space where it had been. Fluff-
ing its wings once, it cocked its head again, fixing them with a
dead black eye, unafraid, giving no sign that anything had happened.

Rand stared at the bird in consternation. "Did you ever see a
raven do that?" he asked quietly.

Mat shook his head without looking away from the raven.
"Never. Nor any other bird, either."

"A vile bird," came a woman's voice from behind them, me-
lodious despite echoes of distaste, "to be mistrusted in the best
of times."

With a shrill cry the raven launched itself into the air so violently that two black feathers drifted down from the roof's
edge.

Startled, Rand and Mat twisted to follow the bird's swift
flight, over the Green and toward the cloud-tipped Mountains
of Mist, tall beyond the Westwood, until it dwindled to a speck
in the west, then vanished from view.

Rand's gaze fell to the woman who had spoken. She, too,
had been watching the flight of the raven, but now she turned
back, and her eyes met his. He could only stare. This had to be
the Lady Moiraine, and she was everything that Mat and Ewin
had said, everything and more.

When he had heard she called Nynaeve child, he had pictured her as old, but she was not. At least, he could not put any
age to her at all. At first he thought she was as young as
Nynaeve, but the longer he looked the more he thought she
was older than that. There was a maturity about her large, dark
eyes, a hint of knowing that no one could have gotten young.
For an instant he thought those eyes were deep pools about to
swallow him up. It was plain why Mat and Ewin named her a
lady from a gleeman's tale, too. She held herself with a grace
and air of command that made him feel awkward and stumble-
footed. She was barely tall enough to come up to his chest, but

her presence was such that her height seemed the proper one, and he felt ungainly in his tallness.

Altogether she was like no one he had ever seen before. The wide hood of her cloak framed her face and dark hair, hanging in soft ringlets. He had never seen a grown woman with her hair unbraided; every girl in the Two Rivers waited eagerly for the Women's Circle of her village to say she was old enough to wear a braid. Her clothes were just as strange. Her cloak was sky-blue velvet, with thick silver embroidery, leaves and vines and flowers, all along the edges. Her dress gleamed faintly as she moved, a darker blue than the cloak, and slashed with cream. A necklace of heavy gold links hung around her neck, while another gold chain, delicate and fastened in her hair, supported a small, sparkling blue stone in the middle of her forehead. A wide belt of woven gold encircled her waist, and on the second finger of her left hand was a gold ring in the shape of a serpent biting its own tail. He had certainly never seen a ring like that, though he recognized the Great Serpent, an even older symbol for eternity than the Wheel of Time.

Fancier than any feastday clothes, Ewin had said, and he was right. No one ever dressed like that in the Two Rivers. Not ever.

"Good morning, Mistress . . . ah . . . Lady Moiraine," Rand said. His face grew hot at his tongue's fumbling.

"Good morning, Lady Moiraine," Mat echoed somewhat more smoothly, but only a little.

She smiled, and Rand found himself wondering if there was anything he might do for her, something that would give him an excuse to stay near her. He knew she was smiling at all of them, but it seemed meant for him alone. It really was just like seeing a gleeman's tale come to life. Mat had a foolish grin on his face.

"You know my name," she said, sounding delighted. As if her presence, however brief, would not be the talk of the village for a year! "But you must call me Moiraine, not lady. And what are your names?"

Ewin leaped forward before either of the others could speak. "My name is Ewin Finngar, my lady. I told them your name; that's how they know. I heard Lan say it, but I wasn't eavesdropping. No one like you has ever come to Emond's Field, before. There's a gleeman in the village for Bel Tine, too. And tonight is Winternight. Will you come to my house? My mother has apple cakes."

"I shall have to see," she replied, putting a hand on Ewin's shoulder. Her eyes twinkled with amusement, though she gave no other sign of it. "I do not know how well I could compete against a gleeman, Ewin. But you must all call me Moiraine." She looked expectantly at Rand and Mat.

"I'm Matrim Cauthon, La . . . ah . . . Moiraine," Mat said. He made a stiff, jerking bow, then went red in the face as he straightened.

Rand had been wondering if he should do something of the sort, the way men did in stories, but with Mat's example, he merely spoke his name. At least he did not stumble over his own tongue this time.

Moiraine looked from him to Mat and back again. Rand thought her smile, a bare curve of the corners of her mouth, was now the sort Egwene wore when she had a secret. "I may have some small tasks to be done from time to time while I am in Emond's Field," she said. "Perhaps you would be willing to assist me?" She laughed as their assents tumbled over one another. "Here," she said, and Rand was surprised when she pressed a coin into his palm, closing his hand tightly around it with both of hers.

"There's no need," he began, but she waved aside his protest as she gave Ewin a coin as well, then pressed Mat's hand around one the same way she had Rand's.

"Of course, there is," she said. "You cannot be expected to work for nothing. Consider this a token, and keep it with you, so you will remember that you have agreed to come to me when I ask it. There is a bond between us now."

"I'll never forget," Ewin piped up.

"Later we must talk," she said, "and you must tell me all about yourselves."

"Lady . . . I mean, Moiraine?" Rand asked hesitantly as she turned away. She stopped and looked back over her shoulder, and he had to swallow before going on. "Why have you come to Emond's Field?" Her expression was unchanged, but suddenly he wished he had not asked, though he could not have said why. He rushed to explain himself, anyway. "I don't mean to be rude. I'm sorry. It's just that no one comes into the Two Rivers except the merchants, and peddlers when the snow isn't too deep to get down from Baerlon. Almost no one. Certainly no one like you. The merchants' guards sometimes say this is the back end of forever, and I suppose it must seem that way to anyone from outside. I just wondered."

Her smile did fade then, slowly, as if something had been recalled to her. For a moment she merely looked at him. "I am a student of history," she said at last, "a collector of old stories. This place you call the Two Rivers has always interested me. Sometimes I study the stories of what happened here long ago, here and at other places."

"Stories?" Rand said. "What ever happened in the Two Rivers to interest someone like—I mean, what could have happened here?"

"And what else would you call it beside the Two Rivers?" Mat added. "That's what it has always been called."

"As the Wheel of Time turns," Moiraine said, half to herself and with a distant look in her eyes, "places wear many names. Men wear many names, many faces. Different faces, but always the same man. Yet no one knows the Great Pattern the Wheel weaves, or even the Pattern of an Age. We can only watch, and study, and hope."

Rand stared at her, unable to say a word, even to ask what she meant. He was not sure she had meant for them to hear. The other two were just as tongue-tied, he noticed. Ewin's mouth hung open.

Moiraine focused on them again, and all three gave a little shake as if waking up. "Later we will talk," she said. None of them said a word. "Later." She moved on toward the Wagon Bridge, appearing to glide over the ground rather than walk, her cloak spreading on either side of her like wings.

As she left, a tall man Rand had not noticed before moved away from the front of the inn and followed her, one hand resting on the long hilt of a sword. His clothes were a dark grayish green that would have faded into leaf or shadow, and his cloak swirled through shades of gray and green and brown as it shifted in the wind. It almost seemed to disappear at times, that cloak, fading into whatever lay beyond it. His hair was long, and gray at the temples, held back from his face by a narrow leather headband. That face was made from stony planes and angles, weathered but unlined despite the gray in his hair. When he moved, Rand could think of nothing but a wolf.

In passing the three youths his gaze ran over them, eyes as cold and blue as a midwinter dawn. It was as if he were weighing them in his mind, and there was no sign on his face of what the scales told him. He quickened his pace until he caught up to Moiraine, then slowed to walk by her shoulder, bending to speak to her. Rand let out a breath he had not realized he had been holding.

"That was Lan," Ewin said throatily, as if he, too, had been holding his breath. It had been that kind of look. "I'll bet he's a Warder."

"Don't be a fool." Mat laughed, but it was a shaky laugh. "Warders are just in stories. Anyway, Warders have swords and armor covered in gold and jewels, and spend all their time up north, in the Great Blight, fighting evil and Trollocs and such."

"He *could* be a Warder," Ewin insisted.

"Did you see any gold or jewels on him?" Mat scoffed. "Do we have Trollocs in the Two Rivers? We have sheep. I wonder what could ever have happened here to interest someone like her."

"Something could have," Rand answered slowly. "They say the inn's been here for a thousand years, maybe more."

"A thousand years of sheep," Mat said.

"A silver penny!" Ewin burst out. "She gave me a whole silver penny! Think what I can buy when the peddler comes."

Rand opened his hand to look at the coin she had given him, and almost dropped it in surprise. He did not recognize the fat silver coin with the raised image of a woman balancing a single flame on her upturned hand, but he had watched while Bran al'Vere weighed out the coins merchants brought from a dozen lands, and he had an idea of its value. That much silver would buy a good horse anywhere in the Two Rivers, with some left over.

He looked at Mat and saw the same stunned expression he knew must be on his own face. Tilting his hand so Mat could see the coin but not Ewin, he raised a questioning eyebrow.

Mat nodded, and for a minute they stared at one another in perplexed wonder.

"What kind of chores does she have?" Rand asked finally.

"I don't know," Mat said firmly, "and I don't care. I won't spend it, either. Even when the peddler comes." With that he thrust his coin into his coat pocket.

Nodding, Rand slowly did the same with his. He was not sure why, but somehow what Mat said seemed right. The coin should not be spent. Not when it came from her. He could not think of anything else silver was good for, but. . . .

"Do you think I should keep mine, too?" Anguished indecision painted Ewin's face.

"Not unless you want to," Mat said.

"I think she gave it to you to spend," Rand said.

Ewin looked at his coin, then shook his head and stuffed the silver penny into his pocket. "I'll keep it," he said mournfully.

"There's still the gleeman," Rand said, and the younger boy brightened.

"If he ever wakes up," Mat added.

"Rand," Ewin asked, "*is* there a gleeman?"

"You'll see," Rand answered with a laugh. It was clear Ewin would not believe until he set eyes on the gleeman. "He has to come down sooner or later."

Shouting drifted across the Wagon Bridge, and when Rand looked to see what was causing it, his laughter became wholehearted. A milling crowd of villagers, from gray-haired oldsters to toddlers barely able to walk, escorted a tall wagon toward the bridge, a huge wagon drawn by eight horses, the outside of its rounded canvas cover hung about with bundles like bunches of grapes. The peddler had come at last. Strangers and a gleeman, fireworks and a peddler. It was going to be the best Bel Tine ever.

CHAPTER
3

The Peddler

Clusters of pots clattered and banged as the peddler's wagon rumbled over the heavy timbers of the Wagon Bridge. Still surrounded by a cloud of villagers and farmers come for Festival, the peddler reined his horses to a stop in front of the inn. From every direction people streamed to swell the numbers around the great wagon, its wheels taller than any of the people with their eyes fastened to the peddler above them on the wagon seat.

The man on the wagon was Padan Fain, a pale, skinny fellow with gangly arms and a massive beak of a nose. Fain, always smiling and laughing as if he knew a joke that no one· else knew, had driven his wagon and team into Emond's Field every spring for as long as Rand could remember.

The door of the inn flew open even as the team halted in a jangle of harness, and the Village Council appeared, led by Master al'Vere and Tam. They marched out deliberately, even Cenn Buie, amid all the excited shouting of the others for pins or lace or books or a dozen other things. Reluctantly the crowd parted to let them to the fore, everyone closing in quickly behind and never stopping their calling to the peddler. Most of all, the villagers called for news.

In the eyes of the villagers, needles and tea and the like were no more than half the freight in a peddler's wagon. Every bit as important was word of outside, news of the world beyond the Two Rivers. Some peddlers simply told what they knew, throwing it out in a heap, a pile of rubbish with which they could not be bothered. Others had to have every word dragged out of them, speaking grudgingly, with a bad grace. Fain, however, spoke freely if often teasingly, and spun out the telling, making a show to rival a gleeman. He enjoyed being the center of attention, strutting around like an under-sized rooster, with every eye on him. It occurred to Rand that Fain might not be best pleased to find a real gleeman in Emond's Field.

The peddler gave the Council and villagers alike exactly the same attention as he fussed with tying his reins off just so, which was to say hardly any attention at all. He nodded casually at no one in particular. He smiled without speaking, and waved absently to people with whom he was particularly friendly, though his friendliness had always been of a peculiarly distant kind, backslapping without ever getting close.

The demands for him to speak grew louder, but Fain waited, fiddling with small tasks about the driver's seat, for the crowd and the anticipation to reach the size he wanted. The Council alone kept silent. They maintained the dignity befitting their position, but increasing clouds of pipesmoke rising above their heads showed the effort of it.

Rand and Mat edged into the crowd, getting as close to the wagon as they could. Rand would have stopped halfway, but Mat wriggled through the press, pulling Rand behind him, until they were right behind the Council.

"I had been thinking you were going to stay out on the farm through the whole Festival," Perrin Aybara shouted at Rand over the clamor. Half a head shorter than Rand, the curly-haired blacksmith's apprentice was so stocky as to seem a man and a half wide, with arms and shoulders thick enough to rival those of Master Luhhan himself. He could easily have pushed through the throng, but that was not his way. He picked his path carefully, offering apologies to people who had only half a mind to notice anything but the peddler. He made the apologies anyway, and tried not to jostle anyone as he worked through the crowd to Rand and Mat. "Imagine it," he said when he finally reached them. "Bel Tine and a peddler, both together. I'll bet there really are fireworks."

"You don't know a quarter of it." Mat laughed.

Perrin eyed him suspiciously, then looked a question at Rand.

"It's true," Rand shouted, then gestured at the growing mass of people, all giving voice. "Later. I'll explain later. Later, I said!"

At that moment Padan Fain stood up on the wagon seat, and the crowd quieted in an instant. Rand's last words exploded into utter silence, catching the peddler with an arm raised dramatically and his mouth open. Everybody turned to stare at Rand. The bony little man on the wagon, prepared to have everyone hanging on his first words, gave Rand a sharp, searching look.

Rand's face reddened, and he wished he were Ewin's size so he did not stand out so clearly. His friends shifted uncomfortably, too. It had only been the year before that Fain had taken notice of them for the first time, acknowledging them as men. Fain did not usually have time for anyone too young to buy a good deal of things off his wagon. Rand hoped he had not been relegated to a child again in the peddler's eyes.

With a loud harrumph, Fain tugged at his heavy cloak. "No, not later," the peddler declaimed, once more throwing up a hand grandly. "I will be telling you now." As he spoke he made broad gestures, casting his words over the crowd. "You are thinking you have had troubles in the Two Rivers, are you? Well, all the world has troubles, from the Great Blight south to the Sea of Storms, from the Aryth Ocean in the west to the Aiel Waste in the east. And even beyond. The winter was harsher than you've ever seen before, cold enough to jell your blood and crack your bones? Ahhh! Winter was cold and harsh everywhere. In the Borderlands they'd be calling your winter spring. But spring does not come, you say? Wolves have killed your sheep? Perhaps wolves have attacked men? Is that the way of it? Well, now. Spring is late everywhere. There are wolves everywhere, all hungry for any flesh they can sink a tooth into, be it sheep or cow or man. But there are things worse than wolves or winter. There are those who would be glad to have only your little troubles." He paused expectantly.

"What could be worse than wolves killing sheep, and men?" Cenn Buie demanded. Others muttered in support.

"Men killing men." The peddler's reply, in portentous tones, brought shocked murmurs that increased as he went on. "It is war I mean. There is war in Ghealdan, war and madness. The snows of the Dhallin Forest are red with the blood of men. Ravens and the cries of ravens fill the air. Armies march to Ghealdan. Nations, great houses and great men, send their soldiers to fight."

"War?" Master al'Vere's mouth fit awkwardly around the unfamiliar word. No one in the Two Rivers had ever had anything to do with a war. "Why are they having a war?"

Fain grinned, and Rand had the feeling he was mocking the villagers' isolation from the world, and their ignorance. The peddler leaned forward as if he were about to impart a secret to the Mayor, but his whisper was meant to carry and did. "The standard of the Dragon has been raised, and men flock to oppose. And to support."

One long gasp left every throat together, and Rand shivered in spite of himself.

"The Dragon!" someone moaned. "The Dark One's loose in Ghealdan!"

"Not the Dark One," Haral Luhhan growled. "The Dragon's not the Dark One. And this is a false Dragon, anyway."

"Let's hear what Master Fain has to say," the Mayor said, but no one would be quieted that easily. People cried out from every side, men and women shouting over one another.

"Just as bad as the Dark One!"

"The Dragon broke the world, didn't he?"

"He started it! He caused the Time of Madness!"

"You know the prophecies! When the Dragon is reborn, your worst nightmares will seem like your fondest dreams!"

"He's just another false Dragon. He must be!"

"What difference does that make? You remember the last false Dragon. He started a war, too. Thousands died, isn't that right, Fain? He laid siege to Illian."

"It's evil times! No one claiming to be the Dragon Reborn for twenty years, and now three in the last five years. Evil times! Look at the weather!"

Rand exchanged looks with Mat and Perrin. Mat's eyes shone with excitement, but Perrin wore a worried frown. Rand could remember every tale he had heard about the men who named themselves the Dragon Reborn, and if they had all proven themselves false Dragons by dying or disappearing without fulfilling any of the prophecies, what they had done was bad enough. Whole nations torn by battle, and cities and towns put to the torch. The dead fell like autumn leaves, and refugees clogged the roads like sheep in a pen. So the peddlers said, and the merchants, and no one in the Two Rivers with any sense doubted it. The world would end, so some said, when the real Dragon was born again.

"Stop this!" the Mayor shouted. "Be quiet! Stop working yourselves to a lather out of your own imaginations. Let Master Fain tell us about this false Dragon." The people began to quieten, but Cenn Buie refused to be silent.

"*Is* this a false Dragon?" the thatcher asked sourly.

Master al'Vere blinked as if taken by surprise, then snapped, "Don't be an old fool, Cenn!" But Cenn had kindled the crowd again.

"He can't be the Dragon Reborn! Light help us, he can't be!"

"You old fool, Buie! You *want* bad luck, don't you?"

"Be naming the Dark One, next! You're taken by the Dragon, Cenn Buie! Trying to bring us all harm!"

Cenn looked around defiantly, trying to stare down the glowers, and raised his voice. "I didn't hear Fain say this was a false Dragon. Did you? Use your eyes! Where are the crops that should be knee high or better? Why is it still winter when spring should be here a month?" There were angry shouts for Cenn to hold his tongue. "I will not be silent! I've no liking for this talk, either, but I won't hide my head under a basket till a Taren Ferry man comes to cut my throat. And I won't dangle on Fain's pleasure, not this time. Speak it out plain, peddler. What have you heard? Eh? Is this man a false Dragon?"

If Fain was perturbed by the news he brought or the upset he had caused, he gave no sign of it. He merely shrugged and laid a skinny finger alongside his nose. "As to that, now, who can say until it is over and done?" He paused with one of his secretive grins, running his eyes over the crowd as if imagining how they would react and finding it funny. "I do know," he said, too casually, "that he can wield the One Power. The others couldn't. But he can channel. The ground opens beneath his enemies' feet, and strong walls crumble at his shout. Lightning comes when he calls and strikes where he points. That I've heard, and from men I believe."

A stunned silence fell. Rand looked at his friends. Perrin seemed to be seeing things he did not like, but Mat *still* looked excited.

Tam, his face only a little less composed than usual, drew the Mayor close, but before he could speak Ewin Finngar burst out.

"He'll go mad and die! In the stories, men who channel the Power always go mad, and then waste away and die. Only women can touch it. Doesn't he know that?" He ducked under a cuff from Master Buie.

"Enough of that from you, boy." Cenn shook a gnarled fist in Ewin's face. "Show a proper respect and leave this to your elders. Get away with you!"

"Hold steady, Cenn," Tam growled. "The boy is just curious. There's no need of this foolishness from you."

"Act your age," Bran added. "And for once remember you're a member of the Council."

Cenn's wrinkled face grew darker with every word from Tam and the Mayor, until it was almost purple. "You know what kind of women he's talking about. Stop frowning at me, Luhhan, and you, too, Crawe. This is a decent village of decent folk, and it's bad enough to have Fain here talking about false Dragons using the Power without this Dragon-possessed fool of a boy bringing Aes Sedai into it. Some things just shouldn't be talked about, and I don't care if you will be letting that fool gleeman tell any kind of tale he wants. It isn't right or decent."

"I never saw or heard or smelled anything that couldn't be talked about," Tam said, but Fain was not finished.

"The Aes Sedai are already into it," the peddler spoke up. "A party of them has ridden south from Tar Valon. Since he can wield the Power, none but Aes Sedai can defeat him, for all the battles they fight, or deal with him once he's defeated. If he is defeated."

Someone in the crowd moaned aloud, and even Tam and Bran exchanged uneasy frowns. Huddles of villagers clumped together, and some pulled their cloaks tighter around themselves, though the wind had actually lessened.

"Of course, he'll be defeated," someone shouted.

"They're always beaten in the end, false Dragons."

"He has to be defeated, doesn't he?"

"What if he isn't?"

Tam had finally managed to speak quietly into the Mayor's ear, and Bran, nodding from time to time and ignoring the hubbub around them, waited until he was finished before raising his own voice.

"All of you listen. Be quiet and listen!" The shouting died to a murmur again. "This goes beyond mere news from outside. It must be discussed by the Village Council. Master Fain, if you will join us inside the inn, we have questions to ask."

"A good mug of hot mulled wine would not go far amiss with me just now," the peddler replied with a chuckle. He jumped down from the wagon, dusted his hands on his coat, and cheerfully righted his cloak. "Will you be looking after my horses, if you please?"

"I want to hear what he has to say!" More than one voice was raised in protest.

"You can't take him off! My wife sent me to buy pins!" That was Wit Congar; he hunched his shoulders at the stares some of the others gave him, but he held his ground.

"We've a right to ask questions, too," somebody back in the crowd shouted. "I—"

"Be silent!" the Mayor roared, producing a startled hush. "When the Council has asked its questions, Master Fain will be back to tell you all his news. And to sell you his pots and pins. Hu! Tad! Stable Master Fain's horses."

Tam and Bran moved in on either side of the peddler, the rest of the Council gathered behind them, and the whole cluster swept into the Winespring Inn, firmly shutting the door in the faces of those who tried to crowd inside after them. Pounding on the door brought only a single shout from the Mayor.

"Go home!"

People milled around in front of the inn muttering about what the peddler had said, and what it meant, and what questions the Council was asking, and why they should be allowed to listen and ask questions of their own. Some peered in through the front windows of the inn, and a few even questioned Hu and Tad, though it was far from clear what they were supposed to know. The two stolid stablemen just grunted in reply and went on methodically removing the team's harness. One by one they led Fain's horses away and, when the last was gone, did not return.

Rand ignored the crowd. He took a seat on the edge of the old stone foundation, gathered his cloak around him, and stared at the inn door. Ghealdan. Tar Valon. The very names were strange and exciting. They were places he knew only from peddlers' news, and tales told by merchants' guards. Aes Sedai and wars and false Dragons: those were the stuff of stories told late at night in front of the fireplace, with one candle making strange shapes on the wall and the wind howling against the shutters. On the whole, he believed he would rather have blizzards and wolves. Still, it must be different out there, beyond the Two Rivers, like living in the middle of a gleeman's tale. An adventure. One long adventure. A whole lifetime of it.

Slowly the villagers dispersed, still muttering and shaking their heads. Wit Congar paused to stare into the now-abandoned wagon as though he might find another peddler hidden inside. Finally only a few of the younger folk were left. Mat and Perrin drifted over to where Rand sat.

"I don't see how the gleeman could beat this," Mat said excitedly. "I wonder if we might get to see this false Dragon?"

Perrin shook his shaggy head. "I don't want to see him. Somewhere else, maybe, but not in the Two Rivers. Not if it means war."

"Not if it means Aes Sedai here, either," Rand added. "Or have you forgotten who caused the Breaking? The Dragon may have started it, but it was Aes Sedai who actually broke the world."

"I heard a story once," Mat said slowly, "from a wool-buyer's guard. He said the Dragon would be reborn in mankind's greatest hour of need, and save us all."

"Well, he was a fool if he believed that," Perrin said firmly. "And you were a fool to listen." He did not sound angry; he was slow to anger. But he sometimes got exasperated with Mat's quicksilver fancies, and there was a touch of that in his voice. "I suppose he claimed we'd all live in a new Age of Legends afterwards, too."

"I didn't say I believed it," Mat protested. "I just heard it. Nynaeve did, too, and I thought she was going to skin me and the guard both. He said—the guard did—that a lot of people do believe, only they're afraid to say so, afraid of the Aes Sedai or the Children of the Light. He wouldn't say any more after Nynaeve lit into us. She told the merchant, and he said it was the guard's last trip with him."

"A good thing, too," Perrin said. "The Dragon going to save us? Sounds like Coplin talk to me."

"What kind of need would be great enough that we'd want the Dragon to save us from it?" Rand mused. "As well ask for help from the Dark One."

"He didn't say," Mat replied uncomfortably. "And he didn't mention any new Age of Legends. He said the world would be torn apart by the Dragon's coming."

"That would surely save us," Perrin said dryly. "Another Breaking."

"Burn me!" Mat growled. "I'm only telling you what the guard said."

Perrin shook his head. "I just hope the Aes Sedai and this Dragon, false or not, stay where they are. Maybe that way the Two Rivers will be spared."

"You think they're really Darkfriends?" Mat was frowning thoughtfully.

"Who?" Rand asked.

"Aes Sedai."

Rand glanced at Perrin, who shrugged. "The stories," he began slowly, but Mat cut him off.

"Not all the stories say they serve the Dark One, Rand."

"Light, Mat," Rand said, "they caused the Breaking. What more do you want?"

"I suppose." Mat sighed, but the next moment he was grinning again. "Old Bili Congar says they don't exist. Aes Sedai. Darkfriends. Says they're just stories. He says he doesn't believe in the Dark One, either."

Perrin snorted. "Coplin talk from a Congar. What else can you expect?"

"Old Bili named the Dark One. I'll bet you didn't know that."

"Light!" Rand breathed.

Mat's grin broadened. "It was last spring, just before the cut-worm got into his fields and nobody else's. Right before everybody in his house came down with yelloweye fever. I heard him do it. He still says he doesn't believe, but whenever I ask him to name the Dark One now, he throws something at me."

"You are just stupid enough to do that, aren't you, Matrim Cauthon?" Nynaeve al'Meara stepped into their huddle, the dark braid pulled over her shoulder almost bristling with anger. Rand scrambled to his feet. Slender and barely taller than Mat's shoulder, at the moment the Wisdom seemed taller than any of them, and it did not matter that she was young and pretty. "I suspected something of the sort about Bili Congar at the time, but I thought you at least had more sense than to try taunting him into such a thing. You may be old enough to be married, Matrim Cauthon, but in truth you shouldn't be off your mother's apron strings. The next thing, you'll be naming the Dark One yourself."

"No, Wisdom," Mat protested, looking as if he would rather be anywhere else than there. "It was old Bil—I mean, Master Congar, not me! Blood and ashes, I—"

"Watch your tongue, Matrim!"

Rand stood up straighter, though her glare was not directed at him. Perrin looked equally abashed. Later one or another of them would almost certainly complain about being scolded by a woman not all that much older than themselves—someone always did after one of Nynaeve's scoldings, if never in her hearing—but the gap in ages always seemed more than wide enough when face to face with her. Especially if she was angry. The stick in her hand was thick at one end and a slender switch at the other, and she was liable to give a flail to anybody she thought was acting the fool—head or hands or legs—no matter their age or position.

The Wisdom so held his attention that at first Rand failed to see she was not alone. When he realized his mistake, he began to think about leaving no matter what Nynaeve would say or do later.

Egwene stood a few paces behind the Wisdom, watching intently. Of a height with Nynaeve, and with the same dark coloring, she could at that moment have been a reflection of Nynaeve's mood, arms crossed beneath her breasts, mouth tight with disapproval. The hood of her soft gray cloak shaded her face, and her big brown eyes held no laughter now.

If there was any fairness, he thought that being two years older than her should give him some advantage, but that was not the way of it. At the best of times he was never very nimble with his tongue when talking to any of the village girls, not like Perrin, but whenever Egwene gave him that intent look, with her eyes as wide as they would go, as if every last ounce of her attention was on him, he just could not seem to make the words go where he wanted. Perhaps he could get away as soon as Nynaeve finished. But he knew he would not, even if he did not understand why.

"If you are done staring like a moonstruck lamb, Rand al'Thor," Nynaeve said, "perhaps you can tell me why you were talking about something even you three great bullcalves ought to have sense enough to keep out of your mouths."

Rand gave a start and pulled his eyes away from Egwene; she had grown a disconcerting smile when the Wisdom began speaking. Nynaeve's voice was tart, but she had the beginnings of a knowing smile on her face, too—until Mat laughed aloud. The Wisdom's smile vanished, and the look she gave Mat cut his laughter off in a strangled croak.

"Well, Rand?" Nynaeve said.

Out of the corner of his eye he saw Egwene still smiling. *What does she think is so funny?* "It was natural enough to talk of it, Wisdom," he said hurriedly. "The peddler—Padan Fain . . . ah . . . Master Fain—brought news of a false Dragon in Ghealdan, and a war, and Aes Sedai. The Council thought it was important enough to talk to him. What else would we be talking about?"

Nynaeve shook her head. "So that's why the peddler's wagon stands abandoned. I heard people rushing to meet it, but I couldn't leave Mistress Ayellin till her fever broke. The Council is questioning the peddler about what's happening in Ghealdan, are they? If I know them, they're asking all the wrong questions and none of the right ones. It will take the Women's Circle to find out anything useful." Settling her cloak firmly on her shoulders she disappeared into the inn.

Egwene did not follow the Wisdom. As the inn door closed behind Nynaeve, the younger woman came to stand in front of Rand. The frowns were gone from her face, but her unblinking

stare made him uneasy. He looked to his friends, but they
moved away, grinning broadly as they abandoned him.

"You shouldn't let Mat get you mixed up in his foolishness,
Rand," Egwene said, as solemn as a Wisdom herself, then
abruptly she giggled. "I haven't seen you look like that since
Cenn Buie caught you and Mat up in his apple trees when you
were ten."

He shifted his feet and glanced at his friends. They stood not
far away, Mat gesturing excitedly as he talked.

"Will you dance with me tomorrow?" That was not what he
had meant to say. He did want to dance with her, but at the
same time he wanted nothing so little as the uncomfortable way
he was sure to feel while he was with her. The way he felt right
then.

The corners of her mouth quirked up in a small smile. "In
the afternoon," she said. "I will be busy in the morning."

From the others came Perrin's exclamation. "A gleeman!"

Egwene turned toward them, but Rand put a hand on her
arm. "Busy? How?"

Despite the chill she pushed back the hood of her cloak and
with apparent casualness pulled her hair forward over her
shoulder. The last time he had seen her, her hair had hung in
dark waves below her shoulders, with only a red ribbon keeping it back from her face; now it was worked into a long braid.

He stared at that braid as if it were a viper, then stole a
glance at the Spring Pole, standing alone on the Green now,
ready for tomorrow. In the morning unmarried women of marriageable age would dance the Pole. He swallowed hard. Somehow, it had never occurred to him that she would reach
marriageable age at the same time that he did.

"Just because someone is old enough to marry," he muttered, "doesn't mean they should. Not right away."

"Of course not. Or ever, for that matter."

Rand blinked. "Ever?"

"A Wisdom almost never marries. Nynaeve has been teaching me, you know. She says I have a talent, that I can learn to
listen to the wind. Nynaeve says not all Wisdoms can, even if
they say they do."

"Wisdom!" he hooted. He failed to notice the dangerous

glint in her eye. "Nynaeve will be Wisdom here for another fifty years at least. Probably more. Are you going to spend the rest of your life as her apprentice?"

"There are other villages," she replied heatedly. "Nynaeve says the villages north of the Taren always choose a Wisdom from away. They think it stops her from having favorites among the village folk."

His amusement melted as fast as it had come. "Outside the Two Rivers? I'd never see you again."

"And you wouldn't like that? You have not given any sign lately that you'd care one way or another."

"No one ever leaves the Two Rivers," he went on. "Maybe somebody from Taren Ferry, but they're all strange anyway. Hardly like Two Rivers folk at all."

Egwene gave an exasperated sigh. "Well, maybe I'm strange, too. Maybe I want to see some of the places I hear about in the stories. Have you ever thought of that?"

"Of course I have. I daydream sometimes, but I know the difference between daydreams and what's real."

"And I do not?" she said furiously, and promptly turned her back on him.

"That wasn't what I meant. I was talking about me. Egwene?"

She jerked her cloak around her, a wall to shut him off, and stiffly walked a few paces away. He rubbed his head in frustration. How to explain? This was not the first time she had squeezed meanings from his words that he never knew were in them. In her present mood, a misstep would only make matters worse, and he was fairly sure that nearly anything he said would be a misstep.

Mat and Perrin came back then. Egwene ignored their coming. They looked at her hesitantly, then crowded close to Rand.

"Moiraine gave Perrin a coin, too," Mat said. "Just like ours." He paused before adding, "And he saw the rider."

"Where?" Rand demanded. "When? Did anybody else see him? Did you tell anyone?"

Perrin raised broad hands in a slowing gesture. "One question at a time. I saw him on the edge of the village, watching the smithy, just at twilight yesterday. Gave me the shivers, he did. I told Master Luhhan, only nobody was there when he looked. He said I was seeing shadows. But he carried his biggest hammer around with him while we were banking the forge-fire and putting the tools up. He's never done that before."

"So he believed you," Rand said, but Perrin shrugged.

"I don't know. I asked him why he was carrying the hammer if all I saw was shadows, and he said something about wolves getting bold enough to come into the village. Maybe he thought that's what I saw, but he ought to know I can tell the difference between a wolf and a man on horseback, even at dusk. I know what I saw, and nobody is going to make me believe different."

"I believe you," Rand said. "Remember, I saw him, too." Perrin gave a satisfied grunt, as if he had not been sure of that.

"What *are* you talking about?" Egwene demanded suddenly.

Rand suddenly wished he had spoken more quietly. He would have if he had realized she was listening. Mat and Perrin, grinning like fools, fell all over themselves telling her of their encounters with the black-cloaked rider, but Rand kept silent. He was sure he knew what she would say when they were done.

"Nynaeve was right," Egwene announced to the sky when the two youths fell silent. "None of you is ready to be off leading strings. People do ride horses, you know. That doesn't make them monsters out of a gleeman's tale." Rand nodded to himself; it was just as he had thought. She rounded on him. "And you've been spreading these tales. Sometimes you have no sense, Rand al'Thor. The winter has been frightening enough without you going about scaring the children."

Rand gave a sour grimace. "I haven't spread anything, Egwene. But I saw what I saw, and it was no farmer out looking for a strayed cow."

Egwene drew a deep breath and opened her mouth, but whatever she had been going to say vanished as the door of the inn opened and a man with shaggy white hair came hurrying out as if pursued.

CHAPTER
4

The Gleeman

The door of the inn banged shut behind the white-haired man, and he spun around to glare at it. Lean, he would have been tall if not for a stoop to his shoulders, but he moved in a spry fashion that belied his apparent age. His cloak seemed a mass of patches, in odd shapes and sizes, fluttering with every breath of air, patches in a hundred colors. It was really quite thick, Rand saw, despite what Master al'Vere had said, with the patches merely sewn on like decorations.

"The gleeman!" Egwene whispered excitedly.

The white-haired man whirled, cloak flaring. His long coat had odd, baggy sleeves and big pockets. Thick mustaches, as snowy as the hair on his head, quivered around his mouth, and his face was gnarled like a tree that had seen hard times. He gestured imperiously at Rand and the others with a long-stemmed pipe, ornately carved, that trailed a wisp of smoke. Blue eyes peered out from under bushy white brows, drilling into whatever he looked at.

Rand stared at the man's eyes almost as much as at the rest of him. Everybody in the Two Rivers had dark eyes, and so did most of the merchants, and their guards, and everyone else he had ever seen. The Congars and the Coplins had made fun of him for his gray eyes, until the day he finally punched Ewal Coplin in the nose; the Wisdom had surely gotten onto him for that. He wondered if there was a place where nobody had dark eyes. *Maybe Lan comes from there, too.*

"What sort of place is this?" the gleeman demanded in a deep voice that sounded in some way larger than that of an ordinary man. Even in the open air it seemed to fill a great room and resonate from the walls. "The yokels in that village on the hill tell me I can get here before dark, neglecting to say that that was only if I left well before noon. When I finally do arrive, chilled to the bone and ready for a warm bed, your innkeeper grumbles about the hour as if I were a wandering swineherd and your Village Council hadn't begged me to display my art at this festival of yours. And he never even told me he was the Mayor." He slowed for a breath, taking them all in with a glare, but he was off again on the instant. "When I came downstairs to smoke my pipe before the fire and have a mug of ale, every man in the common room stares at me as if I were his least favorite brother-in-law seeking to borrow money. One old grandfather starts ranting at me about the kind of stories I should or should not tell, then a girl-child shouts at me to get out, and threatens me with a great club when I don't move quickly enough for her. Who ever heard of treating a gleeman so?"

Egwene's face was a study, her goggle-eyed amaze at a gleeman in the flesh marred by a desire to defend Nynaeve.

"Your pardon, Master Gleeman," Rand said. He knew he was grinning foolishly, himself. "That was our Wisdom, and—"

"That pretty little slip of a girl?" the gleeman exclaimed. "A village Wisdom? Why, at her age she should better be flirting with the young men than foretelling the weather and curing the sick."

Rand shifted uncomfortably. He hoped Nynaeve never overheard the man's opinion. At least, not until he had done with his performing. Perrin winced at the gleeman's words, and Mat whistled soundlessly, as if both had had the same thought as he had.

"The men were the Village Council," Rand went on. "I'm sure they intended no discourtesy. You see, we just learned there's a war in Ghealdan, and a man claiming to be the Dragon Reborn. A false Dragon. Aes Sedai are riding there from Tar Valon. The Council is trying to decide if we might be in danger here."

"Old news, even in Baerlon," the gleeman said dismissively,

"and that is the last place in the world to hear anything." He paused, looking around the village, and dryly added, "Almost the last place." Then his eyes fell on the wagon in front of the inn, standing alone now, with its shafts on the ground. "So. I thought I recognized Padan Fain in there." His voice was still deep, but the resonance had gone, replaced by scorn. "Fain was always one to carry bad news quickly, and the worse, the faster. There's more raven in him than man."

"Master Fain has come often to Emond's Field, Master Gleeman," Egwene said, a hint of disapproval finally breaking through her delight. "He is always full of laughter, and he brings much more good news than bad."

The gleeman eyed her for a moment, then smiled broadly. "Now you're a lovely lass. You should have rose buds in your hair. Unfortunately, I cannot pull roses from the air, not this year, but how would you like to stand beside me tomorrow for a part of my performance? Hand me my flute when I want it, and certain other apparatus. I always choose the prettiest girl I can find as my assistant."

Perrin snickered, and Mat, who had been snickering, laughed out loud. Rand blinked in surprise; Egwene was glaring at him, and he had not even smiled. She straightened around and spoke in a too-calm voice.

"Thank you, Master Gleeman. I would be happy to assist you."

"Thom Merrilin," the gleeman said. They stared. "My name is Thom Merrilin, not Master Gleeman." He hitched the multi-hued cloak up on his shoulders, and abruptly his voice once more seemed to reverberate in a great hall. "Once a Court-bard, I am now indeed risen to the exalted rank of Master Gleeman, yet my name is plain Thom Merrilin, and gleeman is the simple title in which I glory." And he swept a bow so elaborate with flourishes of his cloak that Mat clapped and Egwene murmured appreciatively.

"Master . . . ah . . . Master Merrilin," Mat said, unsure exactly what form of address to take out of what Thom Merrilin had said, "what *is* happening in Ghealdan? Do you know anything about this false Dragon? Or the Aes Sedai?"

"Do I look like a peddler, boy?" the gleeman grumbled, tapping out his pipe on the heel of his palm. He made the pipe disappear somewhere inside his cloak, or his coat; Rand was not sure where it had gone or how. "I am a gleeman, not a newsmonger. And I make a point of never knowing anything about Aes Sedai. Much safer that way."

"But the war," Mat began eagerly, only to be cut off by Master Merrilin.

"In wars, boy, fools kill other fools for foolish causes. That's enough for anyone to know. I am here for my art." Suddenly he thrust a finger at Rand. "You, lad. You're a tall one. Not with your full growth on you yet, but I doubt there's another man in the district with your height. Not many in the village with eyes that color, either, I'll wager. The point is, you're an axe handle across the shoulders and as tall as an Aielman. What's your name, lad?"

Rand gave it hesitantly, not sure whether or not the man was making fun of him, but the gleeman had already turned his attention to Perrin. "And you have almost the size of an Ogier. Close enough. How are you called?"

"Not unless I stand on my own shoulders." Perrin laughed. "I'm afraid Rand and I are just ordinary folk, Master Merrilin, not made-up creatures from your stories. I'm Perrin Aybara."

Thom Merrilin tugged at one of his mustaches. "Well, now. Made-up creatures from my stories. Is that what they are? You lads are widely traveled, then, it seems."

Rand kept his mouth shut, certain they were the butt of a joke, now, but Perrin spoke up.

"We've all of us been as far as Watch Hill, and Deven Ride. Not many around here have gone as far." He was not boasting; Perrin seldom did. He was just telling the truth.

"We've all seen the Mire, too," Mat added, and he did sound boastful. "That's the swamp at the far end of the Waterwood. Nobody at all goes there—it's full of quicksands and bogs—except us. And nobody goes to the Mountains of Mist, either, but we did, once. To the foot of them, anyway."

"As far as that?" the gleeman murmured, brushing at his mustaches now continually. Rand thought he was hiding a smile, and he saw that Perrin was frowning.

"It's bad luck to enter the mountains," Mat said, as if he had to defend himself for not going further. "Everybody knows that."

"That's just foolishness, Matrim Cauthon," Egwene cut in angrily. "Nynaeve says. . . ." She broke off, her cheeks turning pink, and the look she gave Thom Merrilin was not as friendly as it had been. "It is not right to make. . . . It isn't. . . ." Her face went redder, and she fell silent. Mat blinked, as if he was just getting a suspicion of what had been going on.

"You're right, child," the gleeman said contritely. "I apologize humbly. I am here to entertain. Aah, my tongue has always gotten me into trouble."

"Maybe we haven't traveled as far as you," Perrin said flatly, "but what does how tall Rand is have to do with anything?"

"Just this, lad. A little later I will let you try to pick me up, but you won't be able to lift my feet from the ground. Not you, nor your tall friend there—Rand, is it?—nor any other man. Now what do you think of that?"

Perrin snorted a laugh. "I think I can lift you right now." But when he stepped forward Thom Merrilin motioned him back.

"Later, lad, later. When there are more folk to watch. An artist needs an audience."

A score of folk had gathered on the Green since the gleeman appeared from the inn, young men and women down to children who peeked, wide-eyed and silent, from behind the older onlookers. All looked as if they were waiting for miraculous things from the gleeman. The white-haired man looked them over—he appeared to be counting them—then gave a slight shake of his head and sighed.

"I suppose I had better give you a small sample. So you can run tell the others. Eh? Just a taste of what you'll see tomorrow at your festival."

He took a step back, and suddenly leaped into the air, twisting and somersaulting to land facing them atop the old stone foundation. More than that, three balls—red, white, and black—began dancing between his hands even as he landed.

A soft sound came from the watchers, half astonishment, half satisfaction. Even Rand forgot his irritation. He flashed Egwene a grin and got a delighted one in return, then both turned to stare unabashedly at the gleeman.

"You want stories?" Thom Merrilin declaimed. "I have stories, and I will give them to you. I will make them come alive before your eyes." A blue ball joined the others from somewhere, then a green one, and a yellow. "Tales of great wars and great heroes, for the men and boys. For the women and girls, the entire *Aptarigine Cycle*. Tales of Artur Paendrag Tanreall, Artur Hawkwing, Artur the High King, who once ruled all the lands from the Aiel Waste to the Aryth Ocean, and even beyond. Wondrous stories of strange people and strange lands, of the Green Man, of Warders and Trollocs, of Ogier and Aiel. *The Thousand Tales of Anla, the Wise Counselor.* 'Jaem the Giant-Slayer.' *How Susa Tamed Jain Farstrider.* 'Mara and the Three Foolish Kings.'"

"Tell us about Lenn," Egwene called. "How he flew to the moon in the belly of an eagle made of fire. Tell about his daughter Salya walking among the stars."

Rand looked at her out of the corner of his eye, but she seemed intent on the gleeman. She had never liked stories about adventures and long journeys. Her favorites were always the funny ones, or stories about women outwitting people who were supposed to be smarter than everyone else. He was sure she had asked for tales about Lenn and Salya to put a burr under his shirt. Surely she could see the world outside was no place for Two Rivers folk. Listening to tales of adventures, even dreaming about them, was one thing; having them take place around you would be something else again.

"Old stories, those," Thom Merrilin said, and abruptly he was juggling three colored balls with each hand. "Stories from the Age before the Age of Legends, some say. Perhaps even older. But I have *all* stories, mind you now, of Ages that were and will be. Ages when men ruled the heavens and the stars, and Ages when man roamed as brother to the animals. Ages of wonder, and Ages of horror. Ages ended by fire raining from the skies, and Ages doomed by snow and ice covering land and sea. I have all stories, and I will tell all stories. Tales of Mosk the Giant, with his Lance of fire that could reach around the world, and his wars with Elsbet, the Queen of All. Tales of Materese the Healer, Mother of the Wondrous Ind."

The balls now danced between Thom's hands in two intertwining circles. His voice was almost a chant, and he turned slowly as he spoke, as if surveying the onlookers to gauge his effect. "I will tell you of the end of the Age of Legends, of the Dragon, and his attempt to free the Dark One into the world of men. I will tell of the Time of Madness, when Aes Sedai shattered the world; of the Trolloc Wars, when men battled Trollocs for rule of the earth; of the War of the Hundred Years, when men battled men and the nations of our day were wrought. I will tell the adventures of men and women, rich and poor, great and small, proud and humble. *The Siege of the Pillars of the Sky.* 'How Goodwife Karil Cured Her Husband of Snoring.' *King Darith and the Fall of the House of—*"

Abruptly the flow of words and the juggling alike stopped. Thom simply snatched the balls from the air and stopped talking. Unnoticed by Rand, Moiraine had joined the listeners. Lan was at her shoulder, though he had to look twice to see the man. For a moment Thom looked at Moiraine sideways, his face and body still except for making the balls disappear into his capacious coat sleeves. Then he bowed to her, holding his cloak wide. "Your pardon, but you are surely not from this district?"

"Lady!" Ewin hissed fiercely. "The Lady Moiraine."

Thom blinked, then bowed again, more deeply. "Your pardon again . . . ah, Lady. I meant no disrespect."

Moiraine made a small waving-away gesture. "None was perceived, Master Bard. And my name is simply Moiraine. I am indeed a stranger here, a traveler like yourself, far from home and alone. The world can be a dangerous place when one is a stranger."

"The Lady Moiraine collects stories," Ewin put in. "Stories about things that happened in the Two Rivers. Though I don't know what ever happened here to make a story of."

"I trust you will like my stories, as well . . . Moiraine." Thom watched her with obvious wariness. He looked not best pleased to find her there. Suddenly Rand wondered what sort of entertainment a lady like her might be offered in a city like Baerlon, or Caemlyn. Surely it could not be anything better than a gleeman.

"That is a matter of taste, Master Bard," Moiraine replied. "Some stories I like, and some I do not."

Thom's bow was his deepest yet, bending his long body parallel to the ground. "I assure you, none of my stories will displease. All will please and entertain. And you do me too much honor. I am a simple gleeman; that and nothing more."

Moiraine answered his bow with a gracious nod. For an instant she seemed even more the lady Ewin had named her, accepting an offering from one of her subjects. Then she turned away, and Lan followed, a wolf heeling a gliding swan. Thom stared after them, bushy brows drawn down, stroking his long mustaches with a knuckle, until they were halfway up the Green. *He's not pleased at all,* Rand thought.

"Are you going to juggle some more, now?" Ewin demanded.

"Eat fire," Mat shouted. "I want to see you eat fire."

"The harp!" a voice cried from the crowd. "Play the harp!" Someone else called for the flute.

At that moment the door of the inn opened and the Village Council trundled out, Nynaeve in their midst. Padan Fain was not with them, Rand saw; apparently the peddler had decided to remain in the warm common room with his mulled wine.

Muttering about "a strong brandy," Thom Merrilin abruptly jumped down from the old foundation. He ignored the cries of those who had been watching him, pressing inside past the Councilors before they were well out of the doorway.

"Is he supposed to be a gleeman or a king?" Cenn Buie asked in annoyed tones. "A waste of good money, if you ask me."

Bran al'Vere half turned after the gleeman, then shook his head. "That man may be more trouble than he's worth."

Nynaeve, busy gathering her cloak around her, sniffed loudly. "Worry about the gleeman if you want, Brandelwyn al'Vere. At least he is in Emond's Field, which is more than you can say for this false Dragon. But as long as you are worrying, there are others here who *should* excite your worry."

"If you please, Wisdom," Bran said stiffly, "kindly leave who should worry me to my deciding. Mistress Moiraine and Master Lan are guests in my inn, and decent, respectable folk, so I say. Neither of *them* has called me a fool in front of the whole Council. Neither of *them* has told the Council it hasn't a full set of wits among them."

"It seems my estimate was too high by half," Nynaeve retorted. She strode away without a backward glance, leaving Bran's jaw working as he searched for a reply.

Egwene looked at Rand as if she were going to speak, then

darted after the Wisdom instead. Rand knew there must be
some way to stop her from leaving the Two Rivers, but the only
way he could think of was not one he was prepared to take,
even if she was willing. And she had as much as said she was
not willing at all, which made him feel even worse.

"That young woman wants a husband," Cenn Buie growled,
bouncing on his toes. His face was purple, and getting darker.
"She lacks proper respect. We're the Village Council, not boys
raking her yard, and—"

The Mayor breathed heavily through his nose, and suddenly
rounded on the old thatcher. "Be quiet, Cenn! Stop acting like
a black-veiled Aiel!" The skinny man froze on his toes in astonishment. The Mayor never let his temper get the best of
him. Bran glared. "Burn me, but we have better things to be
about than this foolishness. Or do you intend to prove Nynaeve
right?" With that he stumped back into the inn and slammed
the door behind him.

The Council members glanced at Cenn, then moved off in
their separate directions. All but Haral Luhhan, who accompanied the stony-visaged thatcher, talking quietly. The blacksmith was the only one who could ever get Cenn to see reason.

Rand went to meet his father, and his friends trailed after
him.

"I've never seen Master al'Vere so mad," was the first thing
Rand said, getting him a disgusted look from Mat.

"The Mayor and the Wisdom seldom agree," Tam said, "and
they agreed less than usual today. That's all. It's the same in
every village."

"What about the false Dragon?" Mat asked, and Perrin
added eager murmurs. "What about the Aes Sedai?"

Tam shook his head slowly. "Master Fain knew little more
than he had already told. At least, little of interest to us. Battles won or lost. Cities taken and retaken. All in Ghealdan,
thank the Light. It hasn't spread, or had not the last Master
Fain knew."

"Battles interest me," Mat said, and Perrin added, "What
did he say about them?"

"Battles don't interest me, Matrim," Tam said. "But I'm
sure he will be glad to tell you all about them later. What does
interest me is that we shouldn't have to worry about them here,

as far as the Council can tell. We can see no reason for Aes Sedai to come here on their way south. And as for the return journey, they aren't likely to want to cross the Forest of Shadows and swim the White River."

Rand and the others chuckled at the idea. There were three reasons why no one came into the Two Rivers except from the north, by way of Taren Ferry. The Mountains of Mist, in the west, were the first, of course, and the Mire blocked the east just as effectively. To the south was the White River, which got its name from the way rocks and boulders churned its swift waters to froth. And beyond the White lay the Forest of Shadows. Few Two Rivers folk had ever crossed the White, and fewer still returned if they did. It was generally agreed, though, that the Forest of Shadows stretched south for a hundred miles or more without a road or a village, but with plenty of wolves and bears.

"So that's an end to it for us," Mat said. He sounded at least a little disappointed.

"Not quite," Tam said. "Day after tomorrow we will send men to Deven Ride and Watch Hill, and Taren Ferry, too, to arrange for a watch to be kept. Riders along the White and the Taren, both, and patrols between. It should be done today, but only the Mayor agrees with me. The rest can't see asking anyone to spend Bel Tine off riding across the Two Rivers."

"But I thought you said we didn't have to worry," Perrin said, and Tam shook his head.

"I said should not, boy, not did not. I've seen men die because they were sure that what should not happen, would not. Besides, the fighting will stir up all sorts of people. Most will just be trying to find safety, but others will be looking for a way to profit from the confusion. We'll offer any of the first a helping hand, but we must be ready to send the second type on their way."

Abruptly Mat spoke up. "Can we be part of it? I want to, anyway. You know I can ride as well as anyone in the village."

"You want a few weeks of cold, boredom, and sleeping rough?" Tam chuckled. "Likely that's all there will be to it. I hope that's all. We're well out of the way even for refugees. But you can speak to Master al'Vere if your mind is made up. Rand, it's time for us to be getting back to the farm."

Rand blinked in surprise. "I thought we were staying for Winternight."

"Things need seeing to at the farm, and I need you with me."

"Even so, we don't have to leave for hours yet. And I want to volunteer for the patrols, too."

"We are going now," his father replied in a tone that brooked no argument. In a softer voice he added, "We'll be back tomorrow in plenty of time for you to speak to the Mayor. And plenty of time for Festival, too. Five minutes, now, then meet me in the stable."

"Are you going to join Rand and me on the watch?" Mat asked Perrin as Tam left. "I'll bet there's nothing like this ever happened in the Two Rivers before. Why, if we get up to the Taren, we might even see soldiers, or who knows what. Even Tinkers."

"I expect I will," Perrin said slowly, "if Master Luhhan doesn't need me, that is."

"The war is in Ghealdan," Rand snapped. With an effort he lowered his voice. "The war is in Ghealdan, and the Aes Sedai are the Light knows where, but none of it is here. The man in the black cloak is, or have you forgotten him already?" The others exchanged embarrassed looks.

"Sorry, Rand," Mat muttered. "But a chance to do something besides milk my da's cows doesn't come along very often." He straightened under their startled stares. "Well, I do milk them, and every day, too."

"The black rider," Rand reminded them. "What if he hurts somebody?"

"Maybe he's a refugee from the war," Perrin said doubtfully.

"Whatever he is," Mat said, "the watch will find him."

"Maybe," Rand said, "but he seems to disappear when he wants to. It might be better if they knew to look for him."

"We'll tell Master al'Vere when we volunteer for the patrols," Mat said, "he'll tell the Council, and they'll tell the watch."

"The Council!" Perrin said incredulously. "We'd be lucky if the Mayor didn't laugh out loud. Master Luhhan and Rand's father already think the two of us are jumping at shadows."

Rand sighed. "If we're going to do it, we might as well do it now. He won't laugh any louder today than he will tomorrow."

"Maybe," Perrin said with a sidelong glance at Mat, "we should try finding some others who've seen him. We'll see just about everybody in the village tonight." Mat's scowl deepened, but he still did not say anything. All of them understood that Perrin meant they should find witnesses who were more reliable than Mat. "He won't laugh any louder tomorrow," Perrin added when Rand hesitated. "And I'd just as soon have somebody else with us when we go to him. Half the village would suit me fine."

Rand nodded slowly. He could already hear Master al'Vere laughing. More witnesses certainly could not hurt. And if three of them had seen the fellow, others had to have, too. They must have. "Tomorrow, then. You two find whoever you can tonight, and tomorrow we go to the Mayor. After that. . . ." They looked at him silently, no one raising the question of what happened if they could not find anyone else who had seen the black-cloaked man. The question was clear in their eyes, though, and he had no answer. He sighed heavily. "I'd better go, now. My father will be wondering if I fell into a hole."

Followed by their goodbyes, he trotted around to the stableyard where the high-wheeled cart stood propped on its shafts.

The stable was a long, narrow building, topped by a high-peaked, thatched roof. Stalls, their floors covered with straw, filled both sides of the dim interior, lit only by the open double-doors at either end. The peddler's team munched their oats in eight stalls, and Master al'Vere's massive Dhurrans, the team he hired out when farmers had hauling beyond the abilities of their own horses, filled six more, but only three others were occupied. Rand thought he could match up horse and rider with no trouble. The tall, deep-chested black stallion that swung up his head fiercely had to be Lan's. The sleek white mare with an arched neck, her quick steps as graceful as a girl dancing, even in the stall, could only belong to Moiraine. And the third unfamiliar horse, a rangy, slab-sided gelding of a dusty brown, fit Thom Merrilin perfectly.

Tam stood in the rear of the stable, holding Bela by a lead

rope and speaking quietly to Hu and Tad. Before Rand had taken two steps into the stable his father nodded to the stablemen and brought Bela out, wordlessly gathering up Rand as he went.

They harnessed the shaggy mare in silence. Tam appeared so deep in thought that Rand held his tongue. He did not really look forward to trying to convince his father about the black-cloaked rider, much less the Mayor. Tomorrow would have to be time enough, when Mat and the rest had found others who had seen the man. If they found others.

As the cart lurched into motion, Rand took his bow and quiver from the back, awkwardly belting the quiver at his waist as he half trotted alongside. When they reached the last row of houses in the village, he nocked an arrow, carrying it half raised and partly drawn. There was nothing to see except mostly leafless trees, but his shoulders tightened. The black rider could be on them before either of them knew it. There might not be time to draw the bow if he was not already half-way to it.

He knew he could not keep up the tension on the bowstring for long. He had made the bow himself, and Tam was one of the few others in the district who could even draw it all the way to the cheek. He cast around for something to take his mind off thinking about the dark rider. Surrounded by the forest, their cloaks flapping in the wind, it was not easy.

"Father," he said finally, "I don't understand why the Council had to question Padan Fain." With an effort he took his eyes off the woods and looked across Bela at Tam. "It seems to me, the decision you reached could have been made right on the spot. The Mayor frightened everybody half out of their wits, talking about Aes Sedai and the false Dragon here in the Two Rivers."

"People are funny, Rand. The best of them are. Take Haral Luhhan. Master Luhhan is a strong man, and a brave one, but he can't bear to see butchering done. Turns pale as a sheet."

"What does that have to do with anything? Everybody knows Master Luhhan can't stand the sight of blood, and nobody but the Coplins and the Congars thinks anything of it."

"Just this, lad. People don't always think or behave the way you might believe they would. Those folk back there . . . let the hail beat their crops into the mud, and the wind take off every roof in the district, and the wolves kill half their livestock, and they'll roll up their sleeves and start from scratch. They'll grumble, but they won't waste any time with it. But you give them just the thought of Aes Sedai and a false Dragon in Ghealdan, and soon enough they'll start thinking that Ghealdan is not that far the other side of the Forest of Shadows, and a straight line from Tar Valon to Ghealdan wouldn't pass that much to the east of us. As if the Aes Sedai wouldn't take the road through Caemlyn and Lugard instead of traveling cross-country! By tomorrow morning half the village would have been sure the entire war was about to descend on us. It would take weeks to undo. A fine Bel Tine that would make. So Bran gave them the idea before they could get it for themselves.

"They've seen the Council take the problem under consideration, and by now they'll be hearing what we decided. They chose us for the Village Council because they trust we can reason things out in the best way for everybody. They trust our opinions. Even Cenn's, which doesn't say much for the rest of us, I suppose. At any rate, they will hear there isn't anything to worry about, and they'll believe it. It is not that they couldn't reach the same conclusion, or would not, eventually, but this way we won't have Festival ruined, and nobody has to spend weeks worrying about something that isn't likely to happen. If it does, against all odds . . . well, the patrols will give us enough warning to do what we can. I truly don't think it will come to that, though."

Rand puffed out his cheeks. Apparently, being on the Council was more complicated than he had believed. The cart rumbled on along the Quarry Road.

"Did anyone besides Perrin see this strange rider?" Tam asked.

"Mat did, but—" Rand blinked, then stared across Bela's back at his father. "You believe me? I have to go back. I have to tell them." Tam's shout halted him as he turned to run back to the village.

"Hold, lad, hold! Do you think I waited this long to speak for no reason?"

Reluctantly Rand kept on beside the cart, still creaking along behind patient Bela. "What made you change your mind? Why can't I tell the others?"

"They'll know soon enough. At least, Perrin will. Mat, I'm not sure of. Word must be gotten to the farms as best it can, but in another hour there won't be anyone in Emond's Field above sixteen, those who can be responsible about it, at least, who doesn't know a stranger is skulking around and likely not the sort you would invite to Festival. The winter has been bad enough without this to scare the young ones."

"Festival?" Rand said. "If you had seen him you wouldn't want him closer than ten miles. A hundred, maybe."

"Perhaps so," Tam said placidly. "He could be just a refugee from the troubles in Ghealdan, or more likely a thief who thinks the pickings will be easier here than in Baerlon or Taren Ferry. Even so, no one around here has so much they can afford to have it stolen. If the man is trying to escape the war . . . well, that's still no excuse for scaring people. Once the watch is mounted, it should either find him or frighten him off."

"I hope it frightens him off. But why do you believe me now, when you didn't this morning?"

"I had to believe my own eyes then, lad, and I saw nothing." Tam shook his grizzled head. "Only young men see this fellow, it seems. When Haral Luhhan mentioned Perrin jumping shadows, though, it all came out. Jon Thane's oldest son saw him, too, and so did Samel Crawe's boy, Bandry. Well, when four of you say you've seen a thing—and solid lads, all—we start thinking maybe it's there whether we can see it or not. All except Cenn, of course. Anyway, that's why we're going home. With both of us away, this stranger could be up to any kind of mischief there. If not for Festival, I wouldn't come back tomorrow, either. But we can't make ourselves prisoners in our own homes just because this fellow is lurking about."

"I didn't know about Ban or Lem," Rand said. "The rest of us were going to the Mayor tomorrow, but we were worried he wouldn't believe us, either."

"Gray hairs don't mean our brains have curdled," Tam said dryly. "So you keep a sharp eye. Maybe I'll catch sight of him, too, if he shows up again."

Rand settled down to do just that. He was surprised to realize that his step felt lighter. The knots were gone from his shoulders. He was still scared, but it was not so bad as it had been. Tam and he were just as alone on the Quarry Road as they had been that morning, but in some way he felt as if the entire village were with them. That others knew and believed made all the difference. There was nothing the black-cloaked horseman could do that the people of Emond's Field could not handle together.

Rand al'Thor

CHAPTER
5

Winternight

The sun stood halfway down from its noonday high by the time the cart reached the farmhouse. It was not a big house, not nearly so large as some of the sprawling farmhouses to the east, dwellings that had grown over the years to hold entire families. In the Two Rivers that often included three or four generations under one roof, including aunts, uncles, cousins, and nephews. Tam and Rand were considered out of the ordinary as much for being two men living alone as for farming in the Westwood.

Here most of the rooms were on one floor, a neat rectangle with no wings or additions. Two bedrooms and an attic storeroom fitted up under the steeply sloped thatch. If the whitewash was all but gone from the stout wooden walls after the winter storms, the house was still in a tidy state of repair, the thatch tightly mended and the doors and shutters well-hung and snug-fitting.

House, barn, and stone sheep pen formed the points of a triangle around the farmyard, where a few chickens had ventured out to scratch at the cold ground. An open shearing shed and a stone dipping trough stood next to the sheep pen. Hard by the fields between the farmyard and the trees loomed the tall cone of a tight-walled curing shed. Few farmers in the Two Rivers could make do without both wool and tabac to sell when the merchants came.

When Rand took a look in the stone pen, the heavy-horned

herd ram looked back at him, but most of the black-faced flock remained placidly where they lay, or stood with their heads in the feed trough. Their coats were thick and curly, but it was still too cold for shearing.

"I don't think the black-cloaked man came here," Rand called to his father, who was walking slowly around the farmhouse, spear held at the ready, examining the ground intently. "The sheep wouldn't be so settled if that one had been around."

Tam nodded but did not stop. When he had made a complete circuit of the house, he did the same around the barn and the sheep pen, still studying the ground. He even checked the smokehouse and the curing shed. Drawing a bucket of water from the well, he filled a cupped hand, sniffed the water, and gingerly touched it with the tip of his tongue. Abruptly he barked a laugh, then drank it down in a quick gulp.

"I suppose he didn't," he told Rand, wiping his hand on his coat front. "All this about men and horses I can't see or hear just makes me look crossways at everything." He emptied the well water into another bucket and started for the house, the bucket in one hand and his spear in the other. "I'll start some stew for supper. And as long as we're here, we might as well get caught up on a few chores."

Rand grimaced, regretting Winternight in Emond's Field. But Tam was right. Around a farm the work never really got done; as soon as one thing was finished two more always needed doing. He hesitated about it, but kept his bow and quiver close at hand. If the dark rider did appear, he had no intention of facing him with nothing but a hoe.

First was stabling Bela. Once he had unharnessed her and put her into a stall in the barn next to their cow, he set his cloak aside and rubbed the mare down with handfuls of dry straw, then curried her with a pair of brushes. Climbing the narrow ladder to the loft, he pitched down hay for her feed. He fetched a scoopful of oats for her as well, though there was little enough left and might be no more for a long while unless the weather warmed soon. The cow had been milked that morning before first light, giving a quarter of her usual yield; she seemed to be drying up as the winter hung on.

Enough feed had been left to see the sheep for two days—

they should have been in the pasture by now, but there was none worth calling it so—but he topped off their water. Whatever eggs had been laid needed to be gathered, too. There were only three. The hens seemed to be getting cleverer at hiding them.

He was taking a hoe to the vegetable garden behind the house when Tam came out and settled on a bench in front of the barn to mend harness, propping his spear beside him. It made Rand feel better about the bow lying on his cloak a pace from where he stood.

Few weeds had pushed above ground, but more weeds than anything else. The cabbages were stunted, barely a sprout of the beans or peas showed, and there was not a sign of a beet. Not everything had been planted, of course; only part, in hopes the cold might break in time to make a crop of some kind before the cellar was empty. It did not take long to finish hoeing, which would have suited him just fine in years past, but now he wondered what they would do if nothing came up this year. Not a pleasant thought. And there was still firewood to split.

It seemed to Rand like years since there had *not* been firewood to split. But complaining would not keep the house warm, so he fetched the axe, propped up bow and quiver beside the chopping block, and got to work. Pine for a quick, hot flame, and oak for long burning. Before long he was warm enough to put his coat aside. When the pile of split wood grew big enough, he stacked it against the side of the house, beside other stacks already there. Most reached all the way to the eaves. Usually by this time of year the woodpiles were small and few, but not this year. Chop and stack, chop and stack, he lost himself in the rhythm of the axe and the motions of stacking wood. Tam's hand on his shoulder brought him back to where he was, and for a moment he blinked in surprise.

Gray twilight had come on while he worked, and already it was fading quickly toward night. The full moon stood well above the treetops, shimmering pale and bulging as if about to fall on their heads. The wind had grown colder without his noticing, too, and tattered clouds scudded across the darkling sky.

"Let's wash up, lad, and see about some supper. I've already carried in water for hot baths before sleep."

"Anything hot sounds good to me," Rand said, snatching up his cloak and tossing it round his shoulders. Sweat soaked his shirt, and the wind, forgotten in the heat of swinging the axe, seemed to be trying to freeze it now that he had stopped work. He stifled a yawn, shivering as he gathered the rest of his things. "And sleep, too, for that. I might just sleep right through Festival."

"Would you care to make a small wager about that?" Tam smiled, and Rand had to grin back. He would not miss Bel Tine if he had had no sleep in a week. No one would.

Tam had been extravagant with the candles, and a fire crackled in the big stone fireplace, so that the main room had a warm, cheerful feel to it. A broad oaken table was the main feature of the room other than the fireplace, a table long enough to seat a dozen or more, though there had seldom been so many around it since Rand's mother died. A few cabinets and chests, most of them skillfully made by Tam himself, lined the walls, and high-backed chairs stood around the table. The cushioned chair that Tam called his reading chair sat angled before the flames. Rand preferred to do his reading stretched out on the rug in front of the fire. The shelf of books by the door was not nearly as long as the one at the Winespring Inn, but books were hard to come by. Few peddlers carried more than a handful, and those had to be stretched out among everyone who wanted them.

If the room did not look quite so freshly scrubbed as most farm wives kept their homes—Tam's piperack and *The Travels of Jain Farstrider* sat on the table, while another wood-bound book rested on the cushion of his reading chair; a bit of harness to be mended lay on the bench by the fireplace, and some shirts to be darned made a heap on a chair—if not quite so spotless, it was still clean and neat enough, with a lived-in look that was almost as warming and comforting as the fire. Here, it was possible to forget the chill beyond the walls. There was no false Dragon here. No wars or Aes Sedai. No men in black cloaks. The aroma from the stewpot hanging over the fire permeated the room, and filled Rand with ravenous hunger.

His father stirred the stewpot with a long-handled wooden spoon, then took a taste. "A little while longer."

Rand hurried to wash his face and hands; there was a pitcher and basin on the washstand by the door. A hot bath was what he wanted, to take away the sweat and soak the chill out, but that would come when there had been time to heat the big kettle in the back room.

Tam rooted around in a cabinet and came up with a key as long as his hand. He twisted it in the big iron lock on the door. At Rand's questioning look he said, "Best to be safe. Maybe I'm taking a fancy, or maybe the weather is blacking my mood, but. . . ." He sighed and bounced the key on his palm. "I'll see to the back door," he said, and disappeared toward the back of the house.

Rand could not remember either door ever being locked. No one in the Two Rivers locked doors. There was no need. Until now, at least.

From overhead, from Tam's bedroom, came a scraping, as of something being dragged across the floor. Rand frowned. Unless Tam had suddenly decided to move the furniture around, he could only be pulling out the old chest he kept under his bed. Another thing that had never been done in Rand's memory.

He filled a small kettle with water for tea and hung it from a hook over the fire, then set the table. He had carved the bowls and spoons himself. The front shutters had not yet been closed, and from time to time he peered out, but full night had come and all he could see were moon shadows. The dark rider could be out there easily enough, but he tried not to think about that.

When Tam came back, Rand stared in surprise. A thick belt slanted around Tam's waist, and from the belt hung a sword, with a bronze heron on the black scabbard and another on the long hilt. The only men Rand had ever seen wearing swords were the merchants' guards. And Lan, of course. That his father might own one had never even occurred to him. Except for the herons, the sword looked a good deal like Lan's sword.

"Where did that come from?" he asked. "Did you get it from a peddler? How much did it cost?"

Slowly Tam drew the weapon; firelight played along the gleaming length. It was nothing at all like the plain, rough blades Rand had seen in the hands of merchants' guards. No gems or gold adorned it, but it seemed grand to him, nonetheless. The blade, very slightly curved and sharp on only one edge, bore another heron etched into the steel. Short quillons, worked to look like braid, flanked the hilt. It seemed almost fragile compared with the swords of the merchants' guards; most of those were double-edged, and thick enough to chop down a tree.

"I got it a long time ago," Tam said, "a long way from here. And I paid entirely too much; two coppers is too much for one of these. Your mother didn't approve, but she was always wiser than I. I was young then, and it seemed worth the price at the time. She always wanted me to get rid of it, and more than once I've thought she was right, that I should just give it away."

Reflected fire made the blade seem aflame. Rand started. He had often daydreamed about owning a sword. "Give it away? How could you give a sword like that away?"

Tam snorted. "Not much use in herding sheep, now is it? Can't plow a field or harvest a crop with it." For a long minute he stared at the sword as if wondering what he was doing with such a thing. At last he let out a heavy sigh. "But if I am not just taken by a black fancy, if our luck runs sour, maybe in the next few days we'll be glad I tucked it in that old chest, instead." He slid the sword smoothly back into its sheath and wiped his hand on his shirt with a grimace. "The stew should be ready. I'll dish it out while you fix the tea."

Rand nodded and got the tea canister, but he wanted to know everything. Why would Tam have bought a sword? He could not imagine. And where had Tam come by it? How far away? No one ever left the Two Rivers; or very few, at least. He had always vaguely supposed his father must have gone outside—his mother had been an outlander—but a sword . . . ? He had a lot of questions to ask once they had settled at the table.

The tea water was boiling fiercely, and he had to wrap a cloth around the kettle's handle to lift it off the hook. Heat soaked through immediately. As he straightened from the fire, a heavy thump at the door rattled the lock. All thoughts of the sword, or the hot kettle in his hand, flew away.

"One of the neighbors," he said uncertainly. "Master Dautry wanting to borrow. . . ." But the Dautry farm, their nearest neighbor, was an hour away even in the daylight, and Oren

Dautry, shameless borrower that he was, was still not likely to leave his house by dark.

Tam softly placed the stew-filled bowls on the table. Slowly he moved away from the table. Both of his hands rested on his sword hilt. "I don't think—" he began, and the door burst open, pieces of the iron lock spinning across the floor.

A figure filled the doorway, bigger than any man Rand had ever seen, a figure in black mail that hung to his knees, with spikes at wrists and elbows and shoulders. One hand clutched a heavy, scythe-like sword; the other hand was flung up before his eyes as if to shield them from the light.

Rand felt the beginnings of an odd sort of relief. Whoever this was, it was not the black-cloaked rider. Then he saw the curled ram's horns on the head that brushed the top of the doorway, and where mouth and nose should have been was a hairy muzzle. He took in all of it in the space of one deep breath that he let out in a terrified yell as, without thinking, he hurled the hot kettle at that half-human head.

The creature roared, part scream of pain, part animal snarl, as boiling water splashed over its face. Even as the kettle struck, Tam's sword flashed. The roar abruptly became a gurgle, and the huge shape toppled back. Before it finished falling, another was trying to claw its way past. Rand glimpsed a misshapen head topped by spike-like horns before Tam struck again, and two huge bodies blocked the door. He realized his father was shouting at him.

"Run, lad! Hide in the woods!" The bodies in the doorway jerked as others outside tried to pull them clear. Tam thrust a shoulder under the massive table; with a grunt he heaved it over atop the tangle. "There are too many to hold! Out the back! Go! Go! I'll follow!".

Even as Rand turned away, shame filled him that he obeyed so quickly. He wanted to stay and help his father, though he could not imagine how, but fear had him by the throat, and his legs moved on their own. He dashed from the room, toward the back of the house, as fast as he had ever run in his life. Crashes and shouts from the front door pursued him.

He had his hands on the bar across the back door when his eye fell on the iron lock that was never locked. Except that Tam had done just that tonight. Letting the bar stay where it was, he darted to a side window, flung up the sash and threw back the shutters. Night had replaced twilight completely. The full moon and drifting clouds made dappled shadows chase one another across the farmyard.

Shadows, he told himself. Only shadows. The back door creaked as someone outside, or something, tried to push it open. His mouth went dry. A crash shook the door in its frame and lent him speed; he slipped through the window like a hare going to ground, and cowered against the side of the house. Inside the room, wood splintered like thunder.

He forced himself up to a crouch, made himself peer inside, just with one eye, just at the corner of the window. In the dark he could not make out much, but more than he really wanted to see. The door hung askew, and shadowed shapes moved cautiously into the room, talking in low, guttural voices. Rand understood none of what was said; the language sounded harsh, unsuited to a human tongue. Axes and spears and spiked things dully reflected stray glimmers of moonlight. Boots scraped on the floor, and there was a rhythmic click, as of hooves, as well.

He tried to work moisture back into his mouth. Drawing a deep, ragged breath, he shouted as loudly as he could. "They're coming in the back!" The words came out in a croak, but at least they came out. He had not been sure they would. "I'm outside! Run, father!" With the last word he was sprinting away from the farmhouse.

Coarse-voiced shouts in the strange tongue raged from the back room. Glass shattered, loud and sharp, and something thudded heavily to the ground behind him. He guessed one of them had broken through the window rather than try to squeeze through the opening, but he did not look back to see if he was right. Like a fox running from hounds he darted into the nearest moon-cast shadows as if headed for the woods, then dropped to his belly and slithered back to the barn and its larger, deeper shadows. Something fell across his shoulders, and he thrashed about, not sure if he was trying to fight or escape, until he realized he was grappling with the new hoe handle Tam had been shaping.

Idiot! For a moment he lay there, trying to stop panting. *Coplin fool idiot!* At last he crawled on along the back of the barn, dragging the hoe handle with him. It was not much, but it was better than nothing. Cautiously he looked around the corner at the farmyard and the house.

Of the creature that had jumped out after him there was no sign. It could be anywhere. Hunting him, surely. Even creeping up on him at that very moment.

Frightened bleats filled the sheep pen to his left; the flock milled as if trying to find an escape. Shadowed shapes flickered in the lighted front windows of the house, and the clash of steel on steel rang through the darkness. Suddenly one of the windows burst outward in a shower of glass and wood as Tam leaped through it, sword still in hand. He landed on his feet, but instead of running away from the house he dashed toward the back of it, ignoring the monstrous things scrambling after him through the broken window and the doorway.

Rand stared in disbelief. Why was he not trying to get away? Then he understood. Tam had last heard his voice from the rear of the house. "Father!" he shouted. "I'm over here!"

In mid-stride Tam whirled, not running toward Rand, but at an angle away from him. "Run, lad!" he shouted, gesturing with the sword as if to someone ahead of him. "Hide!" A dozen huge forms streamed after him, harsh shouts and shrill howls shivering the air.

Rand pulled back into the shadows behind the barn. There he could not be seen from the house, in case any of the creatures were still inside. He was safe; for the moment, at least. But not Tam. Tam, who was trying to lead those things away from him. His hands tightened on the hoe handle, and he had to clench his teeth to stop a sudden laugh. A hoe handle. Facing one of those creatures with a hoe handle would not be much like playing at quarterstaffs with Perrin. But he could not let Tam face what was chasing him alone.

"If I move like I was stalking a rabbit," he whispered to himself, "they'll never hear me, or see me." The eerie cries echoed in the darkness, and he tried to swallow. "More like a pack of starving wolves." Soundlessly he slipped away from the barn, toward the forest, gripping the hoe handle so hard that his hands hurt.

At first, when the trees surrounded him, he took comfort from them. They helped hide him from whatever the creatures were that had attacked the farm. As he crept through the woods, though, moon shadows shifted, and it began to seem as if the darkness of the forest changed and moved, too. Trees loomed malevolently; branches writhed toward him. But were they just trees and branches? He could almost hear the growling chuckles stifled in their throats while they waited for him. The howls of Tam's pursuers no longer filled the night, but in the silence that replaced them he flinched every time the wind scraped one limb against another. Lower and lower he crouched, and moved more and more slowly. He hardly dared to breathe for fear he might be heard.

Suddenly a hand closed over his mouth from behind, and an iron grip seized his wrist. Frantically he clawed over his shoulder with his free hand for some hold on the attacker.

"Don't break my neck, lad," came Tam's hoarse whisper.

Relief flooded him, turning his muscles to water. When his father released him he fell to his hands and knees, gasping as if he had run for miles. Tam dropped down beside him, leaning on one elbow.

"I wouldn't have tried that if I had thought how much you've grown in the last few years," Tam said softly. His eyes shifted constantly as he spoke, keeping a sharp watch on the darkness. "But I had to make sure you didn't speak out. Some Trollocs can hear like a dog. Maybe better."

"But Trollocs are just. . . ." Rand let the words trail off. Not just a story, not after tonight. Those things could be Trollocs or the Dark One himself for all he knew. "Are you sure?" he whispered. "I mean . . . Trollocs?"

"I'm sure. Though what brought them to the Two Rivers. . . . I never saw one before tonight, but I've talked with men who have, so I know a little. Maybe enough to keep us alive. Listen closely. A Trolloc can see better than a man in the dark, but bright lights blind them, for a time at least. That may be the only reason we got away from so many. Some can track by scent or sound, but they're said to be lazy. If we can keep out of their hands long enough, they should give up."

That made Rand feel only a little better. "In the stories they hate men, and serve the Dark One."

"If anything belongs in the Shepherd of the Night's flocks, lad, it is Trollocs. They kill for the pleasure of killing, so I've been told. But that's the end of my knowledge, except that they cannot be trusted unless they're afraid of you, and then not far."

Rand shivered. He did not think he would want to meet anyone a Trolloc was afraid of. "Do you think they're still hunting for us?"

"Maybe, maybe not. They don't seem very smart. Once we got into the forest, I sent the ones after me off toward the mountains without much trouble." Tam fumbled at his right side, then put his hand close to his face. "Best act as if they are, though."

"You're hurt."

"Keep your voice down. It's just a scratch, and there is nothing to be done about it now, anyway. At least the weather seems to be warming." He lay back with a heavy sigh. "Perhaps it won't be too bad spending the night out."

In the back of his mind Rand had just been thinking fond thoughts of his coat and cloak. The trees cut the worst of the wind, but what gusted through still sliced like a frozen knife. Hesitantly he touched Tam's face, and winced. "You're on fire. I have to get you to Nynaeve."

"In a bit, lad."

"We don't have any time to waste. It's a long way in the dark." He scrambled to his feet and tried to pull his father up. A groan barely stifled by Tam's clenched teeth made Rand hastily ease him back down.

"Let me rest a while, boy. I'm tired."

Rand pounded his fist on his thigh. Snug in the farmhouse, with a fire and blankets, plenty of water and willowbark, he might have been willing to wait for daybreak before hitching Bela and taking Tam into the village. Here was no fire, no blankets, no cart, and no Bela. But those things were still back at the house. If he could not carry Tam to them, perhaps he could bring some of them, at least, to Tam. If the Trollocs were gone. They had to go sooner or later.

He looked at the hoe handle, then dropped it. Instead he drew Tam's sword. The blade gleamed dully in the pale moonlight. The long hilt felt odd in his hand; the weight and heft were strange. He slashed at the air a few times before stopping with a sigh. Slashing at air was easy. If he had to do it against a Trolloc he was surely just as likely to run instead, or freeze stiff so he could not move at all until the Trolloc swung one of those odd swords and. . . . *Stop it! It's not helping anything!*

As he started to rise, Tam caught his arm. "Where are you going?"

"We need the cart," he said gently. "And blankets." He was shocked at how easily he pulled his father's hand from his sleeve. "Rest, and I'll be back."

"Careful," Tam breathed.

He could not see Tam's face in the moonlight, but he could feel his eyes on him. "I will be." *As careful as a mouse exploring a hawk's nest*, he thought.

As silently as another shadow, he slid into the darkness. He thought of all the times he had played tag in the woods with his friends as children, stalking one another, straining not to be heard until he put a hand on someone's shoulder. Somehow he could not make this seem the same.

Creeping from tree to tree, he tried to make a plan, but by the time he reached the edge of the woods he had made and discarded ten. Everything depended on whether or not the Trollocs were still there. If they were gone, he could simply walk up to the house and take what he needed. If they were still there. . . . In that case, there was nothing for it but go back to Tam. He did not like it, but he could do Tam no good by getting killed.

He peered toward the farm buildings. The barn and the sheep pen were only dark shapes in the moonlight. Light spilled from the front windows of the house, though, and through the open front door. *Just the candles father lit, or are there Trollocs waiting?*

He jumped convulsively at a nighthawk's reedy cry, then sagged against a tree, shaking. This was getting him nowhere. Dropping to his belly, he began to crawl, holding the sword awkwardly before him. He kept his chin in the dirt all the way to the back of the sheep pen.

Crouched against the stone wall, he listened. Not a sound disturbed the night. Carefully he eased up enough to look over the wall. Nothing moved in the farmyard. No shadows flickered against the lit windows of the house, or in the doorway. *Bela and the cart first, or the blankets and other things*. It was the light that decided him. The barn was dark. Anything could be waiting inside, and he would have no way of knowing until it was too late. At least he would be able to see what was inside the house.

As he started to lower himself again, he stopped suddenly. There was *no* sound. Most of the sheep might have settled down already and gone back to sleep, though it was not likely, but a few were always awake even in the middle of the night, rustling about, bleating now and again. He could barely make out the shadowy mounds of sheep on the ground. One lay almost beneath him.

Trying to make no noise, he hoisted himself onto the wall until he could stretch out a hand to the dim shape. His fingers touched curly wool, then wetness; the sheep did not move. Breath left him in a rush as he pushed back, almost dropping the sword as he fell to the ground outside the pen. *They kill for fun.* Shakily he scrubbed the wetness from his hand in the dirt.

Fiercely he told himself that nothing had changed. The Trollocs had done their butchery and gone. Repeating that in his mind, he crawled on across the farmyard, keeping as low as he could, but trying to watch every direction, too. He had never thought he would envy an earthworm.

At the front of the house he lay close beside the wall, beneath the broken window, and listened. The dull thudding of blood in his ears was the loudest sound he heard. Slowly he reared up and peered inside.

The stewpot lay upside down in the ashes on the hearth. Splintered, broken wood littered the room; not a single piece of furniture remained whole. Even the table rested at an angle, two legs hacked to rough stubs. Every drawer had been pulled out and smashed; every cupboard and cabinet stood open, many doors hanging by one hinge. Their contents were strewn over the wreckage, and everything was dusted with white. Flour and salt, to judge from the slashed sacks tossed down by the fireplace. Four twisted bodies made a tangle in the remnants of the furnishings. Trollocs.

Rand recognized one by its ram's horns. The others were much the same, even in their differences, a repulsive melange of human faces distorted by muzzles, horns, feathers, and fur. Their hands, almost human, only made it worse. Two wore boots; the others had hooves. He watched without blinking until his eyes burned. None of the Trollocs moved. They had to be dead. And Tam was waiting.

He ran in through the front door and stopped, gagging at the stench. A stable that had not been mucked out in months was the only thing he could think of that might come close to matching it. Vile smears defiled the walls. Trying to breathe through his mouth, he hurriedly began poking through the mess on the floor. There had been a waterbag in one of the cupboards.

A scraping sound behind him sent a chill to his marrow, and he spun, almost falling over the remains of the table. He caught himself, and moaned behind teeth that would have chattered had he not had them clenched until his jaw ached.

One of the Trollocs was getting to its feet. A wolf's muzzle jutted out below sunken eyes. Flat, emotionless eyes, and all too human. Hairy, pointed ears twitched incessantly. It stepped over one of its dead companions on sharp goat hooves. The same black mail the others wore rasped against leather trousers, and one of the huge, scythe-curved swords swung at its side.

It muttered something, guttural and sharp, then said, "Others go away. Narg stay. Narg smart." The words were distorted and hard to understand, coming from a mouth never meant for human speech. Its tone was meant to be soothing, he thought, but he could not take his eyes off the stained teeth, long and sharp, that flashed every time the creature spoke. "Narg know some come back sometime. Narg wait. You no need sword. Put sword down."

Until the Trolloc spoke Rand had not realized that he held Tam's sword wavering before him in both hands, its point aimed at the huge creature. It towered head and shoulders above him, with a chest and arms to dwarf Master Luhhan.

"Narg no hurt." It took a step closer, gesturing. "You put sword down." The dark hair on the backs of its hands was thick, like fur.

"Stay back," Rand said, wishing his voice were steadier. "Why did you do this? Why?"

"*Vlja daeg roghda!*" The snarl quickly became a toothy smile. "Put sword down. Narg no hurt. Myrddraal want talk you." A flash of emotion crossed the distorted face. Fear.

"Others come back, you talk Myrddraal." It took another step, one big hand coming to rest on its own sword hilt. "You put sword down."

Rand wet his lips. Myrddraal! The worst of the stories was walking tonight. If a Fade was coming, it made a Trolloc pale by comparison. He had to get away. But if the Trolloc drew that massive blade he would not have a chance. He forced his lips into a shaky smile. "All right." Grip tightening on the sword, he let both hands drop to his sides. "I'll talk."

The wolf-smile became a snarl, and the Trolloc lunged for him. Rand had not thought anything that big could move so fast. Desperately he brought his sword up. The monstrous body crashed into him, slamming him against the wall. Breath left his lungs in one gasp. He fought for air as they fell to the floor together, the Trolloc on top. Frantically he struggled beneath the crushing weight, trying to avoid thick hands groping for him, and snapping jaws.

Abruptly the Trolloc spasmed and was still. Battered and bruised, half suffocated by the bulk on top of him, for a moment Rand could only lie there in disbelief. Quickly he came to his senses, though, enough to writhe out from under the body, at least. And body it was. The bloodied blade of Tam's sword stood out from the center of the Trolloc's back. He had gotten it up in time after all. Blood covered Rand's hands, as well, and made a blackish smear across the front of his shirt. His stomach churned, and he swallowed hard to keep from being sick. He shook as hard as he had in the worst of his fear, but this time in relief at still being alive.

Others come back, the Trolloc had said. The other Trollocs would be returning to the farmhouse. And a Myrddraal, a Fade. The stories said Fades were twenty feet tall, with eyes of fire, and they rode shadows like horses. When a Fade turned sideways, it disappeared, and no wall could stop them. He had to do what he had come for, and get away quickly.

Grunting with the effort he heaved the Trolloc's body over to get to the sword—and almost ran when open eyes stared at him. It took him a minute to realize they were staring through the glaze of death.

He wiped his hands on a tattered rag—it had been one of Tam's shirts only that morning—and tugged the blade free.

Cleaning the sword, he reluctantly dropped the rag on the floor. There was no time for neatness, he thought with a laugh that he had to clamp his teeth shut to stop. He did not see how they could ever clean the house well enough for it to be lived in again. The horrible stench had probably already soaked right into the timbers. But there was no time to think of that. *No time for neatness. No time for anything, maybe.*

He was sure he was forgetting any number of things they would need, but Tam was waiting, and the Trollocs were coming back. He gathered what he could think of on the run. Blankets from the bedrooms upstairs, and clean cloths to bandage Tam's wound. Their cloaks and coats. A waterbag that he carried when he took the sheep to pasture. A clean shirt. He did not know when he would have time to change, but he wanted to get out of his blood-smeared shirt at the first opportunity. The small bags of willowbark and their other medicines were part of a dark, muddy-looking pile he could not bring himself to touch.

One bucket of the water Tam had brought in still stood by the fireplace, miraculously unspilled and untouched. He filled the waterbag from it, gave his hands a hasty wash in the rest, and made one more quick search for anything he might have forgotten. He found his bow among the wreckage, broken cleanly in two at the thickest point. He shuddered as he let the pieces fall. What he had gathered already would have to do, he decided. Quickly he piled everything outside the door.

The last thing before leaving the house, he dug a shuttered lantern from the mess on the floor. It still held oil. Lighting it from one of the candles, he closed the shutters—partly against the wind, but mostly to keep from drawing attention—and hurried outside with the lantern in one hand and the sword in the other. He was not sure what he would find in the barn. The sheep pen kept him from hoping too much. But he needed the cart to get Tam to Emond's Field, and for the cart he needed Bela. Necessity made him hope a little.

The barn doors stood open, one creaking on its hinges as it shifted in the wind. The interior looked as it always had, at first. Then his eyes fell on empty stalls, the stall doors ripped from their hinges. Bela and the cow were gone. Quickly he went to the back of the barn. The cart lay on its side, half the spokes broken out of its wheels. One shaft was only a foot-long stump.

The despair he had been holding at bay filled him. He was not sure he could carry Tam as far as the village even if his father could bear to be carried. The pain of it might kill Tam more quickly than the fever. Still, it was the only chance left. He had done all he could do here. As he turned to go, his eyes fell on the hacked-off cart shaft lying on the straw-strewn floor. Suddenly he smiled.

Hurriedly he set the lantern and the sword on the straw-covered floor, and in the next instant he was wrestling with the cart, tipping it back over to fall upright with a snap of more breaking spokes, then throwing his shoulder into it to heave it over on the other side. The undamaged shaft stood straight out. Snatching up the sword he hacked at the well-seasoned ash. To his pleased surprise great chips flew with his strokes, and he cut through as quickly as he could have with a good axe.

When the shaft fell free, he looked at the sword blade in wonder. Even the best-sharpened axe would have dulled chopping through that hard, aged wood, but the sword looked as brightly sharp as ever. He touched the edge with his thumb, then hastily stuck it in his mouth. The blade was still razor-sharp.

But he had no time for wonder. Blowing out the lantern—there was no need to have the barn burn down on top of everything else—he gathered up the shafts and ran back to get what he had left at the house.

Altogether it made an awkward burden. Not a heavy one, but hard to balance and manage, the cart shafts shifting and twisting in his arms as he stumbled across the plowed field. Once back in the forest they were even worse, catching on trees and knocking him half off his feet. They would have been easier to drag, but that would leave a clear trail behind him. He intended to wait as long as possible before doing that.

Tam was right where he had left him, seemingly asleep. He hoped it was sleep. Suddenly fearful, he dropped his burdens and put a hand to his father's face. Tam still breathed, but the fever was worse.

The touch roused Tam, but only into a hazy wakefulness. "Is that you, boy?" he breathed. "Worried about you. Dreams of

days gone. Nightmares." Murmuring softly, he drifted off
again.

"Don't worry," Rand said. He lay Tam's coat and cloak over
him to keep off the wind. "I'll get you to Nynaeve just as quick
as I can." As he went on, as much to reassure himself as for
Tam's benefit, he peeled off his bloodstained shirt, hardly even
noticing the cold in his haste to be rid of it, and hurriedly
pulled on the clean one. Throwing his old shirt away made him
feel as if he had just had a bath. "We'll be safe in the village in
no time, and the Wisdom will set everything right. You'll see.
Everything's going to be all right."

That thought was like a beacon as he pulled on his coat and
bent to tend Tam's wound. They would be safe once they
reached the village, and Nynaeve would cure Tam. He just had
to get him there.

A Trolloc attack

CHAPTER
6

The Westwood

I n the moonlight Rand could not really see what he was doing, but Tam's wound seemed to be only a shallow gash along the ribs, no longer than the palm of his hand. He shook his head in disbelief. He had seen his father take more of an injury than that and not even stop work except to wash it off. Hastily he searched Tam from head to foot for something bad enough to account for the fever, but the one cut was all he could find.

Small as it was, that lone cut was still grave enough; the flesh around it burned to the touch. It was even hotter than the rest of Tam's body, and the rest of him was hot enough to make Rand's jaws clench. A scalding fever like that could kill, or leave a man a husk of what he had once been. He soaked a cloth with water from the skin and laid it across Tam's forehead.

He tried to be gentle about washing and bandaging the gash on his father's ribs, but soft groans still interrupted Tam's low muttering. Stark branches loomed around them, threatening as they shifted as in the wind. Surely the Trollocs would go on their way when they failed to find Tam and him, when they came back to the farmhouse and found it still empty. He tried to make himself believe it, but the wanton destruction at the house, the senselessness of it, left little room for belief of that sort. Believing they would give up short of killing everyone and everything they could find was dangerous, a foolish chance he could not afford to take.

Trollocs. Light above, Trollocs! Creatures out of a gleeman's tale coming out of the night to bash in the door. And a Fade. Light shine on me, a Fade!

Abruptly he realized he was holding the untied ends of the bandage in motionless hands. *Frozen like a rabbit that's seen a hawk's shadow,* he thought scornfully. With an angry shake of his head he finished tying the bandage around Tam's chest.

Knowing what he had to do, even getting on with it, did not stop him being afraid. When the Trollocs came back they would surely begin searching the forest around the farm for some trace of the people who had escaped them. The body of the one he had killed would tell them those people were not far off. Who knew what a Fade would do, or could do? On top of that, his father's comment about Trollocs' hearing was as loud in his mind as if Tam had just said it. He found himself resisting the urge to put a hand over Tam's mouth, to still his groans and murmurs. *Some track by scent. What can I do about that? Nothing.* He could not waste time worrying over problems he could do nothing about.

"You have to keep quiet," he whispered in his father's ear. "The Trollocs will be back."

Tam spoke in hushed, hoarse tones. "You're still lovely, Kari. Still lovely as a girl."

Rand grimaced. His mother had been dead fifteen years. If Tam believed she was still alive, then the fever was even worse than Rand had thought. How could he be kept from speaking, now that silence might mean life?

"Mother wants you to be quiet," Rand whispered. He paused to clear his throat of a sudden tightness. She had had gentle hands; he remembered that much. "Kari wants you to be quiet. Here. Drink."

Tam gulped thirstily from the waterskin, but after a few swallows he turned his head aside and began murmuring softly again, too low for Rand to understand. He hoped it was too low to be heard by hunting Trollocs, too.

Hastily he got on with what was needed. Three of the blankets he wove around and between the shafts cut from the cart, contriving a makeshift litter. He would only be able to carry one end, letting the other drag on the ground, but it would have to do. From the last blanket he cut a long strip with his belt knife, then tied one end of the strip to each of the shafts.

As gently as he could, he lifted Tam onto the litter, wincing with every moan. His father had always seemed indestructible. Nothing could harm him; nothing could stop him, or even slow him down. For him to be in this condition almost robbed Rand of what courage he had managed to gather. But he had to keep on. That was all that kept him moving. He had to.

When Tam finally lay on the litter, Rand hesitated, then took the sword belt from his father's waist. When he fastened it around himself, it felt odd there; it made him feel odd. Belt and sheath and sword together only weighed a few pounds, but when he sheathed the blade it seemed to drag at him like a great weight.

Angrily he berated himself. This was no time or place for foolish fancies. It was only a big knife. How many times had he daydreamed about wearing a sword and having adventures? If he could kill one Trolloc with it, he could surely fight off any others as well. Only, he knew all too well that what had happened in the farmhouse had been the purest luck. And his daydream adventures had never included his teeth chattering, or running for his life through the night, or his father at the point of death.

Hastily he tucked the last blanket around Tam, and laid the waterskin and the rest of the cloths beside his father on the litter. With a deep breath he knelt between the shafts and lifted the strip of blanket over his head. It settled across his shoulders and under his arms. When he gripped the shafts and straightened, most of the weight was on his shoulders. It did not seem like very much. Trying to keep a smooth pace, he set out for Emond's Field, the litter scraping along behind him.

He had already decided to make his way to the Quarry Road and follow that to the village. The danger would almost certainly be greater along the road, but Tam would receive no help at all if he got them lost trying to find his way through the woods and the dark.

In the darkness he was almost out onto the Quarry Road

before he knew it. When he realized where he was, his throat tightened like a fist. Hurriedly he turned the litter around and dragged it back into the trees a way, then stopped to catch his breath and let his heart stop pounding. Still panting, he turned east, toward Emond's Field.

Traveling through the trees was more difficult than taking Tam down the road, and the night surely did not help, but going out onto the road itself would be madness. The idea was to reach the village *without* meeting any Trollocs; without even seeing any, if he had his wish. He had to assume the Trollocs were still hunting them, and sooner or later they would realize the two had set off for the village. That was the most likely place to go, and the Quarry Road the most likely route. In truth, he found himself closer to the road than he liked. The night and the shadows under the trees seemed awfully bare cover in which to hide from the eyes of anyone traveling along it.

Moonlight filtering through bare branches gave only enough illumination to fool his eyes into thinking they saw what was underfoot. Roots threatened to trip him at every step, old brambles snagged his legs, and sudden dips or rises in the ground had him half falling as his foot met nothing but air where he expected firm earth, or stumbling when his toe struck dirt while still moving forward. Tam's mutterings broke into a sharp groan whenever one of the shafts bumped too quickly over root or rock.

Uncertainty made him peer into the darkness until his eyes burned, listen as he had never listened before. Every scrape of branch against branch, every rustle of pine needles, brought him to a halt, ears straining, hardly daring to breathe for fear he might not hear some warning sound, for fear he might hear that sound. Only when he was sure it was just the wind would he go on.

Slowly weariness crept into his arms and legs, driven home by a night wind that mocked his cloak and coat. The weight of the litter, so little at the start, now tried to pull him to the ground. His stumbles were no longer all from tripping. The almost constant struggle not to fall took as much out of him as did the actual work of pulling the litter. He had been up before dawn to begin his chores, and even with the trip to Emond's

Field he had done almost a full day's work. On any normal night he would be resting before the fireplace, reading one of Tam's small collection of books before going to bed. The sharp chill soaked into his bones, and his stomach reminded him that he had had nothing to eat since Mistress al'Vere's honeycakes.

He muttered to himself, angry at not taking some food at the farm. A few minutes more could not have made any difference. A few minutes to find some bread and cheese. The Trollocs would not have come back in just a few minutes more. Or just the bread. Of course, Mistress al'Vere would insist on putting a hot meal in front of him once they reached the inn. A steaming plate of her thick lamb stew, probably. And some of that bread she had been baking. And lots of hot tea.

"They came over the Dragonwall like a flood," Tam said suddenly, in a strong, angry voice, "and washed the land with blood. How many died for Laman's sin?"

Rand almost fell from surprise. Wearily he lowered the litter to the ground and untangled himself. The strip of blanket left a burning groove in his shoulders. Shrugging to work the knots out, he knelt beside Tam. Fumbling for the waterbag, he peered through the trees, trying vainly in the dim moonlight to see up and down the road, not twenty paces away. Nothing moved there but shadows. Nothing but shadows.

"There isn't any flood of Trollocs, father. Not now, anyway. We'll be safe in Emond's Field soon. Drink a little water."

Tam brushed aside the waterbag with an arm that seemed to have regained all of its strength. He seized Rand's collar, pulling him close enough to feel the heat of his father's fever in his own cheek. "They called them savages," Tam said urgently. "The fools said they could be swept aside like rubbish. How many battles lost, how many cities burned, before they faced the truth? Before the nations stood together against them?" He loosed his hold on Rand, and sadness filled his voice. "The field at Marath carpeted with the dead, and no sound but the cries of ravens and the buzzing of flies. The topless towers of Cairhien burning in the night like torches. All the way to the Shining Walls they burned and slew before they were turned back. All the way to—"

Rand clamped a hand over his father's mouth. The sound came again, a rhythmic thudding, directionless in the trees, fading then growing stronger again as the wind shifted. Frowning, he turned his head slowly, trying to decide from where it came. A flicker of motion caught the corner of his eye, and in an instant he was crouched over Tam. He was startled to feel the hilt of the sword clutched tight in his hand, but most of him concentrated on the Quarry Road as if the road were the only real thing in the entire world.

Wavering shadows to the east slowly resolved themselves into a horse and rider followed up the road by tall, bulky shapes trotting to keep up with the animal. The pale light of the moon glittered from spearheads and axe blades. Rand never even considered that they might be villagers coming to help. He knew what they were. He could feel it, like grit scraping his bones, even before they drew close enough for moonlight to reveal the hooded cloak swathing the horseman, a cloak that hung undisturbed by the wind. All of the shapes appeared black in the night, and the horse's hooves made the same sounds that any other's would, but Rand knew this horse from any other.

Behind the dark rider came nightmare forms with horns and muzzles and beaks, Trollocs in a double file, all in steps, boots and hooves striking the ground at the same instant as if obeying a single mind. Rand counted twenty as they ran past. He wondered what kind of man would dare turn his back on so many Trollocs. Or on one, for that matter.

The trotting column disappeared westward, thumping footfalls fading into the darkness, but Rand remained where he was, not moving a muscle except to breathe. Something told him to be certain, absolutely certain, they were gone before he moved. At long last he drew a deep breath and began to straighten.

This time the horse made no sound at all. In eerie silence the dark rider returned, his shadowy mount stopping every few steps as it walked slowly back down the road. The wind gusted higher, moaning through the trees; the horseman's cloak lay still as death. Whenever the horse halted, that hooded head swung from side to side as the rider peered into the forest, searching. Exactly opposite Rand the horse stopped again, the shadowed opening of the hood turning toward where he crouched above his father.

Rand's hand tightened convulsively on the sword hilt. He felt the gaze, just as he had that morning, and shivered again from the hatred even if he could not see it. That shrouded man hated everyone and everything, everything that lived. Despite the cold wind, sweat beaded on Rand's face.

Then the horse was moving on, a few soundless steps and stop, until all Rand could see was a barely distinguishable blur in the night far down the road. It could have been anything, but he had not taken his eyes off it for a second. If he lost it, he was afraid the next time he saw the black-cloaked rider might be when that silent horse was on top of him.

Abruptly the shadow was rushing back, passing him in a silent gallop. The rider looked only ahead of him as he sped westward into the night, toward the Mountains of Mist. Toward the farm.

Rand sagged, gulping air and scrubbing cold sweat off his face with his sleeve. He did not care any more about why the Trollocs had come. If he never found out why, that would be fine, just as long as it was all ended.

With a shake he gathered himself, hastily checking his father. Tam was still murmuring, but so softly Rand could not make out the words. He tried to give him a drink, but the water spilled over his father's chin. Tam coughed and choked on the trickle that made it into his mouth, then began muttering again as if there had not been any interruption.

Rand splashed a little more water on the cloth on Tam's forehead, pushed the waterbag back on the litter, and scrambled between the shafts again.

He started out as if he had had a good night's sleep, but the new strength did not last long. Fear masked his tiredness in the beginning, but though the fear remained, the mask melted away quickly. Soon he was back to stumbling forward, trying to ignore hunger and aching muscles. He concentrated on putting one foot in front of the other without tripping.

In his mind he pictured Emond's Field, shutters thrown back and the houses lit for Winternight, people shouting greetings as they passed back and forth on their visits, fiddles filling the streets with "Jaem's Folly" and "Heron on the Wing." Haral Luhhan would have one too many brandies and start singing "The Wind in the Barley" in a voice like a bullfrog—he always did—until his wife managed to shush him, and Cenn Buie would decide to prove he could still dance as well as ever, and Mat would have something planned that would not quite happen the way he intended, and everybody would know he was responsible even if no one could prove it. He could almost smile thinking about how it would be.

After a time Tam spoke up again.

"*Avendesora*. It's said it makes no seed, but they brought a cutting to Cairhien, a sapling. A royal gift of wonder for the king." Though he sounded angry, he was barely loud enough for Rand to understand. Anyone who could hear him would be able to hear the litter scraping across the ground, too. Rand kept on, only half listening. "They never make peace. Never. But they brought a sapling, as a sign of peace. Five hundred years it grew. Five hundred years of peace with those who make no peace with strangers. Why did he cut it down? Why? Blood was the price for *Avendoraldera*. Blood the price for Laman's pride." He faded off into muttering once more.

Tiredly Rand wondered what fever-dream Tam could be having now. *Avendesora*. The Tree of Life was supposed to have all sorts of miraculous qualities, but none of the stories mentioned any sapling, or any "they." There was only the one, and that belonged to the Green Man.

Only that morning he might have felt foolish at musing over the Green Man and the Tree of Life. They were only stories. *Are they? Trollocs were just stories this morning*. Maybe all the stories were as real as the news the peddlers and merchants brought, all the gleeman's tales and all the stories told at night in front of the fireplace. Next he might actually meet the Green Man, or an Ogier giant, or a wild, black-veiled Aielman.

Tam was talking again, he realized, sometimes only murmuring, sometimes loud enough to understand. From time to time he stopped to pant for breath, then went on as if he thought he had been speaking the whole time.

". . . battles are always hot, even in the snow. Sweat heat. Blood heat. Only death is cool. Slope of the mountain . . . only place didn't stink of death. Had to get away from smell of it . . . sight of it. . . . heard a baby cry. Their women fight alongside the men, sometimes, but why they had let her come, I don't . . . gave birth there alone, before she died of her

wounds. . . . covered the child with her cloak, but the wind
. . . blown the cloak away. . . . child, blue with the cold.
Should have been dead, too. . . . crying there. Crying in the
snow. I couldn't just leave a child. . . . no children of our
own. . . . always knew you wanted children. I knew you'd take
it to your heart, Kari. Yes, lass. Rand is a good name. A good
name."

Suddenly Rand's legs lost the little strength they had. Stumbling, he fell to his knees. Tam moaned with the jolt, and the
strip of blanket cut into Rand's shoulders, but he was not aware
of either. If a Trolloc had leaped up in front of him right then,
he would just have stared at it. He looked over his shoulder at
Tam, who had sunk back into wordless murmurs. *Fever-
dreams,* he thought dully. Fevers always brought bad dreams,
and this was a night for nightmares even without a fever.

"You are my father," he said aloud, stretching back a hand
to touch Tam, "and I am——" The fever was worse. Much worse.

Grimly he struggled to his feet. Tam murmured something,
but Rand refused to listen to any more. Throwing his weight
against the improvised harness he tried to put all of his mind
into taking one leaden step after another, into reaching the
safety of Emond's Field. But he could not stop the echo in the
back of his mind. *He's my father. It was just a fever-dream. He's
my father. It was just a fever-dream. Light, who am I?*

CHAPTER
7

Out of the Woods

G ray first light came while Rand still trudged through
the forest. At first he did not really see. When he finally did, he stared at the fading darkness in surprise.
No matter what his eyes told him, he could hardly believe he
had spent all night trying to travel the distance from the farm to
Emond's Field. Of course, the Quarry Road by day, rocks and
all, was a far cry from the woods by night. On the other hand,
it seemed days since he had seen the black-cloaked rider on the
road, weeks since he and Tam had gone in for their supper. He
no longer felt the strip of cloth digging into his shoulders, but
then he felt nothing in his shoulders except numbness, nor in
his feet, for that matter. In between, it was another matter. His
breath came in labored pants that had long since set his throat
and lungs to burning, and hunger twisted his stomach into
queasy sickness.

Tam had fallen silent some time before. Rand was not sure
how long it had been since the murmurs ceased, but he did not
dare halt now to check on Tam. If he stopped he would never
be able to force himself to start out again. Anyway, whatever
Tam's condition, he could do nothing beyond what he was
doing. The only hope lay ahead, in the village. He tried wearily
to increase his pace, but his wooden legs continued their slow
plod. He barely even noticed the cold, or the wind.

Vaguely he caught the smell of woodsmoke. At least he was
almost there if he could smell the village chimneys. A tired

smile had only begun on his face, though, when it turned to a frown. Smoke lay heavy in the air—too heavy. With the weather, a fire might well be blazing on every hearth in the village, but the smoke was still too strong. In his mind he saw again the Trollocs on the road. Trollocs coming from the east, from the direction of Emond's Field. He peered ahead, trying to make out the first houses, and ready to shout for help at the first sight of anyone, even Cenn Buie or one of the Coplins. A small voice in the back of his head told him to hope someone there could still give help.

Suddenly a house became visible through the last bare-branched trees, and it was all he could do to keep his feet moving. Hope turning to sharp despair, he staggered into the village.

Charred piles of rubble stood in the places of half the houses of Emond's Field. Soot-coated brick chimneys thrust like dirty fingers from heaps of blackened timbers. Thin wisps of smoke still rose from the ruins. Grimy-faced villagers, some yet in their night clothes, poked through the ashes, here pulling free a cookpot, there simply prodding forlornly at the wreckage with a stick. What little had been rescued from the flames dotted the streets; tall mirrors and polished sideboards and highchests stood in the dust among chairs and tables buried under bedding, cooking utensils, and meager piles of clothing and personal belongings.

The destruction seemed scattered at random through the village. Five houses marched untouched in one row, while in another place a lone survivor stood surrounded by desolation.

On the far side of the Winespring Water, the three huge Bel Tine bonfires roared, tended by a cluster of men. Thick columns of black smoke bent northward with the wind, flecked by careless sparks. One of Master al'Vere's Dhurran stallions was dragging something Rand could not make out over the ground toward the Wagon Bridge, and the flames.

Before he was well out of the trees, a sooty-faced Haral Luhhan hurried to him, clutching a woodsman's axe in one thick-fingered hand. The burly blacksmith's ash-smeared night-shirt hung to his boots, the angry red welt of a burn across his chest showing through a ragged tear. He dropped to one knee beside the litter. Tam's eyes were closed, and his breathing came low and hard.

"Trollocs, boy?" Master Luhhan asked in a smoke-hoarse voice. "Here, too. Here, too. Well, we may have been luckier than anyone has a right to be, if you can credit it. He needs the Wisdom. Now where in the Light is she? Egwene!"

Egwene, running by with her arms full of bedsheets torn into bandages, looked around at them without slowing. Her eyes stared at something in the far distance; dark circles made them appear even larger than they actually were. Then she saw Rand and stopped, drawing a shuddering breath. "Oh, no, Rand, not your father? Is he . . . ? Come, I'll take you to Nynaeve."

Rand was too tired, too stunned, to speak. All through the night Emond's Field had been a haven, where he and Tam would be safe. Now all he could seem to do was stare in dismay at her smoke-stained dress. He noticed odd details as if they were very important. The buttons down the back of her dress were done up crookedly. And her hands were clean. He wondered why her hands were clean when smudges of soot marked her cheeks.

Master Luhhan seemed to understand what had come over him. Laying his axe across the shafts, the blacksmith picked up the rear of the litter and gave it a gentle push, prodding him to follow Egwene. He stumbled after her as if walking in his sleep. Briefly he wondered how Master Luhhan knew the creatures were Trollocs, but it was a fleeting thought. If Tam could recognize them, there was no reason why Haral Luhhan could not.

"All the stories are real," he muttered.

"So it seems, lad," the blacksmith said. "So it seems."

Rand only half heard. He was concentrating on following Egwene's slender shape. He had pulled himself together just enough to wish she would hurry, though in truth she was keeping her pace to what the two men could manage with their burden. She led them halfway down the Green, to the Calder house. Char blackened the edges of its thatch, and smut stained the whitewashed walls. Of the houses on either side only the foundation stones were left, and two piles of ash and burned timbers. One had been the house of Berin Thane, one of the miller's brothers. The other had been Abell Cauthon's. Mat's father. Even the chimneys had toppled.

"Wait here," Egwene said, and gave them a look as if expecting an answer. When they only stood there, she muttered something under her breath, then dashed inside.

"Mat," Rand said. "Is he . . . ?"

"He's alive," the blacksmith said. He set down his end of the litter and straightened slowly. "I saw him a little while ago. It's a wonder any of us are alive. The way they came after my house, and the forge, you'd have thought I had gold and jewels in there. Alsbet cracked one's skull with a frying pan. She took one look at the ashes of our house this morning and set out hunting around the village with the biggest hammer she could dig out of what's left of the forge, just in case any of them hid instead of running away. I could almost pity the thing if she finds one." He nodded to the Calder house. "Mistress Calder and a few others took in some of those who were hurt, the ones with no home of their own still standing. When the Wisdom's seen Tam, we'll find him a bed. The inn, maybe. The Mayor offered it already, but Nynaeve said the hurt folk would heal better if there weren't so many of them together."

Rand sank to his knees. Shrugging out of his blanket harness, he wearily busied himself with checking Tam's covers. Tam never moved or made a sound, even when Rand's wooden hands jostled him. But he was still breathing, at least. *My father. The other was just the fever talking.* "What if they come back?" he said dully.

"The Wheel weaves as the Wheel wills," Master Luhhan said uneasily. "If they come back. . . . Well, they're gone, now. So we pick up the pieces, build up what's been torn down." He sighed, his face going slack as he knuckled the small of his back. For the first time Rand realized that the heavyset man was as tired as he was himself, if not more so. The blacksmith looked at the village, shaking his head. "I don't suppose today will be much of a Bel Tine. But we'll make it through. We always have." Abruptly he took up his axe, and his face firmed. "There's work waiting for me. Don't you worry, lad. The Wisdom will take good care of him, and the Light will take care of us all. And if the Light doesn't, well, we'll just take care of ourselves. Remember, we're Two Rivers folk."

Still on his knees, Rand looked at the village as the blacksmith walked away, really looked for the first time. Master Luhhan was right, he thought, and was surprised that he was not surprised by what he saw. People still dug in the ruins of their homes, but even in the short time he had been there more of them had begun to move with a sense of purpose. He could almost feel the growing determination. But he wondered. They had seen Trollocs; had they seen the black-cloaked rider? Had they felt his hatred?

Nynaeve and Egwene appeared from the Calder house, and he sprang to his feet. Or rather, he tried to spring to his feet; it was more of a stumbling lurch that almost put him on his face in the dust.

The Wisdom dropped to her knees beside the litter without giving him so much as a glance. Her face and dress were even dirtier than Egwene's, and the same dark circles lined her eyes, though her hands, too, were clean. She felt Tam's face and thumbed open his eyelids. With a frown she pulled down the coverings and eased the bandage aside to look at the wound. Before Rand could see what lay underneath she had replaced the wadded cloth. Sighing, she smoothed the blanket and cloak back up to Tam's neck with a gentle touch, as if tucking a child in for the night.

"There's nothing I can do," she said. She had to put her hands on her knees to straighten up. "I'm sorry, Rand."

For a moment he stood, not understanding, as she started back to the house, then he scrambled after her and pulled her around to face him. "He's dying," he cried.

"I know," she said simply, and he sagged with the matter-of-factness of it.

"You have to do something. You have to. You're the Wisdom."

Pain twisted her face, but only for an instant, then she was all hollow-eyed resolve again, her voice emotionless and firm. "Yes, I am. I know what I can do with my medicines, and I know when it's too late. Don't you think I would do something if I could? But I can't. I can't, Rand. And there are others who need me. People I *can* help."

"I brought him to you as quickly as I could," he mumbled.

Even with the village in ruins, there had been the Wisdom for hope. With that gone, he was empty.

"I know you did," she said gently. She touched his cheek with her hand. "It isn't your fault. You did the best anyone could. I am sorry, Rand, but I have others to tend to. Our troubles are just beginning, I'm afraid."

Vacantly he stared after her until the door of the house closed behind her. He could not make any thought come except that she would not help.

Suddenly he was knocked back a step as Egwene cannoned into him, throwing her arms around him. Her hug was hard enough to bring a grunt from him any other time; now he only looked silently at the door behind which his hopes had vanished.

"I'm so sorry, Rand," she said against his chest. "Light, I wish there was something I could do."

Numbly he put his arms around her. "I know. I . . . I have to do something, Egwene. I don't know what, but I can't just let him. . . ." His voice broke, and she hugged him harder.

"Egwene!" At Nynaeve's shout from the house, Egwene jumped. "Egwene, I need you! And wash your hands again!"

She pushed herself free from Rand's arms. "She needs my help, Rand."

"Egwene!"

He thought he heard a sob as she spun away from him. Then she was gone, and he was left alone beside the litter. For a moment he looked down at Tam, feeling nothing but hollow helplessness. Suddenly his face hardened. "The Mayor will know what to do," he said, lifting the shafts once more. "The Mayor will know." Bran al'Vere always knew what to do. With weary obstinacy he set out for the Winespring Inn.

Another of the Dhurran stallions passed him, its harness straps tied around the ankles of a big shape draped with a dirty blanket. Arms covered with coarse hair dragged in the dirt behind the blanket, and one corner was pushed up to reveal a goat's horn. The Two Rivers was no place for stories to become horribly real. If Trollocs belonged anywhere it was in the world outside, for places where they had Aes Sedai and false Dragons and the Light alone knew what else come to life out of the tales of gleemen. Not the Two Rivers. Not Emond's Field.

As he made his way down the Green, people called to him, some from the ruins of their homes, asking if they could help. He heard them only as murmurs in the background, even when they walked alongside him for a distance as they spoke. Without really thinking about it he managed words that said he needed no help, that everything was being taken care of. When they left him, with worried looks, and sometimes a comment about sending Nynaeve to him, he noticed that just as little. All he let himself be aware of was the purpose he had fixed in his head. Bran al'Vere could do something to help Tam. What that could be he tried not to dwell on. But the Mayor would be able to do something, to think of something.

The inn had almost completely escaped the destruction that had taken half the village. A few scorch marks marred its walls, but the red roof tiles glittered in the sunlight as brightly as ever. All that was left of the peddler's wagon, though, were blackened iron wheel-rims leaning against the charred wagon box, now on the ground. The big round hoops that had held up the canvas cover slanted crazily, each at a different angle.

Thom Merrilin sat cross-legged on the old foundation stones, carefully snipping singed edges from the patches on his cloak with a pair of small scissors. He set down cloak and scissors when Rand drew near. Without asking if Rand needed or wanted help, he hopped down and picked up the back of the litter.

"Inside? Of course, of course. Don't you worry, boy. Your Wisdom will take care of him. I've watched her work, since last night, and she has a deft touch and a sure skill. It could be a lot worse. Some died last night. Not many, perhaps, but any at all are too many for me. Old Fain just disappeared, and that's the worst of all. Trollocs will eat anything. You should thank the Light your father's still here, and alive for the Wisdom to heal."

Rand blotted out the words—*He is my father!*—reducing the voice to meaningless sound that he noticed no more than a fly's buzzing. He could not bear any more sympathy, any more attempts to boost his spirits. Not now. Not until Bran al'Vere told him how to help Tam.

Suddenly he found himself facing something scrawled on the inn door, a curving line scratched with a charred stick, a char-

coal teardrop balanced on its point. So much had happened
that it hardly surprised him to find the Dragon's Fang marked
on the door of the Winespring Inn. Why anyone would want to
accuse the innkeeper or his family of evil, or bring the inn bad
luck, was beyond him, but the night had convinced him of one
thing. Anything was possible. Anything at all.

At a push from the gleeman he lifted the latch, and went in.

The common room was empty except for Bran al'Vere, and
cold, too, for no one had found time to lay a fire. The Mayor
sat at one of the tables, dipping his pen in an inkwell with a
frown of concentration on his face and his gray-fringed head
bent over a sheet of parchment. Nightshirt tucked hastily into
his trousers and bagging around his considerable waist, he absently scratched at one bare foot with the toes of the other. His
feet were dirty, as if he had been outside more than once without bothering about boots, despite the cold. "What's your trouble?" he demanded without looking up. "Be quick with it. I
have two dozen things to do right this minute, and more that
should have been done an hour ago. So I have little time or
patience. Well? Out with it!"

"Master al'Vere?" Rand said. "It's my father."

The Mayor's head jerked up. "Rand? Tam!" He threw down
the pen and knocked over his chair as he leaped up. "Perhaps
the Light hasn't abandoned us altogether. I was afraid you were
both dead. Bela galloped into the village an hour after the Trollocs left, lathered and blowing as if she'd run all the way from
the farm, and I thought. . . . No time for that, now. We'll take
him upstairs." He seized the rear of the litter, shouldering the
gleeman out of the way. "You go get the Wisdom, Master Merrilin. And tell her I said hurry, or I'll know the reason why!
Rest easy, Tam. We'll soon have you in a good, soft bed. Go,
gleeman, go!"

Thom Merrilin vanished through the doorway before Rand
could speak. "Nynaeve wouldn't do anything. She said she
couldn't help him. I knew . . . I hoped you'd think of something."

Master al'Vere looked at Tam more sharply, then shook his
head. "We will see, boy. We will see." But he no longer
sounded confident. "Let's get him into a bed. He can rest easy,
at least."

Rand let himself be prodded toward the stairs at the back of the common room. He tried hard to keep his certainty that somehow Tam would be all right, but it had been thin to begin with, he realized, and the sudden doubt in the Mayor's voice shook him.

On the second floor of the inn, at the front, were half a dozen snug, well-appointed rooms with windows overlooking the Green. Mostly they were used by the peddlers, or people down from Watch Hill or up from Deven Ride, but the merchants who came each year were often surprised to find such comfortable rooms. Three of them were taken now, and the Mayor hurried Rand to one of the unused ones.

Quickly the down comforter and blankets were stripped back on the wide bed, and Tam was transferred to the thick feather mattress, with goose-down pillows tucked under his head. He made no sound beyond hoarse breathing as he was moved, not even a groan, but the Mayor brushed away Rand's concern, telling him to set a fire to take the chill off the room. While Rand dug wood and kindling from the woodbox next to the fireplace, Bran threw back the curtains on the window, letting in the morning light, then began to gently wash Tam's face. By the time the gleeman returned, the blaze on the hearth was warming the room.

"She will not come," Thom Merrilin announced as he stalked into the room. He glared at Rand, his bushy white brows drawing down sharply. "You didn't tell me she had seen him already. She almost took my head off."

"I thought . . . I don't know . . . maybe the Mayor could do something, could make her see. . . ." Hands clenched in anxious fists, Rand turned from the fireplace to Bran. "Master al'Vere, what can I do?" The rotund man shook his head helplessly. He laid a freshly dampened cloth on Tam's forehead and avoided meeting Rand's eye. "I can't just watch him die, Master al'Vere. I have to do something." The gleeman shifted as if to speak. Rand rounded on him eagerly. "Do you have an idea? I'll try anything."

"I was just wondering," Thom said, tamping his long-stemmed pipe with his thumb, "if the Mayor knew who scrawled the Dragon's Fang on his door." He peered into the bowl, then looked at Tam and replaced the unlit pipe between his teeth with a sigh. "Someone seems not to like him anymore. Or maybe it's his guests they don't like."

Rand gave him a disgusted look and turned away to stare into the fire. His thoughts danced like the flames, and like the flames they concentrated fixedly on one thing. He would not give up. He could not just stand there and watch Tam die. *My father*, he thought fiercely. *My father*. Once the fever was gone, that could be cleared up as well. But the fever first. Only, how?

Bran al'Vere's mouth tightened as he looked at Rand's back, and the glare he directed at the gleeman would have given a bear pause, but Thom just waited expectantly as if he had not noticed it.

"It's probably the work of one of the Congars, or a Coplin," the Mayor said finally, "though the Light alone knows which. They're a large brood, and if there's ill to be said of someone, or even if there isn't, they'll say it. They make Cenn Buie sound honey-tongued."

"That wagonload who came in just before dawn?" the gleeman asked. "They hadn't so much as smelled a Trolloc, and all they wanted to know was when Festival was going to start, as if they couldn't see half the village in ashes."

Master al'Vere nodded grimly. "One branch of the family. But none of them are very different. That fool Darl Coplin spent half the night demanding I put Mistress Moiraine and Master Lan out of the inn, out of the village, as if there would be any village at all left without them."

Rand had only half listened to the conversation, but this last tugged him to speak. "What did they do?"

"Why, she called ball lightning out of a clear night sky," Master al'Vere replied. "Sent it darting straight at the Trollocs. You've seen trees shattered by it. The Trollocs stood it no better."

"Moiraine?" Rand said incredulously, and the Mayor nodded.

"Mistress Moiraine. And Master Lan was a whirlwind with that sword of his. His sword? The man himself is a weapon, and in ten places at once, or so it seemed. Burn me, but I still wouldn't believe it if I couldn't step outside and see. . . ." He rubbed a hand over his bald head. "Winternight visits just beginning, our hands full of presents and honeycakes and our heads full of wine, then the dogs snarling, and suddenly the two of them burst out of the inn, running through the village, shouting about Trollocs. I thought they'd had too much wine. After all . . . Trollocs? Then, before anyone knew what was happening, those . . . those things were right in the streets with us, slashing at people with their swords, torching houses, howling to freeze a man's blood." He made a sound of disgust in his throat. "We just ran like chickens with a fox in the henyard till Master Lan put some backbone into us."

"No need to be so hard," Thom said. "You did as well as anyone could. Not every Trolloc lying out there fell to the two of them."

"Umm . . . yes, well." Master al'Vere gave himself a shake. "It's still almost too much to believe. An Aes Sedai in Emond's Field. And Master Lan is a Warder."

"An Aes Sedai?" Rand whispered, "She can't be. I talked to her. She isn't. . . . She doesn't. . . ."

"Did you think they wore signs?" the Mayor said wryly. "'Aes Sedai' painted across their backs, and maybe, 'Danger, stay away'?" Suddenly he slapped his forehead. "Aes Sedai. I'm an old fool, and losing my wits. There's a chance, Rand, if you're willing to take it. I can't tell you to do it, and I don't know if I'd have the nerve, if it were me."

"A chance?" Rand said. "I'll take any chance, if it'll help."

"Aes Sedai can heal, Rand. Burn me, lad, you've heard the stories. They can cure where medicines fail. Gleeman, you should have remembered that better than I. Gleemen's tales are full of Aes Sedai. Why didn't you speak up, instead of letting me flail around?"

"I'm a stranger here," Thom said, looking longingly at his unlit pipe, "and Goodman Coplin isn't the only one who wants nothing to do with Aes Sedai. Best the idea came from you."

"An Aes Sedai," Rand muttered, trying to make the woman who had smiled at him fit the stories. Help from an Aes Sedai was sometimes worse than no help at all, so the stories said, like poison in a pie, and their gifts always had a hook in them, like fishbait. Suddenly the coin in his pocket, the coin Moiraine had given him, seemed like a burning coal. It was all he could do not to rip it out of his coat and throw it out the window.

"Nobody wants to get involved with Aes Sedai, lad," the

Mayor said slowly. "It is the only chance I can see, but it's still no small decision. I cannot make it for you, but I have seen nothing but good from Mistress Moiraine . . . Moiraine Sedai, I should call her, I suppose. Sometimes"—he gave a meaningful look at Tam—"you have to take a chance, even if it's a poor one."

"Some of the stories are exaggerated, in a way," Thom added, as if the words were being dragged from him. "Some of them. Besides, boy, what choice do you have?"

"None," Rand sighed. Tam still had not moved a muscle; his eyes were sunken as if he had been sick a week. "I'll . . . I'll go find her."

"The other side of the bridges," the gleeman said, "where they are . . . disposing of the dead Trollocs. But be careful, boy. Aes Sedai do what they do for reasons of their own, and they aren't always the reasons others think."

The last was a shout that followed Rand through the door. He had to hold onto the sword hilt to keep the scabbard from tangling in his legs as he ran, but he would not take the time to remove it. He clattered down the stairs and dashed out of the inn, tiredness forgotten for the moment. A chance for Tam, however small, was enough to overcome a night without sleep, for a time at least. That the chance came from an Aes Sedai, or what the price of it might be, he did not want to consider. And as for actually facing an Aes Sedai. . . . He took a deep breath and tried to move faster.

The bonfires stood well beyond the last houses to the north, on the Westwood side of the road to Watch Hill. The wind still carried the oily black columns of smoke away from the village, but even so a sickly sweet stink filled the air, like a roast left hours too long on the spit. Rand gagged at the smell, then swallowed hard when he realized its source. A fine thing to do with Bel Tine fires. The men tending the fires had cloths tied over their noses and mouths, but their grimaces made it plain the vinegar dampening the cloths was not enough. Even if it did kill the stench, they still knew the stench was there, and they still knew what they were doing.

Two of the men were untying the harness straps of one of the big Dhurrans from a Trolloc's ankles. Lan, squatting beside the body, had tossed back the blanket enough to reveal the Trolloc's shoulders and goat-snouted head. As Rand trotted up the Warder unfastened a metal badge, a blood-red enameled trident, from one spiked shoulder of the Trolloc's shirt of black mail.

"Ko'bal," he announced. He bounced the badge on his palm and snatched it out of the air with a growl. "That makes seven bands so far."

Moiraine, seated cross-legged on the ground a short distance off, shook her head tiredly. A walking staff, covered from end to end in carved vines and flowers, lay across her knees, and her dress had the rumpled look of having been worn too long. "Seven bands. Seven! That many have not acted together since the Trolloc Wars. Bad news piles on bad news. I am afraid, Lan. I thought we had gained a march, but we may be further behind than ever."

Rand stared at her, unable to speak. An Aes Sedai. He had been trying to convince himself that she would not look any different now that he knew who . . . what he was looking at, and to his surprise she did not. She was no longer quite so pristine, not with wisps of her hair sticking out in all directions and a faint streak of soot across her nose, yet not really different, either. Surely there must be something about an Aes Sedai to mark her for what she was. On the other hand, if outward appearance reflected what was inside, and if the stories were true, then she should look closer to a Trolloc than to a more than handsome woman whose dignity was not dented by sitting in the dirt. And she could help Tam. Whatever the cost, there was that before anything else.

He took a deep breath. "Mistress Moiraine . . . I mean, Moiraine Sedai." Both turned to look at him, and he froze under her gaze. Not the calm, smiling gaze he remembered from the Green. Her face was tired, but her dark eyes were a hawk's eyes. Aes Sedai. Breakers of the world. Puppeteers who pulled strings and made thrones and nations dance in designs only the women from Tar Valon knew.

"A little more light in the darkness," the Aes Sedai murmured. She raised her voice. "How are your dreams, Rand al'Thor?"

He stared at her. "My dreams?"

"A night like that can give a man bad dreams, Rand. If you

have nightmares, you must tell me of it. I can help with bad dreams, sometimes."

"There's nothing wrong with my. . . . It's my father. He's hurt. It's not much more than a scratch, but the fever is burning him up. The Wisdom won't help. She says she can't. But the stories—" She raised an eyebrow, and he stopped and swallowed hard. *Light, is there a story with an Aes Sedai where she isn't a villain?* He looked at the Warder, but Lan appeared more interested in the dead Trolloc than in anything Rand might say. Fumbling his way under her eyes, he went on. "I . . . ah . . . it's said Aes Sedai can heal. If you can help him . . . anything you can do for him . . . whatever the cost. . . . I mean. . . ." He took a deep breath and finished up in a rush. "I'll pay any price in my power if you help him. Anything."

"Any price," Moiraine mused, half to herself. "We will speak of prices later, Rand, if at all. I can make no promises. Your Wisdom knows what she is about. I will do what I can, but it is beyond my power to stop the Wheel from turning."

"Death comes sooner or later to everyone," the Warder said grimly, "unless they serve the Dark One, and only fools are willing to pay that price."

Moiraine made a clucking sound. "Do not be so gloomy, Lan. We have some reason to celebrate. A small one, but a reason." She used the staff to pull herself to her feet. "Take me to your father, Rand. I will help him as much as I am able. Too many here have refused to let me help at all. They have heard the stories, too," she added dryly.

"He's at the inn," Rand said. "This way. And thank you. Thank you!"

They followed, but his pace took him quickly ahead. He slowed impatiently for them to catch up, then darted ahead again and had to wait again.

"Please hurry," he urged, so caught up in actually getting help for Tam that he never considered the temerity of prodding an Aes Sedai. "The fever is burning him up."

Lan glared at him. "Can't you see she's tired? Even with an *angreal,* what she did last night was like running around the village with a sack of stones on her back. I don't know that you are worth it, sheepherder, no matter what she says."

Rand blinked and held his tongue.

"Gently, my friend," Moiraine said. Without slowing her pace, she reached up to pat the Warder's shoulder. He towered over her protectively, as if he could give her strength just by being close. "You think only of taking care of me. Why should he not think the same of his father?" Lan scowled, but fell silent. "I am coming as quickly as I can, Rand, I promise you."

The fierceness of her eyes, or the calm of her voice—not gentle, exactly; more firmly in command—Rand did not know which to believe. Or perhaps they did go together. Aes Sedai. He was committed, now. He matched his stride to theirs, and tried not to think of what the price might be that they would talk about later.

Moiraine

CHAPTER
8

A Place of Safety

While he was still coming through the door Rand's eyes went to his father—his father no matter what *anyone* said. Tam had not moved an inch; his eyes were still shut, and his breath came in labored gasps, low and rasping. The white-haired gleeman cut off a conversation with the Mayor—who was bent over the bed again, tending Tam— and gave Moiraine an uneasy look. The Aes Sedai ignored him. Indeed, she ignored everyone except for Tam, but at him she stared with an intent frown.

Thom stuck his unlit pipe between his teeth, then snatched it out again and glowered at it. "Man cannot even smoke in peace," he muttered. "I had better make sure some farmer doesn't steal my cloak to keep his cow warm. At least I can have my pipe out there." He hurried out of the room.

Lan stared after him, his angular face as expressionless as a rock. "I do not like that man. There is something about him I don't trust. I did not see a hair of him last night."

"He was there," Bran said, watching Moiraine uncertainly. "He must have been. His cloak did not get singed in front of the fireplace."

Rand did not care if the gleeman had spent the night hiding in the stable. "My father?" he said to Moiraine pleadingly.

Bran opened his mouth, but before he could speak Moiraine said, "Leave me with him, Master al'Vere. There is nothing you can do here now except get in my way."

For a minute Bran hesitated, torn between dislike of being ordered about in his own inn and reluctance to disobey an Aes Sedai. Finally, he straightened to clap Rand on the shoulder. "Come along, boy. Let us leave Moiraine Sedai to her . . . ah . . . her. . . . There's plenty you can give me a hand with downstairs. Before you know it Tam will be shouting for his pipe and a mug of ale."

"Can I stay?" Rand spoke to Moiraine, though she did not really seem to be aware of anyone besides Tam. Bran's hand tightened, but Rand ignored him. "Please? I'll keep out of your way. You won't even know I am here. He's my father," he added with a fierceness that startled him and widened the Mayor's eyes in surprise. Rand hoped the others put it down to tiredness, or the strain of dealing with an Aes Sedai.

"Yes, yes," Moiraine said impatiently. She had tossed her cloak and staff carelessly across the only chair in the room, and now she pushed up the sleeves of her gown, baring her arms to her elbows. Her attention never really left Tam, even while she spoke. "Sit over there. And you, too, Lan." She gestured vaguely in the direction of a long bench against the wall. Her eyes traveled slowly from Tam's feet to his head, but Rand had the prickly feeling that she was looking *beyond* him in some fashion. "You may talk if you wish," she went on absently, "but do it quietly. Now, you go, Master al'Vere. This is a sick-room, not a gathering hall. See that I am not disturbed."

The Mayor grumbled under his breath, though not loudly enough to catch her attention, of course, squeezed Rand's shoulder again, then obediently, if reluctantly, closed the door behind him.

Muttering to herself, the Aes Sedai knelt beside the bed and rested her hands lightly on Tam's chest. She closed her eyes, and for a long time she neither moved nor made a sound.

In the stories Aes Sedai wonders were always accompanied by flashes and thunderclaps, or other signs to indicate mighty works and great powers. *The* Power. The One Power, drawn from the True Source that drove the Wheel of Time. That was not something Rand wanted to think about, the Power involved with Tam, himself in the same room where the Power might be used. In the same village was bad enough. For all he could tell, though, Moiraine might just as well have gone to sleep. But he thought Tam's breathing sounded easier. She must be doing something. So intent was he that he jumped when Lan spoke softly.

"That is a fine weapon you wear. Is there by chance a heron on the blade, as well?"

For a moment Rand stared at the Warder, not grasping what it was he was talking about. He had completely forgotten Tam's sword in the lather of dealing with an Aes Sedai. It did not seem so heavy anymore. "Yes, there is. What is she doing?"

"I'd not have thought to find a heron-mark sword in a place like this," Lan said.

"It belongs to my father." He glanced at Lan's sword, the hilt just visible at the edge of his cloak; the two swords did look a good deal alike, except that no herons showed on the Warder's. He swung his eyes back to the bed. Tam's breathing did sound easier; the rasp was gone. He was sure of it. "He bought it a long time ago."

"Strange thing for a sheepherder to buy."

Rand spared a sidelong look for Lan. For a stranger to wonder about the sword was prying. For a Warder to do it. . . . Still, he felt he had to say something. "He never had any use for it, that I know of. He said it *had* no use. Until last night, anyway. I didn't even know he had it till then."

"He called it useless, did he? He must not always have thought so." Lan touched the scabbard at Rand's waist briefly with one finger. "There are places where the heron is a symbol of the master swordsman. That blade must have traveled a strange road to end up with a sheepherder in the Two Rivers."

Rand ignored the unspoken question. Moiraine still had not moved. *Was* the Aes Sedai doing anything? He shivered and rubbed his arms, not sure he really wanted to know what she was doing. An Aes Sedai.

A question of his own popped into his head then, one he did not want to ask, one he needed an answer to. "The Mayor—" He cleared his throat, and took a deep breath. "The Mayor said the only reason there's anything left of the village is because of you and her." He made himself look at the Warder. "If you had been told about a man in the woods . . . a man who made people afraid just by looking at them . . . would that have warned you? A man whose horse doesn't make any noise?

And the wind doesn't touch his cloak? Would you have known what was going to happen? Could you and Moiraine Sedai have stopped it if you'd known about him?"

"Not without half a dozen of my sisters," Moiraine said, and Rand started. She still knelt by the bed, but she had taken her hands from Tam and half turned to face the two of them on the bench. Her voice never raised, but her eyes pinned Rand to the wall. "Had I known when I left Tar Valon that I would find Trollocs and Myrddraal here, I would have brought half a dozen of them, a dozen, if I had to drag them by the scruffs of their necks. By myself, a month's warning would have made little difference. Perhaps none. There is only so much one person can do, even calling on the One Power, and there were probably well over a hundred Trollocs scattered around this district last night. An entire fist."

"It would still have been good to know," Lan said sharply, the sharpness directed at Rand. "When did you see him, exactly, and where?"

"That's of no consequence now," Moiraine said. "I will not have the boy thinking he is to blame for something when he is not. I am as much to blame. That accursed raven yesterday, the way it behaved, should have warned me. And you, too, my old friend." Her tongue clicked angrily. "I was overconfident to the point of arrogance, sure that the Dark One's touch could not have spread so far. Nor so heavily, not yet. So sure."

Rand blinked. "The raven? I don't understand."

"Carrion eaters." Lan's mouth twisted in distaste. "The Dark One's minions often find spies among creatures that feed on death. Ravens and crows, mainly. Rats, in the cities, sometimes."

A quick shiver ran through Rand. Ravens and crows as spies of the Dark One? There were ravens and crows everywhere now. The Dark One's touch, Moiraine had said. The Dark One was always there—he knew that—but if you tried to walk in the Light, tried to live a good life, and did not name him, he could not harm you. That was what everybody believed, what everybody learned with his mother's milk. But Moiraine seemed to be saying. . . .

His glance fell on Tam, and everything else was pushed right out of his head. His father's face was noticeably less flushed than it had been, and his breathing sounded almost normal. Rand would have leaped up if Lan had not caught his arm. "You've done it."

Moiraine shook her head and sighed. "Not yet. I hope it is only not yet. Trolloc weapons are made at forges in the valley called Thakan'dar, on the very slopes of Shayol Ghul itself. Some of them take a taint from that place, a stain of evil in the metal. Those tainted blades make wounds that will not heal unaided, or cause deadly fevers, strange sicknesses that medicines cannot touch. I have soothed your father's pain, but the mark, the taint, is still in him. Left alone, it will grow again, and consume him."

"But you won't leave it alone." Rand's words were half plea, half command. He was shocked to realize he had spoken to an Aes Sedai like that, but she seemed not to notice his tone.

"I will not," she agreed simply. "I am very tired, Rand, and I have had no chance to rest since last night. Ordinarily it would not matter, but for this kind of hurt. . . . This"—she took a small bundle of white silk from her pouch—"is an *angreal.*" She saw his expression. "You know of *angreal,* then. Good."

Unconsciously he leaned back, further away from her and what she held. A few stories mentioned *angreal,* those relics of the Age of Legends that Aes Sedai used to perform their greatest wonders. He was startled to see her unwrap a smooth ivory figurine, age-darkened to deep brown. No longer than her hand, it was a woman in flowing robes, with long hair falling about her shoulders.

"We have lost the making of these," she said. "So much is lost, perhaps never to be found again. So few remain, the Amyrlin Seat almost did not allow me to take this one. It is well for Emond's Field, and for your father, that she did give her permission. But you must not hope too much. Now, even with it, I can do little more than I could have without it yesterday, and the taint is strong. It has had time to fester."

"You can help him," Rand said fervently. "I know you can."

Moiraine smiled, a bare curving of her lips. "We shall see." Then she turned back to Tam. One hand she laid on his forehead; the other cupped the ivory figure. Eyes closed, her face took on a look of concentration. She scarcely seemed to breathe.

"That rider you spoke of," Lan said quietly, "the one who made you afraid—that was surely a Myrddraal."

"A Myrddraal!" Rand exclaimed. "But Fades are twenty feet tall and. . . ." The words faded away under the Warder's mirthless grin.

"Sometimes, sheepherder, stories make things larger than truth. Believe me, the truth is big enough with a Halfman. Halfman, Lurk, Fade, Shadowman; the name depends on the land you're in, but they all mean Myrddraal. Fades are Trolloc spawn, throwbacks almost to the human stock the Dreadlords used to make the Trollocs. Almost. But if the human strain is made stronger, so is the taint that twists the Trollocs. Halfmen have powers of a kind, the sort that stem from the Dark One. Only the weakest Aes Sedai would fail to be a match for a Fade, one against one, but many a good man and true has fallen to them. Since the wars that ended the Age of Legends, since the Forsaken were bound, they have been the brain that tells the Trolloc fists where to strike. In the days of the Trolloc Wars, Halfmen led the Trollocs in battle, under the Dreadlords."

"He scared me," Rand said faintly. "He just looked at me, and. . . ." He shivered.

"No need for shame, sheepherder. They scare me, too. I've seen men who have been soldiers all their lives freeze like a bird facing a snake when they confronted a Halfman. In the north, in the Borderlands along the Great Blight, there is a saying. The look of the Eyeless is fear."

"The Eyeless?" Rand said, and Lan nodded.

"Myrddraal see like eagles, in darkness or in light, but they have no eyes. I can think of few things more dangerous than facing a Myrddraal. Moiraine Sedai and I both tried to kill the one that was here last night, and we failed every time. Halfmen have the Dark One's own luck."

Rand swallowed. "A Trolloc said the Myrddraal wanted to talk to me. I didn't know what it meant."

Lan's head jerked up; his eyes were blue stones. "You *talked* to a Trolloc?"

"Not exactly," Rand stammered. The Warder's gaze held him like a trap. "It talked to me. It said it wouldn't hurt me, that the Myrddraal wanted to talk to me. Then it tried to kill me." He licked his lips and rubbed his hand along the nobby leather of the sword hilt. In short, choppy sentences he explained about returning to the farmhouse. "I killed it, instead," he finished. "By accident, really. It jumped at me, and I had the sword in my hand."

Lan's face softened slightly, if rock could be said to soften. "Even so, that is something to speak of, sheepherder. Until last night there were few men south of the Borderlands who could say they had seen a Trolloc, much less killed one."

"And fewer still who have slain a Trolloc alone and unaided," Moiraine said wearily. "It is done, Rand. Lan, help me up."

The Warder sprang to her side, but he was no quicker than Rand darting to the bed. Tam's skin was cool to the touch, though his face had a pale, washed-out look, as if he had spent far too long out of the sun. His eyes were still closed, but he drew the deep breaths of normal sleep.

"He will be all right now?" Rand asked anxiously.

"With rest, yes," Moiraine said. "A few weeks in bed, and he will be as good as ever." She walked unsteadily, despite holding Lan's arm. He swept her cloak and staff from the chair cushion for her to sit, and she eased herself down with a sigh. With a slow care she rewrapped the *angreal* and returned it to her pouch.

Rand's shoulders shook; he bit his lip to keep from laughing. At the same time he had to scrub a hand across his eyes to clear away tears. "Thank you."

"In the Age of Legends," Moiraine went on, "some Aes Sedai could fan life and health to flame if only the smallest spark remained. Those days are gone, though—perhaps forever. So much was lost; not just the making of *angreal*. So much that could be done which we dare not even dream of, if we remember it at all. There are far fewer of us now. Some talents are all but gone, and many that remain seem weaker. Now there must be both will and strength for the body to draw on, or even the strongest of us can do nothing in the way of Healing. It is fortunate that your father is a strong man, both in body and spirit. As it is, he used up much of his strength in the fight for life, but all that is left now is for him to recuperate. That will take time, but the taint is gone."

"I can never repay you," he told her without taking his eyes from Tam, "but anything I can do for you, I will. Anything at all." He remembered the talk of prices, then, and his promise. Kneeling beside Tam he meant it even more than before, but it still was not easy to look at her. "Anything. As long as it does not hurt the village, or my friends."

Moiraine raised a hand dismissively. "If you think it is necessary. I would like to talk with you, anyway. You will no doubt leave at the same time we do, and we can speak at length then."

"Leave!" he exclaimed, scrambling to his feet. "Is it really that bad? Everyone looked to me as if they were ready to start rebuilding. We are pretty settled folk in the Two Rivers. Nobody ever leaves."

"Rand—"

"And where would we go? Padan Fain said the weather is just as bad everywhere else. He's . . . he was . . . the peddler. The Trollocs. . . ." Rand swallowed, wishing Thom Merrilin had not told him what Trollocs ate. "The best I can see to do is stay right here where we belong, in the Two Rivers, and put things back together. We have crops in the ground, and it has to warm enough for the shearing, soon. I don't know who started this talk about leaving—one of the Coplins, I'll bet—but whoever it was—"

"Sheepherder," Lan broke in, "you talk when you should be listening."

He blinked at both of them. He had been half babbling, he realized, and he had rambled on while she tried to talk. While an Aes Sedai tried to talk. He wondered what to say, how to apologize, but Moiraine smiled while he was still thinking.

"I understand how you feel, Rand," she said, and he had the uncomfortable feeling that she really did. "Think no more of it." Her mouth tightened, and she shook her head. "I have handled this badly, I see. I should have rested, first, I suppose. It is you who will be leaving, Rand. You who must leave, for the sake of your village."

"Me?" He cleared his throat and tried again. "Me?" It

sounded a little better this time. "Why do I have to go? I don't understand any of this. I don't want to go anywhere."

Moiraine looked at Lan, and the Warder unfolded his arms. He looked at Rand from under his leather headband, and Rand had the feeling of being weighed on invisible scales again. "Did you know," Lan said suddenly, "that some homes were not attacked?"

"Half the village is in ashes," he protested, but the Warder waved it away.

"Some houses were only torched to create confusion. The Trollocs ignored them afterwards, and the people who fled from them as well, unless they actually got in the way of the true attack. Most of the people who've come in from the outlying farms never saw a hair of a Trolloc, and that only at a distance. Most never knew there was any trouble until they saw the village."

"I did hear about Darl Coplin," Rand said slowly. "I suppose it just didn't sink in."

"Two farms were attacked," Lan went on. "Yours and one other. Because of Bel Tine everyone who lived at the second farm was already in the village. Many people were saved because the Myrddraal was ignorant of Two Rivers customs. Festival and Winternight made its task all but impossible, but it did not know that."

Rand looked at Moiraine, leaning back in the chair, but she said nothing, only watched him, a finger laid across her lips. "Our farm, and who else's?" he asked finally.

"The Aybara farm," Lan replied. "Here in Emond's Field, they struck first at the forge, and the blacksmith's house, and Master Cauthon's house."

Rand's mouth was suddenly dry. "That's crazy," he managed to get out, then jumped as Moiraine straightened.

"Not crazy, Rand," she said. "Purposeful. The Trollocs did not come to Emond's Field by happenstance, and they did not do what they did for the pleasure of killing and burning, however much that delighted them. They knew what, or rather who, they were after. The Trollocs came to kill or capture young men of a certain age who live near Emond's Field."

"My age?" Rand's voice shook, and he did not care. "Light! Mat. What about Perrin?"

"Alive and well," Moiraine assured him, "if a trifle sooty."

"Ban Crawe and Lem Thane?"

"Were never in any danger," Lan said. "At least, no more than anyone else."

"But they saw the rider, the Fade, too, and they're the same age as I am."

"Master Crawe's house was not even damaged," Moiraine said, "and the miller and his family slept through half the attack before the noise woke them. Ban is ten months older than you, and Lem eight months younger." She smiled dryly at his surprise. "I told you I asked questions. And I also said young men of a *certain* age. You and your two friends are within weeks of one another. It was you three the Myrddraal sought, and none others."

Rand shifted uneasily, wishing she would not look at him like that, as if her eyes could pierce his brain and read what lay in every corner of it. "What would they want with us? We're just farmers, shepherds."

"That is a question that has no answer in the Two Rivers," Moiraine said quietly, "but the answer is important. Trollocs where they have not been seen in almost two thousand years tells us that much."

"Lots of stories tell about Trolloc raids," Rand said stubbornly. "We just never had one here before. Warders fight Trollocs all the time."

Lan snorted. "Boy, I expect to fight Trollocs along the Great Blight, but not here, nearly six hundred leagues to the south. That was as hot a raid last night as I'd expect to see in Shienar, or any of the Borderlands."

"In one of you," Moiraine said, "or all three, there is something the Dark One fears."

"That . . . that's impossible." Rand stumbled to the window and stared out at the village, at the people working among the ruins. "I don't care what's happened, that is just impossible." Something on the Green caught his eye. He stared, then realized it was the blackened stump of the Spring Pole. A fine Bel Tine, with a peddler, and a gleeman, and strangers. He shivered, and shook his head violently. "No. No, I'm a shepherd. The Dark One can't be interested in me."

"It took a great deal of effort," Lan said grimly, "to bring so many Trollocs so far without raising a hue and cry from the Borderlands to Caemlyn and beyond. I wish I knew how they did it. Do you really believe they went to all that bother just to burn a few houses?"

"They will be back," Moiraine added.

Rand had his mouth open to argue with Lan, but that brought him up short. He spun to face her. "Back? Can't you stop them? You did last night, and you were surprised, then. Now you know they are here."

"Perhaps," Moiraine replied. "I could send to Tar Valon for some of my sisters; they might have time to make the journey before we need them. The Myrddraal knows *I* am here, too, and it probably will not attack—not openly, at least—lacking reinforcements, more Myrddraal and more Trollocs. With enough Aes Sedai and enough Warders, the Trollocs can be beaten off, though I cannot say how many battles it will take."

A vision danced in his head, of Emond's Field all in ashes. All the farms burned. And Watch Hill, and Deven Ride, and Taren Ferry. All ashes and blood. "No," he said, and felt a wrenching inside as if he had lost his grip on something. "That's why I have to leave, isn't it? The Trollocs won't come back if I am not here." A last trace of obstinacy made him add, "If they really are after me."

Moiraine's eyebrows raised as if she were surprised that he was not convinced, but Lan said, "Are you willing to bet your village on it, sheepherder? Your whole Two Rivers?"

Rand's stubbornness faded. "No," he said again, and felt that emptiness inside again, too. "Perrin and Mat have to go, too, don't they?" Leaving the Two Rivers. Leaving his home and his father. At least Tam would get better. At least he would be able to hear him say all that on the Quarry Road had been nonsense. "We could go to Baerlon, I suppose, or even Caemlyn. I've heard there are more people in Caemlyn than in the whole Two Rivers. We'd be safe there." He tried out a laugh that sounded hollow. "I used to daydream about seeing Caemlyn. I never thought it would come about like this."

There was a long silence, then Lan said, "I would not count on Caemlyn for safety. If the Myrddraal want you badly enough, they will find a way. Walls are a poor bar to a Halfman. And you would be a fool not to believe they want you very badly indeed."

Rand thought his spirits had sunk as low as they possibly could, but at that they slid deeper.

"There is a place of safety," Moiraine said softly, and Rand's ears pricked up to listen. "In Tar Valon you would be among Aes Sedai and Warders. Even during the Trolloc Wars the forces of the Dark One feared to attack the Shining Walls. The one attempt was their greatest defeat until the very end. And Tar Valon holds all the knowledge we Aes Sedai have gathered since the Time of Madness. Some fragments even date from the Age of Legends. In Tar Valon, if anywhere, you will be able to learn why the Myrddraal want you. Why the Father of Lies wants you. That I can promise."

A journey all the way to Tar Valon was almost beyond thinking. A journey to a place where he would be surrounded by Aes Sedai. Of course, Moiraine had healed Tam—or it looked as if she had, at least—but there were all those stories. It was uncomfortable enough to be in a room with one Aes Sedai, but to be in a city full of them. . . . And she still had not demanded her price. There was always a price, so the stories said.

"How long will my father sleep?" he asked at last. "I . . . I have to tell him. He shouldn't just wake and find me gone." He thought he heard Lan give a sigh of relief. He looked at the Warder curiously, but Lan's face was as expressionless as ever.

"It is unlikely he will wake before we depart," Moiraine said. "I mean to go soon after full dark. Even a single day of delay could be fatal. It will be best if you leave him a note."

"In the night?" Rand said doubtfully, and Lan nodded.

"The Halfman will discover we are gone soon enough. There is no need to make things any easier for it than we must."

Rand fussed with his father's blankets. It was a very long way to Tar Valon. "In that case. . . . In that case, I had better go find Mat and Perrin."

"I will attend to that." Moiraine got to her feet briskly and donned her cloak with suddenly restored vigor. She put a hand on his shoulder, and he tried very hard not to flinch. She did not press hard, but it was an iron grip that held him as surely as a forked stick held a snake. "It will be best if we keep all of this just among us. Do you understand? The same ones who put the Dragon's Fang on the inn door might make trouble if they knew."

"I understand." He drew a relieved breath when she took her hand away.

"I will have Mistress al'Vere bring you something to eat," she went on just as if she had not noticed his reaction. "Then you need to sleep. It will be a hard journey tonight even if you are rested."

The door closed behind them, and Rand stood looking down at Tam—looking at Tam, but seeing nothing. Not until that very minute had he realized that Emond's Field was a part of him as much as he was a part of it. He realized it now because he knew that was what he had felt tearing loose. He was apart from the village, now. The Shepherd of the Night wanted him. It was impossible—he was only a farmer—but the Trollocs had come, and Lan was right about one thing. He could not risk the village on the chance Moiraine was wrong. He could not even tell anyone; the Coplins really would make trouble about something like that. He had to trust an Aes Sedai.

"Don't wake him, now," Mistress al'Vere said, as the Mayor shut the door behind his wife and himself. The cloth-covered tray she carried gave off delicious, warm smells. She set it on the chest against the wall, then firmly moved Rand away from the bed.

"Mistress Moiraine told me what he needs," she said softly, "and it does not include you falling on top of him from exhaustion. I've brought you a bite to eat. Don't let it get cold, now."

"I wish you wouldn't call her that," Bran said peevishly. "Moiraine Sedai is proper. She might get mad."

Mistress al'Vere gave him a pat on the cheek. "You just leave me to worry about that. She and I had a long talk. And keep your voice down. If you wake Tam, you'll have to answer to me *and* Moiraine Sedai." She put an emphasis on Moiraine's title that made Bran's insistence seem foolish. "The two of you keep out of my way." With a fond smile for her husband, she turned to the bed and Tam.

Master al'Vere gave Rand a frustrated look. "She's an Aes Sedai. Half the women in the village act as if she sits in the Women's Circle, and the rest as if she were a Trolloc. Not a one of them seems to realize you have to be careful around Aes Sedai. The men may keep looking at her sideways, but at least they aren't doing anything that might provoke her."

Careful, Rand thought. It was not too late to start being careful. "Master al'Vere," he said slowly, "do you know how many farms were attacked?"

"Only two that I've heard of so far, including your place." The Mayor paused, frowning, then shrugged. "It doesn't seem enough, with what happened here. I should be glad of it, but. . . . Well, we'll probably hear of more before the day is out."

Rand sighed. No need to ask which farms. "Here in the village, did they. . . . I mean, was there anything to show what they were after?"

"After, boy? I don't know that they were after anything, except maybe killing us all. It was just the way I said. The dogs barking, and Moiraine Sedai and Lan running through the streets, then somebody shouted that Master Luhhan's house and the forge were on fire. Abell Cauthon's house flared up—odd that; it's nearly in the middle of the village. Anyway, the next thing the Trollocs were all among us. No, I don't think they were *after* anything." He gave an abrupt bark of a laugh, and cut it short with a wary look at his wife. She did not look around from Tam. "To tell the truth," he went on more quietly, "they seemed almost as confused as we were. I doubt they expected to find an Aes Sedai here, or a Warder."

"I suppose not," Rand said, grimacing.

If Moiraine had told the truth about that, she probably had told the truth about the rest, too. For a moment he thought about asking the Mayor's advice, but Master al'Vere obviously knew little more about Aes Sedai than anyone else in the village. Besides, he was reluctant to tell even the Mayor what was going on—what Moiraine said was going on. He was not sure if he was more afraid of being laughed at or being believed. He rubbed a thumb against the hilt of Tam's sword. His father had been out into the world; he must know more about Aes Sedai than the Mayor did. But if Tam really had been out of the Two Rivers, then maybe what he had said in the Westwood. . . . He scrubbed both hands through his hair, scattering that line of thought.

"You need sleep, lad," the Mayor said.

"Yes, you do," Mistress al'Vere added. "You're almost falling down where you stand."

Rand blinked at her in surprise. He had not even realized she had left his father. He did need sleep; just the thought set off a yawn.

"You can take the bed in the next room," the Mayor said. "There's already a fire laid."

Rand looked at his father; Tam was still deep in sleep, and that made him yawn again. "I'd rather stay in here, if you don't mind. For when he wakes up."

Sickroom matters were in Mistress al'Vere's province, and the Mayor left it to her. She hesitated only a moment before nodding. "But you let him wake on his own. If you bother his sleep. . . ." He tried to say he would do as she ordered, but the words got tangled in yet another yawn. She shook her head with a smile. "You will be asleep yourself in no time at all. If you must stay, curl up next to the fire. And drink a little of that beef broth before you doze off."

"I will," Rand said. He would have agreed to anything that kept him in that room. "And I won't wake him."

"See that you do not," Mistress al'Vere told him firmly, but not in an unkindly way. "I'll bring you up a pillow and some blankets."

When the door finally closed behind them, Rand dragged the lone chair in the room over beside the bed and sat down where he could watch Tam. It was all very well for Mistress al'Vere to talk about sleep—his jaws cracked as he stifled a yawn—but he could not sleep yet. Tam might wake at any time, and maybe only stay awake a short while. Rand had to be waiting when he did.

He grimaced and twisted in the chair, absently shifting the sword hilt out of his ribs. He still felt backward about telling anyone what Moiraine had said, but this was Tam, after all. This was. . . . Without realizing it he set his jaw determinedly. *My father. I can tell my* father *anything.*

He twisted a little more in the chair and put his head against the chairback. Tam was his father, and nobody could tell him what to say or not say to his father. He just had to stay awake until Tam woke up. He just had to. . . .

CHAPTER

9

Tellings of the Wheel

Rand's heart pounded as he ran, and he stared in dismay
at the barren hills surrounding him. This was not just a
place where spring was late in coming; spring had never
come here, and never would come. Nothing grew in the cold
soil that crunched under his boots, not so much as a bit of li-
chen. He scrambled past boulders, twice as tall as he was; dust
coated the stone as if never a drop of rain had touched it. The
sun was a swollen, blood-red ball, more fiery than on the hottest day of summer and bright enough to sear his eyes, but it
stood stark against a leaden cauldron of a sky where clouds of
sharp black and silver roiled and boiled on every horizon. For
all the swirling clouds, though, no breath of breeze stirred
across the land, and despite the sullen sun the air burned cold
like the depths of winter.

Rand looked over his shoulder often as he ran, but he could
not see his pursuers. Only desolate hills and jagged black
mountains, many topped by tall plumes of dark smoke rising to
join the milling clouds. If he could not see his hunters, though,
he could hear them, howling behind him, guttural voices shouting with the glee of the chase, howling with the joy of blood to
come. Trollocs. Coming closer, and his strength was almost
gone.

With desperate haste he scrambled to the top of a knife-
edged ridge, then dropped to his knees with a groan. Below
him a sheer rock wall fell away, a thousand-foot cliff plummet-

ing into a vast canyon. Steamy mists covered the canyon floor, their thick gray surface rolling in grim waves, rolling and breaking against the cliff beneath him, but more slowly than any ocean wave had ever moved. Patches of fog glowed red for an instant as if great fires had suddenly flared beneath, then died. Thunder rumbled in the depths of the valley, and lightning crackled through the gray, sometimes striking up at the sky.

It was not the valley itself that sapped his strength and filled the empty spaces left with helplessness. From the center of the furious vapors a mountain thrust upward, a mountain taller than any he had ever seen in the Mountains of Mist, a mountain as black as the loss of all hope. That bleak stone spire, a dagger stabbing at the heavens, was the source of his desolation. He had never seen it before, but he knew it. The memory of it flashed away like quicksilver when he tried to touch it, but the memory was there. He knew it was there.

Unseen fingers touched him, pulled at his arms and legs, trying to draw him to the mountain. His body twitched, ready to obey. His arms and legs stiffened as if he thought he could dig his fingers and toes into the stone. Ghostly strings entwined around his heart, pulling him, calling him to the spire mountain. Tears ran down his face, and he sagged to the ground. He felt his will draining away like water out of a holed bucket. Just a little longer, and he would go where he was called. He would obey, do as he was told. Abruptly he discovered another emotion: anger. Push him, pull him, he was not a sheep to be prodded into a pen. The anger squeezed itself into one hard knot, and he clung to it as he would have clung to a raft in a flood.

Serve me, a voice whispered in the stillness of his mind. A familiar voice. If he listened hard enough he was sure he would know it. *Serve me.* He shook his head to try to get it out of his head. *Serve me!* He shook his fist at the black mountain. "The Light consume you, Shai'tan!"

Abruptly the smell of death lay thick around him. A figure loomed over him, in a cloak the color of dried blood, a figure with a face. . . . He did not want to see the face that looked down at him. He did not want to think of that face. It hurt to think of it, turned his mind to embers. A hand reached toward him. Not caring if he fell over the edge, he threw himself away.

He had to get away. Far away. He fell, flailing at the air, wanting to scream, finding no breath for screaming, no breath at all.

Abruptly he was no longer in the barren land, no longer falling. Winter-brown grass flattened under his boots; it seemed like flowers. He almost laughed to see scattered trees and bushes, leafless as they were, dotting the gently rolling plain that now surrounded him. In the distance reared a single mountain, its peak broken and split, but this mountain brought no fear or despair. It was just a mountain, though oddly out of place there, with no other in sight.

A broad river flowed by the mountain, and on an island in the middle of that river was a city such as might live in a gleeman's tale, a city surrounded by high walls gleaming white and silver beneath the warm sun. With mingled relief and joy he started for the walls, for the safety and serenity he somehow knew he would find behind them.

As he came closer he made out soaring towers, many joined by wondrous walkways that spanned the open air. High bridges arched from both banks of the river to the island city. Even at a distance he could see lacy stonework on those spans, seemingly too delicate to withstand the swift waters that rushed beneath them. Beyond those bridges lay safety. Sanctuary.

Of a sudden a chill ran along his bones; an icy clamminess settled on his skin, and the air around him turned fetid and dank. Without looking back he ran, ran from the pursuer whose freezing fingers brushed his back and tugged at his cloak, ran from the light-eating figure with the face that. . . . He could not remember the face, except as terror. He did not want to remember the face. He ran, and the ground passed beneath his feet, rolling hills and flat plain . . . and he wanted to howl like a dog gone mad. The city was receding before him. The harder he ran, the further away drifted the white shining walls and haven. They grew smaller, and smaller, until only a pale speck remained on the horizon. The cold hand of his pursuer clutched at his collar. If those fingers touched him he knew he would go mad. Or worse. Much worse. Even as that surety came to him he tripped and fell . . .

"Noooo!" he screamed.

. . . and grunted as paving stones smacked the breath out of him. Wonderingly he got to his feet. He stood on the approaches to one of the marvelous bridges he had seen rearing over the river. Smiling people walked by on either side of him, people dressed in so many colors they made him think of a field of wildflowers. Some of them spoke to him, but he could not understand, though the words sounded as if he should. But the faces were friendly, and the people gestured him onward, over the bridge with its intricate stonework, onward toward the shining, silver-streaked walls and the towers beyond. Toward the safety he knew waited there.

He joined the throng streaming across the bridge and into the city through massive gates set in tall, pristine walls. Within was a wonderland where the meanest structure seemed a palace. It was as though the builders had been told to take stone and brick and tile and create beauty to take the breath of mortal men. There was no building, no monument that did not make him stare with goggling eyes. Music drifted down the streets, a hundred different songs, but all blending with the clamor of the crowds to make one grand, joyous harmony. The scents of sweet perfumes and sharp spices, of wondrous foods and myriad flowers, all floated in the air, as if every good smell in the world were gathered there.

The street by which he entered the city, broad and paved with smooth, gray stone, stretched straight before him toward the center of the city. At its end loomed a tower larger and taller than any other in the city, a tower as white as fresh-fallen snow. That tower was where safety lay, and the knowledge he sought. But the city was such as he had never dreamed of seeing. Surely it would not matter if he delayed just a short time in going to the tower? He turned aside onto a narrower street, where jugglers strolled among hawkers of strange fruits.

Ahead of him down the street was a snow-white tower. The same tower. In just a little while, he thought, and rounded another corner. At the far end of this street, too, lay the white tower. Stubbornly he turned another corner, and another, and each time the alabaster tower met his eyes. He spun to run away from it . . . and skidded to a halt. Before him, the white tower. He was afraid to look over his shoulder, afraid it would be there, too.

The faces around him were still friendly, but shattered hope filled them now, hope he had broken. Still the people gestured him forward, pleading gestures. Toward the tower. Their eyes shone with desperate need, and only he could fulfill it, only he could save them.

Very well, he thought. The tower was, after all, where he wanted to go.

Even as he took his first step forward disappointment faded from those about him, and smiles wreathed every face. They moved with him, and small children strewed his path with flower petals. He looked over his shoulder in confusion, wondering who the flowers were meant for, but behind him were only more smiling people gesturing him on. *They must be for me,* he thought, and wondered why that suddenly did not seem strange at all. But wonderment lasted only a moment before melting away; all was as it should be.

First one, then another of the people began to sing, until every voice was lifted in a glorious anthem. He still could not understand the words, but a dozen interweaving harmonies shouted joy and salvation. Musicians capered through the on-flowing crowd, adding flutes and harps and drums in a dozen sizes to the hymn, and all the songs he had heard before blended in without seam. Girls danced around him, laying garlands of sweet-smelling blossoms across his shoulders, twining them about his neck. They smiled at him, their delight growing with every step he took. He could not help but smile back. His feet itched to join in their dance, and even as he thought of it he was dancing, his steps fitting as if he had known it all from birth. He threw back his head and laughed; his feet were lighter than they had ever been, dancing with. . . . He could not remember the name, but it did not seem important.

It is your destiny, a voice whispered in his head, and the whisper was a thread in the paean.

Carrying him like a twig on the crest of a wave, the crowd flowed into a huge square in the middle of the city, and for the first time he saw that the white tower rose from a great palace of pale marble, sculpted rather than built, curving walls and swelling domes and delicate spires fingering the sky. The whole of it made him gasp in awe. Broad stairs of pristine stone led up from the square, and at the foot of those stairs the people halted, but their song rose ever higher. The swelling voices buoyed his feet. *Your destiny,* the voice whispered, insistent now, eager.

He no longer danced, but neither did he stop. He mounted the stairs without hesitation. This was where he belonged.

Scrollwork covered the massive doors at the top of the stairs, carvings so intricate and delicate that he could not imagine a knife blade fine enough to fit. The portals swung open, and he went in. They closed behind him with an echoing crash like thunder.

"We have been waiting for you," the Myrddraal hissed.

Rand sat bolt upright, gasping for breath and shivering, staring. Tam was still asleep on the bed. Slowly his breathing slowed. Half-consumed logs blazed in the fireplace with a good bed of coals built up around the fire-irons; someone had been there to tend it while he slept. A blanket lay at his feet, where it had fallen when he woke. The makeshift litter was gone, too, and his and Tam's cloaks had been hung by the door.

He wiped cold sweat from his face with a hand that was none too steady and wondered if naming the Dark One in a dream brought his attention the same way that naming him aloud did.

Twilight darkened the window; the moon was well up, round and fat, and evening stars sparkled above the Mountains of Mist. He had slept the day away. He rubbed a sore spot on his side. Apparently he had slept with the sword hilt jabbing him in the ribs. Between that and an empty stomach and the night before, it was no wonder he had had nightmares.

His belly rumbled, and he got up stiffly and made his way to the table where Mistress al'Vere had left the tray. He twitched aside the white napkin. Despite the time he had slept, the beef broth was still warm, and so was the crusty bread. Mistress al'Vere's hand was plain; the tray had been replaced. Once she decided you needed a hot meal, she did not give up till it was inside you.

He gulped down some broth, and it was all he could do to put some meat and cheese between two pieces of bread before stuffing it in his mouth. Taking big bites, he went back to the bed.

Mistress al'Vere had apparently seen to Tam, as well. Tam had been undressed, his clothes now clean and neatly folded on

the bedside table, and a blanket was drawn up under his chin.
When Rand touched his father's forehead, Tam opened his
eyes.

"There you are, boy. Marin said you were here, but I
couldn't even sit up to see. She said you were too tired for her
to wake just so I could look at you. Even Bran can't get around
her when she has her mind set."

Tam's voice was weak, but his gaze was clear and steady. *The
Aes Sedai was right,* Rand thought. With rest he would be as
good as ever.

"Can I get you something to eat? Mistress al'Vere left a
tray."

"She fed me already . . . if you can call it that. Wouldn't let
me have anything but broth. How can a man avoid bad dreams
with nothing but broth in his. . . ." Tam fumbled a hand from
under the cover and touched the sword at Rand's waist. "Then
it wasn't a dream. When Marin told me I was sick, I thought I
had been. . . . But you're all right. That is all that matters.
What of the farm?"

Rand took a deep breath. "The Trollocs killed the sheep. I
think they took the cow, too, and the house needs a good
cleaning." He managed a weak smile. "We were luckier than
some. They burned half the village."

He told Tam everything that had happened, or at least most
of it. Tam listened closely, and asked sharp questions, so he
found himself having to tell about returning to the farmhouse
from the woods, and that brought in the Trolloc he had killed.
He had to tell how Nynaeve had said Tam was dying to explain
why the Aes Sedai had tended him instead of the Wisdom.
Tam's eyes widened at that, an Aes Sedai in Emond's Field.
But Rand could see no need to go over every step of the journey from the farm, or his fears, or the Myrddraal on the road.
Certainly not his nightmares as he slept by the bed. Especially
he saw no reason to mention Tam's ramblings under the fever.
Not yet. Moiraine's story, though: there was no avoiding that.

"Now that's a tale to make a gleeman proud," Tam muttered
when he was done. "What would Trollocs want with you boys?
Or the Dark One, Light help us?"

"You think she was lying? Master al'Vere said she was telling the truth about only two farms being attacked. And about Master Luhhan's house, and Master Cauthon's."

For a moment Tam lay silent before saying, "Tell me what she said. Her exact words, mind, just as she said them."

Rand struggled. Who ever remembered the *exact* words they heard? He chewed at his lip and scratched his head, and bit by bit he brought it out, as nearly as he could remember. "I can't think of anything else," he finished. "Some of it I'm not too sure she didn't say a little differently, but it's close, anyway."

"It's good enough. It has to be, doesn't it? You see, lad, Aes Sedai are tricksome. They don't lie, not right out, but the truth an Aes Sedai tells you is not always the truth you think it is. You take care around her."

"I've heard the stories," Rand retorted. "I'm not a child."

"So you're not, so you're not." Tam sighed heavily, then shrugged in annoyance. "I should be going along with you, just the same. The world outside the Two Rivers is nothing like Emond's Field."

That was an opening to ask about Tam going outside and all the rest of it, but Rand did not take it. His mouth fell open, instead. "Just like that? I thought you would try to talk me out of it. I thought you'd have a hundred reasons I should not go." He realized he had been hoping Tam would have a hundred reasons, and good ones.

"Maybe not a hundred," Tam said with a snort, "but a few did come to mind. Only they don't count for much. If Trollocs are after you, you will be safer in Tar Valon than you could ever be here. Just remember to be wary. Aes Sedai do things for their own reasons, and those are not always the reasons you think."

"The gleeman said something like that," Rand said slowly.

"Then he knows what he's talking about. You listen sharp, think deep, and guard your tongue. That's good advice for any dealings beyond the Two Rivers, but most especially with Aes Sedai. And with Warders. Tell Lan something, and you've as good as told Moiraine. If he's a Warder, then he's bonded to her as sure as the sun rose this morning, and he won't keep many secrets from her, if any."

Rand knew little about the bonding between Aes Sedai and Warders, though it played a big part in every story about Warders he had ever heard. It was something to do with the Power, a gift to the Warder, or maybe some sort of exchange. The Warders got all sorts of benefits, according to the stories. They healed more quickly than other men, and could go longer without food or water or sleep. Supposedly they could sense Trollocs, if they were close enough, and other creatures of the Dark One, too, which explained how Lan and Moiraine had tried to warn the village before the attack. As to what the Aes Sedai got out of it, the stories were silent, but he was not about to believe they did not get something.

"I'll be careful," Rand said. "I just wish I knew why. It doesn't make any sense. Why me? Why us?"

"I wish I knew, too, boy. Blood and ashes, I wish I knew." Tam sighed heavily. "Well, no use trying to put a broken egg back in the shell, I suppose. How soon do you have to go? I'll be back on my feet in a day or two, and we can see about starting a new flock. Oren Dautry has some good stock he might be willing to part with, with the pastures all gone, and so does Jon Thane."

"Moiraine . . . the Aes Sedai said you had to stay in bed. She said weeks." Tam opened his mouth, but Rand went on. "And she talked to Mistress al'Vere."

"Oh. Well, maybe I can talk Marin around." Tam did not sound hopeful of it, though. He gave Rand a sharp look. "The way you avoided answering means you have to leave soon. Tomorrow? Or tonight?"

"Tonight," Rand said quietly, and Tam nodded sadly.

"Yes. Well, if it must be done, best not to delay. But we will see about this 'weeks' business." He plucked at his blankets with more irritation than strength. "Perhaps I'll follow in a few days anyway. Catch you up on the road. We will see if Marin can keep me in bed when I want to get up."

There was a tap at the door, and Lan stuck his head into the room. "Say your goodbyes quickly, sheepherder, and come. There may be trouble."

"Trouble?" Rand said, and the Warder growled at him impatiently.

"Just hurry!"

Hastily Rand snatched up his cloak. He started to undo the sword belt, but Tam spoke up.

"Keep it. You will probably have more need of it than I, though, the Light willing, neither of us will. Take care, lad. You hear?"

Ignoring Lan's continued growls, Rand bent to grab Tam in a hug. "I will come back. I promise you that."

"Of course you will." Tam laughed. He returned the hug weakly, and ended by patting Rand on the back. "I know that. And I'll have twice as many sheep for you to tend when you return. Now go, before that fellow does himself an injury."

Rand tried to hang back, tried to find the words for the question he did not want to ask, but Lan entered the room to catch him by the arm and pull him into the hall. The Warder had donned a dull gray-green tunic of overlapping metal scales. His voice rasped with irritation.

"We have to hurry. Don't you understand the word *trouble*?"

Outside the room Mat waited, cloaked and coated and carrying his bow. A quiver hung at his waist. He was rocking anxiously on his heels, and he kept glancing off toward the stairs with what seemed to be equal parts impatience and fear. "This isn't much like the stories, Rand, is it?" he said hoarsely.

"What kind of trouble?" Rand demanded, but the Warder ran ahead of him instead of answering, taking the steps down two at a time. Mat dashed after him with quick gestures for Rand to follow.

Shrugging into his cloak, he caught up to them downstairs. Only a feeble light filled the common room; half the candles had burned out and most of the rest were guttering. It was empty except for the three of them. Mat stood next to one of the front windows, peeping out as if trying not to be seen. Lan held the door open a crack and peered into the inn yard.

Wondering what they could be watching, Rand went to join him. The Warder muttered at him to take a care, but he did open the door a trifle wider to make room for Rand to look, too.

At first he was not sure exactly what he was seeing. A crowd of village men, some three dozen or so, clustered near the burned-out husk of the peddler's wagon, night pushed back by the torches some of them carried. Moiraine faced them, her back to the inn, leaning with seeming casualness on her walking staff. Hari Coplin stood in the front of the crowd with his brother, Darl, and Bili Congar. Cenn Buie was there, as well, looking uncomfortable. Rand was startled to see Hari shake his fist at Moiraine.

"Leave Emond's Field!" the sour-faced farmer shouted. A few voices in the crowd echoed him, but hesitantly, and no one pushed forward. They might be willing to confront an Aes Sedai from within a crowd, but none of them wanted to be singled out. Not by an Aes Sedai who had every reason to take offense.

"You brought those monsters!" Darl roared. He waved a torch over his head, and there were shouts of, "You brought them!" and "It's your fault!" led by his cousin Bili.

Hari elbowed Cenn Buie, and the old thatcher pursed his lips and gave him a sidelong glare. "Those things . . . those Trollocs didn't appear until after you came," Cenn muttered, barely loud enough to be heard. He swung his head from side to side dourly as if wishing he were somewhere else and looking for a way to get there. "You're an Aes Sedai. We want none of your sort in the Two Rivers. Aes Sedai bring trouble on their backs. If you stay, you will only bring more."

His speech brought no response from the gathered villagers, and Hari scowled in frustration. Abruptly he snatched Darl's torch and shook it in her direction. "Get out!" he shouted. "Or we'll burn you out!"

Dead silence fell, except for the shuffling of a few feet as men drew back. Two Rivers folk could fight back if they were attacked, but violence was far from common, and threatening people was foreign to them, beyond the occasional shaking of a fist. Cenn Buie, Bili Congar, and the Coplins were left out front alone. Bili looked as if he wanted to back away, too.

Hari gave an uneasy start at the lack of support, but he recovered quickly. "Get out!" he shouted again, echoed by Darl and, more weakly, by Bili. Hari glared at the others. Most of the crowd failed to meet his eye.

Suddenly Bran al'Vere and Haral Luhhan moved out of the shadows, stopping apart from both the Aes Sedai and the crowd. In one hand the Mayor casually carried the big wooden maul he used to drive spigots into casks. "Did someone suggest burning my inn?" he asked softly.

The two Coplins took a step back, and Cenn Buie edged

away from them. Bili Congar dived into the crowd. "Not that," Darl said quickly. "We never said that, Bran . . . ah, Mayor."

Bran nodded. "Then perhaps I heard you threatening to harm guests in my inn?"

"She's an Aes Sedai," Hari began angrily, but his words cut off as Haral Luhhan moved.   :

The blacksmith simply stretched, thrusting thick arms over his head, tightening massive fists until his knuckles cracked, but Hari looked at the burly man as if one of those fists had been shaken under his nose. Haral folded his arms across his chest. "Your pardon, Hari. I did not mean to cut you off. You were saying?"

But Hari, shoulders hunched as though he were trying to draw into himself and disappear, seemed to have nothing more to say.

"I'm surprised at you people," Bran rumbled. "Paet al'Caar, your boy's leg was broken last night, but I saw him walking on it today—because of her. Eward Candwin, you were lying on your belly with a gash down your back like a fish for cleaning, till she laid hands on you. Now it looks as if it happened a month ago, and unless I misdoubt there'll barely be a scar. And you, Cenn." The thatcher started to fade back into the crowd, but stopped, held uncomfortably by Bran's gaze. "I'd be shocked to see any man on the Village Council here, Cenn, but you most of all. Your arm would still be hanging useless at your side, a mass of burns and bruises, if not for her. If you have no gratitude, have you no shame?"

Cenn half lifted his right hand, then looked away from it angrily. "I cannot deny what she did," he muttered, and he did sound ashamed. "She helped me, and others," he went on in a pleading tone, "but she's an Aes Sedai, Bran. If those Trollocs didn't come because of her, why did they come? We want no part of Aes Sedai in the Two Rivers. Let them keep their troubles away from us."

A few men, safely back in the crowd, shouted then. "We want no Aes Sedai troubles!" "Send her away!" "Drive her out!" "Why did they come if not because of her?"

A scowl grew on Bran's face, but before he could speak Moiraine suddenly whirled her vine-carved staff above her head, spinning it with both hands. Rand's gasp echoed that of the villagers, for a hissing white flame flared from each end of the staff, standing straight out like spearpoints despite the rod's whirling. Even Bran and Haral edged away from her. She snapped her arms down straight out before her, the staff parallel to the ground, but the pale fire still jetted out, brighter than the torches. Men shied away, held up hands to shield their eyes from the pain of that brilliance.

"Is this what Aemon's blood has come to?" The Aes Sedai's voice was not loud, but it overwhelmed every other sound. "Little people squabbling for the right to hide like rabbits? You have forgotten who you were, forgotten what you were, but I had hoped some small part was left, some memory in blood and bone. Some shred to steel you for the long night coming."

No one spoke. The two Coplins looked as if they never wanted to open their mouths again.

Bran said, "Forgotten who we were? We are who we always have been. Honest farmers and shepherds and craftsmen. Two Rivers folk."

"To the south," Moiraine said, "lies the river you call the White River, but far to the east of here men call it still by its rightful name. Manetherendrelle. In the Old Tongue, Waters of the Mountain Home. Sparkling waters that once coursed through a land of bravery and beauty. Two thousand years ago Manetherendrelle flowed by the walls of a mountain city so lovely to behold that Ogier stonemasons came to stare in wonder. Farms and villages covered this region, and that you call the Forest of Shadows, as well, and beyond. But all of those folk thought of themselves as the people of the Mountain Home, the people of Manetheren.

"Their King was Aemon al Caar al Thorin, Aemon son of Caar son of Thorin, and Eldrene ay Ellan ay Carlan was his Queen. Aemon, a man so fearless that the greatest compliment for courage any could give, even among his enemies, was to say a man had Aemon's heart. Eldrene, so beautiful that it was said the flowers bloomed to make her smile. Bravery and beauty and wisdom and a love that death could not sunder. Weep, if you have a heart, for the loss of them, for the loss of even their memory. Weep, for the loss of their blood."

She fell silent then, but no one spoke. Rand was as bound as the others in the spell she had created. When she spoke again, he drank it in, and so did the rest.

"For nearly two centuries the Trolloc Wars had ravaged the length and breadth of the world, and wherever battles raged, the Red Eagle banner of Manetheren was in the forefront. The men of Manetheren were a thorn to the Dark One's foot and a bramble to his hand. Sing of Manetheren, that would never bend knee to the Shadow. Sing of Manetheren, the sword that could not be broken.

"They were far away, the men of Manetheren, on the Field of Bekkar, called the Field of Blood, when news came that a Trolloc army was moving against their home. Too far to do else but wait to hear of their land's death, for the forces of the Dark One meant to make an end of them. Kill the mighty oak by hacking away its roots. Too far to do else but mourn. But they were the men of the Mountain Home.

"Without hesitation, without thought for the distance they must travel, they marched from the very field of victory, still covered in dust and sweat and blood. Day and night they marched, for they had seen the horror a Trolloc army left behind it, and no man of them could sleep while such a danger threatened Manetheren. They moved as if their feet had wings, marching further and faster than friends hoped or enemies feared they could. At any other day that march alone would have inspired songs. When the Dark One's armies swooped down upon the lands of Manetheren, the men of the Mountain Home stood before it, with their backs to the Tarendrelle."

Some villager raised a small cheer then, but Moiraine kept on as if she had not heard. "The host that faced the men of Manetheren was enough to daunt the bravest heart. Ravens blackened the sky; Trollocs blackened the land. Trollocs and their human allies. Trollocs and Darkfriends in tens of tens of thousands, and Dreadlords to command. At night their cook-fires outnumbered the stars, and dawn revealed the banner of Ba'alzamon at their head. Ba'alzamon, Heart of the Dark. An ancient name for the Father of Lies. The Dark One could not have been free of his prison at Shayol Ghul, for if he had been, not all the forces of humankind together could have stood against him, but there was power there. Dreadlords, and some evil that made that light-destroying banner seem no more than right and sent a chill into the souls of the men who faced it.

"Yet, they knew what they must do. Their homeland lay just across the river. They must keep that host, and the power with it, from the Mountain Home. Aemon had sent out messengers. Aid was promised if they could hold for but three days at the Tarendrelle. Hold for three days against odds that should overwhelm them in the first hour. Yet somehow, through bloody assault and desperate defense, they held through an hour, and the second hour, and the third. For three days they fought, and though the land became a butcher's yard, no crossing of the Tarendrelle did they yield. By the third night no help had come, and no messengers, and they fought on alone. For six days. For nine. And on the tenth day Aemon knew the bitter taste of betrayal. No help was coming, and they could hold the river crossings no more."

"What did they do?" Hari demanded. Torchfires flickered in the chill night breeze, but no one made a move to draw a cloak tighter.

"Aemon crossed the Tarendrelle," Moiraine told them, "destroying the bridges behind him. And he sent word throughout his land for the people to flee, for he knew the powers with the Trolloc horde would find a way to bring it across the river. Even as the word went out, the Trolloc crossing began, and the soldiers of Manetheren took up the fight again, to buy with their lives what hours they could for their people to escape. From the city of Manetheren, Eldrene organized the flight of her people into the deepest forests and the fastness of the mountains.

"But some did not flee. First in a trickle, then a river, then a flood, men went, not to safety, but to join the army fighting for their land. Shepherds with bows, and farmers with pitchforks, and woodsmen with axes. Women went, too, shouldering what weapons they could find and marching side by side with their men. No one made that journey who did not know they would never return. But it was their land. It had been their fathers', and it would be their children's, and they went to pay the price of it. Not a step of ground was given up until it was soaked in blood, but at the last the army of Manetheren was driven back,

back to here, to this place you now call Emond's Field. And here the Trolloc hordes surrounded them."

Her voice held the sound of cold tears. "Trolloc dead and the corpses of human renegades piled up in mounds, but always more scrambled over those charnel heaps in waves of death that had no end. There could be but one finish. No man or woman who had stood beneath the banner of the Red Eagle at that day's dawning still lived when night fell. The sword that could not be broken was shattered.

"In the Mountains of Mist, alone in the emptied city of Manetheren, Eldrene felt Aemon die, and her heart died with him. And where her heart had been was left only a thirst for vengeance, vengeance for her love, vengeance for her people and her land. Driven by grief she reached out to the True Source, and hurled the One Power at the Trolloc army. And there the Dreadlords died wherever they stood, whether in their secret councils or exhorting their soldiers. In the passing of a breath the Dreadlords and the generals of the Dark One's host burst into flame. Fire consumed their bodies, and terror consumed their just-victorious army.

"Now they ran like beasts before a wildfire in the forest, with no thought for anything but escape. North and south they fled. Thousands drowned attempting to cross the Tarendrelle without the aid of the Dreadlords, and at the Manetherendrelle they tore down the bridges in their fright at what might be following them. Where they found people, they slew and burned, but to flee was the need that gripped them. Until, at last, no one of them remained in the lands of Manetheren. They were dispersed like dust before the whirlwind. The final vengeance came more slowly, but it came, when they were hunted down by other peoples, by other armies in other lands. None was left alive of those who did murder at Aemon's Field.

"But the price was high for Manetheren. Eldrene had drawn to herself more of the One Power than any human could ever hope to wield unaided. As the enemy generals died, so did she die, and the fires that consumed her consumed the empty city of Manetheren, even the stones of it, down to the living rock of the mountains. Yet the people had been saved.

"Nothing was left of their farms, their villages, or their great city. Some would say there was nothing left for them, nothing but to flee to other lands, where they could begin anew. They did not say so. They had paid such a price in blood and hope for their land as had never been paid before, and now they were bound to that soil by ties stronger than steel. Other wars would wrack them in years to come, until at last their corner of the world was forgotten and at last they had forgotten wars and the ways of war. Never again did Manetheren rise. Its soaring spires and splashing fountains became as a dream that slowly faded from the minds of its people. But they, and their children, and their children's children, held the land that was theirs. They held it when the long centuries had washed the why of it from their memories. They held it until, today, there is you. Weep for Manetheren. Weep for what is lost forever."

The fires on Moiraine's staff winked out, and she lowered it to her side as if it weighed a hundred pounds. For a long moment the moan of the wind was the only sound. Then Paet al'Caar shouldered past the Coplins.

"I don't know about your story," the long-jawed farmer said. "I'm no thorn to the Dark One's foot, nor ever likely to be, neither. But my Wil is walking because of you, and for that I am ashamed to be here. I don't know if you can forgive me, but whether you will or no, I'll be going. And for me, you can stay in Emond's Field as long as you like."

With a quick duck of his head, almost a bow, he pushed back through the crowd. Others began to mutter then, offering shamefaced penitence before they, too, slipped away one by one. The Coplins, sour-mouthed and scowling once more, looked at the faces around them and vanished into the night without a word. Bili Congar had disappeared even before his cousins.

Lan pulled Rand back and shut the door. "Let's go, boy." The Warder started for the back of the inn. "Come along, both of you. Quickly!"

Rand hesitated, exchanging a wondering glance with Mat. While Moiraine had been telling the story, Master al'Vere's Dhurrans could not have dragged him away, but now something else held his feet. This was the real beginning, leaving the inn and following the Warder into the night. . . . He shook himself, and tried to firm his resolve. He had no choice but to go, but he would come back to Emond's Field, however far or long this journey was.

"What are you waiting for?" Lan asked from the door that led out of the back of the common room. With a start Mat hurried to him.

Trying to convince himself that he was beginning a grand adventure, Rand followed them through the darkened kitchen and out into the stableyard.

Matrim (Mat) Cauthon

CHAPTER
10

Leavetaking

A single lantern, its shutters half closed, hung from a nail on a stall post, casting a dim light. Deep shadows swallowed most of the stalls. As Rand came through the doors from the stableyard, hard on the heels of Mat and the Warder, Perrin leaped up in a rustle of straw from where he had been sitting with his back against a stall door. A heavy cloak swathed him.

Lan barely paused to demand, "Did you look the way I told you, blacksmith?"

"I looked," Perrin replied. "There's nobody here but us. Why would anybody hide—"

"Care and a long life go together, blacksmith." The Warder ran a quick eye around the shadowed stable and the deeper shadows of the hayloft above, then shook his head. "No time," he muttered, half to himself. "Hurry, she says."

As if to suit his words, he strode quickly to where the five horses stood tethered, bridled and saddled at the back of the pool of light. Two were the black stallion and white mare that Rand had seen before. The others, if not quite so tall or so sleek, certainly appeared to be among the best the Two Rivers had to offer. With hasty care Lan began examining cinches and girth straps, and the leather ties that held saddlebags, waterskins, and blanketrolls behind the saddles.

Rand exchanged shaky smiles with his friends, trying hard to look as if he really was eager to be off.

For the first time Mat noticed the sword at Rand's waist, and pointed to it. "You becoming a Warder?" He laughed, then swallowed it with a quick glance at Lan. The Warder apparently took no notice. "Or at least a merchant's guard," Mat went on with a grin that seemed only a little forced. He hefted his bow. "An honest man's weapon isn't good enough for him."

Rand thought about flourishing the sword, but Lan being there stopped him. The Warder was not even looking in his direction, but he was sure the man was aware of everything that went on around him. Instead he said with exaggerated casualness, "It might be useful," as if wearing a sword were nothing out of the ordinary.

Perrin moved, trying to hide something under his cloak. Rand glimpsed a wide leather belt encircling the apprentice blacksmith's waist, with the handle of an axe thrust through a loop on the belt.

"What do you have there?" he asked.

"Merchant's guard, indeed," Mat hooted.

The shaggy-haired youth gave Mat a frown that suggested he had already had more than his fair share of joking, then sighed heavily and tossed back his cloak to uncover the axe. It was no common woodsman's tool. A broad half-moon blade on one side of the head and a curved spike on the other made it every bit as strange for the Two Rivers as Rand's sword. Perrin's hand rested on it with a sense of familiarity, though.

"Master Luhhan made it about two years ago, for a wool-buyer's guard. But when it was done the fellow wouldn't pay what he had agreed, and Master Luhhan would not take less. He gave it to me when"—he cleared his throat, then shot Rand the same warning frown he'd given Mat—"when he found me practicing with it. He said I might as well have it since he couldn't make anything useful from it."

"Practicing," Mat snickered, but held up his hands soothingly when Perrin raised his head. "As you say. It's just as well one of us knows how to use a real weapon."

"That bow is a real weapon," Lan said suddenly. He propped an arm across the saddle of his tall black and regarded them gravely. "So are the slings I've seen you village boys with. Just because you never used them for anything but hunting rabbits or chasing a wolf away from the sheep makes no difference. Anything can be a weapon, if the man or woman who holds it has the nerve and will to make it so. Trollocs aside, you had better have that clear in your minds before we leave the Two Rivers, before we leave Emond's Field, if you want to reach Tar Valon alive."

His face and voice, cold as death and hard as a rough-hewn gravestone, stifled their smiles and their tongues. Perrin grimaced and pulled his cloak back over the axe. Mat stared at his feet and stirred the straw on the stable floor with his toe. The Warder grunted and went back to his checking, and the silence lengthened.

"It isn't much like the stories," Mat said, finally.

"I don't know," Perrin said sourly. "Trollocs, a Warder, an Aes Sedai. What more could you ask?"

"Aes Sedai," Mat whispered, sounding as if he were suddenly cold.

"Do you believe her, Rand?" Perrin asked. "I mean, what would Trollocs want with us?"

As one, they glanced at the Warder. Lan appeared absorbed in the white mare's saddle girth, but the three of them moved back toward the stable door, away from Lan. Even so, they huddled together and spoke softly.

Rand shook his head. "I don't know, but she had it right about our farms being the only ones attacked. And they attacked Master Luhhan's house and the forge first, here in the village. I asked the Mayor. It's as easy to believe they are after us as anything else I can think of." Suddenly he realized they were both staring at him.

"You asked the Mayor?" Mat said incredulously. "She said not to tell anybody."

"I didn't tell him why I was asking," Rand protested. "Do you mean you didn't talk to anybody at all? You didn't let anybody know you're going?"

Perrin shrugged defensively. "Moiraine Sedai said not anybody."

"We left notes," Mat said. "For our families. They'll find them in the morning. Rand, my mother thinks Tar Valon is the next thing to Shayol Ghul." He gave a little laugh to show he did not share her opinion. It was not very convincing. "She'd try to lock me in the cellar if she believed I was even thinking of going there."

"Master Luhhan is stubborn as stone," Perrin added, "and Mistress Luhhan is worse. If you'd seen her digging through what's left of the house, saying she hoped the Trollocs did come back so she could get her hands on them. . . ."

"Burn me, Rand," Mat said, "I know she's an Aes Sedai and all, but the Trollocs were really here. She said not to tell anybody. If an Aes Sedai doesn't know what to do about something like this, who does?"

"I don't know." Rand rubbed at his forehead. His head hurt; he could not get that dream out of his mind. "My father believes her. At least, he agreed that we had to go."

Suddenly Moiraine was in the doorway. "You talked to your father about this journey?" She was clothed in dark gray from head to foot, with a skirt divided for riding astride, and the serpent ring was the only gold she wore now.

Rand eyed her walking staff; despite the flames he had seen, there was no sign of charring, or even soot. "I couldn't go off without letting him know."

She eyed him for a moment with pursed lips before turning to the others. "And did you also decide that a note was not enough?" Mat and Perrin talked on top of each other, assuring her they had only left notes, the way she had said. Nodding, she waved them to silence, and gave Rand a sharp look. "What is done is already woven in the Pattern. Lan?"

"The horses are ready," the Warder said, "and we have enough provisions to reach Baerlon with some to spare. We can leave at any time. I suggest now."

"Not without me." Egwene slipped into the stable, a shawl-wrapped bundle in her arms. Rand nearly fell over his own feet.

Lan's sword had come half out of its sheath; when he saw who it was he shoved the blade back, his eyes suddenly flat. Perrin and Mat began babbling to convince Moiraine they had not told Egwene about leaving. The Aes Sedai ignored them; she simply looked at Egwene, tapping her lips thoughtfully with one finger.

The hood of Egwene's dark brown cloak was pulled up, but not enough to hide the defiant way she faced Moiraine. "I have everything I need here. Including food. And I will not be left behind. I'll probably never get another chance to see the world outside the Two Rivers."

"This isn't a picnic trip into the Waterwood, Egwene," Mat growled. He stepped back when she looked at him from under lowered brows.

"Thank you, Mat. I wouldn't have known. Do you think you three are the only ones who want to see what's outside? I've dreamed about it as long as you have, and I don't intend to miss this chance."

"How did you find out we were leaving?" Rand demanded. "Anyway, you can't go with us. We aren't leaving for the fun of it. The Trollocs are after us." She gave him a tolerant look, and he flushed and stiffened indignantly.

"First," she told him patiently, "I saw Mat creeping about, trying hard not to be noticed. Then I saw Perrin attempting to hide that absurd great axe under his cloak. I knew Lan had bought a horse, and it suddenly occurred to me to wonder why he needed another. And if he could buy one, he could buy others. Putting that with Mat and Perrin sneaking about like bull calves pretending to be foxes . . . well, I could see only one answer. I don't know if I'm surprised or not to find you here, Rand, after all your talk about daydreams. With Mat and Perrin involved, I suppose I should have known you would be in it, too."

"I have to go, Egwene," Rand said. "All of us do, or the Trollocs will come back."

"The Trollocs!" Egwene laughed incredulously. "Rand, if you've decided to see some of the world, well and good, but please spare me any of your nonsensical tales."

"It's true," Perrin said as Mat began, "The Trollocs—"

"Enough," Moiraine said quietly, but it cut their talk as sharply as a knife. "Did anyone else notice all of this?" Her voice was soft, but Egwene swallowed and drew herself up before answering.

"After last night, all they can think about is rebuilding, that and what to do if it happens again. They couldn't see anything else unless it was pushed under their noses. And I told no one what I suspected. No one."

"Very well," Moiraine said after a moment. "You may come with us."

A startled expression darted across Lan's face. It was gone in an instant, leaving him outwardly calm, but furious words erupted from him. "No, Moiraine!"

"It is part of the Pattern, now, Lan."

"It is ridiculous!" he retorted. "There's no reason for her to come along, and every reason for her not to."

"There *is* a reason for it," Moiraine said calmly. "A part of the Pattern, Lan." The Warder's stony face showed nothing, but he nodded slowly.

"But, Egwene," Rand said, "the Trollocs will be chasing us. We won't be safe until we get to Tar Valon."

"Don't try to frighten me off," she said. "I am going."

Rand knew that tone of voice. He had not heard it since she decided that climbing the tallest trees was for children, but he remembered it well. "If you think being chased by Trollocs will be fun," he began, but Moiraine interrupted.

"We have no time for this. We must be as far away as possible by daybreak. If she is left behind, Rand, she could rouse the village before we have gone a mile, and that would surely warn the Myrddraal."

"I would not do that," Egwene protested.

"She can ride the gleeman's horse," the Warder said. "I'll leave him enough to buy another."

"That will not be possible," came Thom Merrilin's resonant voice from the hayloft. Lan's sword left its sheath this time, and he did not put it back as he stared up at the gleeman.

Thom tossed down a blanketroll, then slung his cased flute and harp across his back and shouldered bulging saddlebags. "This village has no use for me, now, while on the other hand, I have never performed in Tar Valon. And though I usually journey alone, after last night I have no objections at all to traveling in company."

The Warder gave Perrin a hard look, and Perrin shifted uncomfortably. "I didn't think of looking in the loft," he muttered.

As the long-limbed gleeman scrambled down the ladder from the loft, Lan spoke, stiffly formal. "Is this part of the Pattern, too, Moiraine Sedai?"

"Everything is a part of the Pattern, my old friend," Moiraine replied softly. "We cannot pick and choose. But we shall see."

Thom put his feet on the stable floor and turned from the ladder, brushing straw from his patch-covered cloak. "In fact," he said in more normal tones, "you might say that I insist on traveling in company. I have given many hours over many mugs of ale to thinking of how I might end my days. A Trolloc's cookpot was not one of the thoughts." He looked askance at the Warder's sword. "There's no need for that. I am not a cheese for slicing."

"Master Merrilin," Moiraine said, "we must go quickly, and almost certainly in great danger. The Trollocs are still out there, and we go by night. Are you sure that you want to travel with us?"

Thom eyed the lot of them with a quizzical smile. "If it is not too dangerous for the girl, it can't be too dangerous for me. Besides, what gleeman would not face a little danger to perform in Tar Valon?"

Moiraine nodded, and Lan scabbarded his sword. Rand suddenly wondered what would have happened if Thom had changed his mind, or if Moiraine had not nodded. The gleeman began saddling his horse as if similar thoughts had never crossed his mind, but Rand noticed that he eyed Lan's sword more than once.

"Now," Moiraine said. "What horse for Egwene?"

"The peddler's horses are as bad as the Dhurrans," the Warder replied sourly. "Strong, but slow plodders."

"Bela," Rand said, getting a look from Lan that made him wish he had kept silent. But he knew he could not dissuade Egwene; the only thing left was to help. "Bela may not be as fast as the others, but she's strong. I ride her sometimes. She can keep up."

Lan looked into Bela's stall, muttering under his breath. "She might be a little better than the others," he said finally. "I don't suppose there is any other choice."

"Then she will have to do," Moiraine said. "Rand, find a saddle for Bela. Quickly, now! We have tarried too long already."

Rand hurriedly chose a saddle and blanket in the tack room,

then fetched Bela from her stall. The mare looked back at him in sleepy surprise when he put the saddle on her back. When he rode her, it was barebacked; she was not used to a saddle. He made soothing noises while he tightened the girth strap, and she accepted the oddity with no more than a shake of her mane.

Taking Egwene's bundle from her, he tied it on behind the saddle while she mounted and adjusted her skirts. They were not divided for riding astride, so her wool stockings were bared to the knee. She wore the same soft leather shoes as all the other village girls. They were not at all suited for journeying to Watch Hill, much less Tar Valon.

"I still think you shouldn't come," he said. "I wasn't making it up about the Trollocs. But I promise I will take care of you."

"Perhaps I'll take care of you," she replied lightly. At his exasperated look she smiled and bent down to smooth his hair. "I know you'll look after me, Rand. We will look after each other. But now you had better look after getting on your horse."

All of the others were already mounted and waiting for him, he realized. The only horse left riderless was Cloud, a tall gray with a black mane and tail that belonged to Jon Thane, or had. He scrambled into the saddle, though not without difficulty as the gray tossed his head and pranced sideways as Rand put his foot in the stirrup, and his scabbard caught in his legs. It was not chance that his friends had not chosen Cloud. Master Thane often raced the spirited gray against merchants' horses, and Rand had never known him to lose, but he had never known Cloud to give anyone an easy ride, either. Lan must have given a huge price to make the miller sell. As he settled in the saddle Cloud's dancing increased, as if the gray were eager to run. Rand gripped the reins firmly and tried to think that he would have no trouble. Perhaps if he convinced himself, he could convince the horse, too.

An owl hooted in the night outside, and the village people jumped before they realized what it was. They laughed nervously and exchanged shamefaced looks.

"Next thing, field mice will chase us up a tree," Egwene said with an unsteady chuckle.

Lan shook his head. "Better if it had been wolves."

"Wolves!" Perrin exclaimed, and the Warder favored him with a flat stare.

"Wolves don't like Trollocs, blacksmith, and Trollocs don't like wolves, or dogs, either. If I heard wolves I would be sure there were no Trollocs waiting out there for us." He moved into the moonlit night, walking his tall black slowly.

Moiraine rode after him without a moment's hesitation, and Egwene kept hard to the Aes Sedai's side. Rand and the gleeman brought up the rear, following Mat and Perrin.

The back of the inn was dark and silent, and dappled moon shadows filled the stableyard. The soft thuds of the hooves faded quickly, swallowed by the night. In the darkness the Warder's cloak made him a shadow, too. Only the need to let him lead the way kept the others from clustering around him. Getting out of the village without being seen was going to be no easy task, Rand decided as he neared the gate. At least, without being seen by villagers. Many windows in the village emitted pale yellow light, and although those glows seemed very small in the night now, shapes moved frequently within them, the shapes of villagers watching to see what this night brought. No one wanted to be caught by surprise again.

In the deep shadows beside the inn, just on the point of leaving the stableyard, Lan abruptly halted, motioning sharply for silence.

Boots rattled on the Wagon Bridge, and here and there on the bridge moonlight glinted off metal. The boots clattered across the bridge, grated on gravel, and approached the inn. No sound at all came from those in the shadow. Rand suspected his friends, at least, were too frightened to make a noise. Like him.

The footsteps halted before the inn in the grayness just beyond the dim light from the common-room windows. It was not until Jon Thane stepped forward, a spear propped on his stout shoulder, an old jerkin sewn all over with steel disks straining across his chest, that Rand saw them for what they were. A dozen men from the village and the surrounding farms, some in helmets or pieces of armor that had lain dust-covered in attics for generations, all with a spear or a woodaxe or a rusty bill.

The miller peered into a common-room window, then turned

with a curt, "It looks right here." The others formed in two ragged ranks behind him, and the patrol marched into the night as if stepping to three different drums.

"Two Dha'vol Trollocs would have them all for breakfast," Lan muttered when the sound of their boots had faded, "but they have eyes and ears." He turned his stallion back. "Come."

Slowly, quietly, the Warder took them back across the stableyard, down the bank through the willows and into the Winespring Water. So close to the Winespring itself the cold, swift water, gleaming as it swirled around the horses' legs, was deep enough to lap against the soles of the riders' boots.

Climbing out on the far bank, the line of horses wound its way under the Warder's deft direction, keeping away from any of the village houses. From time to time Lan stopped, signing them all to be quiet, though no one else heard or saw anything. Each time he did, however, another patrol of villagers and farmers soon passed. Slowly they moved toward the north edge of the village.

Rand peered at the high-peaked houses in the dark, trying to impress them on his memory. *A fine adventurer I am,* he thought. He was not even out of the village yet, and already he was homesick. But he did not stop looking.

They passed beyond the last farmhouses on the outskirts of the village and into the countryside, paralleling the North Road that led to Taren Ferry. Rand thought that surely no night sky elsewhere could be as beautiful as the Two Rivers sky. The clear black seemed to reach to forever, and myriad stars gleamed like points of light scattered through crystal. The moon, only a thin slice less than full, appeared almost close enough to touch, if he stretched, and. . . .

A black shape flew slowly across the silvery ball of the moon. Rand's involuntary jerk on the reins halted the gray. A bat, he thought weakly, but he knew it was not. Bats were a common sight of an evening, darting after flies and bitemes in the twilight. The wings that carried this creature might have the same shape, but they moved with the slow, powerful sweep of a bird of prey. And it was hunting. The way it cast back and forth in long arcs left no doubt of that. Worst of all was the size. For a bat to seem so large against the moon it would have had to be almost within arm's reach. He tried to judge in his mind how far away it must be, and how big. The body of it had to be as large as a man, and the wings. . . . It crossed the face of the moon again, wheeling suddenly downward to be engulfed by the night.

He did not realize that Lan had ridden back to him until the Warder caught his arm. "What are you sitting here and staring at, boy? We have to keep moving." The others waited behind Lan.

Half expecting to be told he was letting fear of the Trollocs overcome his sense, Rand told what he had seen. He hoped that Lan would dismiss it as a bat, or a trick of his eyes.

Lan growled a word, sounding as if it left a bad taste in his mouth. "Draghkar." Egwene and the other Two Rivers folk stared at the sky nervously in all directions, but the gleeman groaned softly.

"Yes," Moiraine said. "It is too much to hope otherwise. And if the Myrddraal has a Draghkar at his command, then he will soon know where we are, if he does not already. We must move more quickly than we can cross-country. We may still reach Taren Ferry ahead of the Myrddraal, and he and his Trollocs will not cross as easily as we."

"A Draghkar?" Egwene said. "What is it?"

It was Thom Merrilin who answered her hoarsely. "In the war that ended the Age of Legends, worse than Trollocs and Halfmen were created."

Moiraine's head jerked toward him as he spoke. Not even the dark could hide the sharpness of her look.

Before anyone could ask the gleeman for more, Lan began giving directions. "We take to the North Road, now. For your lives, follow my lead, keep up and keep together."

He wheeled his horse about, and the others galloped wordlessly after him.

CHAPTER
11

The Road to Taren Ferry

On the hard-packed dirt of the North Road the horses stretched out, manes and tails streaming back in the moonlight as they raced northward, hooves pounding a steady rhythm. Lan led the way, black horse and shadow-clad rider all but invisible in the cold night. Moiraine's white mare, matching the stallion stride for stride, was a pale dart speeding through the dark. The rest followed in a tight line, as if they were all tied to a rope with one end in the Warder's hands.

Rand galloped last in line, with Thom Merrilin just ahead and the others less distinct beyond. The gleeman never turned his head, reserving his eyes for where they ran, not what they ran from. If Trollocs appeared behind, or the Fade on its silent horse, or that flying creature, the Draghkar, it would be up to Rand to sound an alarm.

Every few minutes he craned his neck to peer behind while he clung to Cloud's mane and reins. The Draghkar. . . . Worse than Trollocs and Fades, Thom had said. But the sky was empty, and only darkness and shadows met his eyes on the ground. Shadows that could hide an army.

Now that the gray had been let loose to run, the animal sped through the night like a ghost, easily keeping pace with Lan's stallion. And Cloud wanted to go faster. He wanted to catch the black, strained to catch the black. Rand had to keep a firm hand on the reins to hold him back. Cloud lunged against his restraint as if the gray thought this were a race, fighting him for mastery with every stride. Rand clung to saddle and reins with every muscle taut. Fervently he hoped his mount did not detect how uneasy he was. If Cloud did, he would lose the one real edge he held, however precariously.

Lying low on Cloud's neck, Rand kept a worried eye on Bela and on her rider. When he had said the shaggy mare could stay with the others, he had not meant on the run. She kept up now only by running as he had not thought she could. Lan had not wanted Egwene in their number. Would he slow for her if Bela began to flag? Or would he try to leave her behind? The Aes Sedai and the Warder thought Rand and his friends were important in some way, but for all of Moiraine's talk of the Pattern, he did not think they included Egwene in that importance.

If Bela fell back, he would fall back, too, whatever Moiraine and Lan had to say about it. Back where the Fade and the Trollocs were. Back where the Draghkar was. With all his heart and desperation he silently shouted at Bela to run like the wind, silently tried to will strength into her. *Run!* His skin prickled, and his bones felt as if they were freezing, ready to split open. *The Light help her, run!* And Bela ran.

On and on they sped, northward into the night, time fading into an indistinct blur. Now and again the lights of farmhouses flashed into sight, then disappeared as quickly as imagination. Dogs' sharp challenges faded swiftly behind, or cut off abruptly as the dogs decided they had been chased away. They raced through darkness relieved only by watery pale moonlight, a darkness where trees along the road loomed up without warning, then were gone. For the rest, murk surrounded them, and only a solitary night-bird's cry, lonely and mournful, disturbed the steady pounding of hooves.

Abruptly Lan slowed, then brought the file of horses to a stop. Rand was not sure how long they had been moving, but a soft ache filled his legs from gripping the saddle. Ahead of them in the night, lights sparkled, as if a tall swarm of fireflies held one place among the trees.

Rand frowned at the lights in puzzlement, then suddenly gasped with surprise. The fireflies were windows, the windows of houses covering the sides and top of a hill. It was Watch Hill. He could hardly believe they had come so far. They had probably made the journey as fast as it had ever been traveled. Following Lan's example, Rand and Thom Merrilin dismounted. Cloud stood head down, sides heaving. Lather, almost indistinguishable from the horse's smoky sides, flecked the gray's neck and shoulders. Rand thought that Cloud would not be carrying anyone further that night.

"Much as I would like to put all these villages behind me," Thom announced, "a few hours rest would not go amiss right now. Surely we have enough of a lead to allow that?"

Rand stretched, knuckling the small of his back. "If we're stopping the rest of the night in Watch Hill, we may as well go on up."

A vagrant gust of wind brought a fragment of song from the village, and smells of cooking that made his mouth water. They were still celebrating in Watch Hill. There had been no Trollocs to disturb their Bel Tine. He looked for Egwene. She was leaning against Bela, slumped with weariness. The others were climbing down as well, with many a sigh and much stretching of aching muscles. Only the Warder and the Aes Sedai showed no visible sign of fatigue.

"I could do with some singing," Mat put in tiredly. "And maybe a hot mutton pie at the White Boar." Pausing, he added, "I've never been further than Watch Hill. The White Boar's not nearly as good as the Winespring Inn."

"The White Boar isn't so bad," Perrin said. "A mutton pie for me, too. And lots of hot tea to take the chill off my bones."

"We cannot stop until we are across the Taren," Lan said sharply. "Not for more than a few minutes."

"But the horses," Rand protested. "We'll run them to death if we try to go any further tonight. Moiraine Sedai, surely you—"

He had vaguely noticed her moving among the horses, but he had not paid any real attention to what she did. Now she brushed past him to lay her hands on Cloud's neck. Rand fell silent. Suddenly the horse tossed his head with a soft whicker, nearly pulling the reins from Rand's hands. The gray danced a step sideways, as restive as if he had spent a week in a stable. Without a word Moiraine went to Bela.

"I did not know she could do that," Rand said softly to Lan, his cheeks hot.

"You, of all people, should have suspected it," the Warder replied. "You watched her with your father. She will wash all the fatigue away. First from the horses, then from the rest of you."

"The rest of us. Not you?"

"Not me, sheepherder. I don't need it, not yet. And not her. What she can do for others, she cannot do for herself. Only one of us will ride tired. You had better hope she does not grow too tired before we reach Tar Valon."

"Too tired for what?" Rand asked the Warder.

"You were right about your Bela, Rand," Moiraine said from where she stood by the mare. "She has a good heart, and as much stubbornness as the rest of you Two Rivers folk. Strange as it seems, she may be the least weary of all."

A scream ripped the darkness, a sound like a man dying under sharp knives, and wings swooped low above the party. The night deepened in the shadow that swept over them. With panicked cries the horses reared wildly.

The wind of the Draghkar's wings beat at Rand with a feel like the touch of slime, like chittering in the dank dimness of a nightmare. He had no time even to feel the fear of it, for Cloud exploded into the air with a scream of his own, twisting desperately as if attempting to shake off some clinging thing. Rand, hanging onto the reins, was jerked off his feet and dragged across the ground, Cloud screaming as though the big gray felt wolves tearing at his hocks.

Somehow he maintained his grip on the reins; using the other hand as much as his legs he scrambled onto his feet, taking leaping, staggering steps to keep from being pulled down again. His breath came in ragged pants of desperation. He could not let Cloud get away. He threw out a frantic hand, barely catching the bridle. Cloud reared, lifting him into the air; Rand clung helplessly, hoping against hope that the horse would quieten.

The shock of landing jarred Rand to his teeth, but suddenly the gray was still, nostrils flaring and eyes rolling, stiff-legged and trembling. Rand was trembling as well, and all but hanging from the bridle. *That jolt must have shaken the fool animal, too,* he thought. He took three or four deep, shaky breaths. Only then could he look around and see what had happened to the others.

Chaos reigned among the party. They clutched reins against jerking heads, trying with little success to calm the rearing horses that dragged them about in a milling mass. Only two seemingly had no trouble at all with their mounts. Moiraine sat straight in her saddle, the white mare stepping delicately away from the confusion as if nothing at all out of the ordinary had happened. On foot, Lan scanned the sky, sword in one hand and reins in the other; the sleek black stallion stood quietly beside him.

Sounds of merrymaking no longer came from Watch Hill. Those in the village must have heard the cry, too. Rand knew they would listen awhile, and perhaps watch for what had caused it, then return to their jollity. They would soon forget the incident, its memory submerged by song and food and dance and fun. Perhaps when they heard the news of what had happened in Emond's Field some would remember, and wonder. A fiddle began to play, and after a moment a flute joined in. The village was resuming its celebration.

"Mount!" Lan commanded curtly. Sheathing his sword, he leaped onto the stallion. "The Draghkar would not have showed itself unless it had already reported our whereabouts to the Myrddraal." Another strident shriek drifted down from far above, fainter but no less harsh. The music from Watch Hill silenced raggedly once more. "It tracks us now, marking us for the Halfman. He won't be far."

The horses, fresh now as well as fear-struck, pranced and backed away from those trying to mount. A cursing Thom Merrilin was the first into his saddle, but the others were up soon after. All but one.

"Hurry, Rand!" Egwene shouted. The Draghkar gave shrill voice once more, and Bela ran a few steps before she could rein the mare in. "Hurry!"

With a start Rand realized that instead of trying to mount Cloud he had been standing there staring at the sky in a vain attempt to locate the source of those vile shrieks. More, all unaware, he had drawn Tam's sword as if to fight the flying thing.

His face reddened, making him glad for the night to hide

him. Awkwardly, with one hand occupied by the reins, he resheathed the blade, glancing hastily at the others. Moiraine, Lan, and Egwene all were looking at him, though he could not be sure how much they could see in the moonlight. The rest seemed too absorbed with keeping their horses under control to pay him any mind. He put a hand on the pommel and reached the saddle in one leap, as if he had been doing the like all his life. If any of his friends had noticed the sword, he would surely hear about it later. There would be time enough to worry about it then.

As soon as he was in the saddle they were all off at a gallop again, up the road and by the dome-like hill. Dogs barked in the village; their passage was not entirely unnoticed. *Or maybe the dogs smelled Trollocs,* Rand thought. The barking and the village lights alike vanished quickly behind them.

They galloped in a knot, horses all but jostling together as they ran. Lan ordered them to spread out again, but no one wanted to be even a little alone in the night. A scream came from high overhead. The Warder gave up and let them run clustered.

Rand was close behind Moiraine and Lan, the gray straining in an effort to force himself between the Warder's black and the Aes Sedai's trim mare. Egwene and the gleeman raced on either flank of him, while Rand's friends crowded in behind. Cloud, spurred by the Draghkar's cries, ran beyond anything Rand could do to slow him even had he wished to, yet the gray could not gain so much as a step on the other two horses.

The Draghkar's shriek challenged the night.

Stout Bela ran with neck outstretched and tail and mane streaming in the wind of her running, matching the larger horses' every stride. *The Aes Sedai must have done something more than simply ridding her of fatigue.*

Egwene's face in the moonlight was smiling in excited delight. Her braid streamed behind like the horses' manes, and the gleam in her eyes was not all from the moon, Rand was sure. His mouth dropped open in surprise, until a swallowed biteme set him off into a fit of coughing.

Lan must have asked a question, for Moiraine suddenly shouted over the wind and the pounding of hooves. "I cannot! Most especially not from the back of a galloping horse. They are not easily killed, even when they can be seen. We must run, and hope."

They galloped through a tatter of fog, thin and no higher than the horses' knees. Cloud sped through it in two strides, and Rand blinked, wondering if he had imagined it. Surely the night was too cold for fog. Another patch of ragged gray whisked by them to one side, larger than the first. It had been growing, as if the mist oozed from the ground. Above them, the Draghkar screamed in rage. Fog enveloped the riders for a brief moment and was gone, came again and vanished behind. The icy mist left a chill dampness on Rand's face and hands. Then a wall of pale gray loomed before them, and they were suddenly enshrouded. The thickness of it muffled the sound of their hooves to dullness, and the cries from overhead seemed to come through a wall. Rand could only just make out the shapes of Egwene and Thom Merrilin on either side of him.

Lan did not slow their pace. "There is still only one place we can be going," he called, his voice sounding hollow and directionless.

"Myrddraal are sly," Moiraine replied. "I will use its own slyness against it." They galloped on silently.

Slaty mist obscured both sky and ground, so that the riders, themselves turned to shadow, appeared to float through night clouds. Even the legs of their own horses seemed to have vanished.

Rand shifted in his saddle, shrinking away from the icy fog. Knowing that Moiraine could do things, even seeing her do them, was one thing; having those things leave his skin damp was something else again. He realized he was holding his breath, too, and called himself nine kinds of idiot. He could not ride all the way to Taren Ferry without breathing. She had used the One Power on Tam, and he seemed all right. Still, he had to make himself let that breath go and inhale. The air was heavy, but if colder it was otherwise no different than that on any other foggy night. He told himself that, but he was not sure he believed it.

Lan encouraged them to keep close, now, to stay where each could see the outlines of others in that damp, frosty grayness. Yet the Warder still did not slacken his stallion's dead run. Side by side, Lan and Moiraine led the way through the fog as if they could see clearly what lay ahead. The rest could only trust and follow. And hope.

The shrill cries that had hounded them faded as they galloped, and then were gone, but that gave small comfort. Forest and farmhouses, moon and road were shrouded and hidden. Dogs still barked, hollow and distant in the gray haze, when they passed farms, but there was no other sound save the dull drumming of their horses' hooves. Nothing in that featureless ashen fog changed. Nothing gave any hint of the passage of time except the growing ache in thigh and back.

It had to have been hours, Rand was sure. His hands had clutched his reins until he was not sure he could release them, and he wondered if he would ever walk properly again. He glanced back only once. Shadows in the fog raced behind him, but he could not even be certain of their number. Or even that they really were his friends. The chill and damp soaked through his cloak and coat and shirt, soaked into his bones, so it seemed. Only the rush of air past his face and the gather and stretch of the horse beneath him told him he was moving at all. It must have been hours.

"Slow," Lan called suddenly. "Draw rein."

Rand was so startled that Cloud forced between Lan and Moiraine, forging ahead for half a dozen strides before he could pull the big gray to a halt and stare.

Houses loomed in the fog on all sides, houses strangely tall to Rand's eye. He had never seen this place before, but he had often heard descriptions. That tallness came from high redstone foundations, necessary when the spring melt in the Mountains of Mist made the Taren overflow its banks. They had reached Taren Ferry.

Lan trotted the black warhorse past him. "Don't be so eager, sheepherder."

Discomfited, Rand fell into place without explaining as the party moved deeper into the village. His face was hot, and for the moment the fog was welcome.

A lone dog, unseen in the cold mist, barked at them furiously, then ran away. Here and there a light appeared in a window as some early-riser stirred. Other than the dog, no sound save the muted clops of their horses' hooves disturbed the last hour of the night.

Rand had met few people from Taren Ferry. He tried to recall what little he knew about them. They seldom ventured down into what they called "the lower villages," with their noses up as if they smelled something bad. The few he had met bore strange names, like Hilltop and Stoneboat. One and all, Taren Ferry folk had a reputation for slyness and trickery. If you shook hands with a Taren Ferry man, people said, you counted your fingers afterwards.

Lan and Moiraine stopped before a tall, dark house that looked exactly like any other in the village. Fog swirled around the Warder like smoke as he leaped from his saddle and mounted the stairs that rose to the front door, as high above the street as their heads. At the top of the stairs Lan hammered with his fist on the door.

"I thought he wanted quiet," Mat muttered.

Lan's pounding went on. A light appeared in the window of the next house, and someone shouted angrily, but the Warder kept on with his drumming.

Abruptly the door was flung back by a man in a nightshirt that flapped about his bare ankles. An oil lamp in one hand illumined a narrow face with pointed features. He opened his mouth angrily, then let it stay open as his head swiveled to take in the fog, eyes bulging. "What's this?" he said. "What's this?" Chill gray tendrils curled into the doorway, and he hurriedly stepped back away from them.

"Master Hightower," Lan said. "Just the man I need. We want to cross over on your ferry."

"He never even saw a high tower," Mat snickered. Rand made shushing motions at his friend. The sharp-faced fellow raised his lamp higher and peered down at them suspiciously.

After a minute Master Hightower said crossly, "The ferry goes over in daylight. Not in the night. Not ever. And not in this fog, neither. Come back when the sun's up and the fog's gone."

He started to turn away, but Lan caught his wrist. The ferryman opened his mouth angrily. Gold glinted in the lamplight as the Warder counted out coins one by one into the other's palm. Hightower licked his lips as the coins clinked, and by inches his head moved closer to his hand, as if he could not believe what he was seeing.

"And as much again," Lan said, "when we are safely on the other side. But we leave now."

"Now?" Chewing his lower lip, the ferrety man shifted his feet and peered out at the mist-laden night, then nodded abruptly. "Now it is. Well, let loose my wrist. I have to rouse my haulers. You don't think I pull the ferry across myself, do you?"

"I will wait at the ferry," Lan said flatly. "For a little while." He released his hold on the ferryman.

Master Hightower jerked the handful of coins to his chest and, nodding agreement, hastily shoved the door closed with his hip.

Perrin Aybara

CHAPTER
12

Across the Taren

Lan came down the stairs, telling the company to dismount and lead their horses after him through the fog. Again they had to trust that the Warder knew where he was going. The fog swirled around Rand's knees, hiding his feet, obscuring everything more than a yard away. The fog was not as heavy as it had been outside the town, but he could barely make out his companions.

Still no human stirred in the night except for them. A few more windows than before showed a light, but the thick mist turned most of them to dim patches, and as often as not that hazy glow, hanging in the gray, was all that was visible. Other houses, revealing a little more, seemed to float on a sea of cloud or to thrust abruptly out of the mist while their neighbors remained hidden, so that they could have stood alone for miles around.

Rand moved stiffly from the ache of the long ride, wondering if there was any way he could walk the rest of the way to Tar Valon. Not that walking was much better than riding at that moment, of course, but even so his feet were almost the only part of him that was not sore. At least he was used to walking.

Only once did anyone speak loudly enough for Rand to hear clearly. "You must handle it," Moiraine said in answer to something unheard from Lan. "He will remember too much as it is, and no help for it. If I stand out in his thoughts. . . ."

Rand grumpily shifted his now-sodden cloak on his shoulders, keeping close with the others. Mat and Perrin grumbled to themselves, muttering under their breaths, with bitten-off exclamations whenever one stubbed a toe on something unseen. Thom Merrilin grumbled, too, words like "hot meal" and "fire" and "mulled wine" reaching Rand, but neither the Warder nor the Aes Sedai took notice. Egwene marched along without a word, her back straight and her head high. It was a somewhat painfully hesitant march, to be sure, for she was as unused to riding as the rest.

She was getting her adventure, he thought glumly, and as long as it lasted he doubted if she would notice little things like fog or damp or cold. There must be a difference in what you saw, it seemed to him, depending on whether you sought adventure or had it forced on you. The stories could no doubt make galloping through a cold fog, with a Draghkar and the Light alone knew what else chasing you, sound thrilling. Egwene might be feeling a thrill; he only felt cold and damp and glad to have a village around him again, even if it was Taren Ferry.

Abruptly he walked into something large and warm in the murk: Lan's stallion. The Warder and Moiraine had stopped, and the rest of the party did the same, patting their mounts as much to comfort themselves as the animals. The fog was a little thinner here, enough for them to see one another more clearly than they had in a long while, but not enough to make out much more. Their feet were still hidden by low billows like gray floodwater. The houses seemed to have all been swallowed.

Cautiously Rand led Cloud forward a little way and was surprised to hear his boots scrape on wooden planks. The ferry landing. He backed up carefully, making the gray back as well. He had heard what the Taren Ferry landing was like—a bridge that led nowhere except to the ferryboat. The Taren was supposed to be wide and deep, with treacherous currents that could pull under the strongest swimmer. Much wider than the Winespring Water, he supposed. With the fog added in. . . . It was a relief when he felt dirt under his feet again.

A fierce "Hsst!" from Lan, as sharp as the fog. The Warder gestured at them as he dashed to Perrin's side and threw back the stocky youth's cloak, exposing the great axe. Obediently, if still not understanding, Rand tossed his own cloak over his shoulder to show his sword. As Lan moved swiftly back to his horse, bobbing lights appeared in the mist, and muffled footsteps approached.

Six stolid-faced men in rough clothes followed Master Hightower. The torches they carried burned away a patch of fog around them. When they stopped, all of the party from Emond's Field could be plainly seen, the lot of them surrounded by a gray wall that seemed thicker for the torchlight reflected from it. The ferryman examined them, his narrow head tilted, nose twitching like a weasel sniffing the breeze for a trap.

Lan leaned against his saddle with apparent casualness, but one hand rested ostentatiously on the long hilt of his sword. There was an air about him of a metal spring, compressed, waiting.

Rand hurriedly copied the Warder's pose—at least insofar as putting his hand on his sword. He did not think he could achieve that deadly-seeming slouch. *They'd probably laugh if I tried.*

Perrin eased his axe in its leather loop and planted his feet deliberately. Mat put a hand to his quiver, though Rand was not sure what condition his bowstring was in after being out in all this damp. Thom Merrilin stepped forward grandly and held up one empty hand, turning it slowly. Suddenly he gestured with a flourish, and a dagger twirled between his fingers. The hilt slapped into his palm, and, abruptly nonchalant, he began trimming his fingernails.

A low, delighted laugh floated from Moiraine. Egwene clapped as if watching a performance at Festival, then stopped and looked abashed, though her mouth twitched with a smile just the same.

Hightower seemed far from amused. He stared at Thom, then cleared his throat loudly. "There was mention made of more gold for the crossing." He looked around at them again, a sullen, sly look. "What you gave me before is in a safe place now, hear? It's none of it where you can get at it."

"The rest of the gold," Lan told him, "goes into your hand when we are on the other side." The leather purse hanging at his waist clinked as he gave it a little shake.

For a moment the ferryman's eyes darted, but at last he nodded. "Let's be about it, then," he muttered, and stalked out onto the landing followed by his six helpers. The fog burned away around them as they moved; gray tendrils closed in behind, quickly filling where they had been. Rand hurried to keep up.

The ferry itself was a wooden barge with high sides, boarded by a ramp that could be raised to block off the end. Ropes as thick as a man's wrist ran along each side of it, ropes fastened to massive posts at the end of the landing and disappearing into the night over the river. The ferryman's helpers stuck their torches in iron brackets on the ferry's sides, waited while everyone led their horses aboard, then pulled up the ramp. The deck creaked beneath hooves and shuffling feet, and the ferry shifted with the weight.

Hightower muttered half under his breath, growling for them to keep the horses still and stay to the center, out of the haulers' way. He shouted at his helpers, chivvying them as they readied the ferry to cross, but the men moved at the same reluctant speed whatever he said, and he was halfhearted about it, often cutting off in mid-shout to hold his torch high and peer into the fog. Finally he stopped shouting altogether and went to the bow, where he stood staring into the mist that covered the river. He did not move until one of the haulers touched his arm; then he jumped, glaring.

"What? Oh. You, is it? Ready? About time. Well, man, what are you waiting for?" He waved his arms, heedless of the torch and the way the horses whickered and tried to move back. "Cast off! Give way! Move!" The man slouched off to comply, and Hightower peered once more into the fog ahead, rubbing his free hand uneasily on his coat front.

The ferry lurched as its moorings were loosed and the strong current caught it, then lurched again as the guide-ropes held it. The haulers, three to a side, grabbed hold of the ropes at the front of the ferry and laboriously began walking toward the back, muttering uneasily as they edged out onto the gray-cloaked river.

The landing disappeared as mist surrounded them, tenuous streamers drifting across the ferry between the flickering torches. The barge rocked slowly in the current. Nothing except the steady tread of the haulers, forward to take hold of the ropes and back down again pulling, gave a hint of any other movement. No one spoke. The villagers kept as close to the center of the ferry as they could. They had heard the Taren was far wider than the streams they were used to; the fog made it infinitely vaster in their minds.

After a time Rand moved closer to Lan. Rivers a man could not wade or swim or even see across were nervous-making to someone who had never seen anything broader or deeper than a Waterwood pond. "Would they really have tried to rob us?" he asked quietly. "He acted more as if he were afraid we would rob him."

The Warder eyed the ferryman and his helpers—none appeared to be listening—before answering just as softly. "With the fog to hide them . . . well, when what they do is hidden, men sometimes deal with strangers in ways they wouldn't if there were other eyes to see. And the quickest to harm a stranger are the soonest to think a stranger will harm them. This fellow . . . I believe he might sell his mother to Trollocs for stew meat if the price was right. I'm a little surprised you ask. I heard the way people in Emond's Field speak of those from Taren Ferry."

"Yes, but. . . . Well, everyone says they. . . . But I never thought they would actually. . . ." Rand decided he had better stop thinking that he knew anything at all of what people were like beyond his own village. "He might tell the Fade we crossed on the ferry," he said at last. "Maybe he'll bring the Trollocs over after us."

Lan chuckled dryly. "Robbing a stranger is one thing, dealing with a Halfman something else again. Can you really see him ferrying Trollocs over, especially in this fog, no matter how much gold was offered? Or even talking to a Myrddraal, if he had any choice? Just the thought of it would keep him running for a month. I don't think we have to worry very much about Darkfriends in Taren Ferry. Not here. We are safe . . . for a time, at least. From this lot, anyway. Watch yourself."

Hightower had turned from peering into the fog ahead. Pointed face pushed forward and torch held high, he stared at Lan and Rand as if seeing them clearly for the first time. Deckplanks creaked under the haulers' feet and the occasional stamp of a hoof. Abruptly the ferryman twitched as he realized they were watching him watching them. With a leap he spun back to looking for the far bank, or whatever it was he sought in the fog.

"Say no more," Lan said, so softly Rand almost could not understand. "These are bad days to speak of Trollocs, or Darkfriends, or the Father of Lies, with strange ears to hear. Such talk can bring worse than the Dragon's Fang scrawled on your door."

Rand felt no desire to go on with his questions. Gloom settled on him even more than it had before. Darkfriends! As if Fades and Trollocs and Draghkar were not enough to worry about. At least you could tell a Trolloc at sight.

Abruptly pilings loomed shadowy in the mist before them. The ferry thudded against the far bank, and then the haulers were hurrying to lash the craft fast and let down the ramp at that end with a thump, while Mat and Perrin announced loudly that the Taren was not half as wide as they had heard. Lan led his stallion down the ramp, followed by Moiraine and the others. As Rand, the last, took Cloud down behind Bela, Master Hightower called out angrily.

"Here, now! Here! Where's my gold?"

"It shall be paid." Moiraine's voice came from somewhere in the mist. Rand's boots clumped from the ramp to a wooden landing. "And a silver mark for each of your men," the Aes Sedai added, "for the quick crossing."

The ferryman hesitated, face pushed forward as if he smelled danger, but at the mention of silver the haulers roused themselves. Some paused to seize a torch, but they all thumped down the ramp before Hightower could open his mouth. With a sullen grimace, the ferryman followed his crew.

Cloud's hooves clumped hollowly in the fog as Rand made his way carefully along the landing. The gray mist was as thick here as over the river. At the foot of the landing, the Warder was handing out coins, surrounded by the torches of Hightower and his fellows. Everyone else except Moiraine waited just beyond in an anxious cluster. The Aes Sedai stood looking at the river, though what she could see was beyond Rand. With a shiver he hitched up his cloak, sodden as it was. He was really out of the Two Rivers, now, and it seemed much farther away than the width of a river.

"There," Lan said, handing a last coin to Hightower. "As agreed." He did not put up his purse, and the ferrety-faced man eyed it greedily.

With a loud creak, the landing shivered. Hightower jerked upright, head swiveling back toward the mist-cloaked ferry. The torches remaining on board were a pair of dim, fuzzy points of light. The landing groaned, and with a thunderous crack of snapping wood, the twin glows lurched, then began to revolve. Egwene cried out wordlessly, and Thom cursed.

"It's loose!" Hightower screamed. Grabbing his haulers, he pushed them toward the end of the landing. "The ferry's loose, you fools! Get it! Get it!"

The haulers stumbled a few steps under Hightower's shoves, then stopped. The faint lights on the ferry spun faster, then faster still. The fog above them swirled, sucked into a spiral. The landing trembled. The cracking and splintering of wood filled the air as the ferry began breaking apart.

"Whirlpool," one of the haulers said, his voice filled with awe.

"No whirlpools on the Taren." Hightower sounded empty. "Never been a whirlpool. . . ."

"An unfortunate occurrence." Moiraine's voice was hollow in the fog that made her a shadow as she turned from the river.

"Unfortunate," Lan agreed in a flat tone. "It seems you'll be carrying no one else across the river for a time. An ill thing that you lost your craft in our service." He delved again into his purse, ready in his hand. "This should repay you."

For a moment Hightower stared at the gold, glinting in Lan's hand in the torchlight, then his shoulders hunched and his eyes darted to the others he had carried across. Made indistinct by the fog, the Emond's Fielders stood silently. With a frightened, inarticulate cry, the ferryman snatched the coins from Lan, whirled, and ran into the mist. His haulers were only half a step behind him, their torches quickly swallowed as they vanished upriver.

"There is nothing further to hold us here," the Aes Sedai said as if nothing out of the ordinary had happened. Leading her white mare, she started away from the landing, up the bank.

Rand stood staring at the hidden river. *It could have been happenstance. No whirlpools, he said, but it.* . . . Abruptly he realized everyone else had gone. Hurriedly he scrambled up the gently sloping bank.

In the space of three paces the heavy mist faded away to nothing. He stopped dead and stared back. Along a line running down the shore thick gray hung on one side, on the other shone a clear night sky, still dark though the sharpness of the moon hinted at dawn not far off.

The Warder and the Aes Sedai stood conferring beside their horses a short distance beyond the border of the fog. The others huddled a little apart; even in the moonlit darkness their nervousness was palpable. All eyes were on Lan and Moiraine, and all but Egwene were leaning back as if torn between losing the pair and getting too close. Rand trotted the last few spans to Egwene's side, leading Cloud, and she grinned at him. He did not think the shine in her eyes was all from moonlight.

"It follows the river as if drawn with a pen," Moiraine was saying in satisfied tones. "There are not ten women in Tar Valon who could do that unaided. Not to mention from the back of a galloping horse."

"I don't mean to complain, Moiraine Sedai," Thom said, sounding oddly diffident for him, "but would it not have been better to cover us a little further? Say to Baerlon? If that Draghkar looks on this side of the river, we'll lose everything we have gained."

"Draghkar are not very smart, Master Merrilin," the Aes Sedai said dryly. "Fearsome and deadly dangerous, and with sharp eyes, but little intelligence. It will tell the Myrddraal that this side of the river is clear, but the river itself is cloaked for miles in both directions. The Myrddraal will know the extra effort that cost me. He will have to consider that we may be escaping down the river, and that will slow him. He will have to divide his efforts. The fog should hold long enough that he will never be sure that we did not travel at least partway by boat. I could have extended the fog a little way toward Baerlon, instead, but then the Draghkar could search the river in a matter of hours, and the Myrddraal would know exactly where we were headed."

Thom made a puffing sound and shook his head. "I apologize, Aes Sedai. I hope I did not offend."

"Ah, Moi . . . ah, Aes Sedai." Mat stopped to swallow audibly. "The ferry . . . ah . . . did you . . . I mean . . . I don't understand why. . . ." He trailed off weakly, and there was a silence so deep that the loudest sound Rand heard was his own breathing.

Finally Moiraine spoke, and her voice filled the empty silence with sharpness. "You all want explanations, but if I explained my every action to you, I would have no time for anything else." In the moonlight, the Aes Sedai seemed taller, somehow, almost looming over them. "Know this. I intend to see you safely in Tar Valon. That is the one thing you need to know."

"If we keep standing here," Lan put in, "the Draghkar will not need to search the river. If I remember correctly. . . ." He led his horse on up the riverbank.

As if the Warder's movement had loosened something in his chest, Rand drew a deep breath. He heard others doing the same, even Thom, and remembered an old saying. Better to spit in a wolf's eye than to cross an Aes Sedai. Yet the tension had lessened. Moiraine was not looming over anyone; she barely reached his chest.

"I don't suppose we could rest a bit," Perrin said hopefully, ending with a yawn. Egwene, slumped against Bela, sighed tiredly.

It was the first sound even approaching a complaint that Rand had heard from her. *Maybe now she realizes this isn't some grand adventure after all.* Then he guiltily remembered that, unlike him, she had not slept the day away. "We do need to rest, Moiraine Sedai," he said. "After all, we have ridden all night."

"Then I suggest we see what Lan has for us," Moiraine said. "Come."

She led them on up the bank, into the woods beyond the river. Bare branches thickened the shadows. A good hundred spans from the Taren they came to a dark mound beside a clearing. Here a long-ago flood had undermined and toppled an entire stand of leatherleafs, washing them together into a great, thick tangle, an apparently solid mass of trunks and branches and roots. Moiraine stopped, and suddenly a light appeared low to the ground, coming from under the heap of trees.

Thrusting a stub of a torch ahead of him, Lan crawled out from under the mound and straightened. "No unwelcome visitors," he told Moiraine. "And the wood I left is still dry, so I started a small fire. We will rest warm."

"You expected us to stop here?" Egwene said in surprise.

"It seemed a likely place," Lan replied. "I like to be prepared, just in case."

Moiraine took the torch from him. "Will you see to the horses? When you are done I will do what I can about everyone's tiredness. Right now I want to talk to Egwene. Egwene?"

Rand watched the two women crouch down and disappear under the great pile of tree trunks. There was a low opening, barely big enough to crawl into. The light of the torch vanished.

Lan had included feedbags and a small quantity of oats in the supplies, but he stopped the others from unsaddling their horses. Instead he produced the hobbles he had also packed. "They would rest easier without the saddles, but if we must leave quickly, there may be no time to replace them."

"They don't look to me like they need any rest," Perrin said as he attempted to slip a feedbag over his mount's muzzle. The horse tossed its head before allowing him to put the straps in place. Rand was having difficulties with Cloud, too, taking three tries before he could get the canvas bag over the gray's nose.

"They do," Lan told them. He straightened from hobbling his stallion. "Oh, they can still run. They will run at their fastest, if we let them, right up to the second they drop dead from exhaustion they never even felt. I would rather Moiraine Sedai had not had to do what she did, but it was necessary." He patted the stallion's neck, and the horse bobbed his head as if acknowledging the Warder's touch. "We must go slowly with them for the next few days, until they recover. More slowly than I would like. But with luck it will be enough."

"Is that . . . ?" Mat swallowed audibly. "Is that what she meant? About our tiredness?"

Rand patted Cloud's neck and stared at nothing. Despite what she had done for Tam, he had no desire for the Aes Sedai to use the Power on him. *Light, she as much as admitted sinking the ferry.*

"Something like it." Lan chuckled wryly. "But you will not have to worry about running yourself to death. Not unless things get a lot worse than they are. Just think of it as an extra night's sleep."

The shrill scream of the Draghkar suddenly echoed from above the fog-covered river. Even the horses froze. Again it came, closer now, and again, piercing Rand's skull like needles. Then the cries were fading, until they had faded away entirely.

"Luck," Lan breathed. "It searches the river for us." He gave a quick shrug and abruptly sounded matter-of-fact. "Let's get inside. I could do with some hot tea and something to fill my belly."

Rand was the first to crawl on hands and knees through the opening in the tangle of trees and down a short tunnel. At the end of it, he stopped, still crouching. Ahead was an irregularly shaped space, a woody cave easily large enough to hold them all. The roof of tree trunks and branches came too low to allow any but the women to stand. Smoke from a small fire on a bed of river stones drifted up and through; the draft was enough to keep the space free of smoke, but the interweaving was too thick to let out even a glimmer of the flames. Moiraine and Egwene, their cloaks thrown aside, sat cross-legged, facing one another beside the fire.

"The One Power," Moiraine was saying, "comes from the True Source, the driving force of Creation, the force the Creator made to turn the Wheel of Time." She put her hands together in front of her and pushed them against each other. "*Saidin,* the male half of the True Source, and *saidar,* the female half, work against each other and at the same time together to provide that force. *Saidin*"—she lifted one hand, then let it drop—"is fouled by the touch of the Dark One, like water with a thin slick of rancid oil floating on top. The water is still pure, but it cannot be touched without touching the foulness. Only *saidar* is still safe to be used." Egwene's back was to Rand. He could not see her face, but she was leaning forward eagerly.

Mat poked Rand from behind and muttered something, and he moved on into the tree cavern. Moiraine and Egwene ignored his entry. The other men crowded in behind him, tossing off damp cloaks, settling around the fire, and holding hands out to the warmth. Lan, the last to enter, pulled waterbags and leather sacks from a nook in the wall, took out a kettle, and began to prepare tea. He paid no attention to what the women were saying, but Rand's friends began to stop toasting their hands and stare openly. Thom pretended that all of his interest was engaged in loading his thickly carved pipe, but the way he leaned toward the women gave him away. Moiraine and Egwene acted as if they were alone.

"No," Moiraine said in answer to a question Rand had missed, "the True Source cannot be used up, any more than the river can be used up by the wheel of a mill. The Source is the river; the Aes Sedai, the waterwheel."

"And you really think I can learn?" Egwene asked. Her face shone with eagerness. Rand had never seen her look so beautiful, or so far away from him. "I can become an Aes Sedai?"

Rand jumped up, cracking his head against the low roof of logs. Thom Merrilin grabbed his arm, yanking him back down.

"Don't be a fool," the gleeman murmured. He eyed the women—neither seemed to have noticed—and the look he gave Rand was sympathetic. "It's beyond you now, boy."

"Child," Moiraine said gently, "only a very few can learn to touch the True Source and use the One Power. Some of those can learn to a greater degree, some to a lesser. You are one of the bare handful for whom there is no need to learn. At least, touching the Source will come to you whether you want it or not. Without the teaching you can receive in Tar Valon, though, you will never learn to channel it fully, and you may not survive. Men who have the ability to touch *saidin* born in them die, of course, if the Red Ajah does not find them and gentle them. . . ."

Thom growled deep in his throat, and Rand shifted uncomfortably. Men like those of whom the Aes Sedai spoke were rare—he had only heard of three in his whole life, and thank the Light never in the Two Rivers—but the damage they did before the Aes Sedai found them was always bad enough for the news to carry, like the news of wars, or earthquakes that destroyed cities. He had never really understood what the Ajahs did. According to the stories they were societies among the Aes Sedai that seemed to plot and squabble among themselves more than anything else, but the stories were clear on one point. The Red Ajah held its prime duty to be the prevention of another Breaking of the World, and they did it by hunting down every man who even dreamed of wielding the One Power. Mat and Perrin looked as if they suddenly wished they were back home in their beds.

". . . but some of the women die, too. It is hard to learn without a guide. The women we do not find, those who live, often become . . . well, in this part of the world they might become Wisdoms of their villages." The Aes Sedai paused thoughtfully. "The old blood is strong in Emond's Field, and the old blood sings. I knew you for what you were the moment I saw you. No Aes Sedai can stand in the presence of a woman who can channel, or who is close to her change, and not feel it." She rummaged in the pouch at her belt and produced the small blue gem on a gold chain that she had earlier worn in her hair. "You are very close to your change, your first touching. It will be better if I guide you through it. That way you will avoid the . . . unpleasant effects that come to those who must find their own way."

Egwene's eyes widened as she looked at the stone, and she wet her lips repeatedly. "Is . . . does that have the Power?"

"Of course not," Moiraine snapped. "*Things* do not have the Power, child. Even an *angreal* is only a tool. This is just a pretty blue stone. But it can give off light. Here."

Egwene's hands trembled as Moiraine laid the stone on her fingertips. She started to pull back, but the Aes Sedai held both her hands in one of hers and gently touched the other to the side of Egwene's head.

"Look at the stone," the Aes Sedai said softly. "It is better this way than fumbling alone. Clear your mind of everything but the stone. Clear your mind, and let yourself drift. There is only the stone and emptiness. I will begin it. Drift, and let me guide you. No thoughts. Drift."

Rand's fingers dug into his knees; his jaws clenched until they hurt. *She has to fail. She has to.*

Light bloomed in the stone, just one flash of blue and then gone, no brighter than a firefly, but he flinched as if it had been blinding. Egwene and Moiraine stared into the stone, faces empty. Another flash came, and another, until the azure light pulsed like the beating of a heart. *It's the Aes Sedai,* he thought desperately. *Moiraine's doing it. Not Egwene.*

One last, feeble flicker, and the stone was merely a bauble again. Rand held his breath.

For a moment Egwene continued to stare at the small stone, then she looked up at Moiraine. "I . . . I thought I felt . . . something, but. . . . Perhaps you're mistaken about me. I am sorry I wasted your time."

"I have wasted nothing, child." A small smile of satisfaction flitted across Moiraine's lips. "That last light was yours alone."

"It was?" Egwene exclaimed, then slid immediately back into glumness. "But it was barely there at all."

"Now you are behaving like a foolish village girl. Most who come to Tar Valon must study for many months before they can do what you just did. You may go far. Perhaps even the Amyrlin Seat, one day, if you study hard and work hard."

"You mean . . . ?" With a cry of delight Egwene threw her arms around the Aes Sedai. "Oh, thank you. Rand, did you hear? I'm going to be an Aes Sedai!"

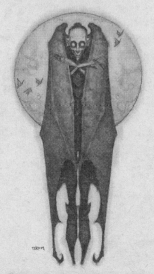

Draghkar

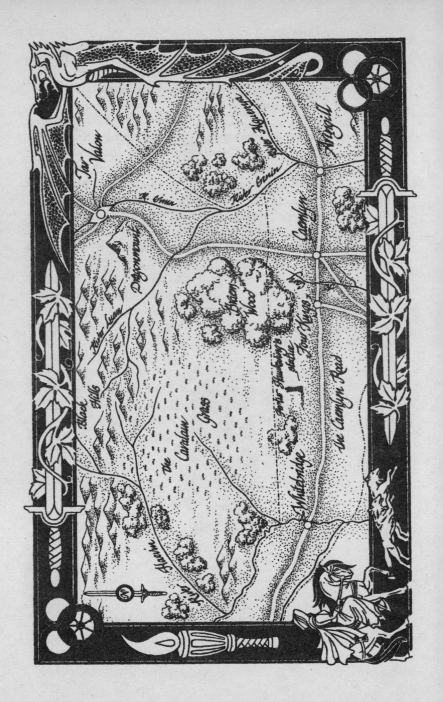

CHAPTER 13

Choices

Before they went to sleep Moiraine knelt by each in turn and laid her hands on their heads. Lan grumbled that he had no need and she should not waste her strength, but he did not try to stop her. Egwene was eager for the experience, Mat and Perrin clearly frightened of it, and frightened to say no. Thom jerked away from the Aes Sedai's hands, but she seized his gray head with a look that allowed no nonsense. The gleeman scowled through the entire thing. She smiled mockingly once she took her hands away. His frown deepened, but he did look refreshed. They all did.

Rand had drawn back into a niche in the uneven wall where he hoped he would be overlooked. His eyes wanted to slide closed once he leaned back against the timber jumble, but he forced himself to watch. He pushed a fist against his mouth to stifle a yawn. A little sleep, an hour or two, and he would be just fine. Moiraine did not forget him, though.

He flinched at the coolness of her fingers on his face, and said, "I don't—" His eyes widened in wonder. Tiredness drained out of him like water running downhill; aches and soreness ebbed to dim memories and vanished. He stared at her with his mouth hanging open. She only smiled and withdrew her hands.

"It is done," she said, and as she stood with a weary sigh he was reminded that she could not do the same for herself. Indeed, she only drank a little tea, refusing the bread and cheese

Lan tried to press on her, before curling up beside the fire. She seemed to fall asleep the instant she wrapped her cloak around her.

The others, all save Lan, were dropping asleep wherever they could find a space to stretch out, but Rand could not imagine why. He felt as if he had already had a full night in a good bed. No sooner did he lean back against the log wall, though, than sleep rolled him under. When Lan poked him awake an hour later he felt as though he had had three days rest.

The Warder awakened them all, except Moiraine, and he sternly hushed any sound that might disturb her. Even so, he allowed them only a short stay in the snug cave of trees. Before the sun was twice its own height above the horizon, all traces that anyone had ever stopped there had been cleared away and they were all mounted and moving north toward Baerlon, riding slowly to conserve the horses. The Aes Sedai's eyes were shadowed, but she sat her saddle upright and steady.

Fog still hung thick over the river behind them, a gray wall resisting the efforts of the feeble sun to burn it away and hiding the Two Rivers from view. Rand watched over his shoulder as he rode, hoping for one last glimpse, even of Taren Ferry, until the fogbank was lost to sight.

"I never thought I'd ever be this far from home," he said when the trees at last hid both the fog and the river. "Remember when Watch Hill seemed a long way?" *Two days ago, that was. It seems like forever.*

"In a month or two, we'll be back," Perrin said in a strained voice. "Think what we'll have to tell."

"Even Trollocs can't chase us forever," Mat said. "Burn me, they can't." He straightened around with a heavy sigh, slumping in his saddle as if he did not believe a word that had been said.

"Men!" Egwene snorted. "You get the adventure you're always prating about, and already you're talking about home." She held her head high, yet Rand noticed a tremor to her voice, now that nothing more was to be seen of the Two Rivers.

Neither Moiraine nor Lan made any attempt to reassure them, not a word to say that of course they would come back. He tried not to think on what that might mean. Even rested, he was full enough of doubts without searching out more. Hunching in his saddle he began a waking dream of tending the sheep alongside Tam in a pasture with deep, lush grass and larks singing of a spring morning. And a trip into Emond's Field, and Bel Tine the way it had been, dancing on the Green with never a care beyond whether he might stumble in the steps. He managed to lose himself in it for a long time.

The journey to Baerlon took almost a week. Lan muttered about the laggardness of their travel, but it was he who set the pace and forced the rest to keep it. With himself and his stallion, Mandarb—he said it meant "Blade" in the Old Tongue— he was not so sparing. The Warder covered twice as much ground as they did, galloping ahead, his color-shifting cloak swirling in the wind, to scout what lay before them, or dropping behind to examine their backtrail. Any others who tried to move at more than a walk, though, got cutting words on taking care of their animals, biting words on how well they would do afoot if the Trollocs did appear. Not even Moiraine was proof against his tongue if she let the white mare pick up her step. Aldieb, the mare was called; in the Old Tongue, "Westwind," the wind that brought the spring rains.

The Warder's scouting never turned up any sign of pursuit, or ambush. He spoke only to Moiraine of what he saw, and that quietly, so it could not be overheard, and the Aes Sedai informed the rest of them of what she thought they needed to know. In the beginning, Rand looked over his shoulder as much as he did ahead. He was not the only one. Perrin fingered his axe often, and Mat rode with an arrow nocked to his bow, in the beginning. But the land behind remained empty of Trollocs or figures in black cloaks, the sky remained empty of Draghkar. Slowly, Rand began to think perhaps they really had escaped.

No very great cover was to be had, even in the thickest parts of the woods. Winter clung as hard north of the Taren as it did in the Two Rivers. Stands of pine or fir or leatherleaf, and here and there a few spicewoods or laurels, dotted a forest of otherwise bare, gray branches. Not even the elders showed a leaf. Only scattered green sprigs of new growth stood out against brown meadows beaten flat by the winter's snows. Here, too, much of what did grow was stinging nettles and coarse thistle and stinkweed. On the bare dirt of the forest floor some of the last snow still hung on, in shady patches and in drifts beneath the low branches of evergreens. Everyone kept their cloaks drawn well about them, for the thin sunlight had no warmth to it and the night cold pierced deep. No more birds flew here than in the Two Rivers, not even ravens.

There was nothing leisurely about the slowness of their movement. The North Road—Rand continued to think of it that way, though he suspected it might have a different name here, north of the Taren—still ran almost due north, but at Lan's insistence their path snaked this way and that through the forest as often as it ran along the hard-packed dirt road. A village, or a farm, or any sign of men or civilization sent them circling for miles to avoid it, though there were few enough of any of those. The whole first day Rand saw no evidence aside from the road that men had ever been in that woods. It came to him that even when he had gone to the foot of the Mountains of Mist he might not have been as far from a human habitation as he was that day.

The first farm he saw—a large frame house and tall barn with high-peaked, thatched roofs, a curl of smoke rising from a stone chimney—was a shock.

"It's no different from back home," Perrin said, frowning at the distant buildings, barely visible through the trees. People moved around the farmyard, as yet unaware of the travelers.

"Of course it is," Mat said. "We're just not close enough to see."

"I tell you, it's no different," Perrin insisted.

"It must be. We're north of the Taren, after all."

"Quiet, you two," Lan growled. "We don't want to be seen, remember? This way." He turned west, to circle the farm through the trees.

Looking back, Rand thought Perrin was right. The farm looked much the same as any around Emond's Field. There was a small boy toting water from the well, and older boys tending sheep behind a rail fence. It even had a curing shed, for tabac. But Mat was right, too. *We're north of the Taren. It must be different.*

Always they halted while light still clung to the sky, to choose a spot sloped for drainage and sheltered from the wind that seldom died completely, only changed direction. Their fire was always small and hidden from only a few yards off, and once tea was brewed, the flames were doused and the coals buried.

At their first stop, before the sun sank, Lan began teaching the boys what to do with the weapons they carried. He started with the bow. After watching Mat put three arrows into a knot the size of a man's head, on the fissured trunk of a dead leatherleaf, at a hundred paces, he told the others to take their turns. Perrin duplicated Mat's feat, and Rand, summoning the flame and the void, the empty calm that let the bow become a part of him, or him of it, clustered his three where the points almost touched one another. Mat gave him a congratulatory clap on the shoulder.

"Now if you all had bows," the Warder said dryly when they started grinning, "and if the Trollocs agreed not to come so close you couldn't use them. . . ." The grins faded abruptly. "Let me see what I can teach you in case they do come that close."

He showed Perrin a bit of how to use that great-bladed axe; raising an axe to someone, or something, that had a weapon was not at all like chopping wood or flailing around in pretend. Setting the big apprentice blacksmith to a series of exercises, block, parry, and strike, he did the same for Rand and his sword. Not the wild leaping about and slashing that Rand had in mind whenever he thought about using it, but smooth motions, one flowing into another, almost a dance.

"Moving the blade is not enough," Lan said, "though some think it is. The mind is part of it, most of it. Blank your mind, sheepherder. Empty it of hate or fear, of everything. Burn them away. You others listen to this, too. You can use it with the axe or the bow, with a spear, or a quarterstaff, or even your bare hands."

Rand stared at him. "The flame and the void," he said wonderingly. "That's what you mean, isn't it? My father taught me about that."

The Warder gave him an unreadable look in return. "Hold the sword as I showed you, sheepherder. I cannot make a mud-footed villager into a blademaster in an hour, but perhaps I can keep you from slicing off your own foot."

Rand sighed and held the sword upright before him in both hands. Moiraine watched without expression, but the next evening she told Lan to continue the lessons.

The meal at evening was always the same as at midday and breakfast, flatbread and cheese and dried meat, except that evenings they had hot tea to wash it down instead of water. Thom entertained them, evenings. Lan would not let the gleeman play harp or flute—no need to rouse the countryside, the Warder said—but Thom juggled and told stories. "Mara and the Three Foolish Kings," or one of the hundreds about Anla the Wise Counselor, or something filled with glory and adventure, like *The Great Hunt of the Horn,* but always with a happy ending and a joyous homecoming.

Yet if the land was peaceful around them, if no Trollocs appeared among the trees, no Draghkar among the clouds, it seemed to Rand that they managed to raise their tension themselves, whenever it was in danger of vanishing.

There was the morning that Egwene awoke and began unbraiding her hair. Rand watched her from the corner of his eye as he made up his blanketroll. Every night when the fire was doused, everyone took to their blankets except for Egwene and the Aes Sedai. The two women always went aside from the others and talked for an hour or two, returning when the others were asleep. Egwene combed her hair out—one hundred strokes; he counted—while he was saddling Cloud, tying his saddlebags and blanket behind the saddle. Then she tucked the comb away, swept her loose hair over her shoulder, and pulled up the hood of her cloak.

Startled, he asked, "What are you doing?" She gave him a sidelong look without answering. It was the first time he had spoken to her in two days, he realized, since the night in the log shelter on the bank of the Taren, but he did not let that stop him. "All your life you've waited to wear your hair in a braid, and now you're giving it up? Why? Because she doesn't braid hers?"

"Aes Sedai don't braid their hair," she said simply. "At least, not unless they want to."

"You aren't an Aes Sedai. You're Egwene al'Vere from Emond's Field, and the Women's Circle would have a fit if they could see you now."

"Women's Circle business is none of yours, Rand al'Thor. And I *will* be an Aes Sedai. Just as soon as I reach Tar Valon."

He snorted. "As soon as you reach Tar Valon. Why? Light, tell me that. You're no Darkfriend."

"Do you think Moiraine Sedai is a Darkfriend? Do you?" She squared around to face him with her fists clenched, and he almost thought she was going to hit him. "After she saved the village? After she saved your father?"

"I don't know what she is, but whatever she is, it doesn't say anything about the rest of them. The stories—"

"Grow up, Rand! Forget the stories and use your eyes."

"My eyes saw her sink the ferry! Deny that! Once you get an idea in your head, you won't budge even if somebody points out you're trying to stand on water. If you weren't such a Light-blinded fool, you'd see—!"

"Fool, am I? Let me tell you a thing or two, Rand al'Thor! You are the muliest, most wool-headed—!"

"You two trying to wake everybody inside ten miles?" the Warder asked.

Standing there with his mouth open, trying to get a word in edgewise, Rand suddenly realized he had been shouting. They both had.

Egwene's face went scarlet to her eyebrows, and she spun away with a muttered, "Men!" that seemed as much for the Warder as for him.

Warily, Rand looked around the camp. Everybody was looking at him, not just the Warder. Mat and Perrin, with their faces white. Thom, tensed as if ready to run or fight. Moiraine. The Aes Sedai's face was expressionless, but her eyes seemed to bore into his head. Desperately, he tried to recall exactly what he had said, about Aes Sedai and Darkfriends.

"It is time to be going," Moiraine said. She turned to Aldieb, and Rand shivered as if he had been let out of a trap. He wondered if he had been.

Two nights later, with the fire burning low, Mat licked the last crumbs of cheese from his fingers and said, "You know, I think we've lost them for good." Lan was off in the night, taking a last look around. Moiraine and Egwene had gone aside for one of their conversations. Thom was half dozing over his pipe, and the young men had the fire to themselves.

Perrin, idly poking the embers with a stick, answered. "If we've lost them, why does Lan keep scouting?" Nearly asleep, Rand rolled over, his back to the fire.

"We lost them back at Taren Ferry." Mat lay back with his fingers laced behind his head, staring at the moon-filled sky. "If they were even really after us."

"You think that Draghkar was chasing us because it liked us?" Perrin asked.

"I say, stop worrying about Trollocs and such," Mat went on as if Perrin had not spoken, "and start thinking about seeing the world. We're out where the stories come from. What do you think a real city ís like?"

"We're going to Baerlon," Rand said sleepily, but Mat snorted.

"Baerlon's all very well, but I've seen that old map Master al'Vere has. If we turn south once we reach Caemlyn, the road leads all the way to Illian, and beyond."

"What's so special about Illian?" Perrin said, yawning.

"For one thing," Mat replied, "Illian isn't full of Aes Se—"

A silence fell, and Rand was suddenly wide awake. Moiraine had come back early. Egwene was with her, but it was the Aes Sedai, standing at the edge of the firelight, who held their attention. Mat lay there on his back, his mouth still open, staring at her. Moiraine's eyes caught the light like dark, polished stones. Abruptly Rand wondered how long she had been standing there.

"The lads were just—" Thom began, but Moiraine spoke right over the top of him.

"A few days respite, and you are ready to give up." Her calm, level voice contrasted sharply with her eyes. "A day or two of quiet, and already you have forgotten Winternight."

"We haven't forgotten," Perrin said. "It's just—" Still not raising her voice, the Aes Sedai treated him as she had the gleeman.

"Is that the way you all feel? You are all eager to run off to Illian and forget about Trollocs, and Halfmen, and Draghkar?" She ran her eyes over them—that stony glint playing against the everyday tone of voice made Rand uneasy—but she gave no one a chance to speak. "The Dark One is after you three, one or all, and if I let you go running off wherever you want to go, he will take you. Whatever the Dark One wants, I oppose, so hear this and know it true. Before I let the Dark One have you, I will destroy you myself."

It was her voice, so matter-of-fact, that convinced Rand. The Aes Sedai would do exactly what she said, if she thought it was necessary. He had a hard time sleeping that night, and he was not the only one. Even the gleeman did not begin snoring till long after the last coals died. For once, Moiraine offered no help.

Those nightly talks between Egwene and the Aes Sedai were a sore point for Rand. Whenever they disappeared into the darkness, aside from the rest for privacy, he wondered what they were saying, what they were doing. What was the Aes Sedai doing to Egwene?

One night, he waited until the other men had all settled down, Thom snoring like a saw cutting an oak knot. Then he slipped away, clutching his blanket around him. Using every bit of skill he had gained stalking rabbits, he moved with the moon shadows until he was crouched at the base of a tall leatherleaf tree, thick with tough, broad leaves, close enough to hear Moiraine and Egwene, where they sat on a fallen log with a small lantern for light.

"Ask," Moiraine was saying, "and if I can tell you now, I will. Understand, there is much for which you are not yet ready, things you cannot learn until you have learned other things which require still others to be learned before them. But ask what you will."

"The Five Powers," Egwene said slowly. "Earth, Wind, Fire, Water, and Spirit. It doesn't seem fair that men should have been strongest in wielding Earth and Fire. Why should they have had the strongest Powers?"

Moiraine laughed. "Is that what you think, child? Is there a rock so hard that wind and water cannot wear it away, a fire so strong that water cannot quench it or wind snuff it out?"

Egwene was silent for a time, digging her toe into the forest floor. "They . . . they were the ones who . . . who tried to free the Dark One and the Forsaken, weren't they? The male Aes Sedai?" She took a deep breath and picked up speed. "The women were not part of it. It was the men who went mad and broke the world."

"You are afraid," Moiraine said grimly. "If you had remained in Emond's Field, you would have become Wisdom, in time. That was Nynaeve's plan, was it not? Or, you would have sat in the Women's Circle and managed the affairs of Emond's Field while the Village Council thought it was doing so. But you did the unthinkable. You left Emond's Field, left the Two Rivers, seeking adventure. You wanted to do it, and at the same time you are afraid of it. And you are stubbornly refusing to let your fear best you. You would not have asked me how a woman becomes an Aes Sedai, otherwise. You would not have thrown custom and convention over the fence, otherwise."

"No," Egwene protested. "I'm not afraid. I do want to become an Aes Sedai."

"Better for you if you were afraid, but I hope you hold to that conviction. Few women these days have the ability to become initiates, much less have the wish to." Moiraine's voice sounded as if she had begun musing to herself. "Surely never before two in one village. The old blood is indeed still strong in the Two Rivers."

In the shadows, Rand shifted. A twig snapped under his foot. He froze instantly, sweating and holding his breath, but neither of the women looked around.

"Two?" Egwene exclaimed. "Who else? Is it Kari? Kari Thane? Lara Ayellan?"

Moiraine gave an exasperated click of her tongue, then said sternly, "You must forget I said that. Her road lies another way, I fear. Concern yourself with your own circumstances. It is not an easy road you have chosen."

"I will not turn back," Egwene said.

"Be that as it may. But you still want reassurance, and I cannot give it to you, not in the way you want."

"I don't understand."

"You want to know that Aes Sedai are good and pure, that it was those wicked men of the legends who caused the Breaking of the World, not the women. Well, it was the men, but they were no more wicked than any men. They were insane, not evil. The Aes Sedai you will find in Tar Valon are human, no different from any other women except for the ability that sets us apart. They are brave and cowardly, strong and weak, kind

and cruel, warm-hearted and cold. Becoming an Aes Sedai will
not change you from what you are."

Egwene drew a heavy breath. "I suppose I was afraid of that,
that I'd be changed by the Power. That and the Trollocs. And
the Fade. And. . . . Moiraine Sedai, in the name of the Light,
why did the Trollocs come to Emond's Field?"

The Aes Sedai's head swung, and she looked straight at
Rand's hiding place. His breath seized in his throat; her eyes
were as hard as when she had threatened them, and he had the
feeling they could penetrate the leatherleaf's thick branches.
Light, what will she do if she finds me listening?

He tried to melt back into the deeper shadows. With his eyes
on the women, a root snagged his foot, and he barely caught
himself from tumbling into dead brush that would have pointed
him out with a crackle of snapping branches like fireworks.
Panting, he scrambled away on all fours, keeping silent as much
by luck as by anything he did. His heart pounded so hard he
thought that might give him away itself. *Fool! Eavesdropping
on an Aes Sedai!*

Back where the others were sleeping, he managed to slip in
among them silently. Lan moved as he dropped to the ground
and jerked his blanket up, but the Warder settled back with a
sigh. He had only been rolling over in his sleep. Rand let out a
long, silent breath.

A moment later Moiraine appeared out of the night, stopping where she could study the slumbering shapes. Moonlight
made a nimbus around her. Rand closed his eyes and breathed
evenly, all the while listening hard for footsteps coming closer.
None did. When he opened his eyes again, she was gone.

When finally sleep came, it was fitful and filled with sweaty
dreams where all the men in Emond's Field claimed to be the
Dragon Reborn and all the women had blue stones in their hair
like the one Moiraine wore. He did not try to overhear
Moiraine and Egwene again.

On into the sixth day the slow journey stretched. The
warmthless sun slid slowly toward the treetops, while a handful
of thin clouds drifted high to the north. The wind gusted higher
for a moment, and Rand pulled his cloak back up onto his
shoulders, muttering to himself. He wondered if they would

ever get to Baerlon. The distance they had traveled from the river already was more than enough to take him from Taren Ferry to the White River, but Lan always said it was just a short journey whenever he was asked, hardly worth calling a journey at all. It made him feel lost.

Lan appeared ahead of them in the woods, returning from one of his forays. He reined in and rode beside Moiraine, his head bent close to hers.

Rand grimaced, but he did not ask any questions. Lan simply refused to acknowledge all such questions aimed at him.

Only Egwene, among the others, even appeared to notice Lan's return, so used to this arrangement had they become, and she kept back, too. The Aes Sedai might have begun acting as if Egwene were in charge of the Emond's Fielders, but that gave her no say when the Warder made his reports. Perrin was carrying Mat's bow, wrapped in the thoughtful silence that seemed to take them all more and more as they got further from the Two Rivers. The horses' slow walk allowed Mat practice juggling three small stones under Thom Merrilin's watchful eye. The gleeman had given lessons each night, too, well as Lan.

Lan finished whatever he had been telling Moiraine, and she twisted in her saddle to look back at the others. Rand tried not to stiffen when her eyes moved across him. Did they linger on him a moment longer than on anyone else? He had the queasy feeling that she knew who had been listening in the darkness that night.

"Hey, Rand," Mat called, "I can juggle four!" Rand waved in reply without looking around. "I told you I'd get to four before you. I— Look!"

They had topped a low hill, and below them, a scant mile away through the stark trees and the stretching shadows of evening, lay Baerlon. Rand gasped, trying to smile and gape at the same time.

A log wall, nearly twenty feet tall, surrounded the town, with wooden watchtowers scattered along its length. Within, rooftops of slate and tile glinted with the sinking sun, and feathers of smoke drifted upward from chimneys. Hundreds of chimneys. There was not a thatched roof to be seen. A broad road ran east from the town, and another west, each with at least a dozen wagons and twice as many ox-carts trudging toward the palisade. Farms lay scattered about the town, thickest to the north while only a few broke the forest to the south, but they might as well not have existed so far as Rand was concerned. *It's bigger than Emond's Field and Watch Hill and Deven Ride all put together! And maybe Taren Ferry, too.*

"So that's a city," Mat breathed, leaning forward across his horse's neck to stare.

Perrin could only shake his head. "How can so many people live in one place?"

Egwene simply stared.

Thom Merrilin glanced at Mat, then rolled his eyes and blew out his mustaches. "City!" he snorted.

"And you, Rand?" Moiraine said. "What do you think of your first sight of Baerlon?"

"I think it's a long way from home," he said slowly, bringing a sharp laugh from Mat.

"You have further to go yet," Moiraine said. "Much further. But there is no other choice, except to run and hide and run again for the rest of your lives. And short lives they would be. You must remember that, when the journey becomes hard. You have no choice."

Rand exchanged glances with Mat and Perrin. By their faces, they were thinking the same thing he was. How could she talk as if they had any choice after what she had said? *The Aes Sedai's made our choices.*

Moiraine went on as if their thoughts were not plain. "The danger begins again here. Watch what you say within those walls. Above all, do not mention Trollocs, or Halfmen, or any such. You must not even think of the Dark One. Some in Baerlon have even less love for Aes Sedai than do the people of Emond's Field, and there may even be Darkfriends." Egwene gasped, and Perrin muttered under his breath. Mat's face paled, but Moiraine went on calmly. "We must attract as little attention as possible." Lan was exchanging his cloak of shifting grays and greens for one of dark brown, more ordinary, though of fine cut and weave. His color-changing cloak made a large bulge in one of his saddlebags. "We do not go by our own names here," Moiraine continued. "Here I am known as Alys, and Lan is Andra. Remember that. Good. Let us be within the walls before night catches us. The gates of Baerlon are closed from sundown to sunrise."

Lan led the way down the hill and through the woods toward the log wall. The road passed half a dozen farms—none lay close, and none of the people finishing their chores seemed to notice the travelers—ending at heavy wooden gates bound with wide straps of black iron. They were closed tight, even if the sun was not down yet.

Lan rode close to the wall and gave a tug to a frayed rope hanging down beside the gates. A bell clanged on the other side of the wall. Abruptly a wizened face under a battered cloth cap peered down suspiciously from atop the wall, glaring between the cut-off ends of two of the logs, a good three spans over their heads.

"What's all this, eh? It's too late in the day to be opening this gate. Too late, I say. Go around to the Whitebridge Gate if you want to—" Moiraine's mare moved out to where the man atop the wall had a clear view of her. Suddenly his wrinkles deepened in a gap-toothed smile, and he seemed to quiver between speaking and doing his duty. "I didn't know it was you, mistress. Wait. I'll be right down. Just wait. I'm coming. I'm coming."

The head dipped out of sight, but Rand could still hear muffled shouts for them to stay where they were, that he was coming. With great creaks of disuse, the right-hand gate slowly swung outward. It stopped when open just wide enough for one horse to pass through at a time, and the gatekeeper poked his head into the gap, flashed his half-toothless smile at them again and darted back out of the way. Moiraine followed Lan through, with Egwene right behind her.

Rand trotted Cloud after Bela and found himself in a narrow street fronted by high wooden fences and warehouses, tall and windowless, broad doors closed up tight. Moiraine and Lan were already on foot, speaking to the wrinkle-faced gatekeeper, so Rand dismounted, too.

The little man, in a much-mended cloak and coat, held his cloth cap crumpled in one hand and ducked his head whenever he spoke. He peered at those dismounting behind Lan and Moiraine, and shook his head. "Downcountry folk." He grinned. "Why, Mistress Alys, you taken up collecting downcountry folk with hay in their hair?" His look took in Thom Merrilin, then. "You ain't a sheepfarmer. I remember letting you go through some days back, I do. Didn't like your tricks downcountry, eh, gleeman?"

"I hope you remembered to forget letting us through, Master Avin," Lan said, pressing a coin into the man's free hand. "And letting us back in, too."

"No need for that, Master Andra. No need for that. You give me plenty when you went out. Plenty." Just the same, Avin made the coin disappear as deftly as if he were a gleeman, too. "I ain't told nobody, and I won't, neither. Especially not them Whitecloaks," he finished with a scowl. He pursed up his lips to spit, then glanced at Moiraine and swallowed, instead.

Rand blinked, but kept his mouth shut. The others did, too, though it appeared to be an effort for Mat. *Children of the Light,* Rand thought wonderingly. Stories told about the Children by peddlers and merchants and merchants' guards varied from admiration to hatred, but all agreed the Children hated Aes Sedai as much as they did Darkfriends. He wondered if this was more trouble already.

"The Children are in Baerlon?" Lan demanded.

"They surely are." The gatekeeper bobbed his head. "Came the same day you left, as I recall. Ain't nobody here likes them at all. Most don't let on, of course."

"Have they said why they are here?" Moiraine asked intently.

"Why they're here, mistress?" Avin was so astonished he forgot to duck his head. "Of course, they said why— Oh, I forgot. You been downcountry. Likely you ain't heard nothing but sheep bleating. They say they're here because of what's going on down in Ghealdan. The Dragon, you know—well, him, as calls himself Dragon. They say the fellow's stirring up evil— which I expect he is—and they're here to stamp it out, only he's down there in Ghealdan, not here. Just an excuse to meddle in other people's business, is what I figure. There's already been the Dragon's Fang on some people's doors." This time he did spit.

"Have they caused much trouble, then?" Lan said, and Avin shook his head vigorously.

"Not that they don't want to, I expect, only the Governor

don't trust them no more than I do. He won't let but maybe ten or so inside the walls at one time, and ain't they mad about that. The rest have a camp a little ways north, I hear. Bet they got the farmers looking over their shoulders. The ones that do come in, they just stalk around in those white cloaks, looking down their noses at honest folk. Walk in the Light, they say, and it's an order. Near come to blows more than once with the wagoneers and miners and smelters and all, and even the Watch, but the Governor wants it all peaceful, and that's how it's been so far. If they're hunting evil, I say why aren't they up in Saldaea? There's some kind of trouble up there, I hear. Or down in Ghealdan? There's been a big battle down there, they say. Real big."

Moiraine drew a soft breath. "I had heard that Aes Sedai were going to Ghealdan."

"Yes, they did, mistress." Avin's head started bobbing again. "They went to Ghealdan, all right, and that's what started this battle, or so I hear. They say some of those Aes Sedai are dead. Maybe all of them. I know some folks don't hold with Aes Sedai, but I say, who else is going to stop a false Dragon? Eh? And those damned fools who think they can be men Aes Sedai or some such. What about them? Course, some say—not the Whitecloaks, mind, and not me, but some folks—that maybe this fellow really is the Dragon Reborn. He can do things, I hear. Use the One Power. There's thousands following him."

"Don't be a fool," Lan snapped, and Avin's face folded into a hurt look.

"I'm only saying what I heard, ain't I? Just what I heard, Master Andra. They say, some do, that he's moving his army east and south, toward Tear." His voice became heavy with meaning. "They say he's named them the People of the Dragon."

"Names mean little," Moiraine said calmly. If anything she had heard disturbed her, she gave no outward sign of it now. "You could call your mule People of the Dragon, if you wanted."

"Not likely, mistress." Avin chuckled. "Not with the White-cloaks around, for sure. I don't expect anybody else would look

kindly on a name like that, neither. I see what you mean, but
. . . oh, no, mistress. Not *my* mule."

"No doubt a wise decision," Moiraine said. "Now we must
be off."

"And don't you worry, mistress," Avin said, with a deep bob
of his head, "I ain't seen nobody." He darted to the gate and
began tugging it closed with quick jerks. "Ain't seen nobody,
and ain't seen nothing." The gate thudded shut, and he pulled
down the locking bar with a rope. "In fact, mistress, this gate
ain't been open in days."

"The Light illumine you, Avin," Moiraine said.

She led them away from the gate, then. Rand looked back,
once, and Avin was still standing in front of the gate. He
seemed to be polishing a coin with an edge of his cloak and
chuckling.

The way led through dirt streets barely the width of two wagons, empty of people, all lined with warehouses and occasional
high, wooden fences. Rand walked a time beside the gleeman.
"Thom, what was all that about Tear, and the People of the
Dragon? Tear is a city all the way down on the Sea of Storms,
isn't it?"

"*The Karaethon Cycle,*" Thom said curtly.

Rand blinked. *The Prophecies of the Dragon.* "Nobody tells
the . . . those stories in the Two Rivers. Not in Emond's Field,
anyway. The Wisdom would skin them alive, if they did."

"I suppose she would, at that," Thom said dryly. He glanced
at Moiraine up ahead with Lan, saw she could not overhear,
and went on. "Tear is the greatest port on the Sea of Storms,
and the Stone of Tear is the fortress that guards it. The Stone is
said to be the first fortress built after the Breaking of the
World, and in all this time it has never fallen, though more than
one army has tried. One of the Prophecies says that the Stone
of Tear will never fall until the People of the Dragon come to
the Stone. Another says the Stone will never fall till the Sword
That Cannot Be Touched is wielded by the Dragon's hand."
Thom grimaced. "The fall of the Stone will be one of the major
proofs that the Dragon has been reborn. May the Stone stand
till I am dust."

"The sword that cannot be touched?"

"That's what it says. I don't know whether it is a sword. Whatever it is, it lies in the Heart of the Stone, the central citadel of the fortress. None but the High Lords of Tear can enter there, and they never speak of what lies inside. Certainly not to gleemen, anyway."

Rand frowned. "The Stone cannot fall until the Dragon wields the sword, but how can he, unless the Stone has already fallen? Is the Dragon supposed to be a High Lord of Tear?"

"Not much chance of that," the gleeman said dryly. "Tear hates anything to do with the Power even more than Amador, and Amador is the stronghold of the Children of the Light."

"Then how can the Prophecy be fulfilled?" Rand asked. "I'd like it well enough if the Dragon was never reborn, but a prophecy that cannot be fulfilled doesn't make much sense. It sounds like a story meant to make people think the Dragon never will be reborn. Is that it?"

"You ask an awful lot of questions, boy," Thom said. "A prophecy that was easily fulfilled would not be worth much, now would it?" Suddenly his voice brightened. "Well, we're here. Wherever here is."

Lan had stopped by a section of head-high wooden fence that looked no different from any other they had passed. He was working the blade of his dagger between two of the boards. Abruptly he gave a grunt of satisfaction, pulled, and a length of the fence swung out like a gate. In fact it was a gate, Rand saw, though one meant to be opened only from the other side. The metal latch that Lan had lifted with his dagger showed that.

Moiraine went through immediately, drawing Aldieb behind her. Lan motioned the others to follow, and brought up the rear, closing the gate behind him.

On the other side of the fence Rand found himself in the stableyard of an inn. A loud bustle and clatter came from the building's kitchen, but what struck him was its size: it covered more than twice as much ground as the Winespring Inn, and was four stories high besides. Well over half the windows were aglow in the deepening twilight. He wondered at this city, that could have so many strangers in it.

No sooner had they come well into the stableyard than three men in dirty canvas aprons appeared at the huge stable's broad, arched doors. One, a wiry fellow and the only one without a manure fork in his hands, came forward waving his arms.

"Here! Here! You can't come in that way! You'll have to go round the front!"

Lan's hand went to his purse again, but even as it did another man, as big around as Master al'Vere, came hurrying out of the inn. Puffs of hair stuck out above his ears, and his sparkling white apron was as good as a sign proclaiming him the innkeeper.

"It's all right, Mutch," the newcomer said. "It's all right. These folk are expected guests. Take care of their horses, now. Good care."

Mutch sullenly knuckled his forehead, then motioned his two companions to come help. Rand and the others hurriedly got their saddlebags and blanketrolls down while the innkeeper turned to Moiraine. He gave her a deep bow, and spoke with a genuine smile.

"Welcome, Mistress Alys. Welcome. It's good to be seeing you, you and Master Andra, both. Very good. Your fine conversation has been missed. Yes, it has. I must say I worried, you going downcountry and all. Well, I mean, at a time like this, with the weather all crazy and wolves howling right up to the walls in the night." Abruptly he slapped both hands against his round belly and shook his head. "Here I go on like this, chattering away, instead of taking you inside. Come. Come. Hot meals and warm beds, that's what you'll be wanting. And the best in Baerlon are right here. The very best."

"And hot baths, too, I trust, Master Fitch?" Moiraine said, and Egwene echoed her fervently. "Oh, yes."

"Baths?" the innkeeper said. "Why, just the best and the hottest in Baerlon. Come. Welcome to the Stag and Lion. Welcome to Baerlon."

CHAPTER
14

The Stag and Lion

Inside, the inn was every bit as busy as the sounds coming from it had indicated and more. The party from Emond's Field followed Master Fitch through the back door, soon weaving around and between a constant stream of men and women in long aprons, platters of food and trays of drink held high. The bearers murmured quick apologies when they got in anyone's way, but they never slowed by a step. One of the men took hurried orders from Master Fitch and disappeared at a run.

"The inn is near full, I'm afraid," the innkeeper told Moiraine. "Almost to the rafters. Every inn in the town is the same. With the winter we just had . . . well, as soon as it cleared enough for them to get down out of the mountains we were inundated—yes, that's the word—inundated by men from the mines and smelters, all telling the most horrible tales. Wolves, and worse. The kind of tales men tell when they've been cooped up all winter. I can't think there's anyone left up there at all, we have that many here. But never fear. Things may be a little crowded, but I'll do my best by you and Master Andra. And your friends, too, of course." He glanced curiously once or twice at Rand and the others; except for Thom their clothes named them country folk, and Thom's gleeman's cloak made him a strange traveling companion as well for "Mistress Alys" and "Master Andra." "I will do my best, you may rest assured."

Rand stared at the bustle around them and tried to avoid being stepped on, though none of the help really seemed to be in any danger of that. He kept thinking of how Master al'Vere and his wife tended the Winespring Inn with sometimes a little assistance from their daughters.

Mat and Perrin craned their necks in interest toward the common room, from which rolled a wave of laughter and singing and jovial shouting whenever the wide door at the end of the hall swung open. Muttering about finding out the news, the Warder grimly disappeared through that swinging door, swallowed by a wave of merriment.

Rand wanted to follow him, but he wanted a bath even more. He could have done with people and laughing right then, but the common room would appreciate his presence more when he was clean. Mat and Perrin apparently felt the same; Mat was scratching surreptitiously.

"Master Fitch," Moiraine said, "I understand there are Children of the Light in Baerlon. Is there likely to be trouble?"

"Oh, never you worry about them, Mistress Alys. They're up to their usual tricks. Claim there's an Aes Sedai in the town." Moiraine lifted an eyebrow, and the innkeeper spread his plump hands. "Don't you worry. They've tried it before. There's no Aes Sedai in Baerlon, and the Governor knows it. The Whitecloaks think if they show an Aes Sedai, some woman they claim is an Aes Sedai, people will let all of them inside the walls. Well, I suppose some would. Some would. But most people know what the Whitecloaks are up to, and they support the Governor. No one wants to see some harmless old woman hurt just so the Children can have an excuse for whipping up a frenzy."

"I am glad to hear it," Moiraine said dryly. She put a hand on the innkeeper's arm. "Is Min still here? I wish to talk with her, if she is."

Master Fitch's answer was lost to Rand in the arrival of attendants to lead them to the baths. Moiraine and Egwene vanished behind a plump woman with a ready smile and an armload of towels. The gleeman and Rand and his friends found themselves following a slight, dark-haired fellow, Ara by name.

Rand tried asking Ara about Baerlon, but the man barely

said two words together except to say Rand had a funny accent, and then the first sight of the bath chamber drove all thoughts of talk right out of Rand's head. A dozen tall, copper bathtubs sat in a circle on the tiled floor, which sloped down slightly to a drain in the center of the big stone-walled room. A thick towel, neatly folded, and a large cake of yellow soap sat on a stool behind each tub, and big black iron cauldrons of water stood heating over fires along one wall. On the opposite wall logs blazing in a deep fireplace added to the general warmth.

"Almost as good as the Winespring Inn back home," Perrin said loyally, if not exactly with a great attention to truth.

Thom barked a laugh, and Mat sniggered, "Sounds like we brought a Coplin with us and didn't know it."

Rand shrugged out of his cloak and stripped off his clothes while Ara filled four of the copper tubs. None of the others was far behind Rand in choosing a bathtub. Once their clothes were all in piles on the stools, Ara brought them each a large bucket of hot water and a dipper. That done, he sat on a stool by the door, leaning back against the wall with his arms crossed, apparently lost in his own thoughts.

There was little in the way of conversation while they lathered and sluiced away a week of grime with dippers of steaming water. Then it was into the tubs for a long soak; Ara had made the water hot enough that settling in was a slow process of luxuriant sighs. The air in the room went from warm to misty and hot. For a long time there was no sound except the occasional long, relaxing exhalation as tight muscles loosened and a chill that they had come to think permanent was drawn out of their bones.

"Need anything else?" Ara asked suddenly. He did not have much room to talk about people's accents; he and Master Fitch both sounded as if they had a mouth full of mush. "More towels? More hot water?"

"Nothing," Thom said in his reverberant voice. Eyes closed, he gave an indolent wave of his hand. "Go and enjoy the evening. At a later time I will see that you receive more than adequate recompense for your services." He settled lower in the tub, until the water covered everything but his eyes and nose.

Ara's eyes went to the stools behind the tubs, where their clothes and belongings were stacked. He glanced at the bow, but lingered longest over Rand's sword and Perrin's axe. "Is there trouble downcountry, too?" he said abruptly. "In the Rivers, or whatever you call it?"

"The Two Rivers," Mat said, pronouncing each separate word distinctly. "It's the Two Rivers. As for trouble, why—"

"What do you mean, too?" Rand asked. "Is there some kind of trouble here?"

Perrin, enjoying his soak, murmured, "Good! Good!" Thom raised himself back up a little, and opened his eyes.

"Here?" Ara snorted. "Trouble? Miners having fistfights in the streets in the dark of the morning aren't trouble. Or. . . ." He stopped and eyed them a moment. "I meant the Ghealdan kind of trouble," he said finally. "No, I suppose not. Nothing but sheep downcountry, is there? No offense. I just meant it's quiet down there. Still, it's been a strange winter. Strange things in the mountains. I heard the other day there were Trollocs up in Saldaea. But that's the Borderlands then, isn't it?" He finished with his mouth still open, then snapped it shut, appearing surprised that he had said so much.

Rand had tensed at the word *Trollocs,* and tried to hide it by wringing his washcloth out over his head. As the fellow went on he relaxed, but not everyone kept his mouth shut.

"Trollocs?" Mat chortled. Rand splashed water at him, but Mat just wiped it off of his face with a grin. "You just let me tell you about Trollocs."

For the first time since climbing into his tub, Thom spoke. "Why don't you not? I am a little tired of hearing my own stories back from you."

"He's a gleeman," Perrin said, and Ara gave him a scornful look.

"I saw the cloak. You going to perform?"

"Just a minute," Mat protested. "What's this about me telling Thom's stories? Are you all—?"

"You just don't tell them as well as Thom," Rand cut him off hastily, and Perrin hopped in. "You keep adding in things, trying to make it better, and they never do."

"And you get it all mixed up, too," Rand added. "Best leave it to Thom."

They were all talking so fast that Ara stared at them with his mouth hanging open. Mat stared, too, as if everyone else had suddenly gone crazy. Rand wondered how to shut him up short of jumping on him.

The door banged open to admit Lan, brown cloak slung over one shoulder, along with a gust of cooler air that momentarily thinned the mist.

"Well," the Warder said, rubbing his hands, "this is what I have been waiting for." Ara picked up a bucket, but Lan waved it away. "No, I will see to myself." Dropping his cloak on one of the stools, he bundled the bath attendant out of the room, despite the fellow's protests, and shut the door firmly after him. He waited there a moment, his head cocked to listen, and when he turned back to the rest of them his voice was stony and his eyes stabbed at Mat. "It's a good thing I got back when I did, farmboy. Don't you listen to what you are told?"

"I didn't do anything," Mat protested. "I was just going to tell him about the Trollocs, not about. . . ." He stopped, and leaned back from the Warder's eyes, flat against the back of the tub.

"Don't talk about Trollocs," Lan said grimly. "Don't even think about Trollocs." With an angry snort he began filling himself a bathtub. "Blood and ashes, you had better remember, the Dark One has eyes and ears where you least expect. And if the Children of the Light heard Trollocs were after you, they'd be burning to get their hands on you. To them, it would be as much as naming you Darkfriend. It may not be what you are used to, but until we get where we are going, keep your trust small unless Mistress Alys or I tell you differently." At his emphasis on the name Moiraine was using, Mat flinched.

"There was something that fellow wouldn't tell us," Rand said. "Something he thought was trouble, but he wouldn't say what it was."

"Probably the Children," Lan said, pouring more hot water into his tub. "Most people consider them trouble. Some don't, though, and he did not know you well enough to risk it. You might have gone running to the Whitecloaks, for all he knew."

Rand shook his head; this place already sounded worse than Taren Ferry could possibly be.

"He said there were Trollocs in . . . in Saldaea, wasn't it?" Perrin said.

Lan hurled his empty bucket to the floor with a crash. "You will talk about it, won't you? There are always Trollocs in the Borderlands, blacksmith. Just you put it in the front of your mind that we want no more attention than mice in a field. Concentrate on that. Moiraine wants to get you all to Tar Valon alive, and I will do it if it can be done, but if you bring any harm to her. . . ."

The rest of their bathing was done in silence, and dressing afterwards, too.

When they left the bath chamber, Moiraine was standing at the end of the hall with a slender girl not much taller than herself. At least, Rand thought it was a girl, though her dark hair was cut short and she wore a man's shirt and trousers. Moiraine said something, and the girl looked at the men sharply, then nodded to Moiraine and hurried away.

"Well, now," Moiraine said as they drew closer, "I am sure a bath has given you all an appetite. Master Fitch has given us a private dining room." She talked on inconsequentially as she turned to lead the way, about their rooms and the crowding in the town, and how the innkeeper hoped Thom would favor the common room with some music and a story or two. She never mentioned the girl, if girl it had been.

The private dining room had a polished oak table with a dozen chairs around it, and a thick rug on the floor. As they entered, Egwene, freshly gleaming hair combed out around her shoulders, turned from warming her hands at the fire crackling on the hearth. Rand had had plenty of time for thought during the long silence in the bath chamber. Lan's constant admonitions not to trust anyone, and especially Ara being afraid to trust them, had made him think of just how alone they really were. It seemed they could not trust anyone but themselves, and he was still not too sure how far they could trust Moiraine, or Lan. Just themselves. And Egwene was still Egwene. Moiraine said it would have happened to her anyway, this touching the True Source. She had no control over it, and that meant it was not her fault. And she was still Egwene.

He opened his mouth to apologize, but Egwene stiffened and turned her back before he could get a word out. Staring sullenly at her back, he swallowed what he had been going to say.

All right, then. If she wants to be like that, there's nothing I can do.

Master Fitch bustled in then, followed by four women in white aprons as long as his, with a platter holding three roast chickens and others bearing silver, and pottery dishes, and covered bowls. The women began setting the table immediately, while the innkeeper bowed to Moiraine.

"My apologies, Mistress Alys, for making you wait like this, but with so many people in the inn, it's a wonder anybody gets served at all. I am afraid the food isn't what it should be, either. Just the chickens, and some turnips and henpeas, with a little cheese for after. No, it just isn't what it should be. I truly do apologize."

"A feast." Moiraine smiled. "For these troubled times, a feast indeed, Master Fitch."

The innkeeper bowed again. His wispy hair, sticking out in all directions as if he constantly ran his hands through it, made the bow comical, but his grin was so pleasant that anyone who laughed would be laughing with him, not at him. "My thanks, Mistress Alys. My thanks." As he straightened he frowned and wiped an imagined bit of dust from the table with a corner of his apron. "It isn't what I would have laid before you a year ago, of course. Not nearly. The winter. Yes. The winter. My cellars are emptying out, and the market is all but bare. And who can blame the farm folk? Who? There's certainly no telling when they'll harvest another crop. No telling at all. It's the wolves get the mutton and beef that should go on people's tables, and. . . ."

Abruptly he seemed to realize that this was hardly the conversation to settle his guests to a comfortable meal. "How I do run on. Full of old wind, that's me. Old wind. Mari, Cinda, let these good people eat in peace." He made shooing gestures at the women and, as they scurried from the room, swung back to bow to Moiraine yet again. "I hope you enjoy your meal, Mistress Alys. If there's anything else you need, just speak it, and I will fetch it. Just you speak it. It is a pleasure serving you and Master Andra. A pleasure." He gave one more deep bow and was gone, closing the door softly behind him.

Lan had slouched against the wall through all of this as if half asleep. Now he leaped up and was at the door in two long strides. Pressing an ear to a door panel, he listened intently for a slow count of thirty, then snatched open the door and stuck his head into the hall. "They're gone," he said at last, closing the door. "We can talk safely."

"I know you say not to trust anyone," Egwene said, "but if you suspect the innkeeper, why stay here?"

"I suspect him no more than anyone else," Lan replied. "But then, until we reach Tar Valon, I suspect everyone. There, I'll suspect only half."

Rand started to smile, thinking the Warder was making a joke. Then he realized there was not a trace of humor on Lan's face. He really would suspect people in Tar Valon. Was anywhere safe?

"He exaggerates," Moiraine told them soothingly. "Master Fitch is a good man, honest and trustworthy. But he does like to talk, and with the best will in the world he might let something slip to the wrong ear. And I have never yet stopped at an inn where half the maids did not listen at doors and spend more time gossiping than making beds. Come, let us be seated before our meal gets cold."

They took places around the table, with Moiraine at the head and Lan at the foot, and for a while everyone was too busy filling their plates for talk. It might not have been a feast, but after close to a week of flatbread and dried meat, it tasted like one.

After a time, Moiraine asked, "What did you learn in the common room?" Knives and forks stilled, suspended in midair, and all eyes turned to the Warder.

"Little that's good," Lan replied. "Avin was right, at least as far as talk has it. There was a battle in Ghealdan, and Logain was the victor. A dozen different stories are floating about, but they all agree on that."

Logain? That must be the false Dragon. It was the first time Rand had heard a name put to the man. Lan sounded almost as if he knew him.

"The Aes Sedai?" Moiraine asked quietly, and Lan shook his head.

"I don't know. Some say they were all killed, some say none." He snorted. "Some even say they went over to Logain.

There's nothing reliable, and I did not care to show too much interest."

"Yes," Moiraine said. "Little that is good." With a deep breath she brought her attention back to the table. "And what of our own circumstances?"

"There, the news is better. No odd happenings, no strangers around who might be Myrddraal, certainly no Trollocs. And the Whitecloaks are busy trying to make trouble for Governor Adan because he won't cooperate with them. They will not even notice us unless we advertise ourselves."

"Good," Moiraine said. "That agrees with what the bath maid said. Gossip does have its points. Now," she addressed the entire company, "we have a long journey still ahead of us, but the last week has not been easy, either, so I propose to remain here tonight and tomorrow night, and leave early the following morning." All the younger folk grinned; a city for the first time. Moiraine smiled, but she still said, "What does Master Andra say to that?"

Lan eyed the grinning faces flatly. "Well enough, if they remember what I've told them for a change."

Thom snorted through his mustaches. "These country folk loose in a . . . a city." He snorted again and shook his head.

With the crowding at the inn there were only three rooms to be had, one for Moiraine and Egwene, and two to take the men. Rand found himself sharing with Lan and Thom, on the fourth floor at the back, close up under the overhanging eaves, with a single small window that overlooked the stableyard. Full night had fallen, and light from the inn made a pool outside. It was a small room to begin, and an extra bed set up for Thom made it smaller, though all three were narrow. And hard, Rand found when he threw himself down on his. Definitely not the best room.

Thom stayed only long enough to uncase his flute and harp, then left already practicing grand poses. Lan went with him.

It was strange, Rand thought as he shifted uncomfortably on the bed. A week ago he would have been downstairs like a falling rock for just the chance he might see a gleeman perform, for just the rumor of it. But he had heard Thom tell his stories every night for a week, and Thom would be there tomorrow night, and the next, and the hot bath had loosened kinks in muscles that he had thought would be there forever, and his first hot meal in a week oozed lethargy into him. Sleepily he wondered if Lan really did know the false Dragon, Logain. A muffled shout came from belowstairs, the common room greeting Thom's arrival, but Rand was already asleep.

The stone hallway was dim and shadowy, and empty except for Rand. He could not tell where the light came from, what little there was of it; the gray walls were bare of candles or lamps, nothing at all to account for the faint glow that seemed to just be there. The air was still and dank, and somewhere in the distance water dripped with a steady, hollow plonk. Wherever this was, it was not the inn. Frowning, he rubbed at his forehead. Inn? His head hurt, and thoughts were hard to hold on to. There had been something about . . . an inn? It was gone, whatever it was.

He licked his lips and wished he had something to drink. He was awfully thirsty, dry-as-dust thirsty. It was the dripping sound that decided him. With nothing to choose by except his thirst, he started toward that steady *plonk—plonk—plonk.*

The hallway stretched on, without any crossing corridor and without the slightest change in appearance. The only features at all were the rough doors set at regular intervals in pairs, one on either side of the hall, the wood splintered and dry despite the damp in the air. The shadows receded ahead of him, staying the same, and the dripping never came any closer. After a long time he decided to try one of those doors. It opened easily, and he stepped through into a grim, stone-walled chamber.

One wall opened in a series of arches onto a gray stone balcony, and beyond that was a sky such as he had never seen. Striated clouds in blacks and grays, reds and oranges, streamed by as if storm winds drove them, weaving and interweaving endlessly. *No one* could ever have seen a sky like that; it could not exist.

He pulled his eyes away from the balcony, but the rest of the room was no better. Odd curves and peculiar angles, as if the chamber had been melted almost haphazardly out of the stone, and columns that seemed to grow out of the gray floor. Flames roared on the hearth like a forge-fire with the bellows pumping, but gave no heat. Strange oval stones made the fireplace; they just looked like stones, wet-slick despite the fire, when he looked straight at them, but when he glimpsed them from the corner of his eye they seemed to be faces instead, the faces of men and women writhing in anguish, screaming silently. The high-backed chairs and the polished table in the middle of the room were perfectly ordinary, but that in itself emphasized the rest. A single mirror hung on the wall, but that was not ordinary at all. When he looked at it he saw only a blur where his reflection should have been. Everything else in the room was shown true, but not him.

A man stood in front of the fireplace. He had not noticed the man when he first came in. If he had not known it was impossible, he would have said no one had been there until he actually looked at the man. Dressed in dark clothes of a fine cut, he seemed in the prime of his maturity, and Rand supposed women would have found him good-looking.

"Once more we meet face-to-face," the man said and, just for an instant, his mouth and eyes became openings into endless caverns of flame.

With a yell Rand hurled himself backwards out of the room, so hard that he stumbled across the hall and banged into the door there, knocking it open. He twisted and grabbed at the doorhandle to keep from falling to the floor—and found himself staring wide-eyed into a stone room with an impossible sky through the arches leading to a balcony, and a fireplace. . . .

"You cannot get away from me that easily," the man said.

Rand twisted, scrambling back out of the room, trying to regain his feet without slowing down. This time there was no corridor. He froze half crouched not far from the polished table, and looked at the man by the fireplace. It was better than looking at the fireplace stones, or at the sky.

"This is a dream," he said as he straightened. Behind him he heard the click of the door closing. "It's some kind of nightmare." He shut his eyes, thinking about waking up. When he was a child the Wisdom had said if you could do that in a nightmare, it would go away. *The . . . Wisdom? What?* If only his thoughts would stop sliding away. If only his head would stop hurting, then he could think straight.

He opened his eyes again. The room was still as it had been, the balcony, the sky. The man by the fireplace.

"Is it a dream?" the man said. "Does it matter?" Once again, for a moment, his mouth and eyes became peepholes into a furnace that seemed to stretch forever. His voice did not change; he did not seem to notice it happening at all.

Rand jumped a little this time, but he managed to keep from yelling. *This is a dream. It has to be.* All the same, he stepped backwards all the way to the door, never taking his eyes off the fellow by the fire, and tried the handle. It did not move; the door was locked.

"You seem thirsty," the man by the fire said. "Drink."

On the table was a goblet, shining gold and ornamented with rubies and amethysts. It had not been there before. He wished he could stop jumping. It was only a dream. His mouth felt like dust.

"I am, a little," he said, picking up the goblet. The man leaned forward intently, one hand on the back of a chair, watching him. The smell of spiced wine drove home to Rand just how thirsty he was, as if he had had nothing to drink in days. *Have I?*

With the wine halfway to his mouth, he stopped. Whispers of smoke were rising from the chairback between the man's fingers. And those eyes watched him so sharply, flickering rapidly in and out of flames.

Rand licked his lips and put the wine back on the table, untasted. "I'm not as thirsty as I thought." The man straightened abruptly, his face without expression. His disappointment could not have been more plain if he had cursed. Rand wondered what was in the wine. But that was a stupid question, of course. This was all a dream. *Then why won't it stop?* "What do you want?" he demanded. "Who are you?"

Flames rose in the man's eyes and mouth; Rand thought he could hear them roar. "Some call me Ba'alzamon."

Rand found himself facing the door, jerking frantically at the handle. All thought of dreams had vanished. The Dark One. The doorhandle would not budge, but he kept twisting.

"Are you the one?" Ba'alzamon said suddenly. "You cannot hide it from me forever. You cannot even hide yourself from me, not on the highest mountain or in the deepest cave. I know you down to the smallest hair."

Rand turned to face the man—to face Ba'alzamon. He swallowed hard. A nightmare. He reached back to give the door-handle one last pull, then stood up straighter.

"Are you expecting glory?" Ba'alzamon said. "Power? Did they tell you the Eye of the World would serve you? What glory or power is there for a puppet? The strings that move you have been centuries weaving. Your father was chosen by the White Tower, like a stallion roped and led to his business. Your mother was no more than a brood mare to their plans. And those plans lead to your death."

Rand's hands knotted in fists. "My father is a good man, and my mother was a good woman. Don't you talk about them!"

The flames laughed. "So there is some spirit in you after all. Perhaps you *are* the one. Little good it will do you. The Amyrlin Seat will use you until you are consumed, just as Davian was used, and Yurian Stonebow, and Guaire Amalasan, and Raolin Darksbane. Just as Logain is being used. Used until there is nothing left of you."

"I don't know. . . ." Rand swung his head from side to side. That one moment of clear thinking, born in anger, was gone. Even as he groped for it again he could not remember how he had reached it the first time. His thoughts spun around and around. He seized one like a raft in the whirlpool. He forced the words out, his voice strengthening the further he went. "You . . . are bound . . . in Shayol Ghul. You and all the Forsaken . . . bound by the Creator until the end of time."

"The end of time?" Ba'alzamon mocked. "You live like a beetle under a rock, and you think your slime is the universe. The death of time will bring me power such as you could not dream of, worm."

"You are bound—"

"Fool, I have never been bound!" The fires of his face roared so hot that Rand stepped back, sheltering behind his hands. The sweat on his palms dried from the heat. "I stood at Lews Therin Kinslayer's shoulder when he did the deed that named him. It was I who told him to kill his wife, and his children, and all his blood, and every living person who loved him or whom he loved. It was I who gave him the moment of sanity to know what he had done. Have you ever heard a man scream his soul away, worm? He could have struck at me, then. He could not have won, but he could have tried. Instead he called down his precious One Power upon himself, so much that the earth split open and reared up Dragonmount to mark his tomb.

"A thousand years later I sent the Trollocs ravening south, and for three centuries they savaged the world. Those blind fools in Tar Valon said I was beaten in the end, but the Second Covenant, the Covenant of the Ten Nations, was shattered beyond remaking, and who was left to oppose me then? I whispered in Artur Hawkwing's ear, and the length and breadth of the land Aes Sedai died. I whispered again, and the High King sent his armies across the Aryth Ocean, across the World Sea, and sealed two dooms. The doom of his dream of one land and one people, and a doom yet to come. At his deathbed I was there when his councilors told him only Aes Sedai could save his life. I spoke, and he ordered his councilors to the stake. I spoke, and the High King's last words were to cry that Tar Valon must be destroyed.

"When men such as these could not stand against me, what chance do you have, a toad crouching beside a forest puddle. You will serve me, or you will dance on Aes Sedai strings until you die. And then you *will* be mine. The dead belong to me!"

"No," Rand muttered, "this is a dream. It is a dream!"

"Do you think you are safe from me in your dreams? Look!" Ba'alzamon pointed commandingly, and Rand's head turned to follow, although he did not turn it; he did not want to turn.

The goblet was gone from the table. Where it had been, crouched a large rat, blinking at the light, sniffing the air warily. Ba'alzamon crooked his finger, and with a squeak the rat arched its back, forepaws lifting into the air while it balanced awkwardly on its hind feet. The finger curved more, and the rat toppled over, scrabbling frantically, pawing at nothing, squealing shrilly, its back bending, bending, bending. With a sharp snap like the breaking of a twig, the rat trembled violently and was still, lying bent almost double.

Rand swallowed. "Anything can happen in a dream," he mumbled. Without looking he swung his fist back against the door again. His hand hurt, but he still did not wake up.

"Then go to the Aes Sedai. Go to the White Tower and tell them. Tell the Amyrlin Seat of this . . . dream." The man laughed; Rand felt the heat of the flames on his face. "That is one way to escape them. They will not use you, then. No, not

when they know that I know. But will they let you live, to
spread the tale of what they do? Are you a big enough fool to
believe they will? The ashes of many like you are scattered on
the slopes of Dragonmount."

"This is a dream," Rand said, panting. "It's a dream, and I
am going to wake up."

"Will you?" Out of the corner of his eye he saw the man's
finger move to point at him. "Will you, indeed?" The finger
crooked, and Rand screamed as he arched backwards, every
muscle in his body forcing him further. "Will you ever wake
again?"

*   *   *

Convulsively Rand jerked up in the darkness, his hands tightening on cloth. A blanket. Pale moonlight shone through the
single window. The shadowed shapes of the other two beds. A
snore from one of them, like canvas ripping: Thom Merrilin. A
few coals gleamed among the ashes on the hearth.

It had been a dream, then, like that nightmare in the Winespring Inn the day of Bel Tine, everything that he had heard
and done all jumbled in together with old tales and nonsense
from nowhere. He pulled the blanket up around his shoulders,
but it was not cold that made him shake. His head hurt, too.
Perhaps Moiraine could do something to stop these dreams.
She said she could help with nightmares.

With a snort he lay back. Were the dreams really bad enough
for him to ask the help of an Aes Sedai? On the other hand,
could anything he did now get him in any deeper? He had left
the Two Rivers, come away with an Aes Sedai. But there had
not been any choice, of course. So did he have any choice but
to trust her? An Aes Sedai? It was as bad as the dreams, thinking about it. He huddled under his blanket, trying to find the
calmness of the void the way Tam had taught him, but sleep
was a long time returning.

CHAPTER
15

Strangers and Friends

S unlight streaming across his narrow bed finally woke
Rand out of a deep but restless sleep. He pulled a pillow
over his head, but it did not really shut out the light, and
he did not really want to go back to sleep. There had been
more dreams after the first. He could not remember any but
the first, but he knew he wanted no more.

With a sigh he tossed the pillow aside and sat up, wincing as
he stretched. All the aches he thought had soaked out in the
bath were back. And his head still hurt, too. It did not surprise
him. A dream like that was enough to give anybody a head-
ache. The others had already faded, but not that one.

The other beds were empty. Light poured in through the
window at a steep angle; the sun stood well above the horizon.
By this hour back on the farm he would have already fixed
something to eat and been well into his chores. He scrambled
out of bed, muttering angrily to himself. A city to see, and they
did not even wake him. At least someone had seen that there
was water in the pitcher, and still warm, too.

He washed and dressed quickly, hesitating a moment over
Tam's sword. Lan and Thom had left their saddlebags and
blanketrolls behind in the room, of course, but the Warder's
sword was nowhere to be seen. Lan had worn his sword in
Emond's Field even before there was any hint of trouble. He
thought he would take the older man's lead. Telling himself it
was not because he had often daydreamed about walking the

streets of a real city wearing a sword, he belted it on and tossed his cloak over his shoulder like a sack.

Taking the stairs two at a time, he hurried down to the kitchen. That was surely the quickest place to get a bite, and on his only day in Baerlon he did not want to waste any more time than he already had. *Blood and ashes, but they could have waked me.*

Master Fitch was in the kitchen, confronting a plump woman whose arms were covered in flour to her elbows, obviously the cook. Rather, she was confronting him, shaking her finger under his nose. Serving maids and scullions, potboys and spitboys, hurried about their tasks, elaborately ignoring what was going on in front of them.

". . . my Cirri is a good cat," the cook was saying sharply, "and I won't hear a word otherwise, do you hear? Complaining about him doing his job too well, that's what you're doing, if you ask me."

"I have had complaints," Master Fitch managed to get in. "Complaints, mistress. Half the guests—"

"I won't hear of it. I just won't hear of it. If they want to complain about my cat, let *them* do the cooking. My poor old cat, who's just doing his job, and me, we'll go somewhere where we're appreciated, see if we don't." She untied her apron and started to lift it over her head.

"No!" Master Fitch yelped, and leaped to stop her. They danced in a circle with the cook trying to take her apron off and the innkeeper trying to put it back on her. "No, Sara," he panted. "There's no need for this. No need, I say! What would I do without you? Cirri's a fine cat. An excellent cat. He's the best cat in Baerlon. If anyone else complains, I'll tell them to be thankful the cat is doing his job. Yes, thankful. You mustn't go. Sara? Sara!"

The cook stopped their circling and managed to snatch her apron free of him. "All right, then. All right." Clutching the apron in both hands, she still did not retie it. "But if you expect me to have anything ready for midday, you'd best get out of here and let me get to it. This may be your inn, but it's my kitchen. Unless you want to do the cooking?" She made as if to hand the apron to him.

Master Fitch stepped back with his hands spread wide. He

opened his mouth, then stopped, looking around for the first time. The kitchen help still studiously ignored the cook and the innkeeper, and Rand began an intensive search of his coat pockets, though except for the coin Moiraine had given him there was nothing in them but a few coppers and a handful of odds and ends. His pocket knife and sharpening stone. Two spare bowstrings and a piece of string he had thought might be useful.

"I am sure, Sara," Master Fitch said carefully, "that everything will be up to your usual excellence." With that he took one last suspicious look at the kitchen help, then left with as much dignity as he could manage.

Sara waited until he was gone before briskly tying her apron strings again, then fastened her eye on Rand. "I suppose you want something to eat, eh? Well, come on in." She gave him a quick grin. "I don't bite, I don't, no matter what you may have seen as you shouldn't. Ciel, get the lad some bread and cheese and milk. That's all there is right now. Sit yourself, lad. Your friends have all gone out, except one lad I understand wasn't feeling well, and I expect you'll be wanting to do the same."

One of the serving maids brought a tray while Rand took a stool at the table. He began eating as the cook went back to kneading her bread dough, but she was not finished talking.

"You mustn't take any mind of what you saw, now. Master Fitch is a good enough man, though the best of you aren't any bargains. It's the folk complaining as has him on edge, and what do they have to complain about? Would they rather find live rats than dead ones? Though it isn't like Cirri to leave his handiwork behind. And over a dozen? Cirri wouldn't let so many get into the inn, he wouldn't. It's a clean place, too, and not one to be so troubled. And all with backs broken." She shook her head at the strangeness of it all.

The bread and cheese turned to ashes in Rand's mouth. "Their backs were broken?"

The cook waved a floury hand. "Think on happier things, that's my way of looking. There's a gleeman, you know. In the common room right this minute. But then, you came with him, didn't you? You are one of those as came with Mistress Alys last evening, aren't you? I thought you were. I won't get much chance to see this gleeman myself, I'm thinking, not with the inn as full as it is, and most of them riffraff down from the mines." She gave the dough an especially heavy thump. "Not the sort we'd let in most times, only the whole town is filled up with them. Better than some they could be, though, I suppose. Why, I haven't seen ·a gleeman since before the winter, and. . . ."

Rand ate mechanically, not tasting anything, not listening to what the cook said. Dead rats, with their backs broken. He finished his breakfast hastily, stammered his thanks, and hurried out. He had to talk to someone.

The common room of the Stag and Lion shared little except its purpose with the same room at the Winespring Inn. It was twice as wide and three times as long, and colorful pictures of ornate buildings with gardens of tall trees and bright flowers were painted high on the walls. Instead of one huge fireplace, a hearth blazed on each wall, and scores of tables filled the floor, with almost every chair, bench, or stool taken.

Every man among the crowd of patrons with pipes in their teeth and mugs in their fists leaned forward with his attention on one thing: Thom, standing atop a table in the middle of the room, his many-colored cloak tossed over a nearby chair. Even Master Fitch held a silver tankard and a polishing cloth in motionless hands.

". . . prancing, silver hooves and proud, arched necks," Thom proclaimed, while somehow seeming not only to be riding a horse, but to be one of a long procession of riders. "Silken manes flutter with tossed heads. A thousand streaming banners whip rainbows against an endless sky. A hundred brazen-throated trumpets shiver the air, and drums rattle like thunder. Wave on wave, cheers roll from watchers in their thousands, roll across the rooftops and towers of Illian, crash and break unheard around the thousand ears of riders whose eyes and hearts shine with their sacred quest. The Great Hunt of the Horn rides forth, rides to seek the Horn of Valere that will summon the heroes of the Ages back from the grave to battle for the Light. . . ."

It was what the gleeman had called Plain Chant, those nights beside the fire on the ride north. Stories, he said, were told in three voices, High Chant, Plain Chant, and Common, which meant simply telling it the way you might tell your neighbor about your crop. Thom told stories in Common, but he did not bother to hide his contempt for the voice.

Rand closed the door without going in and slumped against the wall. He would get no advice from Thom. Moiraine—what *would* she do if she knew?

He became aware of people staring at him as they passed, and realized he was muttering under his breath. Smoothing his coat, he straightened. He had to talk to somebody. The cook had said one of the others had not gone out. It was an effort not to run.

When he rapped on the door of the room where the other boys had slept and poked his head in, only Perrin was there, lying on his bed and still not dressed. He twisted his head on the pillow to look at Rand, then closed his eyes again. Mat's bow and quiver were propped in the corner.

"I heard you weren't feeling well," Rand said. He came in and sat on the next bed. "I just wanted to talk. I. . . ." He did not know how to bring it up, he realized. "If you're sick," he said, half standing, "maybe you ought to sleep. I can go."

"I don't know if I'll ever sleep again." Perrin sighed. "I had a bad dream, if you must know, and couldn't get back to sleep. Mat will be quick enough to tell you. He laughed this morning, when I told them why I was too tired to go out with him, but he dreamed, too. I listened to him for most of the night, tossing and muttering, and you can't tell me he got a good night's sleep." He threw a thick arm across his eyes. "Light, but I'm tired. Maybe if I just stay here for an hour or two, I'll feel like getting up. Mat will never let me hear the end of it if I miss seeing Baerlon because of a dream."

Rand slowly lowered himself to the bed again. He licked his lips, then said quickly, "Did he kill a rat?"

Perrin lowered his arm and stared at him. "You, too?" he said finally. When Rand nodded, he said, "I wish I was back home. He told me . . . he said. . . . What are we going to do? Have you told Moiraine?"

"No. Not yet. Maybe I won't. I don't know. What about you?"

"He said. . . . Blood and ashes, Rand, I don't know." Perrin raised up on his elbow abruptly. "Do you think Mat had the same dream? He laughed, but it sounded forced, and he looked funny when I said I couldn't sleep because of a dream."

"Maybe he did," Rand said. Guiltily, he felt relieved he was not the only one. "I was going to ask Thom for advice. He's seen a lot of the world. You . . . you don't think we should tell Moiraine, do you?"

Perrin fell back on his pillow. "You've heard the stories about Aes Sedai. Do you think we can trust Thom? If we can trust anybody. Rand, if we get out of this alive, if we ever get back home, and you hear me say anything about leaving Emond's Field, even to go as far as Watch Hill, you kick me. All right?"

"That's no way to talk," Rand said. He put on a smile, as cheerful as he could make it. "Of course we'll get home. Come on, get up. We're in a city, and we have a whole day to see it. Where are your clothes?"

"You go. I just want to lie here awhile." Perrin put his arm back across his eyes. "You go ahead. I'll catch you up in an hour or two."

"It's your loss," Rand said as he got up. "Think of what you might miss." He stopped at the door. "Baerlon. How many times have we talked about seeing Baerlon one day?" Perrin lay there with his eyes covered and did not say a word. After a minute Rand stepped out and closed the door behind him.

In the hallway he leaned against the wall, his smile fading. His head still hurt; it was worse, not better. He could not work up much enthusiasm for Baerlon, either, not now. He could not summon enthusiasm about anything.

A chambermaid came by, her arms full of sheets, and gave him a concerned look. Before she could speak he moved off down the hall, shrugging into his cloak. Thom would not be finished in the common room for hours yet. He might as well see what he could. Perhaps he could find Mat, and see if Ba'alzamon had been in his dreams, too. He went downstairs more slowly this time, rubbing his temple.

The stairs ended near the kitchen, so he took that way out, nodding to Sara but hurrying on when she seemed about to take up where she had left off. The stableyard was empty except for Mutch, standing in the stable door, and one of the other ostlers carrying a sack on his shoulder into the stable.

Rand nodded to Mutch, too, but the stableman gave him a tru-
culent look and went inside. He hoped the rest of the city was
more like Sara and less like Mutch. Ready to see what a city
was like, he picked up his step.

At the open stableyard gates, he stopped and stared. People
packed the street like sheep in a pen, people swathed to the
eyes in cloaks and coats, hats pulled down against the cold,
weaving in and out at a quick step as though the wind whistling
over the rooftops blew them along, elbowing past one another
with barely a word or a glance. *All strangers,* he thought. *None
of them know each other.*

The smells were strange, too, sharp and sour and sweet all
mixed in a hodgepodge that had him rubbing his nose. Even at
the height of Festival he had never seen so many people so
jammed together. Not even half so many. And this was only
one street. Master Fitch and the cook said the whole city was
full. The whole city . . . like this?

He backed slowly away from the gate, away from the street
full of people. It really was not right to go off and leave Perrin
sick in bed. And what if Thom finished his storytelling while
Rand was off in the city? The gleeman might go out himself,
and Rand needed to talk to someone. Much better to wait a
bit. He breathed a sigh of relief as he turned his back on the
swarming street.

Going back inside the inn did not appeal to him, though, not
with his headache. He sat on an upended barrel against the
back of the inn and hoped the cold air might help his head.

Mutch came to the stable door from time to time to stare at
him, and even across the stableyard he could make out the fellow's disapproving scowl. Was it country people the man did
not like? Or had he been embarrassed by Master Fitch greeting
them after he had tried to chase them off for coming in the
back way? *Maybe he's a Darkfriend,* he thought, expecting to
chuckle at the idea, but it was not a funny thought. He rubbed
his hand along the hilt of Tam's sword. There was not much left
that was funny at all.

"A shepherd with a heron-mark sword," said a low, woman's
voice. "That's almost enough to make me believe anything.
What trouble are you in, downcountry boy?"

Startled, Rand jumped to his feet. It was the crop-haired

young woman who had been with Moiraine when he came out
of the bath chamber, still dressed in a boy's coat and breeches.
She was a little older than he was, he thought, with dark eyes
even bigger than Egwene's, and oddly intent.

"You are Rand, aren't you?" she went on. "My name is
Min."

"I'm not in trouble," he said. He did not know what
Moiraine had told her, but he remembered Lan's admonition
not to attract any notice. "What makes you think I'm in trouble? The Two Rivers is a quiet place, and we're all quiet people. No place for trouble, unless it has to do with crops, or
sheep."

"Quiet?" Min said with a faint smile. "I've heard men talk
about you Two Rivers folk. I've heard the jokes about wooden-
headed sheepherders, and then there are men who have actually been downcountry."

"Wooden-headed?" Rand said, frowning. "What jokes?"

"The ones who know," she went on as if he had not spoken,
"say you walk around all smiles and politeness, just as meek
and soft as butter. On the surface, anyway. Underneath, they
say, you're all as tough as old oak roots. Prod too hard, they
say, and you dig up stone. But the stone isn't buried very deep
in you, or in your friends. It's as if a storm has scoured away
almost all the covering. Moiraine didn't tell me everything, but
I see what I see."

Old oak roots? Stone? It hardly sounded like the sort of
thing the merchants or their people would say. That last made
him jump, though.

He looked around quickly; the stableyard was empty, and
the nearest windows were closed. "I don't know anybody
named—what was it again?"

"Mistress Alys, then, if you prefer," Min said with an
amused look that made his cheeks color. "There's no one close
enough to hear."

"What makes you think Mistress Alys has another name?"

"Because she told me," Min said, so patiently that he
blushed again. "Not that she had a choice, I suppose. I saw she
was . . . different . . . right away. When she stopped here before, on her way downcountry. She knew about me. I've talked
to . . . others like her before."

"'Saw'?" Rand said.

"Well, I don't suppose you'll go running to the Children. Not considering who your traveling companions are. The White-cloaks wouldn't like what I do any more than they like what she does."

"I don't understand."

"She says I see pieces of the Pattern." Min gave a little laugh and shook her head. "Sounds too grand, to me. I just see things when I look at people, and sometimes I know what they mean. I look at a man and a woman who've never even talked to one another, and I know they'll marry. And they do. That sort of thing. She wanted me to look at you. All of you to-gether."

Rand shivered. "And what did you see?"

"When you're all in a group? Sparks swirling around you, thousands of them, and a big shadow, darker than midnight. It's so strong, I almost wonder why everybody can't see it. The sparks are trying to fill the shadow, and the shadow is trying to swallow the sparks." She shrugged. "You are all tied together in something dangerous, but I can't make any more of it."

"All of us?" Rand muttered. "Egwene, too? But they weren't after—I mean—"

Min did not seem to notice his slip. "The girl? She's part of it. And the gleeman. All of you. You're in love with her." He stared at her. "I can tell that even without seeing any images. She loves you, too, but she's not for you, or you for her. Not the way you both want."

"What's that supposed to mean?"

"When I look at her, I see the same as when I look at . . . Mistress Alys. Other things, things I don't understand, too, but I know what *that* means. She won't refuse it."

"This is all foolishness," Rand said uncomfortably. His head-ache was fading to numbness; his head felt packed with wool. He wanted to get away from this girl and the things she saw. And yet. . . . "What do you see when you look at . . . the rest of us?"

"All sorts of things," Min said, with a grin as if she knew what he really wanted to ask. "The War . . . ah . . . Master Andra has seven ruined towers around his head, and a babe in a cradle holding a sword, and. . . ." She shook her head. "Men like him—you understand?—always have so many images they crowd one another. The strongest images around the gleeman are a man—not him—juggling fire, and the White Tower, and that doesn't make any sense at all for a man. The strongest things I see about the big, curly-haired fellow are a wolf, and a broken crown, and trees flowering all around him. And the other one—a red eagle, an eye on a balance scale, a dagger with a ruby, a horn, and a laughing face. There are other things, but you see what I mean. This time I can't make up or down out of any of it." She waited then, still grinning, until he finally cleared his throat and asked.

"What about me?"

Her grin stopped just short of outright laughter. "The same kind of things as the rest. A sword that isn't a sword, a golden crown of laurel leaves, a beggar's staff, you pouring water on sand, a bloody hand and a white-hot iron, three women standing over a funeral bier with you on it, black rock wet with blood—"

"All right," he broke in uneasily. "You don't have to list it all."

"Most of all, I see lightning around you, some striking at you, some coming out of you. I don't know what any of it means, except for one thing. You and I will meet again." She gave him a quizzical look, as if she did not understand that either.

"Why shouldn't we?" he said. "I'll be coming back this way on my way home."

"I suppose you will, at that." Suddenly her grin was back, wry and mysterious, and she patted his cheek. "But if I told you everything I saw, you'd be as curly-haired as your friend with the shoulders."

He jerked back from her hand as if it were red-hot. "What do you mean? Do you see anything about rats? Or dreams?"

"Rats! No, no rats. As for dreams, maybe it's your idea of a dream, but I never thought it was mine."

He wondered if she was crazy, grinning like that. "I have to go," he said, edging around her. "I . . . I have to meet my friends."

"Go, then. But you won't escape."

He didn't exactly break into a run, but every step he took was quicker than the step before.

"Run, if you want," she called after him. "You can't escape from me."

Her laughter sped him across the stableyard and out into the street, into the hubbub of people. Her last words were too close to what Ba'alzamon had said. He blundered into people as he hurried through the crowd, earning hard looks and hard words, but he did not slow down until he was several streets away from the inn.

After a time he began to pay attention again to where he was. His head felt like a balloon, but he stared and enjoyed anyway. He thought Baerlon was a grand city, if not exactly in the same way as cities in Thom's stories. He wandered up broad streets, most paved with flagstone, and down narrow, twisting lanes, wherever chance and the shifting of the crowd took him. It had rained during the night, and the streets that were unpaved had already been churned to mud by the crowds, but muddy streets were nothing new to him. None of the streets in Emond's Field was paved.

There certainly were no palaces, and only a few houses were very much bigger than those back home, but every house had a roof of slate or tile as fine as the roof of the Winespring Inn. He supposed there would be a palace or two in Caemlyn. As for inns, he counted nine, not one smaller than the Winespring and most as large as the Stag and Lion, and there were plenty of streets he had not seen yet.

Shops dotted every street, with awnings out front sheltering tables covered with goods, everything from cloth to books to pots to boots. It was as if a hundred peddlers' wagons had spilled out their contents. He stared so much that more than once he had to hurry on at the suspicious look of a shopkeeper. He had not understood the first shopkeeper's stare. When he did understand, he started to get angry until he remembered that here he was the stranger. He could not have bought much, anyway. He gasped when he saw how many coppers were exchanged for a dozen discolored apples or a handful of shriveled turnips, the sort that would be fed to the horses in the Two Rivers, but people seemed eager to pay.

There were certainly more than enough people, to his estimation. For a while the sheer number of them almost overwhelmed him. Some wore clothes of finer cut than anyone in the Two Rivers—almost as fine as Moiraine's—and quite a few had long, fur-lined coats that flapped around their ankles. The miners everybody at the inn kept talking about, they had the hunched look of men who grubbed underground. But most of the people did not look any different from those he had grown up with, not in dress or in face. He had expected they would, somehow. Indeed, some of them had so much the look of the Two Rivers in their faces that he could imagine they belonged to one family or another that he knew around Emond's Field. A toothless, gray-haired fellow with ears like jug handles, sitting on a bench outside one of the inns and peering mournfully into an empty tankard, could easily have been Bili Congar's close cousin. The lantern-jawed tailor sewing in front of his shop might have been Jon Thane's brother, even to the same bald spot on the back of his head. A near mirror image of Samel Crawe pushed past Rand as he turned a corner, and. . . .

In disbelief he stared at a bony little man with long arms and a big nose, shoving hurriedly through the crowd in clothes that looked like a bundle of rags. The man's eyes were sunken and his dirty face gaunt, as if he had not eaten or slept in days, but Rand could swear. . . . The ragged man saw him then, and froze in mid-step, heedless of people who all but stumbled over him. The last doubt in Rand's mind vanished.

"Master Fain!" he shouted. "We all thought you were—"

As quick as a blink the peddler darted away, but Rand dodged after him, calling apologies over his shoulder to the people he bumped. Through the crowd he just caught sight of Fain dashing into an alleyway, and he turned after.

A few steps into the alleyway the peddler had stopped in his tracks. A tall fence made it into a dead end. As Rand skidded to a halt, Fain rounded on him, crouching warily and backing away. He flapped grimy hands at Rand to stay back. More than one rip showed in his coat, and his cloak was worn and tattered as if it had seen much harder use than it was meant for.

"Master Fain?" Rand said hesitantly. "What is the matter? It's me, Rand al'Thor, from Emond's Field. We all thought the Trollocs had taken you."

Fain gestured sharply and, still in a crouch, ran a few crabbed steps toward the open end of the alley. He did not try to pass

Rand, or even come close to him. "Don't!" he rasped. His head
shifted constantly as he tried to see everything in the street beyond
Rand. "Don't mention"—his voice dropped to a hoarse whisper,
and he turned his head away, watching Rand with quick, sidelong
glances—"*them*. There be Whitecloaks in the town."

"They have no reason to bother us," Rand said. "Come back
to the Stag and Lion with me. I'm staying there with friends.
You know most of them. They'll be glad to see you. We all
thought you were dead."

"Dead?" the peddler snapped indignantly. "Not Padan Fain.
Padan Fain knows which way to jump and where to land." He
straightened his rags as if they were feastday clothes. "Always
have, and always will. I'll live a long time. Longer than—"
Abruptly his face tightened and his hands clutched hold of his
coat front. "They burned my wagon, and all my goods. Had no
cause to be doing that, did they? I couldn't get to my horses.
My horses, but that fat old innkeeper had them locked up in his
stable. I had to step quick not to get my throat slit, and what
did it get me? All that I've got left is what I stand up in. Now,
is that fair? Is it, now?"

"Your horses are safe in Master al'Vere's stable. You can get
them anytime. If you come to the inn with me, I'm sure
Moiraine will help you get back to the Two Rivers."

"Aaaaah! She's . . . she's the Aes Sedai, is she?" A guarded
look came over Fain's face. "Maybe, though. . . ." He paused,
licking his lips nervously. "How long will you be at this—What
was it? What did you call it?—the Stag and Lion?"

"We leave tomorrow," Rand said. "But what does that have
to do with—?"

"You just don't know," Fain whined, "standing there with a
full belly and a good night's sleep in a soft bed. I've hardly slept a
wink since that night. My boots are all worn out with running,
and as for what I've had to eat. . . ." His face twisted. "I don't
want to be within miles of an Aes Sedai," he spat the last words,
"not miles and miles, but I may have to. I've no choice, have I?
The thought of her eyes on me, of her even knowing where I
am. . . ." He reached toward Rand as if he wanted to grab his
coat, but his hands stopped short, fluttering, and he actually took
a step back. "Promise me you won't tell her. She frightens me.

There's no need to be telling her, no reason for an Aes Sedai to even be knowing I'm alive. You have to promise. You have to!"

"I promise," Rand said soothingly. "But there's no reason for you to be afraid of her. Come with me. The least you'll get is a hot meal."

"Maybe. Maybe." Fain rubbed his chin pensively. "Tomorrow, you say? In that time. . . . You won't forget your promise? You won't be letting her . . . ?"

"I won't let her hurt you," Rand said, wondering how he could stop an Aes Sedai, whatever she wanted to do.

"She won't hurt me," Fain said. "No, she won't. I won't be letting her." Like a flash he hared past Rand into the crowd.

"Master Fain!" Rand called. "Wait!"

He dashed out of the alley just in time to catch sight of a ragged coat disappearing around the next corner. Still calling, he ran after it, darted around the corner. He only had time to see a man's back before he crashed into it and they both went down in a heap in the mud.

"Can't you watch where you're going?" came a mutter from under him, and Rand scrambled up in surprise.

"Mat?"

Mat sat up with a baleful glare and began scraping mud off his cloak with his hands. "You must really be turning into a city man. Sleep all morning and run right over people." Climbing to his feet, he stared at his muddy hands, then muttered and wiped them off on his cloak. "Listen, you'll never guess who I thought I just saw."

"Padan Fain," Rand said.

"Padan Fa— How did you know?"

"I was talking to him, but he ran off."

"So the Tro—" Mat stopped to look around warily, but the crowd was passing them by with never a glance. Rand was glad he had learned a little caution. "So they didn't get him. I wonder why he left Emond's Field, without a word like that? Probably started running then, too, and didn't stop until he got here. But why was he running just now?"

Rand shook his head and wished he had not. It felt as though it might fall off. "I don't know, except that he's afraid of M . . . Mistress Alys." All this watching what you said was not easy.

"He doesn't want her to know he's here. He made me promise I wouldn't tell her."

"Well, his secret is safe with me," Mat said. "I wish she didn't know where I was, either."

"Mat?" People still streamed by without paying them any heed, but Rand lowered his voice anyway, and leaned closer. "Mat, did you have a nightmare last night? About a man who killed a rat?"

Mat stared at him without blinking. "You, too?" he said finally. "And Perrin, I suppose. I almost asked him this morning, but. . . . He must have. Blood and ashes! Now somebody's making us dream things. Rand, I wish *nobody* knew where I was."

"There were dead rats all over the inn this morning." He did not feel as afraid at saying it as he would have earlier. He did not feel much of anything. "Their backs were broken." His voice rang in his own ears. If he was getting sick, he might have to go to Moiraine. He was surprised that even the thought of the One Power being used on him did not bother him.

Mat took a deep breath, hitching his cloak, and looked around as if searching for somewhere to go. "What's happening to us, Rand? What?"

"I don't know. I'm going to ask Thom for advice. About whether to tell . . . anyone else."

"No! Not her. Maybe him, but not her."

The sharpness of it took Rand by surprise. "Then you believed him?" He did not need to say which "him" he meant; the grimace on Mat's face said he understood.

"No," Mat said slowly. "It's the chances, that's all. If we tell her, and he was lying, then maybe nothing happens. Maybe. But maybe just him being in our dreams is enough for. . . . I don't know." He stopped to swallow. "If we don't tell her, maybe we'll have some more dreams. Rats or no rats, dreams are better than. . . . Remember the ferry? I say we keep quiet."

"All right." Rand remembered the ferry—and Moiraine's threat, too—but somehow it seemed a long time ago. "All right."

"Perrin won't say anything, will he?" Mat went on, bouncing on his toes. "We have to get back to him. If he tells her, she'll figure it out about all of us. You can bet on it. Come on." He started off briskly through the crowd.

Rand stood there looking after him until Mat came back and grabbed him. At the touch on his arm he blinked, then followed his friend.

"What's the matter with you?" Mat asked. "You going to sleep again?"

"I think I have a cold," Rand said. His head was as tight as a drum, and almost as empty.

"You can get some chicken soup when we get back to the inn," Mat said. He kept up a constant chatter as they hunted through the packed streets. Rand made an effort to listen, and even to say something now and then, but it *was* an effort. He was not tired; he did not want to sleep. He just felt as if he were drifting. After a while he found himself telling Mat about Min.

"A dagger with a ruby, eh?" Mat said. "I like that. I don't know about the eye, though. Are you sure she wasn't making it up? It seems to me she would know what it all means if she really is a soothsayer."

"She didn't say she's a soothsayer," Rand said. "I believe she does see things. Remember, Moiraine was talking to her when we finished our baths. And she knows who Moiraine is."

Mat frowned at him. "I thought we weren't supposed to use that name."

"No," Rand muttered. He rubbed his head with both hands. It was so hard to concentrate on anything.

"I think maybe you really are sick," Mat said, still frowning. Suddenly he pulled Rand to a stop by his coat sleeve. "Look at them."

Three men in breastplates and conical steel caps, burnished till they shone like silver, were making their way down the street toward Rand and Mat. Even the mail on their arms gleamed. Their long cloaks, pristine white and embroidered on the left breast with a golden sunburst, just cleared the mud and puddles of the street. Their hands rested on their sword hilts, and they looked around them as if looking at things that had wriggled out from under a rotting log. Nobody looked back, though. Nobody even seemed to notice them. Just the same, the three did not have to push through the crowd; the bustle parted to either side of the white-cloaked men as if by happenstance, leaving them to walk in a clear space that moved with them.

"Do you suppose they're Children of the Light?" Mat asked

in a loud voice. A passerby looked hard at Mat, then quickened his pace.

Rand nodded. Children of the Light. Whitecloaks. Men who hated Aes Sedai. Men who told people how to live, causing trouble for those who refused to obey. If burned farms and worse could be called as mild as trouble. *I should be afraid,* he thought. *Or curious.* Something, at any rate. Instead he stared at them passively.

"They don't look like so much to me," Mat said. "Full of themselves, though, aren't they?"

"They don't matter," Rand said. "The inn. We have to talk to Perrin."

"Like Eward Congar. He always has his nose in the air, too." Suddenly Mat grinned, a twinkle in his eye. "Remember when he fell off the Wagon Bridge and had to tramp home dripping wet? That took him down a peg for a month."

"What does that have to do with Perrin?"

"See that?" Mat pointed to a cart resting on its shafts in an alleyway just ahead of the Children. A single stake held a dozen stacked barrels in place on the flat bed. "Watch." Laughing, he darted into a cutler's shop to their left.

Rand stared after him, knowing he should do something. That look in Mat's eyes always meant one of his tricks. But oddly, he found himself looking forward to whatever Mat was going to do. Something told him that feeling was wrong, that it was dangerous, but he smiled in anticipation anyway.

In a minute Mat appeared above him, climbing half out of an attic window onto the tile roof of the shop. His sling was in his hands, already beginning to whirl. Rand's eyes went back to the cart. Almost immediately there was a sharp crack, and the stake holding the barrels broke just as the Whitecloaks came abreast of the alley. People jumped out of the way as the barrels rolled down the cart shafts with an empty rumble and jounced into the street, splashing mud and muddy water in every direction. The three Children jumped no less quickly than anyone else, their superior looks replaced by surprise. Some passersby fell down, making more splashes, but the three moved agilely, avoiding the barrels with ease. They could not avoid the flying mud that splattered their white cloaks, though.

A bearded man in a long apron hurried out of the alley, waving his arms and shouting angrily, but one look at the three trying vainly to shake the mud from their cloaks and he vanished back into the alley even faster than he had come out. Rand glanced up at the shop roof; Mat was gone. It had been an easy shot for any Two Rivers lad, but the effect was certainly all that could be hoped for. He could not help laughing; the humor seemed to be wrapped in wool, but it was still funny. When he turned back to the street, the three Whitecloaks were staring straight at him.

"You find something funny, yes?" The one who spoke stood a little in front of the others. He wore an arrogant, unblinking look, with a light in his eyes as if he knew something important, something no one else knew.

Rand's laughter cut off short. He and the Children were alone with the mud and the barrels. The crowd that had been all around them had found urgent business up or down the street.

"Does fear of the Light hold your tongue?" Anger made the Whitecloak's narrow face seem even more pinched. He glanced dismissively at the sword hilt sticking out from Rand's cloak. "Perhaps you are responsible for this, yes?" Unlike the others he had a golden knot beneath the sunburst on his cloak.

Rand moved to cover the sword, but instead swept his cloak back over his shoulder. In the back of his head was a frantic wonder at what he was doing, but it was a distant thought. "Accidents happen," he said. "Even to the Children of the Light."

The narrow-faced man raised an eyebrow. "You are that dangerous, youngling?" He was not much older than Rand.

"Heron-mark, Lord Bornhald," one of the others said warningly.

The narrow-faced man glanced at Rand's sword hilt again—the bronze heron was plain—and his eyes widened momentarily. Then his gaze rose to Rand's face, and he sniffed dismissively. "He is too young. You are not from this place, yes?" he said coldly to Rand. "You come from where?"

"I just arrived in Baerlon." A tingling thrill ran along Rand's arms and legs. He felt flushed, almost warm. "You wouldn't know of a good inn, would you?"

"You avoid my questions," Bornhald snapped. "What evil is

in you that you do not answer me?" His companions moved up
to either side of him, faces hard and expressionless. Despite the
mudstains on their cloaks, there was nothing funny about them
now.

The tingling filled Rand; the heat had grown to a fever. He
wanted to laugh, it felt so good. A small voice in his head
shouted that something was wrong, but all he could think of
was how full of energy he felt, nearly bursting with it. Smiling,
he rocked on his heels and waited for what was going to happen. Vaguely, distantly, he wondered what it would be.

The leader's face darkened. One of the others drew his
sword enough for an inch of steel to show and spoke in a voice
quivering with anger. "When the Children of the Light ask
questions, you gray-eyed bumpkin, we expect answers, or—"
He cut off as the narrow-faced man threw an arm across his
chest. Bornhald jerked his head up the street.

The Town Watch had arrived, a dozen men in round steel
caps and studded leather jerkins, carrying quarterstaffs as if
they knew how to use them. They stood watching, silently,
from ten paces off.

"This town has lost the Light," growled the man who had
half drawn his sword. He raised his voice to shout at the Watch.
"Baerlon stands in the Shadow of the Dark One!" At a gesture
from Bornhald he slammed his blade back into its scabbard.

Bornhald turned his attention back to Rand. The light of
knowing burned in his eyes. "Darkfriends do not escape us,
youngling, even in a town that stands in the Shadow. We will
meet again. You may be sure of it!"

He spun on his heel and strode away, his two companions
close behind, as if Rand had ceased to exist. For the moment,
at least. When they reached the crowded part of the street, the
same seemingly accidental pocket as before opened around
them. The Watchmen hesitated, eyeing Rand, then shouldered
their quarterstaffs and followed the white-cloaked three. They
had to push their way into the crowd, shouting, "Make way for
the Watch!" Few did make way, except grudgingly.

Rand still rocked on his heels, waiting. The tingle was so
strong that he almost quivered; he felt as if he were burning up.

Mat came out of the shop, staring at him. "You aren't sick,"
he said finally. "You are crazy!"

Rand drew a deep breath, and abruptly it was all gone like a pricked bubble. He staggered as it vanished, the realization of what he had just done flooding in on him. Licking his lips, he met Mat's stare. "I think we had better go back to the inn, now," he said unsteadily.

"Yes," Mat said. "Yes. I think we better had."

The street had begun to fill up again, and more than one passerby stared at the two boys and murmured something to a companion. Rand was sure the story would spread. A crazy man had tried to start a fight with three Children of the Light. That was something to talk about. *Maybe the dreams are driving me crazy.*

The two lost their way several times in the haphazard streets, but after a while they fell in with Thom Merrilin, making a grand procession all by himself through the throng. The gleeman said he was out to stretch his legs and for a bit of fresh air, but whenever anyone looked twice at his colorful cloak he would announce in a resounding voice, "I am at the Stag and Lion, tonight only."

It was Mat who began disjointedly telling Thom about the dream and their worry over whether or not to tell Moiraine, but Rand joined in, for there were differences in exactly how they remembered it. *Or maybe each dream was a little different,* he thought. The major part of the dreams was the same, though.

. They had not gone far in the telling before Thom started paying full attention. When Rand mentioned Ba'alzamon, the gleeman grabbed them each by a shoulder with a command to hold their tongues, raised on tiptoe to look over the heads of the crowd, then hustled them out of the press to a dead-end alley that was empty except for a few crates and a slat-ribbed, yellow dog huddled out of the cold.

Thom stared out at the crowd, looking for anyone stopping to listen, before turning his attention to Rand and Mat. His blue eyes bored into theirs, between flickering away to watch the mouth of the alley. "Don't ever say that name where strangers can hear." His voice was low, but urgent. "Not even where a stranger *might* hear. It is a very dangerous name, even where Children of the Light are not wandering the streets."

Mat snorted. "I could tell you about Children of the Light," he said with a wry look at Rand.

Thom ignored him. "If only one of you had had this dream. . . ." He tugged at his mustache furiously. "Tell me everything you can remember about it. Every detail." He kept up his wary watch while he listened.

". . . he named the men he said had been used," Rand said finally. He thought he had told everything else. "Guaire Amalasan. Raolin Darksbane."

"Davian," Mat added before he could go on. "And Yurian Stonebow."

"And Logain," Rand finished.

"Dangerous names," Thom muttered. His eyes seemed to drill at them even more intently than before. "Nearly as dangerous as that other, one way and another. All dead, now, except for Logain. Some long dead. Raolin Darksbane nearly two thousand years. But dangerous just the same. Best you don't say them aloud even when you're alone. Most people wouldn't recognize a one of them, but if the wrong person overhears. . . ."

"But who were they?" Rand said.

"Men," Thom murmured. "Men who shook the pillars of heaven and rocked the world on its foundations." He shook his head. "It doesn't matter. Forget about them. They are dust now."

"Did the . . . were they used, like he said?" Mat asked. "And killed?"

"You might say the White Tower killed them. You might say that." Thom's mouth tightened momentarily, then he shook his head again. "But used . . . ? No, I cannot see that. The Light knows the Amyrlin Seat has enough plots going, but I can't see that."

Mat shivered. "He said so many things. Crazy things. All that about Lews Therin Kinslayer, and Artur Hawkwing. And the Eye of the World. What in the Light is that supposed to be?"

"A legend," the gleeman said slowly. "Maybe. As big a legend as the Horn of Valere, at least in the Borderlands. Up there, young men go hunting the Eye of the World the way young men from Illian hunt the Horn. Maybe a legend."

"What do we do, Thom?" Rand said. "Do we tell her? I don't want any more dreams like that. Maybe she could do something."

"Maybe we wouldn't like what she did," Mat growled.

Thom studied them, considering and stroking his mustache with a knuckle. "I say hold your peace," he said finally. "Don't tell anyone, for the time, at least. You can always change your mind, if you have to, but once you tell, it's done, and you're tied up worse than ever with . . . with her." Suddenly he straightened, his stoop almost disappearing. "The other lad! You say he had the same dream? Does he have sense enough to keep his mouth shut?"

"I think so," Rand said at the same time that Mat said, "We were going back to the inn to warn him."

"The Light send we're not too late!" Cloak flapping around his ankles, patches fluttering in the wind, Thom strode out of the alley, looking back over his shoulder without stopping. "Well? Are your feet pegged to the ground?"

Rand and Mat hurried after him, but he did not wait for them to catch up. This time he did not pause for people who looked at his cloak, or those who hailed him as a gleeman, either. He clove through the crowded streets as if they were empty, Rand and Mat half running to follow in his wake. In much less time than Rand expected they were hurrying up to the Stag and Lion.

As they started in, Perrin came speeding out, trying to throw his cloak around his shoulders as he ran. He nearly fell in his effort not to carom into them. "I was coming looking for you two," he panted when he had caught his balance.

Rand grabbed him by the arm. "Did you tell anyone about the dream?"

"Say that you didn't," Mat demanded.

"It's very important," Thom said.

Perrin looked at them in confusion. "No, I haven't. I didn't even get out of bed until less than an hour ago." His shoulders slumped. "I've given myself a headache trying not to think about it, much less talk about it. Why did you tell him?" He nodded at the gleeman.

"We had to talk to somebody or go crazy," Rand said.

"I will explain later," Thom added with a significant look at the people passing in and out of the Stag and Lion.

"All right," Perrin replied slowly, still looking confused. Suddenly he slapped his head. "You almost made me forget why I was looking for you, not that I don't wish I could. Nynaeve is inside."

"Blood and ashes!" Mat yelped. "How did she get here? Moiraine. . . . The ferry. . . ."

Perrin snorted. "You think a little thing like a sunken ferry could stop her? She rooted Hightower out—I don't know how he got back over the river, but she said he was hiding in his bedroom and didn't want to go near the river—anyway, she bullied him into finding a boat big enough for her and her horse and rowing her across. Himself. She only gave him time to find one of his haulers to work another set of oars."

"Light!" Mat breathed.

"What is she doing here?" Rand wanted to know. Mat and Perrin both gave him a scornful look.

"She came after us," Perrin said. "She's with . . . with Mistress Alys right now, and it's cold enough in there to snow."

"Couldn't we just go somewhere else for a while?" Mat asked. "My da says, only a fool puts his hand in a hornet nest until he absolutely has to."

Rand cut in. "She can't make us go back. Winternight should have been enough to make her see that. If she doesn't, we will have to make her."

Mat's eyebrows lifted higher with every word, and when Rand finished he let out a low whistle. "You ever try to make Nynaeve see something she doesn't want to see? I have. I say we stay away till night, and sneak in then."

"From my observation of the young woman," Thom said, "I don't think she will stop until she has had her say. If she is not allowed to have it soon, she might keep on until she attracts attention none of us wants."

That brought them all up short. They exchanged glances, drew deep breaths, and marched inside as if to face Trollocs.

CHAPTER
16

The Wisdom

Perrin led the way into the depths of the inn. Rand was so intent on what he intended to say to Nynaeve that he did not see Min until she seized his arm and pulled him to one side. The others kept on a few steps down the hall before realizing he had stopped, then they halted, too, half impatient to go on, half reluctant to do so.

"We don't have time for that, boy," Thom said gruffly.

Min gave the white-haired gleeman a sharp look. "Go juggle something," she snapped, drawing Rand further away from the others.

"I really don't have time," Rand told her. "Certainly not for any more fool talk about escaping and the like." He tried to get his arm loose, but every time he pulled free, she grabbed it again.

"And I don't have time for your foolishness, either. Will you be still!" She gave the others a quick look, then moved closer, lowering her voice. "A woman arrived a little while ago—shorter than I, young, with dark eyes and dark hair in a braid down to her waist. She's part of it, right along with the rest of you."

For a minute Rand just stared at her. *Nynaeve? How can she be involved? Light, how can I be involved?* "That's . . . impossible."

"You know her?" Min whispered.

"Yes, and she can't be mixed in . . . in whatever it is you. . . ."

"The sparks, Rand. She met Mistress Alys coming in, and there were sparks, with just the two of them. Yesterday I couldn't see sparks without at least three or four of you together, but today it's all sharper, and more furious." She looked at Rand's friends, waiting impatiently, and shivered before turning back to him. "It's almost a wonder the inn doesn't catch fire. You're all in more danger today than yesterday. Since she came."

Rand glanced at his friends. Thom, his brows drawn down in a bushy V, was leaning forward on the point of taking some action to hurry him along. "She won't do anything to hurt us," he told Min. "I have to go, now." He succeeded in getting his arm back, this time.

Ignoring her squawk, he joined the others, and they started off again down the corridor. Rand looked back once. Min shook her fist at him and stamped her foot.

"What did she have to say?" Mat asked.

"Nynaeve is part of it," Rand said without thinking, then shot Mat a hard look that caught him with his mouth open. Then understanding slowly spread across Mat's face.

"Part of what?" Thom said softly. "Does that girl know something?"

While Rand was still trying to gather in his head what to say, Mat spoke up. "Of course she's part of it," he said grumpily. "Part of the same bad luck we've been having since Winternight. Maybe having the Wisdom show up is no great affair to you, but I'd as soon have the Whitecloaks here, myself."

"She saw Nynaeve arrive," Rand said. "Saw her talking to Mistress Alys, and thought she might have something to do with us." Thom gave him a sidelong look and ruffled his mustaches with a snort, but the others seemed to accept Rand's explanation. He did not like keeping secrets from his friends, but Min's secret could be as dangerous for her as any of theirs was for them.

Perrin stopped suddenly in front of a door, and despite his size he seemed oddly hesitant. He drew a deep breath, looked at his companions, took another breath, then slowly opened the door and went in. One by one the rest of them followed. Rand was the last, and he closed the door behind him with the utmost reluctance.

It was the room where they had eaten the night before. A blaze crackled on the hearth, and a polished silver tray sat in the middle of the table holding a gleaming silver pitcher and cups. Moiraine and Nynaeve sat at opposite ends of the table, neither taking her eyes from the other. All the other chairs were empty. Moiraine's hands rested on the table, as still as her face. Nynaeve's braid was thrown over her shoulder, the end gripped in one fist; she kept giving it little tugs the way she did when she was being even more stubborn than usual with the Village Council. *Perrin was right.* Despite the fire it seemed freezing cold, and all coming from the two women at the table.

Lan was leaning against the mantel, staring into the flames and rubbing his hands for warmth. Egwene, her back flat against the wall, had her cloak on with the hood pulled up. Thom, Mat, and Perrin stopped uncertainly in front of the door.

Shrugging uncomfortably, Rand walked to the table. *Sometimes you have to grab the wolf by the ears,* he reminded himself. But he remembered another old saying, too. *When you have a wolf by the ears, it's as hard to let go as to hold on.* He felt Moiraine's eyes on him, and Nynaeve's, and his face became hot, but he sat down anyway, halfway between the two.

For a minute the room was as still as a carving, then Egwene and Perrin, and finally Mat, made their reluctant way to the table and took seats—toward the middle, with Rand. Egwene tugged her hood further forward, enough to half hide her face, and they all avoided looking at anyone.

"Well," Thom snorted, from his place beside the door. "At least that much is done."

"Since everyone is here," Lan said, leaving the fireplace and filling one of the silver cups with wine, "perhaps you will finally take this." He proffered the cup to Nynaeve; she looked at it suspiciously. "There is no need to be afraid," he said patiently. "You saw the innkeeper bring the wine, and neither of us has had a chance to put anything in it. It is quite safe."

The Wisdom's mouth tightened angrily at the word *afraid,* but she took the cup with a murmured, "Thank you."

"I am interested," he said, "in how you found us."

"So am I." Moiraine leaned forward intently. "Perhaps you are willing to speak now that Egwene and the boys have been brought to you?"

Nynaeve sipped the wine before answering the Aes Sedai. "There was nowhere for you to go except Baerlon. To be safe, though, I followed your trail. You certainly cut back and forth enough. But then, I suppose you would not care to risk meeting decent people."

"You . . . followed our trail?" Lan said, truly surprised for the first time that Rand could remember. "I must be getting careless."

"You left very little trace, but I can track as well as any man in the Two Rivers, except perhaps Tam al'Thor." She hesitated, then added, "Until my father died, he took me hunting with him, and taught me what he would have taught the sons he never had." She looked at Lan challengingly, but he only nodded with approval.

"If you can follow a trail I have tried to hide, he taught you well. Few can do that, even in the Borderlands." ,

Abruptly Nynaeve buried her face in her cup. Rand's eyes widened. She was blushing. Nynaeve never showed herself even the least bit disconcerted. Angry, yes; outraged, often; but never out of countenance. But she was certainly red-cheeked now, and trying to hide in the wine.

"Perhaps now," Moiraine said quietly, "you will answer a few of my questions. I have answered yours freely enough."

"With a great sackful of gleeman's tales," Nynaeve retorted. "The only *facts* I can see are that four young people have been carried off, for the Light alone knows what reason, by an Aes Sedai."

"You have been told that isn't known here," Lan said sharply. "You must learn to guard your tongue."

"Why should I?" Nynaeve demanded. "Why should I help hide you, or what you are? I've come to take Egwene and the boys back to Emond's Field, not help you spirit them away."

Thom broke in, in a scornful voice. "If you want them to see their village again—or you, either—you had better be more careful. There are those in Baerlon who would kill her"—he jerked his head toward Moiraine—"for what she is. Him, too."

He indicated Lan, then abruptly moved forward to put his fists on the table. He loomed over Nynaeve, and his long mustaches and thick eyebrows suddenly seemed threatening.

Her eyes widened, and she started to lean back, away from him; then her back stiffened defiantly. Thom did not appear to notice; he went right on in an ominously soft voice. "They'd swarm over this inn like murderous ants on a rumor, a whisper. Their hate is that strong, their desire to kill or take any like these two. And the girl? The boys? You? You are all associated with them, enough for the Whitecloaks, anyway. You wouldn't like the way they ask questions, especially when the White Tower is involved. Whitecloak Questioners assume you're guilty before they start, and they have only one sentence for that kind of guilt. They don't care about finding the truth; they think they know that already. All they go after with their hot irons and pincers is a confession. Best you remember some secrets are too dangerous for saying aloud, even when you think you know who hears." He straightened with a muttered, "I seem to tell that to people often of late."

"Well put, gleeman," Lan said. The Warder had that weighing look in his eyes again. "I'm surprised to find you so concerned."

Thom shrugged. "It's known I arrived with you, too. I don't care for the thought of a Questioner with a hot iron telling me to repent my sins and walk in the Light."

"That," Nynaeve put in sharply, "is just one more reason for them to come home with me in the morning. Or this afternoon, for that matter. The sooner we're away from you and on our way back to Emond's Field, the better."

"We can't," Rand said, and was glad that his friends all spoke up at the same time. That way Nynaeve's glare had to be spread around; she spared no one as it was. But he had spoken first, and they all fell silent, looking at him. Even Moiraine sat back in her chair, watching him over steepled fingers. It was an effort for him to meet the Wisdom's eyes. "If we go back to Emond's Field, the Trollocs will come back, too. They're . . . hunting us. I don't know why, but they are. Maybe we can find out why in Tar Valon. Maybe we can find out how to stop it. It's the only way."

Nynaeve threw up her hands. "You sound just like Tam. He

had himself carried to the village meeting and tried to convince everybody. He'd already tried with the Village Council. The Light knows how your . . . Mistress Alys"—she invested the name with a wagonload of scorn—"managed to make him believe; he has a mite of sense, usually, more than most men. In any case, the Council is a pack of fools most of the time, but not foolish enough for that, and neither was anyone else. They agreed you had to be found. Then Tam wanted to be the one to come after you, and him not able to stand by himself. Foolishness must run in your family."

Mat cleared his throat, then mumbled, "What about my da? What did he say?"

"He's afraid you'll try your tricks with outlanders and get your head thumped. He seemed more afraid of that than of . . . Mistress Alys, here. But then, he was never much brighter than you."

Mat seemed unsure how to take what she had said, or how to reply, or even whether to reply.

"I expect," Perrin began hesitantly. "I mean, I suppose Master Luhhan was not too pleased about my leaving, either."

"Did you expect him to be?" Nynaeve shook her head disgustedly and looked at Egwene. "Maybe I should not be surprised at this harebrained idiocy from you three, but I thought others had more judgment."

Egwene sat back so she was shielded by Perrin. "I left a note," she said faintly. She tugged at the hood of her cloak as if she was afraid her unbound hair showed. "I explained everything." Nynaeve's face darkened.

Rand sighed. The Wisdom was on the point of one of her tongue-lashings, and it looked as if it might be a first-rate one. If she took a position in the heat of anger—if she said she intended to see them back in Emond's Field no matter what anybody said, for instance—she would be nearly impossible to budge. He opened his mouth.

"A note!" Nynaeve began, just as Moiraine said, "You and I must still talk, Wisdom."

If Rand could have stopped himself, he would have, but the words poured out as if it were a floodgate he had opened instead of his mouth. "All this is very well, but it doesn't change anything. We can't go back. We have to go on." He spoke more slowly toward the end, and his voice sank, so he finished in a whisper, with the Wisdom and the Aes Sedai both looking at him. It was the sort of look he received if he came on women talking Women's Circle business, the sort that said he had stepped in where he did not belong. He sat back, wishing he was somewhere else.

"Wisdom," Moiraine said, "you must believe that they are safer with me than they would be back in the Two Rivers."

"Safer!" Nynaeve tossed her head dismissively. "You are the one who brought them here, where the Whitecloaks are. The same Whitecloaks who, if the gleeman tells the truth, may harm them because of *you*. Tell me how they are safer, Aes Sedai."

"There are many dangers from which I cannot protect them," Moiraine agreed, "any more than you can protect them from being struck by lightning if they go home. But it is not lightning of which they must be afraid, nor even Whitecloaks. It is the Dark One, and minions of the Dark One. From those things I *can* protect. Touching the True Source, touching *saidar*, gives me that protection, as it does to every Aes Sedai." Nynaeve's mouth tightened skeptically. Moiraine's grew tighter, too, with anger, but she went on, her voice hard on the edge of patience. "Even those poor men who find themselves wielding the Power for a short time gain that much, though sometimes touching *saidin* protects, and sometimes the taint makes them more vulnerable. But I, or any Aes Sedai, can extend my protection to those close by me. No Fade can harm them as long as they are as close to me as they are right now. No Trolloc can come within a quarter of a mile without Lan knowing it, feeling the evil of it. Can you offer them half as much if they return to Emond's Field with you?"

"You stand up straw men," Nynaeve said. "We have a saying in the Two Rivers. 'Whether the bear beats the wolf or the wolf beats the bear, the rabbit always loses.' Take your contest somewhere else and leave Emond's Field folk out of it."

"Egwene," Moiraine said after a moment, "take the others and leave the Wisdom alone with me for a while." Her face was impassive; Nynaeve squared herself at the table as if getting ready for an all-in wrestling match.

Egwene bounced to her feet, her desire to be dignified obviously warring with her desire to avoid a confrontation with the Wisdom over her unbraided hair. She had no difficulty gathering up everyone by eye, though. Mat and Perrin scraped back their chairs hurriedly, making polite murmurs while trying not to actually run on their way out. Even Lan started for the door at a signal from Moiraine, drawing Thom with him.

Rand followed, and the Warder shut the door behind them, then took up guard across the hallway. Under Lan's eyes the others moved on down the hall a short distance; they were not to be allowed even the slightest chance of eavesdropping. When they had gone far enough to suit him, Lan leaned back against the wall. Even without his color-shifting cloak, he was so still that it would be easy not to notice him until you were right on him.

The gleeman muttered something about better things to do with his time and left with a stern, "Remember what I said," over his shoulder to the boys. No one else seemed inclined to leave.

"What did he mean?" Egwene asked absently, her eyes on the door that hid Moiraine and Nynaeve. She kept fiddling with her hair as if torn between continuing to hide the fact that it was no longer braided and pushing back the hood of her cloak.

"He gave us some advice," Mat said.

Perrin gave him a sharp look. "He said not to open our mouths until we were sure what we were going to say."

"That sounds like good advice," Egwene said, but clearly she was not really interested.

Rand was engrossed in his own thoughts. How could Nynaeve possibly be part of it?. How could any of them be involved with Trollocs, and Fades, and Ba'alzamon appearing in their dreams? It was crazy. He wondered if Min had told Moiraine about Nynaeve. *What are they saying in there??*

He had no idea how long he had been standing there when the door finally opened. Nynaeve stepped out, and gave a start when she saw Lan. The Warder murmured something that made her toss her head angrily, then he slipped past her through the door.

She turned toward Rand, and for the first time he realized the others had all quietly disappeared. He did not want to face the Wisdom alone, but he could not get away now that he had met Nynaeve's eye. *A particularly searching eye,* he thought, puzzled. *What did they say?* He drew himself up as she came closer.

She indicated Tam's sword. "That seems to fit you, now, though I would like it better if it did not. You've grown, Rand."

"In a week?" He laughed, but it sounded forced, and she shook her head as if he did not understand. "Did she convince you?" he asked. "It really is the only way." He paused, thinking of Min's sparks. "Are you coming with us?"

Nynaeve's eyes opened wide. "Coming with you! Why would I do that? Mavra Mallen came up from Deven Ride to see to things till I return, but she'll be wanting to get back as soon as she can. I still hope to make you see sense and come home with me."

"We can't." He thought he saw something move at the still-open door, but they were alone in the hallway.

"You told me that, and she did, too." Nynaeve frowned. "If *she* wasn't mixed up in it. . . . Aes Sedai are not to be trusted, Rand."

"You sound as if you really do believe us," he said slowly. "What happened at the village meeting?"

Nynaeve looked back at the doorway before answering; there was no movement there now. "It was a shambles, but there is no need for her to know we can't handle our affairs any better than that. And I believe only one thing: you are all in danger as long as you are with her."

"Something happened," he insisted. "Why do you want us to go back if you think there's even a chance we are right? And why you, at all? As soon send the Mayor himself as the Wisdom."

"You *have* grown." She smiled, and for a moment her amusement had him shifting his feet. "I can think of a time when you would not have questioned where I chose to go or what I chose to do, wherever or whatever it was. A time just a week ago."

He cleared his throat and pressed on stubbornly. "It doesn't make sense. Why are you really here?"

She half glanced at the still-empty doorway, then took his arm. "Let's walk while we talk." He let himself be led away, and when they were far enough from the door not to be over-heard, she began again. "As I said, the meeting was a shambles. Everybody agreed someone had to be sent after you, but the village split into two groups. One wanted you rescued, though there was considerable argument over how that was to be done considering that you were with a . . . the likes of *her*."

He was glad she was remembering to watch what she said. "The others believed Tam?" he said.

"Not exactly, but they thought you shouldn't be among strangers, either, especially not with someone like *her*. Either way, though, almost every man wanted to be one of the party. Tam, and Bran al'Vere, with the scales of office around his neck, and Haral Luhhan, till Alsbet made him sit down. Even Cenn Buie. The Light save me from men who think with the hair on their chests. Though I don't know as there are any other kind." She gave a hearty sniff, and looked up at him, an accusing glance. "At any rate, I could see it would be another day, perhaps more, before they came to any decision, and somehow . . . somehow I was sure we did not dare wait that long. So I called the Women's Circle together and told them what had to be done. I cannot say they liked it, but they saw the right of it. And that is why I am here; because the men around Emond's Field are stubborn wool-heads. They're probably still arguing about who to send, though I left word I would take care of it."

Nynaeve's story explained her presence, but it did nothing to reassure him. She was still determined to bring them back with her.

"What did she say to you in there?" he asked. Moiraine would surely have covered every argument, but if there was one she had missed, he would make it.

"More of the same," Nynaeve replied. "And she wanted to know about you boys. To see if she could reason out why you . . . have attracted the kind of attention you have . . . she *said*." She paused, watching him out of the corner of her eye. "She tried to disguise it, but most of all she wanted to know if any of you was born outside the Two Rivers."

His face was suddenly as taut as a drumhead. He managed a hoarse chuckle. "She does think of some odd things. I hope you assured her we're all Emond's Field born."

"Of course," she replied. There had only been a heartbeat's pause before she spoke, so brief he would have missed it if he had not been watching for it.

He tried to think of something to say, but his tongue felt like a piece of leather. *She knows.* She was the Wisdom, after all, and the Wisdom was supposed to know everything about everyone. *If she knows, it was no fever-dream. Oh, Light help me, father!*

"Are you all right?" Nynaeve asked.

"He said . . . said I . . . wasn't his son. When he was delirious . . . with the fever. He said he found me. I thought it was just. . . ." His throat began to burn, and he had to stop.

"Oh, Rand." She stopped and took his face in both hands. She had to reach up to do it. "People say strange things in a fever. Twisted things. Things that are not true, or real. Listen to me. Tam al'Thor ran away seeking adventure when he was a boy no older than you. I can just remember when he came back to Emond's Field, a grown man with a red-haired, outlander wife and a babe in swaddling clothes. I remember Kari al'Thor cradling that child in her arms with as much love given and delight taken as I have ever seen from any woman with a babe. Her child, Rand. You. Now you straighten up and stop this foolishness."

"Of course," he said. *I was born outside the Two Rivers.* "Of course." Maybe Tam had been having a fever-dream, and maybe he had found a baby after a battle. "Why didn't you tell her?"

"It is none of any outlander's business."

"Were any of the others born outside?" As soon as the question was out, he shook his head. "No, don't answer. It's none of my business, either." But it would be nice to know if Moiraine had some special interest in him, over and above what she had in the whole lot of them. *Would it?*

"No, it isn't your business," Nynaeve agreed. "It might not mean anything. She could just be searching blindly for a reason, any reason, why those things are after you. After *all* of you."

Rand managed a grin. "Then you do believe they're chasing us."

Nynaeve shook her head wryly. "You've certainly learned how to twist words since you met her."

"What are you going to do?" he asked.

She studied him; he met her eyes steadily. "Today, I am going to have a bath. For the rest, we will have to see, won't we?"

Nynaeve al'Meara

CHAPTER
17

Watchers and Hunters

After the Wisdom left him, Rand made his way to the common room. He needed to hear people laughing, to forget what Nynaeve had said and the trouble she might cause alike.

The room was crowded indeed, but no one was laughing, though every chair and bench was filled and people lined the walls. Thom was performing again, standing on a table against the far wall, his gestures grand enough to fill the big room. It was *The Great Hunt of the Horn* again, but no one complained, of course. There were so many tales to be told about each of the Hunters, and so many Hunters to tell of, that no two tellings were ever the same. The whole of it in one telling would have taken a week or more. The only sound competing with the gleeman's voice and harp was the crackling of the fires in the fireplaces.

". . . To the eight corners of the world, the Hunters ride, to the eight pillars of heaven, where the winds of time blow and fate seizes the mighty and the small alike by the forelock. Now, the greatest of the Hunters is Rogosh of Talmour, Rogosh Eagle-eye, famed at the court of the High King, feared on the slopes of Shayol Ghul. . . ." The Hunters were always mighty heroes, all of them.

Rand spotted his two friends and squeezed onto a place Perrin made for him on the end of their bench. Kitchen smells drifting into the room reminded him that he was hungry, but even the people who had food in front of them gave it little attention. The maids who should have been serving stood entranced, clutching their aprons and looking at the gleeman, and nobody seemed to mind at all. Listening was better than eating, no matter how good the food.

". . . since the day of her birth has the Dark One marked Blaes as his own, but not of this mind is she—no Darkfriend, Blaes of Matuchin! Strong as the ash she stands, lithe as the willow branch, beautiful as the rose. Golden-haired Blaes. Ready to die before she yields. But hark! Echoing from the towers of the city, trumpets blare, brazen and bold. Her heralds proclaim the arrival of a hero at her court. Drums thunder and cymbals sing! Rogosh Eagle-eye comes to do homage . . ."

"The Bargain of Rogosh Eagle-eye" wound its way to an end, but Thom paused only to wet his throat from a mug of ale before launching into "Lian's Stand." In turn that was followed by "The Fall of Aleth-Loriel," and "Gaidal Cain's Sword," and "The Last Ride of Buad of Albhain." The pauses grew longer as the evening wore on, and when Thom exchanged the harp for his flute, everyone knew it was the end of storytelling for the night. Two men joined Thom, with a drum and a hammered dulcimer, but sitting beside the table while he remained atop it.

The three young men from Emond's Field began clapping their hands with the first note of "The Wind That Shakes the Willow," and they were not the only ones. It was a favorite in the Two Rivers, and in Baerlon, too, it seemed. Here and there voices even took up the words, not so off-key as for anyone to hush them.

> "My love is gone, carried away
> by the wind that shakes the willow,
> and all the land is beaten hard
> by the wind that shakes the willow.
> But I will hold her close to me
> in heart and dearest memory,
> and with her strength to steel my soul,
> her love to warm my heart-strings,
> I will stand where we once sang,
> though cold wind shakes the willow."

The second song was not so sad. In fact, "Only One Bucket

of Water" seemed even more merry than usual by comparison, which might have been the gleeman's intent. People rushed to clear tables from the floor to make room for dancing, and began kicking up their heels until the walls shook from the stomping and whirling. The first dance ended with laughing dancers leaving the floor holding their sides, and new people taking their places.

Thom played the opening notes of "Wild Geese on the Wing," then paused for people to take their places for the reel.

"I think I'll try a few steps," Rand said, getting to his feet. Perrin popped up right behind him. Mat was the last to move, and so found himself staying behind to guard the cloaks, along with Rand's sword and Perrin's axe.

"Remember I want a turn, too," Mat called after them.

The dancers formed two long lines facing each other, men in one, women in the other. First the drum and then the dulcimer took up the beat, and all the dancers began bending their knees in time. The girl across from Rand, her dark hair in braids that made him think of home, gave him a shy smile, and then a wink that was not shy at all. Thom's flute leaped into the tune, and Rand moved forward to meet the dark-haired girl; she threw back her head and laughed as he spun her around and passed her on to the next man in line.

Everyone in the room was laughing, he thought as he danced around his next partner, one of the serving maids with her apron flapping wildly. The only unsmiling face he saw was on a man huddled by one of the fireplaces, and that fellow had a scar that crossed his whole face from one temple to the opposite jaw, giving his nose a slant and drawing the corner of his mouth down. The man met his gaze and grimaced, and Rand looked away in embarrassment. Maybe with that scar the fellow could not smile.

He caught his next partner as she spun, and whirled her in a circle before passing her on. Three more women danced with him as the music gained speed, then he was back with the first dark-haired girl for a fast promenade that changed the lines about completely. She was still laughing, and she gave him another wink.

The scar-faced man was scowling at him. His step faltered and his cheeks grew hot. He had not meant to embarrass the fellow; he really did not think he had stared. He turned to meet his next partner and forgot all about the man. The next woman to dance into his arms was Nynaeve.

He stumbled through the steps, almost tripping over his own feet, nearly stepping on hers. She danced gracefully enough to make up for his clumsiness, smiling the while.

"I thought you were a better dancer," she laughed as they changed partners.

He had only a moment to gather himself before they changed again, and he found himself dancing with Moiraine. If he had thought he was stumble-footed with the Wisdom, it was nothing to how he felt with the Aes Sedai. She glided across the floor smoothly, her gown swirling about her; he almost fell twice. She gave him a sympathetic smile, which made it worse rather than helping. It was a relief to go to his next partner in the pattern, even if it was Egwene.

He regained some of his poise. After all, he had danced with her for years. Her hair still hung unbraided, but she had gathered it back with a red ribbon. *Probably couldn't decide whether to please Moiraine or Nynaeve,* he thought sourly. Her lips were parted, and she looked as if she wanted to say something, but she never spoke, and he was not about to speak first. Not after the way she had cut off his earlier attempt in the private dining room. They stared at one another soberly and danced apart without a word.

He was glad enough to return to the bench when the reel was done. The music for another dance, a jig, began while he was sitting down. Mat hurried to join in, and Perrin slid onto the bench as he was leaving.

"Did you see her?" Perrin began before he was even seated. "Did you?"

"Which one?" Rand asked. "The Wisdom, or Mistress Alys? I danced with both of them."

"The Ae . . . Mistress Alys, too?" Perrin exclaimed. "I danced with Nynaeve. I didn't even know she danced. She never does at any of the dances back home."

"I wonder," Rand said thoughtfully, "what the Women's Circle would say about the Wisdom dancing? Maybe that's why."

Then the music and the clapping and the singing were too loud for any further talk. Rand and Perrin joined in the clapping as the dancers circled the floor. Several times he became aware of the scar-faced man staring at him. The man had a right to be touchy, with that scar, but Rand did not see anything he could do now that would not make matters worse. He concentrated on the music and avoided looking at the fellow.

The dancing and singing went on into the night. The maids finally did remember their duties; Rand was glad to wolf down some hot stew and bread. Everyone ate where they sat or stood. Rand joined in three more dances, and he managed his steps better when he found himself dancing with Nynaeve again, and with Moiraine, as well. This time they both complimented him on his dancing, which made him stammer. He danced with Egwene again, too; she stared at him, dark-eyed and always seeming on the point of speaking, but never saying a word. He was just as silent as she, but he was sure he did not scowl at her, no matter what Mat said when he returned to the bench.

Toward midnight Moiraine left. Egwene, after one harried look from the Aes Sedai to Nynaeve, hurried after her. The Wisdom watched them with an unreadable expression, then deliberately joined in another dance before she left, too, with a look as if she had gained a point on the Aes Sedai.

Soon Thom was putting his flute into its case and arguing good-naturedly with those who wanted him to stay longer. Lan came by to gather up Rand and the others.

"We have to make an early start," the Warder said, leaning close to be heard over the noise, "and we will need all the rest we can get."

"There's a fellow been staring at me," Mat said. "A man with a scar across his face. You don't think he could be a . . . one of the *friends* you warned us about?"

"Like this?" Rand said, drawing a finger across his nose to the corner of his mouth. "He stared at me, too." He looked around the room. People were drifting away, and most of those still left clustered around Thom. "He's not here, now."

"I saw the man," Lan said. "According to Master Fitch, he's a spy for the Whitecloaks. He's no worry to us." Maybe he was not, but Rand could see something was bothering the Warder.

Rand glanced at Mat, who had the stiff expression on his face that always meant he was hiding something. *A Whitecloak spy.*

Could Bornhald want to get back at us that much? "We're leaving early?" he said. "Really early?" Maybe they could be gone before anything came of it.

"At first light," the Warder replied.

As they left the common room, Mat singing snatches of song under his breath, and Perrin stopping now and again to try out a new step he had learned, Thom joined them in high spirits. Lan's face was expressionless as they headed for the stairs.

"Where is Nynaeve sleeping?" Mat asked. "Master Fitch said we got the last rooms."

"She has a bed," Thom said dryly, "in with Mistress Alys and the girl."

Perrin whistled between his teeth, and Mat muttered, "Blood and ashes! I wouldn't be in Egwene's shoes for all the gold in Caemlyn!"

Not for the first time, Rand wished Mat could think seriously about something for more than two minutes. Their own shoes were not very comfortable right then. "I'm going to get some milk," he said. Maybe it would help him sleep. *Maybe I won't dream tonight.*

Lan looked at him sharply. "There's something wrong tonight. Don't wander far. And remember, we leave whether you are awake enough to sit your saddle or have to be tied on."

The Warder started up the stairs; the others followed him, their jollity subdued. Rand stood in the hall alone. After having so many people around, it was lonely indeed.

He hurried to the kitchen, where a scullery maid was still on duty. She poured a mug of milk from a big stone crock for him.

As he came out of the kitchen, drinking, a shape in dull black started toward him down the length of the hall, raising pale hands to toss back the dark cowl that had hidden the face beneath. The cloak hung motionless as the figure moved, and the face. . . . A man's face, but pasty white, like a slug under a rock, and eyeless. From oily black hair to puffy cheeks was as smooth as an eggshell. Rand choked, spraying milk.

"You are one of them, boy," the Fade said, a hoarse whisper like a file softly drawn across bone.

Dropping the mug, Rand backed away. He wanted to run, but it was all he could do to make his feet take one halting step at a time. He could not break free of that eyeless face; his gaze was held, and his stomach curdled. He tried to shout for help, to scream; his throat was like stone. Every ragged breath hurt.

The Fade glided closer, in no hurry. Its strides had a sinuous, deadly grace, like a viper, the resemblance emphasized by the overlapping black plates of armor down its chest. Thin, bloodless lips curved in a cruel smile, made more mocking by the smooth, pale skin where eyes should have been. The voice made Bornhald's seem warm and soft. "Where are the others? I know they are here. Speak, boy, and I will let you live."

Rand's back struck wood, a wall or a door—he could not make himself look around to see which. Now that his feet had stopped, he could not make them start again. He shivered, watching the Myrddraal slither nearer. His shaking grew harder with every slow stride.

"Speak, I say, or—"

From above came a quick clatter of boots, from the stairs up the hall, and the Myrddraal cut off, whirling. The cloak hung still. For an instant the Fade's head tilted, as if that eyeless gaze could pierce the wooden wall. A sword appeared in a dead-white hand, blade as black as the cloak. The light in the hall seemed to grow dimmer in the presence of that blade. The pounding of boots grew louder, and the Fade spun back to Rand, an almost boneless movement. The black blade rose; narrow lips peeled back in a rictus snarl.

Trembling, Rand knew he was going to die. Midnight steel flashed at his head . . . and stopped.

"You belong to the Great Lord of the Dark." The breathy grating of that voice sounded like fingernails scratched across a slate. "You are his."

Spinning in a black blur, the Fade darted down the hall away from Rand. The shadows at the end of the hall reached out and embraced it, and it was gone.

Lan leaped down the last stairs, landing with a crash, sword in hand.

Rand struggled to find his voice. "Fade," he gasped. "It was. . . ." Abruptly he remembered his sword. With the Myrddraal facing him he had never thought of it. He fumbled the heron-mark blade out now, not caring if it was too late. "It ran that way!"

Lan nodded absently; he seemed to be listening to something

else. "Yes. It's going; fading. No time to pursue it, now. We're leaving, sheepherder."

More boots stumbled down the stairs; Mat and Perrin and Thom, hung about with blankets and saddlebags. Mat was still buckling his bedroll, with his bow awkward under his arm.

"Leaving?" Rand said. Sheathing his sword, he took his things from Thom. "Now? In the night?"

"You want to wait for the Halfman to come back, sheepherder?" the Warder said impatiently. "For half a dozen of them? It knows where we are, now."

"I will ride with you again," Thom told the Warder, "if you have no great objections. Too many people remember that I arrived with you. I fear that before tomorrow this will be a bad place to be known as your friend."

"You can ride with us, or ride to Shayol Ghul, gleeman." Lan's scabbard rattled from the force with which he rammed his sword home.

A stableman came darting past them from the rear door, and then Moiraine appeared with Master Fitch, and behind them Egwene, with her bundled shawl in her arms. And Nynaeve. Egwene looked frightened almost to tears, but the Wisdom's face was a mask of cool anger.

"You must take this seriously," Moiraine was telling the innkeeper. "You will certainly have trouble here by morning. Darkfriends, perhaps; perhaps worse. When it comes, quickly make it clear that we are gone. Offer no resistance. Just let whoever it is know that we left in the night, and they should bother you no further. It is us they are after."

"Never you worry about trouble," Master Fitch replied jovially. "Never a bit. If any come around my inn trying to make trouble for my guests . . . well, they'll get short shrift from the lads and I. Short shrift. And they'll hear not a word about where you've gone or when, or even if you were ever here. I've no use for that kind. Not a word will be spoken about you by any here. Not a word!"

"But—"

"Mistress Alys, I really must see to your horses if you're going to leave in good order." He pulled loose from her grip on his sleeve and trotted in the direction of the stables.

Moiraine sighed vexedly. "Stubborn, stubborn man. He will not listen."

"You think Trollocs might come here hunting for us?" Mat asked.

"Trollocs!" Moiraine snapped. "Of course not! There are other things to fear, not the least of which is how we were found." Ignoring Mat's bristle, she went right on. "The Fade cannot believe we will remain here, now that we know it has found us, but Master Fitch takes Darkfriends too lightly. He thinks of them as wretches hiding in the shadows, but Darkfriends can be found in the shops and streets of every city, and in the highest councils, too. The Myrddraal may send them to see if he can learn of our plans." She turned on her heel and left, Lan close behind her.

As they started for the stableyard, Rand fell in beside Nynaeve. She had her saddlebags and blankets, too. "So you're coming after all," he said. *Min was right.*

"*Was* there something down here?" she asked quietly. "*She* said it was—" She stopped abruptly and looked at him.

"A Fade," he answered. He was amazed that he could say it so calmly. "It was in the hall with me, and then Lan came."

Nynaeve shrugged her cloak against the wind as they left the inn. "Perhaps there is something after you. But I came to see you safely back in Emond's Field, all of you, and I will not leave till that is done. I won't leave you alone with *her* sort." Lights moved in the stables where the ostlers were saddling the horses.

"Mutch!" the innkeeper shouted from the stable door where he stood with Moiraine. "Stir your bones!" He turned back to her, appearing to attempt to soothe her rather than really listening when she spoke, though he did it deferentially, with bows interspersed among the orders called to the stablemen.

The horses were led out, the stablemen grumbling softly about the hurry and the lateness. Rand held Egwene's bundle, handing it up to her when she was on Bela's back. She looked back at him with wide, fear-filled eyes. *At least she doesn't think it's an adventure anymore.*

He was ashamed as soon as he thought it. She was in danger because of him and the others. Even riding back to Emond's Field alone would be safer than going on. "Egwene, I. . . ."

The words died in his mouth. She was too stubborn to just turn back, not after saying she was going all the way to Tar Valon. *What about what Min saw? She's part of it. Light, part of what?*

"Egwene," he said, "I'm sorry. I can't seem to think straight anymore."

She leaned down to grip his hand hard. In the light from the stable he could see her face clearly. She did not look as frightened as she had.

Once they were all mounted, Master Fitch insisted on leading them to the gates, the stablemen lighting the way with their lamps. The round-bellied innkeeper bowed them on their way with assurances that he would keep their secrets, and invitations to come again. Mutch watched them leave as sourly as he had watched them arrive.

There was one, Rand thought, who would not give short shrift to anyone, or any kind of shrift. Mutch would tell the first person who asked him when they had gone and everything else he could think of concerning them. A little distance down the street, he looked back. One figure stood, lamp raised high, peering after them. He did not need to see the face to know it was Mutch.

The streets of Baerlon were abandoned at that hour of the night; only a few faint glimmers here and there escaped tightly closed shutters, and the light of the moon in its last quarter waxed and waned with the wind-driven clouds. Now and again a dog barked as they passed an alleyway, but no other sound disturbed the night except their horses' hooves and the wind whistling across the rooftops. The riders held an even deeper silence, huddled in their cloaks and their own thoughts.

The Warder led the way, as usual, with Moiraine and Egwene close behind. Nynaeve kept near the girl, and the others brought up the rear in a tight cluster. Lan kept the horses moving at a brisk walk.

Rand watched the streets around them warily, and he noticed his friends doing the same. Shifting moon shadows recalled the shadows at the end of the hall, the way they had seemed to reach out to the Fade. An occasional noise in the distance, like a barrel toppling, or another dog barking, jerked every head around. Slowly, bit by bit as they made their way through the

town, they all bunched their horses closer to Lan's black stallion and Moiraine's white mare.

At the Caemlyn Gate Lan dismounted and hammered with
his fist on the door of a small square stone building squatting
against the wall. A weary Watchman appeared, rubbing sleepily
at his face. As Lan spoke, his sleepiness vanished, and he
stared past the Warder to the others.

"You want to leave?" he exclaimed. "Now? In the night?
You must be mad!"

"Unless there is some order from the Governor that pro-
hibits our leaving," Moiraine said. She had dismounted as well,
but she stayed back from the door, out of the light that spilled
into the dark street.

"Not exactly, mistress." The Watchman peered at her,
frowning as he tried to make out her face. "But the gates stay
shut from sundown to sunup. No one to come in except in
daylight. That's the order. Anyway, there're wolves out there.
Killed a dozen cows in the last week. Could kill a man just as
easy."

"No one to come in, but nothing about leaving," Moiraine
said as if that settled the matter. "You see? We are not asking
you to disobey the Governor."

Lan pressed something into the Watchman's hand. "For your
trouble," he murmured.

"I suppose," the Watchman said slowly. He glanced at his
hand; gold glinted before he hastily stuffed it in his pocket. "I
suppose leaving wasn't mentioned at that. Just a minute." He
stuck his head back inside. "Arin! Dar! Get out here and help
me open the gate. There's people want to leave. Don't argue.
Just do it."

Two more of the Watch appeared from inside, stopping to
stare in sleepy surprise at the party of eight waiting to leave.
Under the first Watchman's urgings they shuffled over to heave
at the big wheel that raised the thick bar across the gates, then
turned their efforts to cranking the gates open. The crank-and-
ratchet made a rapid clicking sound, but the well-oiled gates
swung outward silently. Before they were even a quarter open,
though, a cold voice spoke out of the darkness.

"What is this? Are these gates not ordered closed until sunrise?"

Five white-cloaked men walked into the light from the guard-house door. Their cowls were drawn up to hide their faces, but each man rested his hand on his sword, and the golden suns on their left breasts were a plain announcement of who they were. Mat muttered under his breath. The Watchmen stopped their cranking and exchanged uneasy looks.

"This is none of your affair," the first Watchman said belligerently. Five white hoods turned to regard him, and he finished in a weaker tone. "The Children hold no sway here. The Governor—"

"The Children of the Light," the white-cloaked man who had first spoken said softly, "hold sway wherever men walk in the Light. Only where the Shadow of the Dark One reigns are the Children denied, yes?" He swung his hood from the Watchman to Lan, then suddenly gave the Warder a second, more wary, look.

The Warder had not moved; in fact, he seemed completely at ease. But not many people could look at the Children so uncaringly. Lan's stony face could as well have been looking at a bootblack. When the Whitecloak spoke again, he sounded suspicious.

"What kind of people want to leave town walls in the night during times like these? With wolves stalking the darkness, and the Dark One's handiwork seen flying over the town?" He eyed the braided leather band that crossed Lan's forehead and held his long hair back. "A northerner, yes?"

Rand hunched lower in his saddle. A Draghkar. It had to be that, unless the man just named anything he did not understand as the Dark One's handiwork. With a Fade at the Stag and Lion, he should have expected a Draghkar, but at the moment he was hardly thinking about it. He thought he recognized the Whitecloak's voice.

"Travelers," Lan replied calmly. "Of no interest to you or yours."

"Everyone is of interest to the Children of the Light."

Lan shook his head slightly. "Are you really after more trouble with the Governor? He has limited your numbers in the town, even had you followed. What will he do when he discovers you're harassing honest citizens at his gates?" He turned to the Watchmen. "Why have you stopped?" They hesitated, put their hands back on the crank, then hesitated again when the Whitecloak spoke.

"The Governor does not know what happens under his nose. There is evil he does not see, or smell. But the Children of the Light see." The Watchmen looked at one another; their hands opened and closed as if regretting the spears left inside the guardhouse. "The Children of the Light smell the evil." The Whitecloak's eyes turned to the people on horseback. "We smell it, and root it out. Wherever it is found."

Rand tried to make himself even smaller, but the movement drew the man's attention.

"What have we here? Someone who does not wish to be seen? What do you—? Ah!" The man brushed back the hood of his white cloak, and Rand was looking at the face he had known would be there. Bornhald nodded with obvious satisfaction. "Clearly, Watchman, I have saved you from a great disaster. These are Darkfriends you were about to help escape from the Light. You should be reported to your Governor for discipline, or perhaps given to the Questioners to discover your true intent this night." He paused, eyeing the Watchman's fear; it seemed to have no effect on him. "You would not wish that, no? Instead, I will take these ruffians to our camp, that they may be questioned in the Light—instead of you, yes?"

"You will take me to your camp, Whitecloak?" Moiraine's voice came suddenly from every direction at once. She had moved back into the night at the Children's approach, and shadows clumped around her. "You will question me?" Darkness wreathed her as she took a step forward; it made her seem taller. "You will bar my way?"

Another step, and Rand gasped. She *was* taller, her head level with his where he sat on the gray's back. Shadows clung about her face like thunderclouds.

"Aes Sedai!" Bornhald shouted, and five swords flashed from their sheaths. "Die!" The other four hesitated, but he slashed at her in the same motion that cleared his sword.

Rand cried out as Moiraine's staff rose to intercept the blade. That delicately carved wood could not possibly stop hard-swung steel. Sword met staff, and sparks sprayed in a fountain, a hissing roar hurling Bornhald back into his white-cloaked companions. All five went down in a heap. Tendrils of smoke rose from

Bornhald's sword, on the ground beside him, blade bent at a right angle where it had been melted almost in two.

"You dare attack me!" Moiraine's voice roared like a whirlwind. Shadow spun in on her, draped her like a hooded cloak; she loomed as high as the town wall. Her eyes glared down, a giant staring at insects.

"Go!" Lan shouted. In one lightning move he snatched the reins of Moiraine's mare and leaped into his own saddle. "Now!" he commanded. His shoulders brushed either gate as his stallion tore through the narrow opening like a flung stone.

For a moment Rand remained frozen, staring. Moiraine's head and shoulders stood above the wall, now. Watchmen and Children alike cowered away from her, huddling with their backs against the front of the guardhouse. The Aes Sedai's face was lost in the night, but her eyes, as big as full moons, shone with impatience as well as anger when they touched him. Swallowing hard, he booted Cloud in the ribs and galloped after the others.

Fifty paces from the wall, Lan drew them up, and Rand looked back. Moiraine's shadowed shape towered high over the log palisade, head and shoulders a deeper darkness against the night sky, surrounded by a silver nimbus from the hidden moon. As he watched, mouth hanging open, the Aes Sedai stepped over the wall. The gates began swinging shut frantically. As soon as her feet were on the ground outside, she was suddenly her normal size again.

"Hold the gates!" an unsteady voice shouted inside the wall. Rand thought it was Bornhald. "We must pursue them, and take them!" But the Watchmen did not slow the pace of closing. The gates slammed shut, and moments later the bar crashed into place, sealing them. *Maybe some of those other Whitecloaks aren't as eager to confront an Aes Sedai as Bornhald.*

Moiraine hurried to Aldieb, stroking the white mare's nose once before she tucked her staff under the girth strap. Rand did not need to look this time to know there was not even a nick in the staff.

"You were taller than a giant," Egwene said breathlessly, shifting on Bela's back. No one else spoke, though Mat and Perrin edged their horses away from the Aes Sedai.

"Was I?" Moiraine said absently as she swung into her saddle.

"I saw you," Egwene protested.

"The mind plays tricks in the night; the eye sees what is not there."

"This is no time for games," Nynaeve began angrily, but Moiraine cut her off.

"No time for games indeed. What we gained at the Stag and Lion we may have lost here." She looked back at the gate and shook her head. "If only I could believe the Draghkar was on the ground." With a self-deprecatory sniff she added, "Or if only the Myrddraal were truly blind. If I am wishing, I might as well wish for the truly impossible. No matter. They know the way we must go, but with luck we will stay a step ahead of them. Lan!"

The Warder moved off eastward down the Caemlyn Road, and the rest followed close behind, hooves thudding rhythmically on the hard-packed earth.

They kept to an easy pace, a fast walk the horses could maintain for hours without any Aes Sedai help. Before they had been even one hour on their way, though, Mat cried out, pointing back the way they had come.

"Look there!"

They all drew rein and stared.

Flames lit the night over Baerlon as if someone had built a house-size bonfire, tinting the undersides of the cloud with red. Sparks whipped into the sky on the wind.

"I warned him," Moiraine said, "but he would not take it seriously." Aldieb danced sideways, an echo of the Aes Sedai's frustration. "He would not take it seriously."

"The inn?" Perrin said. "That's the Stag and Lion? How can you be sure?"

"How far do you want to stretch coincidence?" Thom asked. "It could be the Governor's house, but it isn't. And it isn't a warehouse, or somebody's kitchen stove, or your grandmother's haystack."

"Perhaps the Light shines on us a little this night," Lan said, and Egwene rounded on him angrily.

"How can you say that? Poor Master Fitch's inn is burning! People may be hurt!"

"If they have attacked the inn," Moiraine said, "perhaps our exit from the town and my . . . display went unnoticed."

"Unless that's what the Myrddraal wants us to think," Lan added.

Moiraine nodded in the darkness. "Perhaps. In any case, we must press on. There will be little rest for anyone tonight."

"You say that so easily, Moiraine," Nynaeve exclaimed. "What about the people at the inn? People must be hurt, and the innkeeper has lost his livelihood, because of you! For all your talk about walking in the Light you're ready to go on without sparing a thought for him. His trouble is because of you!"

"Because of those three," Lan said angrily. "The fire, the injured, the going on—all because of those three. The fact that the price must be paid is proof that it is worth paying. The Dark One wants those boys of yours, and anything he wants this badly, he must be kept from. Or would you rather let the Fade have them?"

"Be at ease, Lan," Moiraine said. "Be at ease. Wisdom, you think I can help Master Fitch and the people at the inn? Well, you are right." Nynaeve started to say something, but Moiraine waved it away and went on. "I can go back by myself and give some help. Not too much, of course. That would draw attention to those I helped, attention they would not thank me for, especially with the Children of the Light in the town. And that would leave only Lan to protect the rest of you. He is very good, but it will take more than him if a Myrddraal and a fist of Trollocs find you. Of course, we could all return, though I doubt I can get all of us back into Baerlon unnoticed. And that would expose all of you to whomever set that fire, not to mention the Whitecloaks. Which alternative would you choose, Wisdom, if you were I?"

"I would do something," Nynaeve muttered unwillingly.

"And in all probability hand the Dark One his victory," Moiraine replied. "Remember what—who—it is that he wants. We are in a war, as surely as anyone in Ghealdan, though thousands fight there and only eight of us here. I will have gold sent to Master Fitch, enough to rebuild the Stag and Lion, gold that cannot be traced to Tar Valon. And help for any who were hurt, as well. Any more than that will only endanger them. It is

far from simple, you see. Lan." The Warder turned his horse
and took up the road again.

From time to time Rand looked back. Eventually all he could
see was the glow on the clouds, and then even that was lost in
the darkness. He hoped Min was all right.

All was still pitch-dark when the Warder finally led them off
the packed dirt of the road and dismounted. Rand estimated
there were no more than a couple of hours till dawn. They
hobbled the horses, still saddled, and made a cold camp.

"One hour," Lan warned as everyone except him was wrapping up in their blankets. He would stand guard while they
slept. "One hour, and we must be on our way." Silence settled
over them.

After a few minutes Mat spoke in a whisper that barely
reached Rand. "I wonder what Dav did with that badger."
Rand shook his head silently, and Mat hesitated. Finally he
said, "I thought we were safe, you know, Rand. Not a sign of
anything since we crossed the Taren, and there we were in a
city, with walls around us. I thought we were safe. And then
that dream. And a Fade. Are we ever going to be safe again?"

"Not until we get to Tar Valon," Rand said. "That's what
she told us."

"Will we be safe then?" Perrin asked softly, and all three of
them looked to the shadowy mound that was the Aes Sedai.
Lan had melded into the darkness; he could have been anywhere.

Rand yawned suddenly. The others twitched nervously at the
sound. "I think we'd better get some sleep," he said. "Staying
awake won't answer anything."

Perrin spoke quietly. "She should have done something."

No one answered.

Rand squirmed onto his side to avoid a root, tried his back,
then rolled off of a stone onto his belly and another root. It was
not a good campsite they had stopped at, not like the spots the
Warder had chosen on the way north from the Taren. He fell
asleep wondering if the roots digging into his ribs would make
him dream, and woke at Lan's touch on his shoulder, ribs aching, and grateful that if any dreams had come he did not remember them.

It was still the dark just before dawn, but once the blankets were rolled and strapped behind their saddles Lan had them riding east again. As the sun rose they made a bleary-eyed breakfast on bread and cheese and water, eating while they rode, huddled in their cloaks against the wind. All except Lan, that is. He ate, but he was not bleary-eyed, and he did not huddle. He had changed back into his shifting cloak, and it whipped around him, fluttering through grays and greens, and the only mind he paid it was to keep it clear of his sword-arm. His face remained without expression, but his eyes searched constantly, as if he expected an ambush any moment.

Egwene al'Vere

CHAPTER
18

The Caemlyn Road

The Caemlyn Road was not very different from the North Road through the Two Rivers. It was considerably wider, of course, and showed the wear of much more use, but it was still hard-packed dirt, lined on either side by trees that would not have been at all out of place in the Two Rivers, especially since only the evergreens carried a leaf.

The land itself was different, though, for by midday the road entered low hills. For two days the road ran through the hills—cut right through them, sometimes, if they were wide enough to have made the road go much out of its way and not so big as to have made digging through too difficult. As the angle of the sun shifted each day it became apparent that the road, for all it appeared straight to the eye, curved slowly southward as it ran east. Rand had daydreamed over Master al'Vere's old map—half the boys in Emond's Field had daydreamed over it—and as he remembered, the road curved around something called the Hills of Absher until it reached Whitebridge.

From time to time Lan had them dismount atop one of the hills, where he could get a good view of the road both ahead and behind, and the surrounding countryside as well. The Warder would study the view while the others stretched their legs or sat under the trees and ate.

"I used to like cheese," Egwene said on the third day after leaving Baerlon. She sat with her back to the bole of a tree, grimacing over a dinner that was once again the same as break-

fast, as supper would be. "Not a chance of tea. Nice hot tea."
She pulled her cloak tighter and shifted around the tree in a
vain effort to avoid the swirling wind.

"Flatwort tea and andilay root," Nynaeve was saying to
Moiraine, "are best for fatigue. They clear the head and dim
the burn in tired muscles."

"I am sure they do," the Aes Sedai murmured, giving
Nynaeve a sidelong glance.

Nynaeve's jaw tightened, but she continued in the same tone.
"Now, if you must go without sleep. . . ."

"No tea!" Lan said sharply to Egwene. "No fire! We can't
see them yet, but they are back there, somewhere, a Fade or
two and their Trollocs, and they know we are taking this road.
No need to tell them exactly where we are."

"I wasn't asking," Egwene muttered into her cloak. "Just
regretting."

"If they know we're on the road," Perrin asked, "why don't
we go straight across to Whitebridge?"

"Even Lan cannot travel as fast cross-country as by road,"
Moiraine said, interrupting Nynaeve, "especially not through
the Hills of Absher." The Wisdom gave an exasperated sigh.
Rand wondered what she was up to; after ignoring the Aes
Sedai completely for the first day, Nynaeve had spent the last
two trying to talk to her about herbs. Moiraine moved away
from the Wisdom as she went on. "Why do you think the road
curves to avoid them? And we would have to come back to this
road eventually. We might find them ahead of us instead of
following."

Rand looked doubtful, and Mat muttered something about
"the long way round."

"Have you seen a farm this morning?" Lan asked. "Or even
the smoke from a chimney? You haven't, because it's all wil-
derness from Baerlon to Whitebridge, and Whitebridge is
where we must cross the Arinelle. That is the only bridge span-
ning the Arinelle south of Maradon, in Saldaea."

Thom snorted and blew out his mustaches. "What is to stop
them from having someone, something, at Whitebridge already?"

From the west came the keening wail of a horn. Lan's head
whipped around to stare back down the road behind them.

Rand felt a chill. A part of him remained calm enough to think, ten miles, no more.

"Nothing stops them, gleeman," the Warder said. "We trust to the Light and luck. But now we know for certain there are Trollocs behind us."

Moiraine dusted her hands. "It is time for us to move on." The Aes Sedai mounted her white mare.

That set off a scramble for the horses, speeded by a second winding of the horn. This time others answered, the thin sounds floating out of the west like a dirge. Rand made ready to put Cloud to a gallop right away, and everyone else settled their reins with the same urgency. Everyone except Lan and Moiraine. The Warder and the Aes Sedai exchanged a long look.

"Keep them moving, Moiraine Sedai," Lan said finally. "I will return as soon as I am able. You will know if I fail." Putting a hand on Mandarb's saddle, he vaulted to the back of the black stallion and galloped down the hill. Heading west. The horns sounded again.

"The Light go with you, last Lord of the Seven Towers," Moiraine said almost too softly for Rand to hear. Drawing a deep breath, she turned Aldieb to the east. "We must go on," she said, and started off at a slow, steady trot. The others followed her in a tight file.

Rand twisted once in his saddle to look for Lan, but the Warder was already lost to sight among the low hills and leafless trees. Last Lord of the Seven Towers, she had called him. He wondered what that meant. He had not thought anyone besides himself had heard, but Thom was chewing the ends of his mustaches, and he had a speculative frown on his face. The gleeman seemed to know a great many things.

The horns called and answered once more behind them. Rand shifted in his saddle. They were closer this time; he was sure of it. Eight miles. Maybe seven. Mat and Egwene looked over their shoulders, and Perrin hunched as if he expected something to hit him in the back. Nynaeve rode up to speak to Moiraine.

"Can't we go any faster?" she asked. "Those horns are getting closer."

The Aes Sedai shook her head. "And why do they let us

know they are there? Perhaps so we will hurry on without thinking of what might be ahead."

They kept on at the same steady pace. At intervals the horns gave cry behind them, and each time the sound was closer. Rand tried to stop thinking of how close, but the thought came unbidden at every brazen wail. Five miles, he was thinking anxiously, when Lan suddenly burst around the hill behind them at a gallop.

He came abreast of Moiraine, reining in the stallion. "At least three fists of Trollocs, each led by a Halfman. Maybe five."

"If you were close enough to see them," Egwene said worriedly, "they could have seen you. They could be right on your heels."

"He was not seen." Nynaeve drew herself up as everyone looked at her. "I have followed his trail, remember."

"Hush," Moiraine commanded. "Lan is telling us there are perhaps five hundred Trollocs behind us." A stunned silence followed, then Lan spoke again.

"And they are closing the gap. They will be on us in an hour or less."

Half to herself, the Aes Sedai said, "If they had that many before, why were they not used at Emond's Field? If they did not, how did they come here since?"

"They are spread out to drive us before them," Lan said, "with scouts quartering ahead of the main parties."

"Driving us toward what?" Moiraine mused. As if to answer her a horn sounded in the distance to the west, a long moan that was answered this time by others, all ahead of them. Moiraine stopped Aldieb; the others followed her lead, Thom and the Emond's Field folk looking around fearfully. Horns cried out before them, and behind. Rand thought they held a note of triumph.

"What do we do now?" Nynaeve demanded angrily. "Where do we go?"

"All that is left is north or south," Moiraine said, more thinking aloud than answering the Wisdom. "To the south are the Hills of Absher, barren and dead, and the Taren, with no way to cross, and no traffic by boat. To the north, we can reach the Arinelle before nightfall, and there will be a chance of a trader's boat. If the ice has broken at Maradon."

"There is a place the Trollocs will not go," Lan said, but Moiraine's head whipped around sharply.

"No!" She motioned to the Warder, and he put his head close to hers so their talk could not be overheard.

The horns winded, and Rand's horse danced nervously.

"They're trying to frighten us," Thom growled, attempting to steady his mount. He sounded half angry and half as if the Trollocs were succeeding. "They're trying to scare us until we panic and run. They'll have us, then."

Egwene's head swung with every blast of a horn, staring first ahead of them, then behind, as if looking for the first Trollocs. Rand wanted to do the same thing, but he tried to hide it. He moved Cloud closer to her.

"We go north," Moiraine announced.

The horns keened shrilly as they left the road and trotted into the surrounding hills.

The hills were low, but the way was all up and down, with never a flat stretch, beneath bare-branched trees and through dead undergrowth. The horses climbed laboriously up one slope only to canter down the other. Lan set a hard pace, faster than they had used on the road.

Branches lashed Rand across the face and chest. Old creepers and vines caught his arms, and sometimes snagged his foot right out of the stirrup. The keening horns came ever closer, and ever more frequently.

As hard as Lan pushed them, they were not getting farther on very quickly. They traveled two feet up or down for every one forward, and every foot was a scrambling effort. And the horns were coming nearer. *Two miles,* he thought. *Maybe less.*

After a time Lan began peering first one way then another, the hard planes of his face as close to worry as Rand had seen them. Once the Warder stood in his stirrups to stare back the way they had come. All Rand could see were trees. Lan settled back into his saddle and unconsciously pushed back his cloak to clear his sword as he resumed searching the forest.

Rand met Mat's eye questioningly, but Mat only grimaced at the Warder's back and shrugged helplessly.

Lan spoke, then, over his shoulder. "There are Trollocs

nearby." They topped a hill and started down the other side. "Some of the scouts, sent ahead of the rest. Probably. If we come on them, stay with me at all costs, and do as I do. We must keep on the way we are going."

"Blood and ashes!" Thom muttered. Nynaeve motioned to Egwene to keep close.

Scattered stands of evergreens provided the only real cover, but Rand tried to peer in every direction at once, his imagination turning gray tree trunks caught out of the corner of his eye into Trollocs. The horns were closer, too. And directly behind them. He was sure of it. Behind and coming closer.

They topped another hill.

Below them, just starting up the slope, marched Trollocs carrying poles tipped with great loops of rope or long hooks. Many Trollocs. The line stretched far to either side, the ends out of sight, but at its center, directly in front of Lan, a Fade rode.

The Myrddraal seemed to hesitate as the humans appeared atop the hill, but in the next instant it produced a sword with the black blade Rand remembered so queasily, and waved it over its head. The line of Trollocs scrambled forward.

Even before the Myrddraal moved, Lan's sword was in his hand. "Stay with me!" he cried, and Mandarb plunged down the slope toward the Trollocs. "For the Seven Towers!" he shouted.

Rand gulped and booted the gray forward; the whole group of them streamed after the Warder. He was surprised to find Tam's sword in his fist. Caught up by Lan's cry, he found his own. "Manetheren! Manetheren!"

Perrin took it up. "Manetheren! Manetheren!"

But Mat shouted, *"Carai an Caldazar! Carai an Ellisande! Al Ellisande!"*

The Fade's head turned from the Trollocs to the riders charging toward him. The black sword froze over its head, and the opening of its cowl swiveled, searching among the oncoming horsemen.

Then Lan was on the Myrddraal, as the human folk fell on the Trolloc line. Warder's blade met black steel from the forges at Thakan'dar with a clang like a great bell, the toll echoing in the hollow, a flash of blue light filling the air like sheet lightning.

Beast-muzzled almost-men swarmed around each of the humans, catchpoles and hooks flailing. Only Lan and the Myrddraal did they avoid; those two fought in a clear circle, black horses matching step for step, swords matching stroke for stroke. The air flashed and pealed.

Cloud rolled his eyes and screamed, rearing and lashing out with his hooves at the snarling, sharp-toothed faces surrounding him. Heavy bodies crowded shoulder-to-shoulder around him. Digging his heels in ruthlessly, Rand forced the gray on regardless, swinging his sword with little of the skill Lan had tried to impart, hacking as if hewing wood. *Egwene!* Desperately he searched for her as he kicked the gray onward, slashing a path through the hairy bodies as though chopping undergrowth.

Moiraine's white mare dashed and cut at the slightest touch of the Aes Sedai's hand on the reins. Her face was as hard as Lan's as her staff lashed out. Flame enveloped Trollocs, then burst with a roar that left misshapen forms unmoving on the ground. Nynaeve and Egwene rode close to the Aes Sedai with frantic urgency, teeth bared almost as fiercely as the Trollocs', belt knives in hand. Those short blades would be no use at all if a Trolloc came close. Rand tried to turn Cloud toward them, but the gray had the bit in his teeth. Screaming and kicking, Cloud struggled forward however hard Rand tugged at the reins.

Around the three women a space opened as Trollocs tried to flee from Moiraine's staff, but as they attempted to avoid her, she sought them out. Fires roared, and the Trollocs howled in rage and fury. Above roar and howl crashed the tolling of the Warder's sword against the Myrddraal's; the air flared blue around them, flared again. Again.

A noose on the end of a pole swept at Rand's head. With an awkward slash, he cut the catchpole in two, then hacked the goat-faced Trolloc that held it. A hook caught his shoulder from behind and tangled in his cloak, jerking him backwards. Frantically, almost losing his sword, he clutched the pommel of his saddle to keep his seat. Cloud twisted, shrieking. Rand hung onto saddle and reins desperately; he could feel himself slipping, inch by inch, falling to the hook. Cloud swung around; for an instant Rand saw Perrin, half out of his saddle, struggling to wrest his axe away from three Trollocs. They had him by one arm and both legs. Cloud plunged, and only Trollocs filled Rand's eyes.

A Trolloc dashed in and seized Rand's leg, forcing his foot free of the stirrup. Panting, he let go of the saddle to stab it. Instantly the hook pulled him out of the saddle, to Cloud's hindquarters; his death-grip on the reins was all that kept him from the ground. Cloud reared and shrieked. And in that same moment the pulling vanished. The Trolloc at his leg threw up its hands and screamed. All of the Trollocs screamed, a howl like all the dogs in the world gone mad.

Around the humans Trollocs fell writhing to the ground, tearing at their hair, clawing their own faces. All of the Trollocs. Biting at the ground, snapping at nothing, howling, howling, howling.

Then Rand saw the Myrddraal. Still upright in the saddle of its madly dancing horse, black sword still flailing, it had no head.

"It won't die until nightfall," Thom had to shout, between heavy breaths, over the unrelenting screams. "Not completely. That is what I've heard, anyway."

"Ride!" Lan shouted angrily. The Warder had already gathered Moiraine and the other two women and had them halfway up the next hill. "This is not all of them!" Indeed, the horns dirged again, above the shrieks of the Trollocs on the ground, to east and west and south.

For a wonder, Mat was the only one who had been unhorsed. Rand trotted toward him, but Mat tossed a noose away from him with a shudder, gathered his bow, and scrambled into his saddle unaided, though rubbing at his throat.

The horns bayed like hounds with the scent of a deer. Hounds closing in. If Lan had set a hard pace before, he doubled it now, till the horses scrabbled uphill faster than they had gone down before, then nearly threw themselves at the other side. But still the horns came ever nearer, until the guttural shouts of pursuit were heard whenever the horns paused, until eventually the humans reached a hilltop just as Trollocs appeared on the next hill behind them. The hilltop blackened with Trollocs, snouted, distorted faces howling, and three Myrddraal overawed them all. Only a hundred spans separated the two parties.

Rand's heart shriveled like an old grape. *Three!*

The Myrddraal's black swords rose as one; Trollocs boiled down the slope, thick, triumphant cries rising, catchpoles bobbing above as they ran.

Moiraine climbed down from Aldieb's back. Calmly she removed something from her pouch, unwrapped it. Rand glimpsed dark ivory. The *angreal*. With *angreal* in one hand and staff in the other, the Aes Sedai set her feet, facing the onrushing Trollocs and the Fades' black swords, raised her staff high, and stabbed it down into the earth.

The ground rang like an iron kettle struck by a mallet. The hollow clang dwindled, faded away. For an instant then, it was silent. Everything was silent. The wind died. The Trolloc cries stilled; even their charge forward slowed and stopped. For a heartbeat, everything waited. Slowly the dull ringing returned, changing to a low rumble, growing until the earth moaned.

The ground trembled beneath Cloud's hooves. This was Aes Sedai work like the stories told about; Rand wished he were a hundred miles away. The tremble became a shaking that set the trees around them quivering. The gray stumbled and nearly fell. Even Mandarb and riderless Aldieb staggered as if drunk, and those who rode had to cling to reins and manes, to anything, to keep their seats.

The Aes Sedai still stood as she had begun, holding the *angreal* and her upright staff thrust into the hilltop, and neither she nor the staff moved an inch, for all that the ground shook and shivered around her. Now the ground rippled, springing out from in front of her staff, lapping toward the Trollocs like ripples on a pond, ripples that grew as they ran, toppling old bushes, flinging dead leaves into the air, growing, becoming waves of earth, rolling toward the Trollocs. Trees in the hollow lashed like switches in the hands of small boys. On the far slope Trollocs fell in heaps, tumbled over and over by the raging earth.

Yet as if the ground were not rearing all around them, the Myrddraal moved forward in a line, their dead-black horses never missing a step, every hoof in unison. Trollocs rolled on the ground all about the black steeds, howling and grabbing at the hillside that heaved them up, but the Myrddraal came slowly on.

Moiraine lifted her staff, and the earth stilled, but she was not done. She pointed to the hollow between the hills, and flame gouted from the ground, a fountain twenty feet high. She flung her arms wide, and the fire raced to left and right as far as the eye could see, spreading into a wall separating humans and Trollocs. The heat made Rand put his hands in front of his face, even on the hilltop. The Myrddraal's black mounts, whatever strange powers they had, screamed at the fire, reared and fought their riders as the Myrddraal beat at them, trying to force them through the flames.

"Blood and ashes," Mat said faintly. Rand nodded numbly.

Abruptly Moiraine wavered and would have fallen had Lan not leaped from his horse to catch her. "Go on," he told the others. The harshness of his voice was at odds with the gentle way he lifted the Aes Sedai to her saddle. "That fire won't burn forever. Hurry! Every minute counts!"

The wall of flame roared as if it would indeed burn forever, but Rand did not argue. They galloped northward as fast as they could make their horses go. The horns in the distance shrilled out disappointment, as if they already knew what had happened, then fell silent.

Lan and Moiraine soon caught up with the others, though Lan led Aldieb by the reins while the Aes Sedai swayed and held the pommel of her saddle with both hands. "I will be all right soon," she said to their worried looks. She sounded tired yet confident, and her gaze was as compelling as ever. "I am not at my strongest when working with Earth and Fire. A small thing."

The two of them moved into the lead again at a fast walk. Rand did not think Moiraine could stay in the saddle at any faster pace. Nynaeve rode foward beside the Aes Sedai, steadying her with a hand. For a time as the party went on across the hills the two women whispered, then the Wisdom delved into her cloak and handed a small packet to Moiraine. Moiraine unfolded it and swallowed the contents. Nynaeve said something more, then fell back with the others, ignoring their questioning looks. Despite their circumstances, Rand thought she had a slight look of satisfaction.

He did not really care what the Wisdom was up to. He rubbed the hilt of his sword continually, and whenever he realized what he was doing, he stared down at it in wonder. *So that's what a battle is like.* He could not remember much of it, not any particular part. Everything ran together in his head, a melted mass of hairy faces and fear. Fear and heat. It had seemed as hot as a midsummer noon while it was going on. He could not understand that. The icy wind was trying to freeze beads of perspiration all over his face and body.

He glanced at his two friends. Mat was scrubbing sweat off his face with the edge of his cloak. Perrin, staring at something in the distance and not liking what he was seeing, appeared unaware of the beads glistening on his forehead.

The hills grew smaller, and the land began to level out, but instead of pressing on, Lan stopped. Nynaeve moved as if to rejoin Moiraine, but the Warder's look kept her away. He and the Aes Sedai rode ahead and put their heads together, and from Moiraine's gestures it became apparent they were arguing. Nynaeve and Thom stared at them, the Wisdom frowning worriedly, the gleeman muttering under his breath and pausing to stare back the way they had come, but everyone else avoided looking at them altogether. Who knew what might come out of an argument between an Aes Sedai and a Warder?

After a few minutes Egwene spoke to Rand quietly, casting an uneasy eye at the still-arguing pair. "Those things you were shouting at the Trollocs." She stopped as if unsure how to proceed.

"What about them?" Rand asked. He felt a little awkward—warcries were all right for Warders; Two Rivers folk did not do things like that, whatever Moiraine said—but if she made fun of him over it. . . . "Mat must have repeated that story ten times."

"And badly," Thom put in. Mat grunted in protest.

"However he told it," Rand said, "we've all heard it any number of times. Besides, we had to shout something. I mean, that's what you do at a time like that. You heard Lan."

"And we have a right," Perrin added thoughtfully. "Moiraine says we're all descended from those Manetheren people. They fought the Dark One, and we're fighting the Dark One. That gives us a right."

Egwene sniffed as if to show what she thought of that. "I

wasn't talking about that. What . . . what was it you were shouting, Mat?"

Mat shrugged uncomfortably. "I don't remember." He stared at them defensively. "Well, I don't. It's all foggy. I don't know what it was, or where it came from, or what it means." He gave a self-deprecating laugh. "I don't suppose it means anything."

"I . . . I think it does," Egwene said slowly. "When you shouted, I thought—just for a minute—I thought I understood you. But it's all gone, now." She sighed and shook her head. "Perhaps you're right. Strange what you can imagine at a time like that, isn't it?"

"*Carai an Caldazar,*" Moiraine said. They all twisted to stare at her. "*Carai an Ellisande. Al Ellisande.* For the honor of the Red Eagle. For the honor of the Rose of the Sun. The Rose of the Sun. The ancient warcry of Manetheren, and the warcry of its last king. Eldrene was called the Rose of the Sun." Moiraine's smile took in Egwene and Mat both, though her gaze may have rested a moment longer on him than on her. "The blood of Arad's line is still strong in the Two Rivers. The old blood still sings."

Mat and Egwene looked at each other, while everyone else looked at them both. Egwene's eyes were wide, and her mouth kept quirking into a smile that she bit back every time it began, as if she was not sure just how to take this talk of the old blood. Mat was sure, from the scowling frown on his face.

Rand thought he knew what Mat was thinking. The same thing he was thinking. If Mat was a descendant of the ancient kings of Manetheren, maybe the Trollocs were really after him and not all three of them. The thought made him ashamed. His cheeks colored, and when he caught a guilty grimace on Perrin's face, he knew Perrin had been having the same thought.

"I can't say that I have ever heard the like of this," Thom said after a minute. He shook himself and became brusque. "Another time I might even make a story out of it, but right now. . . . Do you intend to remain here for the rest of the day, Aes Sedai?"

"No," Moiraine replied, gathering her reins.

A Trolloc horn keened from the south as if to emphasize her

word. More horns answered, east and west. The horses whickered and sidled about nervously.

"They have passed the fire," Lan said calmly. He turned to Moiraine. "You are not strong enough for what you intend, not yet, not without rest. And neither Myrddraal nor Trolloc will enter that place."

Moiraine raised a hand as if to cut him off, then sighed and let it fall instead. "Very well," she said irritably. "You are right, I suppose, but I would rather there was any other choice." She pulled her staff from under the girth strap of her saddle. "Gather in around me, all of you. As close as you can. Closer."

Rand urged Cloud nearer the Aes Sedai's mare. At Moiraine's insistence they kept on crowding closer in a circle around her until every horse had its head stretched over the croup or withers of another. Only then was the Aes Sedai satisfied. Then, without speaking, she stood in the stirrups and swung her staff over their heads, stretching to make certain it covered everyone.

Rand flinched each time the staff passed over him. A tingle ran through him with every pass. He could have followed the staff without seeing it, just by following the shivers as it moved over people. It was no surprise to him that Lan was the only one not affected.

Abruptly Moiraine thrust the staff out to the west. Dead leaves whirled into the air and branches whipped as if a dust-devil ran along the line she pointed to. As the invisible whirlwind vanished from sight she settled back into her saddle with a sigh.

"To the Trollocs," she said, "our scents and our tracks will seem to follow that. The Myrddraal will see through it in time, but by then. . . ."

"By then," Lan said, "we will have lost ourselves."

"Your staff is very powerful," Egwene said, earning a sniff from Nynaeve.

Moiraine made a clicking sound. "I have told you, child, things do not have power. The One Power comes from the True Source, and only a living mind can wield it. This is not even an *angreal*, merely an aid to concentration." Wearily she slid the staff back under her girth strap. "Lan?"

"Follow me," the Warder said, "and keep quiet. It will ruin everything if the Trollocs hear us."

He led the way north again, not at the crashing pace they had been making, but rather in the quick walk with which they had traveled the Caemlyn Road. The land continued to flatten, though the forest remained as thick.

Their path was no longer straight, as it had been before, for Lan chose out a route that meandered over hard ground and rocky outcrops, and he no longer let them force their way through tangles of brush, instead taking the time to make their way around. Now and again he dropped to the rear, intently studying the trail they made. If anyone so much as coughed, it drew a sharp grunt from him.

Nynaeve rode beside the Aes Sedai, concern battling dislike on her face. And there was a hint of something more, Rand thought, almost as if the Wisdom saw some goal in sight. Moiraine's shoulders were slumped, and she held her reins and the saddle with both hands, swaying with every step Aldieb took. It was plain that laying the false trail, small as that might have seemed beside producing an earthquake and a wall of flame, had taken a great deal out of her, strength she no longer had to lose.

Rand almost wished the horns would start again. At least they were a way of telling how far back the Trollocs were. And the Fades.

He kept looking behind them, and so was not the first to see what lay ahead. When he did, he stared, perplexed. A great, irregular mass stretched off to either side out of sight, in most places as high as the trees that grew right up to it, with even taller spires here and there. Leafless vines and creepers covered it all in thick layers. A cliff? *The vines will make climbing easy, but we'll never get the horses up.*

Suddenly, as they rode a little closer, he saw a tower. It was clearly a tower, not some kind of rock formation, with an odd, pointed dome on the top. "A city!" he said. And a city wall, and the spires were guard towers on the wall. His jaw dropped. It had to be ten times as big as Baerlon. Fifty times as big.

Mat nodded. "A city," he agreed. "But what's a city doing in the middle of a forest like this?"

"And without any people," Perrin said. When they looked at

him, he pointed to the wall. "Would people let vines grow over everything like that? You know how creepers can tear down a wall. Look how it's fallen."

What Rand saw adjusted itself in his mind again. It was as Perrin said. Under almost every low place in the wall was a brush-covered hill; rubble from the collapsed wall above. No two of the guard towers were the same height.

"I wonder what city it was," Egwene mused. "I wonder what happened to it. I don't remember anything from papa's map."

"It was called Aridhol," Moiraine said. "In the days of the Trolloc Wars, it was an ally of Manetheren." Staring at the massive walls, she seemed almost unaware of the others, even of Nynaeve, who supported her in the saddle with a hand on her arm. "Later Aridhol died, and this place was called by another name."

"What name?" Mat asked.

"Here," Lan said. He stopped Mandarb in front of what had once been a gate wide enough for fifty men to march through abreast. Only the broken, vine-encrusted watchtowers remained; of the gates there was no sign. "We enter here." Trolloc horns shrieked in the distance. Lan peered in the direction of the sound, then looked at the sun, halfway down toward the treetops in the west. "They have discovered it's a false trail. Come, we must find shelter before dark."

"What name?" Mat asked again.

Moiraine answered as they rode into the city. "Shadar Logoth," she said. "It is called Shadar Logoth."

CHAPTER
19

Shadow's Waiting

Broken paving stones crunched under the horses' hooves as Lan led the way into the city. The entire city was broken, what Rand could see of it, and as abandoned as Perrin had said. Not so much as a pigeon moved, and weeds, mainly old and dead, sprouted from cracks in walls as well as pavement. More buildings had roofs fallen in than had them whole. Tumbled walls spilled fans of brick and stone into the streets. Towers stopped, abrupt and jagged, like broken sticks. Uneven rubble hills with a few stunted trees growing on their slopes could have been the remains of palaces or of entire blocks of the city.

Yet what was left standing was enough to take Rand's breath. The largest building in Baerlon would have vanished in the shadows of almost anything here. Pale marble palaces topped with huge domes met him wherever he looked. Every building appeared to have at least one dome; some had four or five, and each one shaped differently. Long walks lined by columns ran hundreds of paces to towers that seemed to reach the sky. At every intersection stood a bronze fountain, or the alabaster spire of a monument, or a statue on a pedestal. If the fountains were dry, most of the spires toppled, and many of the statues broken, what remained was so great that he could only marvel.

And I thought Baerlon was a city! Burn me, but Thom must have been laughing up his sleeve. Moiraine and Lan, too.

He was so caught up in staring that he was taken by surprise when Lan suddenly stopped in front of a white stone building that had once been twice as big as the Stag and Lion in Baerlon. There was nothing to say what it had been when the city lived and was great, perhaps even an inn. Only a hollow shell remained of the upper floors—the afternoon sky was visible through empty window frames, glass and wood alike long since gone—but the ground floor seemed sound enough.

Moiraine, hands still on the pommel, studied the building intently before nodding. "This will do."

Lan leaped from his saddle and lifted the Aes Sedai down in his arms. "Bring the horses inside," he commanded. "Find a room in the back to use for a stable. Move, farmboys. This isn't the village green." He vanished inside carrying the Aes Sedai.

Nynaeve scrambled down and hurried after him, clutching her bag of herbs and ointments. Egwene was right behind her. They left their mounts standing.

"'Bring the horses inside,'" Thom muttered wryly, and puffed out his mustaches. He climbed down, stiff and slow, knuckled his back, and gave a long sigh, then took Aldieb's reins. "Well?" he said, lifting an eyebrow at Rand and his friends.

They hurried to dismount, and gathered up the rest of the horses. The doorway, without anything to say there had ever been a door in it, was more than big enough to get the animals through, even two abreast.

Inside was a huge room, as wide as the building, with a dirty tile floor and a few ragged wall hangings, faded to a dull brown, that looked as if they would fall apart at a touch. Nothing else. Lan had made a place in the nearest corner for Moiraine with his cloak and hers. Nynaeve, muttering about the dust, knelt beside the Aes Sedai, digging in her bag, which Egwene held open.

"I may not like her, it is true," Nynaeve was saying to the Warder as Rand, leading Bela and Cloud, came in behind Thom, "but I help anyone who needs my help, whether I like them or not."

"I made no accusation, Wisdom. I only said, have a care with your herbs."

She gave him a look from the corner of her eye. "The fact is, she needs my herbs, and so do you." Her voice was acerbic to start, and grew more tart as she spoke. "The fact is, she can only do so much, even with her One Power, and she has done about as much as she can without collapsing. The fact is, your sword cannot help her now, Lord of the Seven Towers, but my herbs can."

Moiraine laid a hand on Lan's arm. "Be at ease, Lan. She means no harm. She simply does not know." The Warder snorted derisively.

Nynaeve stopped digging in her bag and looked at him, frowning, but it was to Moiraine she spoke. "There are many things I don't know. What thing is this?"

"For one," Moiraine replied, "all I truly need is a little rest. For another, I agree with you. Your skills and knowledge will be more useful than I thought. Now, if you have something that will help me sleep for an hour and not leave me groggy—?"

"A weak tea of foxtail, marisin, and—"

Rand missed the last of it as he followed Thom into a room behind the first, a chamber just as big and even emptier. Here was only the dust, thick and undisturbed until they came. Not even the tracks of birds or small animals marked the floor.

Rand began to unsaddle Bela and Cloud, and Thom, Aldieb and his gelding, and Perrin, his horse and Mandarb. All but Mat. He dropped his reins in the middle of the room. There were two doorways from the room besides the one by which they had entered.

"Alley," Mat announced, drawing his head back in from the first. They could all see that much from where they were. The second doorway was only a black rectangle in the rear wall. Mat went through slowly, and came out much faster, vigorously brushing old cobwebs out of his hair. "Nothing in there," he said, giving the alleyway another look.

"You going to take care of your horse?" Perrin said. He had already finished his own and was lifting the saddle from Mandarb. Strangely, the fierce-eyed stallion gave him no trouble at all, though he did watch Perrin. "Nobody is going to do it for you."

Mat gave the alley one last look and went to his horse with a sigh.

As Rand laid Bela's saddle on the floor, he noticed that Mat had taken on a glum stare. His eyes seemed a thousand miles away, and he was moving by rote.

"Are you all right, Mat?" Rand said. Mat lifted the saddle from his horse, and stood holding it. "Mat? Mat!"

Mat gave a start and almost dropped the saddle. "What? Oh. I . . . I was just thinking."

"Thinking?" Perrin hooted from where he was replacing Mandarb's bridle with a hackamore. "You were asleep."

Mat scowled. "I was thinking about . . . about what happened back there. About those words I. . . ." Everybody turned to look at him then, not just Rand, and he shifted uneasily. "Well, you heard what Moiraine said. It's as if some dead man was speaking with my mouth. I don't like it." His scowl grew deeper when Perrin chuckled.

"Aemon's warcry, she said—right? Maybe you're Aemon come back again. The way you go on about how dull Emond's Field is, I'd think you would like that—being a king and hero reborn."

"Don't say that!" Thom drew a deep breath; everybody stared at him now. "That is dangerous talk, stupid talk. The dead can be reborn, or take a living body, and it is not something to speak of lightly." He took another breath to calm himself before going on. "The old blood, she said. The blood, not a dead man. I've heard that it can happen, sometimes. Heard, though I never really thought. . . . It was your roots, boy. A line running from you to your father to your grandfather, right on back to Manetheren, and maybe beyond. Well, now you know your family is old. You ought to let it go at that and be glad. Most people don't know much more than that they had a father."

Some of us can't even be sure of that, Rand thought bitterly. *Maybe the Wisdom was right. Light, I hope she was.*

Mat nodded at what the gleeman said. "I suppose I should. Only . . . do you think it has anything to do with what's happened to us? The Trollocs and all? I mean . . . oh, I don't know what I mean."

"I think you ought to forget about it, and concentrate on getting out of here safely." Thom produced his long-stemmed pipe from inside his cloak. "And I think I am going to have a smoke." With a waggle of the pipe in their direction, he disappeared into the front room.

"We are all in this together, not just one of us," Rand told Mat.

Mat gave himself a shake, and laughed, a short bark. "Right. Well, speaking of being in things together, now that we're done with the horses, why don't we go see a little more of this city. A real city, and no crowds to jostle your elbow and poke you in the ribs. Nobody looking down their long noses at us. There's still an hour, maybe two, of daylight left."

"Aren't you forgetting the Trollocs?" Perrin said.

Mat shook his head scornfully. "Lan said they wouldn't come in here, remember? You need to listen to what people say."

"I remember," Perrin said. "And I do listen. This city—Aridhol?—was an ally of Manetheren. See? I listen."

"Aridhol must have been the greatest city in the Trolloc Wars," Rand said, "for the Trollocs to still be afraid of it. They weren't afraid to come into the Two Rivers, and Moiraine said Manetheren was—how did she put it?—a thorn to the Dark One's foot."

Perrin raised his hands. "Don't mention the Shepherd of the Night. Please?"

"What do you say?" Mat laughed. "Let's go."

"We should ask Moiraine," Perrin said, and Mat threw up his hands.

"Ask Moiraine? You think she'll let us out of her sight? And what about Nynaeve? Blood and ashes, Perrin, why not ask Mistress Luhhan while you're about it?"

Perrin nodded reluctant agreement, and Mat turned to Rand with a grin. "What about you? A real city? With palaces!" He gave a sly laugh. "And no Whitecloaks to stare at us."

Rand gave him a dirty look, but he hesitated only a minute. Those palaces were like a gleeman's tale. "All right."

Stepping softly so as not to be heard in the front room, they left by the alley, following it away from the front of the building to a street on the other side. They walked quickly, and when they were a block away from the white stone building Mat suddenly broke into a capering dance.

"Free." He laughed. "Free!" He slowed until he was turning

a circle, staring at everything and still laughing. The afternoon shadows stretched long and jagged, and the sinking sun made the ruined city golden. "Did you ever even dream of a place like this? Did you?"

Perrin laughed, too, but Rand shrugged uncomfortably. This was nothing like the city in his first dream, but just the same. . . . "If we're going to see anything," he said, "we had better get on with it. There isn't much daylight left."

Mat wanted to see everything, it seemed, and he pulled the others along with his enthusiasm. They climbed over dusty fountains with basins wide enough to hold everybody in Emond's Field and wandered in and out of structures chosen at random, but always the biggest they could find. Some they understood, and some not. A palace was plainly a palace, but what was a huge building that was one round, white dome as big as a hill outside and one monstrous room inside? And a walled place, open to the sky and big enough to have held all of Emond's Field, surrounded by row on row on row of stone benches?

Mat grew impatient when they found nothing but dust, or rubble, or colorless rags of wall hangings that crumbled at a touch. Once some wooden chairs stood stacked against a wall; they all fell to bits when Perrin tried to pick one up.

The palaces, with their huge, empty chambers, some of which could have held the Winespring Inn with room to spare on every side and above as well, made Rand think too much of the people who had once filled them. He thought everybody in the Two Rivers could have stood under that round dome, and as for the place with the stone benches. . . . He could almost imagine he could see the people in the shadows, staring in disapproval at the three intruders disturbing their rest.

Finally even Mat tired, grand as the buildings were, and remembered that he had had only an hour's sleep the night before. Everyone began to remember that. Yawning, they sat on the steps of a tall building fronted by row on row of tall stone columns and argued about what to do next.

"Go back," Rand said, "and get some sleep." He put the back of his hand against his mouth. When he could talk again, he said, "Sleep. That's all I want."

"You can sleep anytime," Mat said determinedly. "Look at where we are. A ruined city. Treasure."

"Treasure?" Perrin's jaws cracked. "There isn't any treasure here. There isn't anything but dust."

Rand shaded his eyes against the sun, a red ball sitting close to the rooftops. "It's getting late, Mat. It'll be dark soon."

"There could be treasure," Mat maintained stoutly. "Anyway, I want to climb one of the towers. Look at that one over there. It's whole. I'll bet you could see for miles from up there. What do you say?"

"The towers are not safe," said a man's voice behind them.

Rand leaped to his feet and spun around clutching his sword hilt, and the others were just as quick.

A man stood in the shadows among the columns at the top of the stairs. He took half a step forward, raised his hand to shield his eyes, and stepped back again. "Forgive me," he said smoothly. "I have been quite a long time in the dark inside. My eyes are not yet used to the light."

"Who are you?" Rand thought the man's accent sounded odd, even after Baerlon; some words he pronounced strangely, so Rand could barely understand them. "What are you doing here? We thought the city was empty."

"I am Mordeth." He paused as if expecting them to recognize the name. When none of them gave any sign of doing so, he muttered something under his breath and went on. "I could ask the same questions of you. There has been no one in Aridhol for a long time. A long, long time. I would not have thought to find three young men wandering its streets."

"We're on our way to Caemlyn," Rand said. "We stopped to take shelter for the night."

"Caemlyn," Mordeth said slowly, rolling the name around his tongue, then shook his head. "Shelter for the night, you say? Perhaps you will join me."

"You still haven't said what you're doing here," Perrin said.

"Why, I am a treasure hunter, of course."

"Have you found any?" Mat demanded excitedly.

Rand thought Mordeth smiled, but in the shadows he could not be sure. "I have," the man said. "More than I expected. Much more. More than I can carry away. I never expected to find three strong, healthy young men. If you will help me move what I *can* take to where my horses are, you may each have a share of the rest. As much as you can carry. Whatever I leave will be gone, carried off by some other treasure hunter, before I can return for it."

"I told you there must be treasure in a place like this," Mat exclaimed. He darted up the stairs. "We'll help you carry it. Just take us to it." He and Mordeth moved deeper into the shadows among the columns.

Rand looked at Perrin. "We can't leave him." Perrin glanced at the sinking sun, and nodded.

They went up the stairs warily, Perrin easing his axe in its belt loop. Rand's hand tightened on his sword. But Mat and Mordeth were waiting among the columns, Mordeth with arms folded, Mat peering impatiently into the interior.

"Come," Mordeth said. "I will show you the treasure." He slipped inside, and Mat followed. There was nothing for the others to do but go on.

The hall inside was shadowy, but almost immediately Mordeth turned aside and took some narrow steps that wound around and down through deeper and deeper dark until they fumbled their way in pitch-blackness. Rand felt along the wall with one hand, unsure there would be a step below until his foot met it. Even Mat began to feel uneasy, judging by his voice when he said, "It's awfully dark down here."

"Yes, yes," Mordeth replied. The man seemed to be having no trouble at all with the dark. "There are lights below. Come."

Indeed the winding stairs abruptly gave way to a corridor dimly lit by scattered, smoky torches set in iron sconces on the walls. The flickering flames and shadows gave Rand his first good look at Mordeth, who hurried on without pausing, motioning them to follow.

There was something odd about him, Rand thought, but he could not pick out what it was, exactly. Mordeth was a sleek, somewhat overfed man, with drooping eyelids that made him seem to be hiding behind something and staring. Short, and completely bald, he walked as if he were taller than any of them. His clothes were certainly like nothing Rand had ever seen before, either. Tight black breeches and soft red boots with the tops turned down at his ankles. A long, red vest thickly embroidered in gold, and a snowy white shirt with wide sleeves, the points of his cuffs hanging almost to his knees. Certainly not the kind of clothes in which to hunt through a ruined city in search of treasure. But it was not that which made him seem strange, either.

Then the corridor ended in a tile-walled room, and he forgot about any oddities Mordeth might have. His gasp was an echo of his friends'. Here, too, light came from a few torches staining the ceiling with their smoke and giving everyone more than one shadow, but that light was reflected a thousand times by the gems and gold piled on the floor, mounds of coins and jewelry, goblets and plates and platters, gilded, gem-encrusted swords and daggers, all heaped together carelessly in waist-high mounds.

With a cry Mat ran forward and fell to his knees in front of one of the piles. "Sacks," he said breathlessly, pawing through the gold. "We'll need sacks to carry all of this."

"We can't carry it all," Rand said. He looked around helplessly; all the gold the merchants brought to Emond's Field in a year would not have made the thousandth part of just one of those mounds. "Not now. It's almost dark."

Perrin pulled an axe free, carelessly tossing back the gold chains that had been tangled around it. Jewels glittered along its shiny black handle, and delicate gold scrollwork covered the twin blades. "Tomorrow, then," he said, hefting the axe with a grin. "Moiraine and Lan will understand when we show them this."

"You are not alone?" Mordeth said. He had let them rush past him into the treasure room, but now he followed. "Who else is with you?"

Mat, wrist deep in the riches before him, answered absently. "Moiraine and Lan. And then there's Nynaeve, and Egwene, and Thom.. He's a gleeman. We're going to Tar Valon."

Rand caught his breath. Then the silence from Mordeth made him look at the man.

Rage twisted Mordeth's face, and fear, too. His lips pulled back from his teeth. "Tar Valon!" He shook clenched fists at them. "Tar Valon! You said you were going to this . . . this . . . Caemlyn! You lied to me!"

"If you still want," Perrin said to Mordeth, "we'll come back tomorrow and help you." Carefully he set the axe back on the heap of gem-encrusted chalices and jewelry. "If you want."

"No. That is. . . ." Panting, Mordeth shook his head as if he could not decide. "Take what you want. Except. . . . Except. . . ."

Suddenly Rand realized what had been nagging at him about the man. The scattered torches in the hallway had given each of them a ring of shadows, just as the torches in the treasure room did. Only. . . . He was so shocked he said it out loud. "You don't have a shadow."

A goblet fell from Mat's hand with a crash.

Mordeth nodded, and for the first time his fleshy eyelids opened all the way. His sleek face suddenly appeared pinched and hungry. "So." He stood straighter, seeming taller. "It is decided." Abruptly there was no seeming to it. Like a balloon Mordeth swelled, distorted, head pressed against the ceiling, shoulders butting the walls, filling the end of the room, cutting off escape. Hollow-cheeked, teeth bared in a rictus snarl, he reached out with hands big enough to engulf a man's head.

With a yell Rand leaped back. His feet tangled in a gold chain, and he crashed to the floor, the wind knocked out of him. Struggling for breath, he struggled at the same time for his sword, fighting his cloak, which had become wrapped around the hilt. The yells of his friends filled the room, and the clash of gold platters and goblets clattering across the floor. Suddenly an agonized scream shivered in Rand's ears.

Almost sobbing, he managed to inhale at last, just as he got the sword out of its sheath. Cautiously, he got to his feet, wondering which of his friends had given that scream. Perrin looked back at him wide-eyed from across the room, crouched and holding his axe back as if about to chop down a tree. Mat peered around the side of a treasure pile, clutching a dagger snatched from the trove.

Something moved in the deepest part of the shadows left by the torches, and they all jumped. It was Mordeth, clutching his knees to his chest and huddled as deep into the furthest corner as he could get.

"He tricked us," Mat panted. "It was some kind of trick."

Mordeth threw back his head and wailed; dust sifted down as

the walls trembled. "You are all dead!" he cried. "All dead!"
And he leaped up, diving across the room.

Rand's jaw dropped, and he almost dropped the sword as
well. As Mordeth dove through the air, he stretched out and
thinned, like a tendril of smoke. As thin as a finger he struck a
crack in the wall tiles and vanished into it. A last cry hung in
the room as he vanished, fading slowly away after he was gone.

"You are all dead!"

"Let's get out of here," Perrin said faintly, firming his grip
on his axe while he tried to face every direction at once. Gold
ornaments and gems scattered unnoticed under his feet.

"But the treasure," Mat protested. "We *can't* just leave it
now."

"I don't want anything of his," Perrin said, still turning one
way after another. He raised his voice and shouted at the walls.
"It's your treasure, you hear? We are not taking any of it!"

Rand stared angrily at Mat. "Do you want him coming after
us? Or are you going to wait here stuffing your pockets until he
comes back with ten more like him?"

Mat just gestured to all the gold and jewels. Before he could
say anything, though, Rand seized one of his arms and Perrin
grabbed the other. They hustled him out of the room, Mat
struggling and shouting about the treasure.

Before they had gone ten steps down the hall, the already
dim light behind them began to fail. The torches in the treasure
room were going out. Mat stopped shouting. They hastened
their steps. The first torch outside the room winked out, then
the next. By the time they reached the winding stairs there was
no need to drag Mat any longer. They were all running, with
the dark closing in behind them. Even the pitch-black of the
stairs only made them hesitate an instant, then they sped up-
wards, shouting at the top of their lungs. Shouting to scare anything that might be waiting; shouting to remind themselves they
were still alive.

They burst out into the hall above, sliding and falling on the
dusty marble, scrambling out through the columns, to tumble
down the stairs and land in a bruised heap in the street.

Rand untangled himself and picked Tam's sword up from the
pavement, looking around uneasily. Less than half of the sun
still showed above the rooftops. Shadows reached out like dark

hands, made blacker by the remaining light, nearly filling the street. He shivered. The shadows looked like Mordeth, reaching.

"At least we're out of it." Mat got up from the bottom of the pile, dusting himself off in a shaky imitation of his usual manner. "And at least I—"

"Are we?" Perrin said.

Rand knew it was not his imagination this time. The back of his neck prickled. Something was watching them from the darkness in the columns. He spun around, staring at the buildings across the way. He could feel eyes on him from there, too. His grip tightened on his sword hilt, though he wondered what good it would be. Watching eyes seemed to be everywhere. The others looked around warily; he knew they could feel it, too.

"We stay in the middle of the street," he said hoarsely. They met his eyes; they looked as frightened as he felt. He swallowed hard. "We stay in the middle of the street, keep out of shadows as much as we can, and walk fast."

"Walk very fast," Mat agreed fervently.

The watchers followed them. Or else there were lots of watchers, lots of eyes staring out of almost every building. Rand could not see anything move, hard as he tried, but he could feel the eyes, eager, hungry. He did not know which would be worse. Thousands of eyes, or just a few, following them.

In the stretches where the sun still reached them, they slowed, just a little, squinting nervously into the darkness that always seemed to lay ahead. None of them was eager to enter the shadows; no one was really sure something might not be waiting. The watchers' anticipation was a palpable thing whenever shadows stretched across the street, barring their way. They ran through those dark places shouting. Rand thought he could hear dry, rustling laughter.

At last, with twilight falling, they came in sight of the white stone building they had left what seemed like days ago. Suddenly the watching eyes departed. Between one step and the next, they vanished in a blink. Without a word Rand broke into a trot, followed by his friends, then a full run that only ended when they hared through the doorway and collapsed, panting.

A small fire burned in the middle of the tile floor, the smoke vanishing through a hole in the ceiling in a way that reminded Rand unpleasantly of Mordeth. Everyone except Lan was there, gathered around the flames, and their reactions varied considerably. Egwene, warming her hands at the fire, gave a start as the three burst into the room, clutching her hands to her throat; when she saw who it was, a relieved sigh spoiled her attempt at a withering look. Thom merely muttered something around his pipestem, but Rand caught the word "fools" before the gleeman went back to poking the flames with a stick.

"You wool-headed witlings!" the Wisdom snapped. She bristled from head to foot; her eyes glittered, and bright spots of red burned on her cheeks. "Why under the Light did you run off like that? Are you all right? Have you no sense at all? Lan is out looking for you now, and you'll be luckier than you deserve if he does not pound some sense into the lot of you when he gets back."

The Aes Sedai's face betrayed no agitation at all, but her hands had loosed a white-knuckled grip on her dress at the sight of them. Whatever Nynaeve had given her must have helped, for she was on her feet. "You should not have done what you did," she said in a voice as clear and serene as a Waterwood pond. "We will speak of it later. Something happened out there, or you would not be falling all over one another like this. Tell me."

"You said it was safe," Mat complained, scrambling to his feet. "You said Aridhol was an ally of Manetheren, and Trollocs wouldn't come into the city, and—"

Moiraine stepped forward so suddenly that Mat cut off with his mouth open, and Rand and Perrin paused in getting up, halfway crouched or on their knees. "Trollocs? Did you see Trollocs inside the walls?"

Rand swallowed. "Not Trollocs," he said, and all three began talking excitedly, all at the same time.

Everyone began in a different place. Mat started with finding the treasure, sounding almost as if he had done it alone, while Perrin began explaining why they had gone off in the first place without telling anyone. Rand jumped right to what he thought was important, meeting the stranger among the columns. But they were all so excited that nobody told anything in the order it happened; whenever one of them thought of something, he blurted it out with no regard for what came before or after, or for who was saying what. The watchers. They all babbled about the watchers.

It made the whole tale close to incoherent, but their fear came through. Egwene began casting uneasy glances at the empty windows fronting the street. Out there the last remnants of twilight were fading; the fire seemed very small and dim. Thom took his pipe from between his teeth and listened with his head cocked, frowning. Moiraine's eyes showed concern, but not an undue amount. Until. . . .

Suddenly the Aes Sedai hissed, and grabbed Rand's elbow in a tight grip. "Mordeth! Are you sure of that name? Be very sure, all of you. Mordeth?"

They murmured a chorused "Yes," taken aback by the Aes Sedai's intensity.

"Did he touch you?" she asked them all. "Did he give you anything, or did you do anything for him? I must know."

"No," Rand said. "None of us. None of those things."

Perrin nodded agreement, and added, "All he did was try to kill us. Isn't that enough? He swelled up until he filled half the room, shouted that we were all dead men, then vanished." He moved his hand to demonstrate. "Like smoke." Egwene gave a squeak.

Mat twisted away petulantly. "Safe, you said! All that talk about Trollocs not coming here. What were we supposed to think?"

"Apparently you did not think at all," she said, coolly composed once more. "Anyone who thinks would be wary of a place that Trollocs are afraid to enter."

"Mat's doing," Nynaeve said, certainty in her voice. "He's always talking some mischief or other, and the others lose the little wits they were born with when they're around him."

Moiraine nodded briefly, but her eyes remained on Rand and his two friends. "Late in the Trolloc Wars, an army camped within these ruins—Trollocs, Darkfriends, Myrddraal, Dreadlords, thousands in all. When they did not come out, scouts were sent inside the walls. The scouts found weapons, bits of armor, and blood splattered everywhere. And messages scratched on walls in the Trolloc tongue, calling on the Dark One to aid them in their last hour. Men who came later found no trace of the blood or the messages. They had been scoured away. Halfmen and Trollocs remember still. That is what keeps them outside this place."

"And this is where you picked for us to hide?" Rand said in disbelief. "We'd be safer out there trying to outrun them."

"If you had not gone running off," Moiraine said patiently, "you would know that I set wards around this building. A Myrddraal would not even know these wards were there, for it is a different kind of evil they are meant to stop, but what resides in Shadar Logoth will not cross them, or even come too near. In the morning it will be safe for us to go; these things cannot stand the light of the sun. They will be hiding deep in the earth."

"Shadar Logoth?" Egwene said uncertainly. "I thought you said this city was called Aridhol."

"Once it was called Aridhol," Moiraine replied, "and was one of the Ten Nations, the lands that made the Second Covenant, the lands that stood against the Dark One from the first days after the Breaking of the World. In the days when Thorin al Toren al Ban was King of Manetheren, the King of Aridhol was Balwen Mayel, Balwen Ironhand. In a twilight of despair during the Trolloc Wars, when it seemed the Father of Lies must surely conquer, the man called Mordeth came to Balwen's court."

"The same man?" Rand exclaimed, and Mat said, "It couldn't be!" A glance from Moiraine silenced them. Stillness filled the room except for the Aes Sedai's voice.

"Before Mordeth had been long in the city he had Balwen's ear, and soon he was second only to the King. Mordeth whispered poison in Balwen's ear, and Aridhol began to change. Aridhol drew in on itself, hardened. It was said that some would rather see Trollocs come than the men of Aridhol. The victory of the Light is all. That was the battlecry Mordeth gave them, and the men of Aridhol shouted it while their deeds abandoned the Light.

"The story is too long to tell in full, and too grim, and only fragments are known, even in Tar Valon. How Thorin's son, Caar, came to win Aridhol back to the Second Covenant, and Balwen sat his throne, a withered shell with the light of madness in his eyes, laughing while Mordeth smiled at his side and ordered the deaths of Caar and the embassy as Friends of the Dark. How Prince Caar came to be called Caar One-Hand. How he escaped the dungeons of Aridhol and fled alone to the Borderlands with Mordeth's unnatural assassins at his heels. How there he met Rhea, who did not know who he was, and married her, and set the skein in the Pattern that led to his death at her hands, and hers by her own hand before his tomb, and the fall of Aleth-loriel. How the armies of Manetheren came to avenge Caar and found the gates of Aridhol torn down, no living thing inside the walls, but something worse than death. No enemy had come to Aridhol but Aridhol. Suspicion and hate had given birth to something that fed on that which created it, something locked in the bedrock on which the city stood. Mashadar waits still, hungering. Men spoke of Aridhol no more. They named it Shadar Logoth, the Place Where the Shadow Waits, or more simply, Shadow's Waiting.

"Mordeth alone was not consumed by Mashadar, but he was snared by it, and he, too, has waited within these walls through the long centuries. Others have seen him. Some he has influenced through gifts that twist the mind and taint the spirit, the taint waxing and waning until it rules . . . or kills. If ever he convinces someone to accompany him to the walls, to the boundary of Mashadar's power, he will be able to consume the soul of that person. Mordeth will leave, wearing the body of the one he worse than killed, to wreak his evil on the world again."

"The treasure," Perrin mumbled when she stopped. "He wanted us to help carry the treasure to his horses." His face was haggard. "I'll bet they were supposed to be outside the city somewhere." Rand shivered.

"But we are safe, now, aren't we?" Mat asked. "He didn't give us anything, and he didn't touch us. We're safe, aren't we, with the wards you set?"

"We are safe," Moiraine agreed. "He cannot cross the ward lines, nor can any other denizen of this place. And they must hide from the sunlight, so we can leave safely once it is day. Now, try to sleep. The wards will protect us until Lan returns."

"He has been gone a long time." Nynaeve looked worriedly at the night outside. Full dark had fallen, as black as pitch.

"Lan will be well," Moiraine said soothingly, and spread her blankets beside the fire while she spoke. "He was pledged to fight the Dark One before he left the cradle, a sword placed in his infant hands. Besides, I would know the minute of his death and the way of it, just as he would know mine. Rest, Nynaeve. All will be well." But as she was rolling herself into her blankets, she paused, staring at the street as if she, too, would have liked to know what kept the Warder.

Rand's arms and legs felt like lead and his eyes wanted to slide shut on their own, yet sleep did not come quickly, and once it did, he dreamed, muttering and kicking off his blankets. When he woke, it was suddenly, and he looked around for a moment before he remembered where he was.

The moon was up, the last thin sliver before the new moon, its faint light defeated by the night. Everyone else was still asleep, though not all soundly. Egwene and his two friends twisted and murmured inaudibly. Thom's snores, soft for once, were broken from time to time by half-formed words. There was still no sign of Lan.

Suddenly he felt as if the wards were no protection at all. Anything at all could be out there in the dark. Telling himself he was being foolish, he added wood to the last coals of the fire. The blaze was too small to give much warmth, but it gave more light.

He had no idea what had awakened him from his unpleasant dream. He had been a little boy again, carrying Tam's sword and with a cradle strapped to his back, running through empty streets, pursued by Mordeth, who shouted that he only wanted his hand. And there had been an old man who watched them and cackled with mad laughter the whole time.

He gathered his blankets and lay back, staring at the ceiling. He wanted very much to sleep, even if he had more dreams like the last one, but he could not make his eyes close.

Suddenly the Warder trotted silently out of the darkness into the room. Moiraine came awake and sat up as if he had rung a bell. Lan opened his hand; three small objects fell to the tiles in front of her with the clink of iron. Three blood-red badges in the shape of horned skulls.

"There are Trollocs inside the walls," Lan said. "They will be here in little more than an hour. And the Dha'vol are the worst of them." He began waking the others.

Moiraine smoothly began folding her blankets. "How many? Do they know we are here?" She sounded as if there were no urgency at all.

"I don't think they do," Lan replied. "There are well over a hundred, frightened enough to kill anything that moves, including one another. The Halfmen are having to drive them—four just to handle one fist—and even the Myrddraal seem to want nothing more than to pass through the city and out as quickly as possible. They are not going out of their way to search, and they're so slipshod that if they were not heading nearly straight for us I would say we had nothing to worry about." He hesitated.

"There is something else?"

"Only this," Lan said slowly. "The Myrddraal forced the Trollocs into the city. What forced the Myrddraal?"

Everyone had been listening in silence. Now Thom cursed under his breath, and Egwene breathed a question. "The Dark One?"

"Don't be a fool, girl," Nynaeve snapped. "The Dark One is bound in Shayol Ghul by the Creator."

"For the time being, at least," Moiraine agreed. "No, the Father of Lies is not out there, but we must leave in any case."

Nynaeve eyed her narrowly. "Leave the protection of the wards, and cross Shadar Logoth in the night."

"Or stay here and face the Trollocs," Moiraine said. "To hold them off here would require the One Power. It would destroy the wards and attract the very thing the wards are meant to protect against. Besides, as well build a signal fire atop one of those towers for every Halfman within twenty miles. To leave is not what I would choose to do, but we are the hare, and it is the hounds who dictate the chase."

"What if there are more outside the walls?" Mat asked. "What are we going to do?"

"We will use my original plan," Moiraine said. Lan looked at her. She held up a hand and added, "Which I was too tired to carry out before. But I am rested, now, thanks to the Wisdom. We will make for the river. There, with our backs guarded by the water, I can raise a smaller ward that will hold the Trollocs and Halfmen back until we can make rafts and cross over. Or better yet, we may even be able to hail a trader's boat coming down from Saldaea."

The faces of the Emond's Fielders looked blank. Lan noticed.

"Trollocs and Myrddraal loathe deep water. Trollocs are terrified of it. Neither can swim. A Halfman will not wade anything more than waist deep, especially if it's moving. Trollocs won't do even that if they can find any way to avoid it."

"So once we get across the river we're safe," Rand said, and the Warder nodded.

"The Myrddraal will find it almost as hard to make the Trollocs build rafts as it was to drive them into Shadar Logoth, and if they try to make them cross the Arinelle that way, half will run away and the rest probably drown."

"Get to your horses," Moiraine said. "We are not across the river yet."

Myrddraal

CHAPTER
20

Dust on the Wind

As they left the white stone building on their nervously shifting horses, the icy wind came in gusts, moaning across the rooftops, whipping cloaks like banners, driving thin clouds across the thin sliver of the moon. With a quiet command to stay close, Lan led off down the street. The horses danced and tugged at the reins, eager to be away.

Rand looked up warily at the buildings they passed, looming now in the night with their empty windows like eye sockets. Shadows seemed to move. Occasionally there was a clatter—rubble toppled by the wind. *At least the eyes are gone.* His relief was momentary. Why *are they gone?*

Thom and the Emond's Fielders made a cluster with him, all keeping close enough to touch one another. Egwene's shoulders were hunched, as if she were trying to ease Bela's hooves to the pavement. Rand did not even want to breathe. Sound might attract attention.

Abruptly he realized that a distance had opened ahead of them, separating them from the Warder and the Aes Sedai. The two were indistinct shapes a good thirty paces ahead.

"We're falling behind," he murmured, and booted Cloud to a quicker step. A thin tendril of silver-gray fog drifted low across the street ahead of him.

"Stop!" It was a strangled shout from Moiraine, sharp and urgent, but pitched not to carry far.

Uncertain, he pulled up short. The splinter of fog lay completely across the street now, slowly fattening as if more were oozing out of the buildings on either side of the street. It was as thick as a man's arm now. Cloud whickered and tried to back further away as Egwene and Thom and the others came up on him. Their horses, too, tossed their heads and bridled against coming too near the fog.

Lan and Moiraine rode slowly toward the fog, grown to as big around as a leg, stopping on the other side, well back. The Aes Sedai studied the branch of mist that separated them. Rand shrugged at a sudden itch of fear between his shoulder blades. A faint light accompanied the fog, growing as the foggy tentacle became fatter, but still only a little more than the moonlight. The horses shifted uneasily, even Aldieb and Mandarb.

"What is it?" Nynaeve asked.

"The evil of Shadar Logoth," Moiraine replied. "Mashadar. Unseeing, unthinking, moving through the city as aimlessly as a worm burrows through the earth. If it touches you, you will die." Rand and the others let their horses dance a few quick steps back, but not too far. As much as Rand would have given to be free of the Aes Sedai, she was as safe as home compared to what lay around them.

"Then how do we join you?" Egwene said. "Can you kill it . . . clear a way?"

Moiraine's laugh was bitter and short. "Mashadar is vast, girl, as vast as Shadar Logoth itself. The whole White Tower could not kill it. If I damaged it enough to let you pass, drawing that much of the One Power would pull the Halfmen like a trumpet call. And Mashadar would rush in to heal whatever harm I did, rush in and perhaps catch us in its net."

Rand exchanged looks with Egwene, then asked her question again. Moiraine sighed before answering.

"I do not like it, but what must be done, must be done. This thing will not be above ground everywhere. Other streets will be clear. See that star?" She twisted in her saddle to point to a red star low in the eastern sky. "Keep on toward that star, and it will bring you to the river. Whatever happens, keep moving toward the river. Go as quickly as you can, but above all make no noise. There are still the Trollocs, remember. And four Halfmen."

"But how will we find you again?" Egwene protested.

"I will find you," Moiraine said. "Be assured, I can find you. Now be off. This thing is utterly mindless, but it can sense food." Indeed, ropes of silver-gray had lifted from the larger body. They drifted, wavering, like the tentacles of a hundredarms on the bottom of a Waterwood pond.

When Rand looked up from the thick trunk of opaque mist, the Warder and the Aes Sedai were gone. He licked his lips and met his companions' eyes. They were as nervous as he was. And something worse: they all seemed to be waiting for someone else to move first. Night and ruins surrounded them. The Fades were out there, somewhere, and the Trollocs, maybe around the next corner. The tentacles of fog drifted nearer, halfway to them now, and no longer wavering. They had chosen their intended prey. Suddenly he missed Moiraine very much.

Everyone was still staring, wondering which way to go. He turned Cloud, and the gray broke into a half trot, tugging against the reins to go faster. As if moving first had made him the leader, everyone followed.

With Moiraine gone, there was no one to protect them should Mordeth appear. And the Trollocs. And. . . . Rand forced himself to stop thinking. He would follow the red star. He could hold onto that thought.

Three times they had to backtrack from a street blocked from side to side by a hill of stone and brick the horses could never have crossed. Rand could hear the others breathing, short and sharp, just shy of panic. He gritted his teeth to stop his own panting. *You have to at least make them think you're not afraid. You're doing a good job, wool-head! You'll get everybody out safely.*

They rounded the next corner. A wall of fog bathed the broken pavement with a light as bright as a full moon. Streamers as thick as their horses broke off toward them. Nobody waited. Wheeling, they galloped away in a tight knot with no heed for the clatter of hooves they raised.

Two Trollocs stepped into the street before them, not ten spans away.

For an instant the humans and the Trollocs just stared at one another, each more surprised than the other. Another pair of

Trollocs appeared, and another, and another, colliding with the ones in front, folding into a shocked mass at the sight of the humans. Only for an instant did they remain frozen, though. Guttural howls echoed from the buildings, and the Trollocs bounded forward. The humans scattered like quail.

Rand's gray reached full gallop in three strides. "This way!" he shouted, but he heard the same cry from five throats. A hasty glance over his shoulder showed him his companions disappearing in as many directions, Trollocs pursuing them all.

Three Trollocs ran at his own heels, catchpoles waving in the air. His skin crawled as he realized they were matching Cloud stride for stride. He dropped low on Cloud's neck and urged the gray on, chased by thick cries.

The street narrowed ahead, broken-topped buildings leaning out drunkenly. Slowly the empty windows filled with a silvery glow, a dense mist bulging outward. Mashadar.

Rand risked a glance over his shoulder. The Trollocs still ran less than fifty paces back; the light from the fog was enough to see them clearly. A Fade rode behind them now, and they seemed to flee the Halfman as much as to pursue Rand. Ahead of Rand, half a dozen gray tendrils wavered from the windows, a dozen, feeling the air. Cloud tossed his head and screamed, but Rand dug his heels in brutally, and the horse lunged forward wildly.

The tendrils stiffened as Rand galloped between them, but he crouched low on Cloud's back and refused to look at them. The way beyond was clear. *If one of them touches me. . . . Light!* He booted Cloud harder, and the horse leaped forward into the welcome shadows. With Cloud still running, he looked back as soon as the glow of Mashadar began to lessen.

The waving gray tentacles of Mashadar blocked half the street, and the Trollocs were balking, but the Fade snatched a whip from its saddlebow, cracking it over the heads of the Trollocs with a sound like a lightning bolt, popping sparks in the air. Crouching, the Trollocs lurched after Rand. The Halfman hesitated, black cowl studying Mashadar's reaching arms, before it, too, spurred forward.

The thickening tentacles of fog swung uncertainly for a moment, then struck like vipers. At least two latched to each Trolloc, bathing them in gray light; muzzled heads went back to scream, but fog rolled over open mouths, and in, eating the howls. Four leg-thick tentacles whipped around the Fade, and the Halfman and its black horse twitched as if dancing, till the cowl fell back, baring that pale, eyeless face. The Fade shrieked.

There was no sound from that cry, any more than from the Trollocs, but something came through, a piercing whine just beyond hearing, like all the hornets in the world, digging into Rand's ears with all the fear that could exist. Cloud convulsed, as if he, too, heard, and ran harder than ever. Rand hung on, panting, his throat as dry as sand.

After a time he realized he could no longer hear the silent shriek of the Fade dying, and suddenly the clatter of his gallop seemed as loud as shouts. He reined Cloud hard, stopping beside a jagged wall, right where two streets met. A nameless monument reared in the darkness before him.

Slumped in the saddle, he listened, but there was nothing to hear except the blood pounding in his ears. Cold sweat beaded on his face, and he shivered as the wind flailed his cloak.

Finally he straightened. Stars spangled the sky where the clouds did not hide them, but the red star low in the east was easy to mark. *Is anybody else alive to see it?* Were they free, or in the Trollocs' hands? *Egwene, Light blind me, why didn't you follow me?* If they were alive and free, they would be following that star. If not. . . . The ruins were vast; he could search for days without finding anyone, if he could keep away from the Trollocs. And the Fades, and Mordeth, and Mashadar. Reluctantly he decided to make for the river.

He gathered the reins. On the crossing street, one stone fell against another with a sharp click. He froze, not even breathing. He was hidden in the shadows, one step from the corner. Frantically he thought of backing up. What was behind him? What would make a noise and give him away? He could not remember, and he was afraid to take his eyes from the corner of the building.

Darkness bulked at that corner, with the longer darkness of a shaft sticking out of it. Catchpole! Even as the thought flashed into Rand's head, he dug his heels into Cloud's ribs and his sword flew from the scabbard; a wordless shout accompanied his charge, and he swung the sword with all of his might. Only a desperate effort stopped the blade short. With a yelp Mat tumbled back, half falling off his horse and nearly dropping his bow.

Rand drew a deep breath and lowered his sword. His arm shook. "Have you seen anybody else?" he managed.

Mat swallowed hard before pulling himself awkwardly back into his saddle. "I . . . I. . . . Just Trollocs." He put a hand to his throat, and licked his lips. "Just Trollocs. You?"

Rand shook his head. "They must be trying to reach the river. We better do the same." Mat nodded silently, still feeling his throat, and they started toward the red star.

Before they had covered a hundred spans the keening cry of a Trolloc horn rose behind them in the depths of the city. Another answered, from outside the walls.

Rand shivered, but he kept to his slow pace, watching the darkest places and avoiding them when he could. After one jerk at his reins as if he might gallop off, Mat did the same. Neither horn sounded again, and it was in silence that they came to an opening in the vine-shrouded wall where a gate had once been. Only the towers remained, standing broken-topped against the black sky.

Mat hesitated at the gateway, but Rand said softly, "Is it any safer in here than out there?" He did not slow the gray, and after a moment Mat followed him out of Shadar Logoth, trying to look every way at once. Rand let out a slow breath; his mouth was dry. *We're going to make it. Light, we're going to make it!*

The walls vanished behind, swallowed by the night and the forest. Listening for the slightest sound, Rand kept the red star dead ahead.

Suddenly Thom galloped by from behind, slowing only long enough to shout, "Ride, you fools!" A moment later hunting cries and crashes in the brush behind him announced the presence of Trollocs on his trail.

Rand dug in his heels, and Cloud sprang after the gleeman's gelding. *What happens when we get to the river without Moiraine? Light, Egwene!*

Perrin sat his horse in the shadows, watching the open gateway, some little distance off yet, and absently ran his thumb along the blade of his axe. It seemed to be a clear way out of the ruined city, but he had sat there for five minutes studying it. The wind tossed his shaggy curls and tried to carry his cloak away, but he pulled the cloak back around him without really noticing what he was doing.

He knew that Mat, and almost everyone else in Emond's Field, considered him slow of thought. It was partly because he was big and usually moved carefully—he had always been afraid he might accidentally break something or hurt somebody, since he was so much bigger than the boys he grew up with—but he really did prefer to think things all the way through if he could. Quick thinking, careless thinking, had put Mat into hot water one time after another, and Mat's quick thinking usually managed to get Rand, or him, or both, in the cookpot alongside Mat, too.

His throat tightened. *Light, don't think about being in a cookpot.* He tried to order his thoughts again. Careful thought was the way.

There had been some sort of square in front of the gate once, with a huge fountain in its middle. Part of the fountain was still there, a cluster of broken statues standing in a big, round basin, and so was the open space around it. To reach the gate he would have to ride nearly a hundred spans with only the night to shield him from searching eyes. That was not a pleasant thought, either. He remembered those unseen watchers too well.

He considered the horns he had heard in the city a little while earlier. He had almost turned back, thinking some of the others might have been taken, before realizing that he could not do anything alone if they had been captured. *Not against— what did Lan say—a hundred Trollocs and four Fades. Moiraine Sedai said get to the river.*

He went back to consideration of the gate. Careful thought had not given him much, but he had made his decision. He rode out of the deeper shadow into the lesser darkness.

As he did, another horse appeared from the far side of the square and stopped. He stopped, too, and felt for his axe; it gave him no great sense of comfort. If that dark shape was a Fade. . . .

"Rand?" came a soft, hesitant call.

He let out a long, relieved breath. "It's Perrin, Egwene," he called back, just as softly. It still sounded too loud in the darkness.

The horses came together near the fountain.

"Have you seen anybody else?" they both asked at the same time, and both answered by shaking their heads.

"They'll be all right," Egwene muttered, patting Bela's neck. "Won't they?"

"Moiraine Sedai and Lan will look after them," Perrin replied. "They will look after all of us once we get to the river." He hoped it was so.

He felt a great relief once they were beyond the gate, even if there *were* Trollocs in the forest. Or Fades. He stopped that line of thought. The bare branches were not enough to keep him from guiding on the red star, and they were beyond Mordeth's reach now. That one had frightened him worse than the Trollocs ever had.

Soon they would reach the river and meet Moiraine, and she would put them beyond the Trollocs' reach as well. He believed it because he needed to believe. The wind scraped branches together and rustled the leaves and needles on the evergreens. A nighthawk's lonely cry drifted in the dark, and he and Egwene moved their horses closer together as though they were huddling for warmth. They were very much alone.

A Trolloc horn sounded somewhere behind them, quick, wailing blasts, urging the hunters to hurry, hurry. Then thick, half-human howls rose on their trail, spurred on by the horn. Howls that grew sharper as they caught the human scent.

Perrin put his horse to a gallop, shouting, "Come on!" Egwene came, both of them booting their horses, heedless of noise, heedless of the branches that slapped at them.

As they raced through the trees, guided as much by instinct as by the dim moonlight, Bela fell behind. Perrin looked back. Egwene kicked the mare and flailed her with the reins, but it was doing no good. By their sounds, the Trollocs were coming closer. He drew in enough not to leave her behind.

"Hurry!" he shouted. He could make out the Trollocs now, huge dark shapes bounding through the trees, bellowing and snarling to chill the blood. He gripped the haft of his axe, hanging at his belt, until his knuckles hurt. "Hurry, Egwene! Hurry!"

Suddenly his horse screamed, and he was falling, tumbling out of the saddle as the horse dropped away beneath him. He flung out his hands to brace himself and splashed headfirst into icy water. He had ridden right off the edge of a sheer bluff into the Arinelle.

The shock of freezing water ripped a gasp from him, and he swallowed more than a little before he managed to fight his way to the surface. He felt more than heard another splash, and thought that Egwene must have come right after him. Panting and blowing, he treaded water. It was not easy to keep afloat; his coat and cloak were already sodden, and his boots had filled. He looked around for Egwene, but saw only the glint of moonlight on the black water, ruffled by the wind.

"Egwene? Egwene!"

A spear flashed right in front of his eyes and threw water in his face. Others splashed into the river around him, too. Guttural voices raised in argument on the riverbank, and the Trolloc spears stopped coming, but he gave up on calling for the time being.

The current washed him downriver, but the thick shouts and snarls followed along the bank, keeping pace. Undoing his cloak, he let the river take it. A little less weight to drag him down. Doggedly, he set out swimming for the far bank. There were no Trollocs there. He hoped.

He swam the way they did back home, in the ponds in the Waterwood, stroking with both hands, kicking with both feet, keeping his head out of the water. At least, he tried to keep his head out of the water; it was not easy. Even without the cloak, his coat and boots each seemed to weigh as much as he did. And the axe dragged at his waist, threatening to roll him over if it did not pull him under. He thought about letting the river have that, too; he thought about it more than once. It would be easy, much easier than struggling out of his boots, for instance. But every time he thought of it, he thought of crawling out on the far bank to find Trollocs waiting. The axe would not do him much good against half a dozen Trollocs—or even against one, maybe—but it was better than his bare hands.

After a while he was not even certain he would be able to lift the axe if Trollocs were there. His arms and legs became leaden; it was an effort to move them, and his face no longer came as far out of the river with each stroke. He coughed from water that went up his nose. *A day at the forge has no odds on this,* he thought wearily, and just then his kicking foot struck something. It was not until he kicked it again that he realized what it was. The bottom. He was in the shallows. He was across the river.

Sucking air through his mouth, he got to his feet, splashing about as his legs almost gave way. He fumbled his axe out of its loop as he floundered ashore, shivering in the wind. He did not see any Trollocs. He did not see Egwene, either. Just a few scattered trees along the riverbank, and a moonlight ribbon on the water.

When he had his breath again, he called their names again and again. Faint shouts from the far side answered him; even at that distance he could make out the harsh voices of Trollocs. His friends did not answer, though.

The wind surged, its moan drowning out the Trollocs, and he shivered. It was not cold enough to freeze the water soaking his clothes, but it felt as if it was; it sliced to the bone with an icy blade. Hugging himself was only a gesture that did not stop the shivering. Alone, he climbed tiredly up the riverbank to find shelter against the wind.

Rand patted Cloud's neck, soothing the gray with whispers. The horse tossed his head and danced on quick feet. The Trollocs had been left behind—or so it seemed—but Cloud had the smell of them thick in his nostrils. Mat rode with an arrow nocked, watching for surprises out of the night, while Rand and Thom peered through the branches, searching for the red star that was their guide. Keeping it in view had been easy enough, even with all the branches overhead, so long as they were riding straight toward it. But then more Trollocs had appeared, ahead, and they went galloping off to the side with both packs howling after them. The Trollocs could keep up with a horse, but only for a hundred paces or so, and finally they left the pursuit and the howls behind. But with all the twists and turns, they had lost the guiding star.

"I still say it's over there," Mat said, gesturing off to his right. "We were going north at the end, and that means east is that way."

"There it is," Thom said abruptly. He pointed through the tangled branches to their left, straight at the red star. Mat mumbled something under his breath.

Out of the corner of his eye Rand caught the movement as a Trolloc leaped out from behind a tree without a sound, swinging its catchpole. Rand dug his heels in, and the gray bounded forward just as two more plunged from the shadows after the first. A noose brushed the back of Rand's neck, sending a shiver down his spine.

An arrow took one of the bestial faces in the eye, then Mat swung in beside him as their horses pounded through the trees. They were running toward the river, he realized, but he was not sure it was going to do any good. The Trollocs sped after them, almost close enough to reach out and grab the streaming tails of their horses. Half a step gained, and the catchpoles could drag them both out of their saddles.

He leaned low on the gray's neck to put that much more distance between his own neck and the nooses. Mat's face was nearly buried in his horse's mane. But Rand wondered where Thom was. Had the gleeman decided he was better off on his own, since all three Trollocs had fastened on the boys?

Suddenly Thom's gelding galloped out of the night, hard behind the Trollocs. The Trollocs had only time enough to look back in surprise before the gleeman's hands whipped back and then forward. Moonlight flashed off steel. One Trolloc tumbled forward, rolling over and over before landing in a heap, while a second dropped to its knees with a scream, clawing at its back with both hands. The third snarled, baring a muzzleful of sharp teeth, but as its companions toppled it whirled away into the darkness. Thom's hand made the whip-like motion again, and the Trolloc shrieked, but the shrieks faded into the distance as it ran.

Rand and Mat pulled up and stared at the gleeman.

"My best knives," Thom muttered, but he made no effort to get down and retrieve them. "That one will bring others. I hope the river isn't too far. I hope. . . ." Instead of saying what else he hoped, he shook his head and set off at a quick canter. Rand and Mat fell in behind him.

Soon they reached a low bank where trees grew right to the edge of the night-black water, its moon-streaked surface riffled by the wind. Rand could not see the far side at all. He did not like the idea of crossing on a raft in the dark, but he liked the idea of staying on this side even less. *I'll swim if I have to.*

Somewhere away from the river a Trolloc horn brayed, sharp, quick, and urgent in the darkness. It was the first sound from the horns since they had left the ruins. Rand wondered if it meant some of the others had been captured.

"No use staying here all night," Thom said. "Pick a direction. Upriver, or down?"

"But Moiraine and the others could be anywhere," Mat protested. "Any way we choose could just take us further away."

"So it could." Clucking to his gelding, Thom turned downriver, heading along the bank. "So it could." Rand looked at Mat, who shrugged, and they turned after him.

For a time nothing changed. The bank was higher in some places, lower in others, the trees grew thicker, or thinned out in small clearings, but the night and the river and the wind were all the same, cold and black. And no Trollocs. That was one change Rand was glad to forgo.

Then he saw a light ahead, just a single point. As they drew closer he could see that the light was well above the river, as if it were in a tree. Thom quickened the pace and began to hum under his breath.

Finally they could make out the source of the light, a lantern hoisted atop one of the masts of a large trader's boat, tied up for the night beside a small clearing in the trees. The boat, a good eighty feet long, shifted slightly with the current, tugging against the mooring ropes tied to trees. The rigging hummed and creaked in the wind. The lantern doubled the moonlight on the deck, but no one was in sight.

"Now that," Thom said as he dismounted, "is better than an Aes Sedai's raft, isn't it?" He stood with his hands on his hips, and even in the dark his smugness was apparent. "It doesn't look as if this vessel is made to carry horses, but considering the danger he's in, which we are going to warn him of, the captain may be reasonable. Just let me do all the talking. And bring your blankets and saddlebags, just in case."

Rand climbed down and began untying the things behind his saddle. "You don't mean to leave without the others, do you?"

Thom had no chance to say what he meant to do. Into the clearing burst two Trollocs, howling and waving their catchpoles, with four more right behind. The horses reared and whinnied. Shouts in the distance said more Trollocs were on the way.

"Onto the boat!" Thom shouted. "Quick! Leave all that! Run!" Suiting his own words, he ran for the boat, patches flapping and instrument cases on his back banging together. "You on the boat!" he shouted. "Wake up, you fools! Trollocs!"

Rand jerked his blanketroll and saddlebags free of the last thong and was right on the gleeman's heels. Tossing his burdens over the rail, he vaulted after them. He just had time to see a man curled up on the deck, beginning to sit up as if he had only that moment awakened, when his feet came down right on top of the fellow. The man grunted loudly, Rand stumbled, and a hooked catchpole slammed into the railing just where he had come over. Shouts rose all over the boat, and feet pounded along the deck.

Hairy hands caught the railing beside the catchpole, and a goat-horned head lifted above it. Off balance, stumbling, Rand still managed to draw his sword and swing. With a scream the Trolloc dropped away.

Men ran everywhere on the boat, shouting, hacking mooring lines with axes. The boat lurched and swung as if eager to be off. Up in the bow three men struggled with a Trolloc. Someone thrust over the side with a spear, though Rand could not see what he was stabbing at. A bowstring snapped, and snapped again. The man Rand had stepped on scrabbled away from him on hands and knees, then flung up his hands when he saw Rand looking at him.

"Spare me!" he cried. "Take whatever you want, take the boat, take everything, but spare me!"

Suddenly something slammed across Rand's back, smashing him to the deck. His sword skittered away from his outstretched hand. Openmouthed, gasping for a breath that would not come, he tried to reach the sword. His muscles responded with agonized slowness; he writhed like a slug. The fellow who wanted to be spared gave one frightened, covetous look at the sword, then vanished into the shadows.

Painfully Rand managed to look over his shoulder, and knew his luck had run out. A wolf-muzzled Trolloc stood balanced on the railing, staring down at him and holding the splintered end of the catchpole that had knocked the wind out of him. Rand struggled to reach the sword, to move, to get away, but his arms and legs moved jerkily, and only half as he wanted. They wobbled and went in odd directions. His chest felt as if it were strapped with iron bands; silver spots swam in his eyes. Frantically he hunted for some way to escape. Time seemed to slow as the Trolloc raised the jagged pole as if to spear him with it. To Rand the creature appeared to be moving as if in a dream. He watched the thick arm go back; he could already feel the broken haft ripping through his spine, feel the pain of it tearing him open. He thought his lungs would burst. *I'm going to die! Light help me, I'm going to . . . !* The Trolloc's arm started forward, driving the splintered shaft, and Rand found the breath for one yell. "No!"

Suddenly the ship lurched, and a boom swung out of the shadows to catch the Trolloc across the chest with a crunch of breaking bones, sweeping it over the side.

For a moment Rand lay panting and staring up at the boom swinging back and forth above him. *That has to have used up my luck,* he thought. *There can't be any more after that.*

Shakily he got to his feet and picked up his sword, for once holding it in both hands the way Lan had taught him, but there was nothing left on which to use it. The gap of black water between the boat and the bank was widening quickly; the cries of the Trollocs were fading behind in the night.

As he sheathed his sword and slumped against the railing, a stocky man in a coat that hung to his knees strode up the deck to glare at him. Long hair that fell to his thick shoulders and a beard that left his upper lip bare framed a round face. Round but not soft. The boom swung out again, and the bearded man spared part of his glare for that as he caught it; it made a crisp *splat* against his broad palm.

"Gelb!" he bellowed. "Fortune! Where do you be, Gelb?" He spoke so fast, with all the words running together, that

Rand could barely understand him. "You can no hide from me on my own ship! Get Floran Gelb out here!"

A crewman appeared with a bull's-eye lantern, and two more pushed a narrow-faced man into the circle of light it cast. Rand recognized the fellow who had offered him the boat. The man's eyes shifted from side to side, never meeting those of the stocky man. The captain, Rand thought. A bruise was coming up on Gelb's forehead where one of Rand's boots had caught him.

"Were you no supposed to secure this boom, Gelb?" the captain asked with surprising calm, though just as fast as before.

Gelb looked truly surprised. "But I did. Tied it down tight. I admit I'm a little slow about things now and then, Captain Domon, but I get them done."

"So you be slow, do you? No so slow at sleeping. Sleeping when you should be standing watch. We could be murdered to a man, for all of you."

"No, Captain, no. It was him." Gelb pointed straight at Rand. "I was on guard, just like I was supposed to be, when he sneaked up and hit me with a club." He touched the bruise on his head, winced, and glared at Rand. "I fought him, but then the Trollocs came. He's in league with them, Captain. A Darkfriend. In league with the Trollocs."

"In league with my aged grandmother!" Captain Domon roared. "Did I no warn you the last time, Gelb? At White-bridge, off you do go! Get out of my sight before I put you off now." Gelb darted out of the lantern light, and Domon stood opening and closing his hands while he stared at nothing. "These Trollocs do be following me. Why will they no leave me be? Why?"

Rand looked over the rail and was shocked to find the river-bank no longer in sight. Two men manned the long steering oar that stuck out over the stern, and there were six sweeps work-ing to a side now, pulling the ship like a waterbug further out into the river.

"Captain," Rand said, "we have friends back there. If you go back and pick them up, I am sure they'll reward you."

The captain's round face swung toward Rand, and when Thom and Mat appeared he included them in his expressionless stare as well.

"Captain," Thom began with a bow, "allow me to—"

"You come below," Captain Domon said, "where I can see what manner of thing be hauled up on my deck. Come. Fortune desert me, somebody secure this horn-cursed boom!" As crewmen rushed to take the boom, he stumped off toward the stern of the boat. Rand and his two companions followed.

Captain Domon had a tidy cabin in the stern, reached by climbing down a short ladder, where everything gave the impression of being in its proper place, right down to the coats and cloaks hanging from pegs on the back of the door. The cabin stretched the width of the ship, with a broad bed built against one side and a heavy table built out from the other. There was only one chair, with a high back and sturdy arms, and the captain took that himself, motioning the others to find places on various chests and benches that were the only other furnishings. A loud harrumph stopped Mat from sitting on the bed.

"Now," said the captain when they were all seated. "My name be Bayle Domon, captain and owner of the *Spray,* which be this ship. Now who be you, and where be you going out here in the middle of nowhere, and why should I no throw you over the side for the trouble you've brought me?"

Rand still had as much trouble as before in following Domon's rapid speech. When he worked out the last part of what the captain had said he blinked in surprise. *Throw us over the side?*

Mat hurriedly said, "We didn't mean to cause you any trouble. We're on our way to Caemlyn, and then to—"

"And then where the wind takes us," Thom interrupted smoothly. "That's how gleemen travel, like dust on the wind. I am a gleeman, you understand, Thom Merrilin by name." He shifted his cloak so the multihued patches stirred, as if the captain could have missed them. "These two country louts want to become my apprentices, though I am not yet sure I want them." Rand looked at Mat, who grinned.

"That be all very well, man," Captain Domon said placidly, "but it tells me nothing. Less. Fortune prick me, that place be on no road to Caemlyn from anywhere I ever heard tell of."

"Now that is a story," Thom said, and he straightaway began to unfold it.

According to Thom, he had been trapped by the winter snows in a mining town in the Mountains of Mist beyond Baerlon. While there he heard legends of a treasure dating from the Trolloc Wars, in the lost ruin of a city called Aridhol. Now it just so happened that he had earlier learned the location of Aridhol from a map given him many years ago by a dying friend in Illian whose life he had once saved, a man who expired breathing that the map would make Thom rich, which Thom never believed until he heard the legends. When the snows melted enough, he set out with a few companions, including his two would-be apprentices, and after a journey of many hardships they actually found the ruined city. But it turned out the treasure had belonged to one of the Dreadlords themselves, and Trollocs had been sent to fetch it back to Shayol Ghul. Almost every danger they really had faced—Trollocs, Myrddraal, Draghkar, Mordeth, Mashadar—assailed them at one point or another of the story, though the way Thom told it they all seemed to be aimed at him personally, and to have been handled by him with the greatest adroitness. With much derring-do, mostly by Thom, they escaped, pursued by Trollocs, though they became separated in the night, until finally Thom and his two companions sought refuge on the last place left to them, Captain Domon's most welcome ship.

As the gleeman finished up, Rand realized his mouth had been hanging open for some time and shut it with a click. When he looked at Mat, his friend was staring wide-eyed at the gleeman.

Captain Domon drummed his fingers on the arm of his chair. "That be a tale many folk would no believe. Of course, I did see the Trollocs, did I no."

"Every word true," Thom said blandly, "from one who lived it."

"Happen you have some of this treasure with you?"

Thom spread his hands regretfully. "Alas, what little we managed to carry away was with our horses, which bolted when those last Trollocs appeared. All I have left are my flute and my harp, a few coppers, and the clothes on my back. But believe me, you want no part of that treasure. It has the taint of the Dark One. Best to leave it to the ruins and the Trollocs."

"So you've no money to pay your passage. I'd no let my own

brother sail with me if he could no pay his passage, especially if he brought Trollocs behind him to hack up my railings and cut up my rigging. Why should I no let you swim back where you came from, and be rid of you?"

"You wouldn't just put us ashore?" Mat said. "Not with Trollocs there?"

"Who said anything about shore?" Domon replied dryly. He studied them a moment, then spread his hands flat on the table. "Bayle Domon be a reasonable man. I'd no toss you over the side if there be a way out of it. Now, I see one of your apprentices has a sword. I need a good sword, and fine fellow that I be, I'll let you have passage far as Whitebridge for it."

Thom opened his mouth, and Rand spoke up quickly, "No!" Tam had not given it to him to trade away. He ran his hand down the hilt, feeling the bronze heron. As long as he had it, it was as if Tam were with him.

Domon shook his head. "Well, if it be no, it be no. But Bayle Domon no give free passage, not to his own mother."

Reluctantly Rand emptied his pocket. There was not much, a few coppers and the silver coin Moiraine had given him. He held it out to the captain. After a second, Mat sighed and did the same. Thom glared, but a smile replaced it so quickly that Rand was not sure it had been there at all.

Captain Domon deftly plucked the two fat silver coins out of the boys' hands and produced a small set of scales and a clinking bag from a brass-bound chest behind his chair. After careful weighing, he dropped the coins in the bag and returned them each some smaller silver and copper. Mostly copper. "As far as Whitebridge," he said, making a neat entry in a leather-bound ledger.

"That's a dear passage just to Whitebridge," Thom grumbled.

"Plus damages to my vessel," the captain answered placidly. He put the scales and the bag back in the chest and closed it in a satisfied way. "Plus a bit for bringing Trollocs down on me so I must run downriver in the night when there be shallows aplenty to pile me up."

"What about the others?" Rand asked. "Will you take them, too? They should have reached the river by now, or they soon will, and they'll see that lantern on your mast."

Captain Domon's eyebrows rose in surprise. "Happen you think we be standing still, man? Fortune prick me, we be three, four miles downriver from where you came aboard. Trollocs make those fellows put their backs into the oars—they know Trollocs better than they like—and the current helps, too. But it makes no nevermind. I'd no put in again tonight if my old grandmother was on the riverbank. I may no put in again at all until I reach Whitebridge. I've had my fill of Trollocs dogging my heels long before tonight, and I'll have no more can I help it."

Thom leaned forward interestedly. "You have had encounters with Trollocs before? Lately?"

Domon hesitated, eyeing Thom narrowly, but when he spoke he merely sounded disgusted. "I wintered in Saldaea, man. Not my choice, but the river froze early and the ice broke up late. They say you can see the Blight from the highest towers in Maradon, but I've no mind for that. I've been there before, and there always be talk of Trollocs attacking a farm or the like. This winter past, though, there be farms burning every night. Aye, and whole villages, too, betimes. They even came right up to the city walls. And if that no be bad enough, the people be all saying it meant the Dark One be stirring, that the Last Days be come." He gave a shiver, and scratched at his head as if the thought made his scalp itch. "I can no wait to get back where people think Trollocs be just tales, the stories I tell be traveler's lies."

Rand stopped listening. He stared at the opposite wall and thought about Egwene and the others. It hardly seemed right for him to be safe on the *Spray* while they were still back there in the night somewhere. The captain's cabin did not seem so comfortable as before.

He was surprised when Thom pulled him to his feet. The gleeman pushed Mat and him toward the ladder with apologies over his shoulder to Captain Domon for the country louts. Rand climbed up without a word.

Once they were on deck Thom looked around quickly to make sure he would not be overheard, then growled, "I could have gotten us passage for a few songs and stories if you two hadn't been so quick to show silver."

"I'm not so sure," Mat said. "He sounded serious about throwing us in the river to me."

Rand walked slowly to the rail and leaned against it, staring back up the night-shrouded river. He could not see anything but black, not even the riverbank. After a minute Thom put a hand on his shoulder, but he did not move.

"There isn't anything you can do, lad. Besides, they're likely safe with the . . . with Moiraine and Lan by this time. Can you think of any better than those two for getting the lot of them clear?"

"I tried to talk her out of coming," Rand said.

"You did what you could, lad. No one could ask more."

"I told her I'd take care of her. I should have tried harder." The creak of the sweeps and the hum of the rigging in the wind made a mournful tune. "I should have tried harder," he whispered.

Trollocs

CHAPTER
21

Listen to the Wind

S unrise creeping across the River Arinelle found its way into the hollow not far from the riverbank where Nynaeve sat with her back against the trunk of a young oak, breathing the deep breath of sleep. Her horse slept, too, head down and legs spraddled in the manner of horses. The reins were wrapped around her wrist. As sunlight fell on the horse's eyelids, the animal opened its eyes and raised its head, jerking the reins. Nynaeve came awake with a start.

For a moment she stared, wondering where she was, then stared around even more wildly when she remembered. But there were only the trees, and her horse, and a carpet of old, dry leaves across the bottom of the hollow. In the deepest dimness, some of last year's shadowshand mushrooms made rings on a fallen log.

"The Light preserve you, woman," she murmured, sagging back, "if you can't stay awake one night." She untied the reins and massaged her wrist as she stood. "You could have awakened in a Trolloc cookpot."

The dead leaves rustled as she climbed to the lip of the hollow and peeped over. No more than a handful of ash trees stood between her and the river. Their fissured bark and bare branches made them seem dead. Beyond, the wide blue-green water flowed by. Empty. Empty of anything. Scattered clumps of evergreens, willows and firs, dotted the far bank, and there seemed to be fewer trees altogether than on her side. If

Moiraine or any of the younglings were over there, they were well hidden. Of course, there was no reason they had to have crossed, or tried to cross, in sight of where she was. They could be anywhere ten miles upriver or down. *If they're alive at all, after last night.*

Angry with herself for thinking of the possibility, she slid back down into the hollow. Not even Winternight, or the battle before Shadar Logoth, had prepared her for last night, for that thing, Mashadar. All that frantic galloping, wondering if anyone else was still alive, wondering when she was going to come face-to-face with a Fade, or Trollocs. She had heard Trollocs growling and shouting in the distance, and the quivering shrieks of Trolloc horns had chilled her deeper than the wind ever could, but aside from that first encounter in the ruins she saw Trollocs only once, and that once she was outside. Ten or so of them seemed to spring out of the ground not thirty spans in front of her, bounding toward her on the instant, howling and shouting, brandishing hooked catchpoles. Yet as she pulled her horse around, they fell silent, lifting muzzles to sniff at the air. She watched, too astonished to run, as they turned their backs and vanished into the night. And that had been the most frightening of all.

"They know the smell of who they want," she told her horse, standing in the hollow, "and it is not me. The Aes Sedai is right, it seems, the Shepherd of the Night swallow her up."

Reaching a decision, she set out downriver, leading her horse. She moved slowly, keeping a wary watch on the forest around her; just because the Trollocs had not wanted her last night did not mean they would let her go if she stumbled on them again. As much attention as she gave the woods, she gave even more to the ground in front of her. If the others had crossed below her during the night, she should see some signs of them, signs she might miss from horseback. She might even come on them all still on this side. If she found neither, the river would take her to Whitebridge eventually, and there was a road from Whitebridge to Caemlyn, and all the way to Tar Valon if need be.

The prospect was almost enough to daunt her. Before this she had been no further from Emond's Field than had the boys. Taren Ferry had seemed strange to her; Baerlon would have had her staring in wonder if she had not been so set on finding Egwene and the others. But she allowed none of that to weaken her resolve. Sooner or later she would find Egwene and the boys. Or find a way to make the Aes Sedai answer for whatever had happened to them. One or the other, she vowed.

At intervals she found tracks, plenty of them, but usually her best efforts could not say whether those who made them had been searching or chasing or pursued. Some had been made by boots that could have belonged to humans or Trollocs either one. Others were hoofprints, like goats or oxen; those were Trollocs for sure. But never a clear sign that she could definitely say came from any of those she sought.

She had covered perhaps four miles when the wind brought her a whiff of woodsmoke. It came from further downriver, and not too far, she thought. She hesitated only a moment before tying her horse to a fir tree, well back from the river in a small, thick stand of evergreens that should keep the animal hidden. The smoke could mean Trollocs, but the only way to find out was to look. She tried not to think about the use Trollocs might be making of a fire.

Crouching, she slipped from tree to tree, mentally cursing the skirts she had to hold up out of the way. Dresses were not made for stalking. The sound of a horse slowed her, and when she finally peered cautiously around the trunk of an ash, the Warder was dismounting from his black warhorse in a small clearing on the bank. The Aes Sedai sat on a log beside a small fire where a kettle of water was just coming to a boil. Her white mare browsed behind her among sparse weeds. Nynaeve remained where she was.

"They are all gone," Lan announced grimly. "Four Halfmen started south about two hours before dawn, as near as I can tell—they don't leave much trace behind—but the Trollocs have vanished. Even the corpses, and Trollocs are not known for carrying off their dead. Unless they're hungry."

Moiraine tossed a handful of something into the boiling water and moved the kettle from the fire. "One could always hope they had gone back into Shadar Logoth and been consumed by it, but that would be too much to wish for."

The delicious odor of tea drifted to Nynaeve. *Light, don't let my stomach grumble.*

"There was no clear sign of the boys, or any of the others. The tracks are too muddled to tell anything." In her concealment, Nynaeve smiled; the Warder's failure was a slight vindication of her own. "But this other is important, Moiraine," Lan went on, frowning. He waved away the Aes Sedai's offer of tea and began marching up and down in front of the fire, one hand on his sword hilt and his cloak changing colors as he turned. "I could accept Trollocs in the Two Rivers, even a hundred Trollocs. But this? There must have been almost a thousand in the hunt for us yesterday."

"We were very lucky that not all stayed to search Shadar Logoth. The Myrddraal must have doubted we would hide there, but they also feared to return to Shayol Ghul leaving even the slightest chance uncovered. The Dark One was never a lenient master."

"Don't try to evade it. You know what I am saying. If those thousand were here to be sent into the Two Rivers, why were they not? There is only one answer. They were sent only after we crossed the Taren, when it was known that one Myrddraal and a hundred Trollocs were no longer enough. How? How were they sent? If a thousand Trollocs can be brought so far south from the Blight, so quickly, unseen—not to mention being taken off the same way—can ten thousand be sent into the heart of Saldaea, or Arafel, or Shienar? The Borderlands could be overrun in a year."

"The whole world will be overrun in five if we do not find those boys," Moiraine said simply. "The question worries me, also, but I have no answers. The Ways are closed, and there has not been an Aes Sedai powerful enough to Travel since the Time of Madness. Unless one of the Forsaken is loose—the Light send it is not so, yet or ever—there is still no one who can. In any case, I do not think all the Forsaken together could move a thousand Trollocs. Let us deal with the problems that face us here and now; everything else must wait."

"The boys." It was not a question.

"I have not been idle while you were away. One is across the river, and alive. As for the others, there was a faint trace downriver, but it faded away as I found it. The bond had been broken for hours before I began my search."

Crouched behind her tree, Nynaeve frowned in puzzlement.

Lan stopped his pacing. "You think the Halfmen heading south have them?"

"Perhaps." Moiraine poured herself a cup of tea before going on. "But I will not admit the possibility of them being dead. I cannot. I dare not. You know how much is at stake. I must have those young men. That Shayol Ghul will hunt them, I expect. Opposition from within the White Tower, even from the Amyrlin Seat, I accept. There are always Aes Sedai who will accept only one solution. But. . . ." Suddenly she put her cup down and sat up straight, grimacing. "If you watch the wolf too hard," she muttered, "a mouse will bite you on the ankle." And she looked right at the tree behind which Nynaeve was hiding. "Mistress al'Meara, you may come out now, if you wish."

Nynaeve scrambled to her feet, hastily dusting dead leaves from her dress. Lan had spun to face the tree as soon as Moiraine's eyes moved; his sword was in his hand before she finished speaking Nynaeve's name. Now he sheathed it again with more force than was strictly necessary. His face was almost as expressionless as ever, but Nynaeve thought there was a touch of chagrin about the set of his mouth. She felt a stab of satisfaction; the Warder had not known she was there, at least.

Satisfaction lasted only a moment, though. She fastened her eyes on Moiraine and walked toward her purposefully. She wanted to remain cold and calm, but her voice quivered with anger. "What have you meshed Egwene and the boys in? What filthy Aes Sedai plots are you planning to use them in?"

The Aes Sedai picked up her cup and calmly sipped her tea. When Nynaeve was close, though, Lan put out an arm to bar her way. She tried to brush the obstruction aside, and was surprised when the Warder's arm moved no more than an oak branch would have. She was not frail, but his muscles were like iron.

"Tea?" Moiraine offered.

"No, I don't want any tea. I would not drink your tea if I was dying of thirst. You won't use any Emond's Field folk in your dirty Aes Sedai schemes."

"You have very little room to talk, Wisdom." Moiraine showed more interest in her hot tea than in anything she was saying. "You can wield the One Power yourself, after a fashion."

Nynaeve pushed at Lan's arm again; it still did not move, and she decided to ignore it. "Why don't you try claiming I am a Trolloc?"

Moiraine's smile was so knowing that Nynaeve wanted to hit her. "Do you think I can stand face-to-face with a woman who can touch the True Source and channel the One Power, even if only now and then, without knowing what she is? Just as you sensed the potential in Egwene. How do you think I knew you were behind that tree? If I had not been distracted, I would have known the moment you came close. You certainly are not a Trolloc, for me to feel the evil of the Dark One. So what did I sense, Nynaeve al'Meara, Wisdom of Emond's Field and unknowing wielder of the One Power?"

Lan was looking down at Nynaeve in a way she did not like; surprised and speculative, it seemed to her, though nothing had changed about his face but his eyes. Egwene *was* special; she had always known that. Egwene would make a fine Wisdom. *They're working together,* she thought, *trying to put me off balance.* "I won't listen to any more of this. You—"

"You must listen," Moiraine said firmly. "I had my suspicions in Emond's Field even before I met you. People told me how upset the Wisdom was that she had not predicted the hard winter and the lateness of spring. They told me how good she was at foretelling weather, at telling the crops. They told me how wonderful her cures were, how she sometimes healed injuries, that should have been crippling, so well there was barely a scar, and not a limp or a twinge. The only ill word I heard about you was from a few who thought you too young for the responsibility, and that only strengthened my suspicions. So much skill so young."

"Mistress Barran taught me well." She tried looking at Lan, but his eyes still made her uncomfortable, so she settled for staring over the Aes Sedai's head at the river. *How dare the village gossip in front of an outlander!* "Who said I was too young?" she demanded.

Moiraine smiled, refusing to be diverted. "Unlike most women who claim to listen to the wind, you actually can, sometimes. Oh, it has nothing to do with the wind, of course. It is of Air and Water. It is not something you needed to be taught; it was born into you, just as it was born into Egwene. But you have learned to handle it, which she still has to learn. Two minutes after I came face-to-face with you, I knew. Do you remember how I suddenly asked you if you were the Wisdom? Why, do you think? There was nothing to distinguish you from any other pretty young woman getting ready for Festival. Even looking for a young Wisdom I expected someone half again your age."

Nynaeve remembered that meeting all too well; this woman, more self-possessed than anyone in the Women's Circle, in a dress more beautiful than any she had ever seen, addressing her as a child. Then Moiraine had suddenly blinked as if surprised and out of a clear sky asked. . . .

She licked lips gone abruptly dry. They were both looking at her, the Warder's face as unreadable as a stone, the Aes Sedai's sympathetic yet intent. Nynaeve shook her head. "No! No, it's impossible. I would know. You are just trying to trick me, and it will not work."

"Of course you do not know," Moiraine said soothingly. "Why should you even suspect? All of your life you have heard about listening to the wind. In any case, you would as soon announce to all of Emond's Field that you were a Darkfriend as admit to yourself, even in the deepest recesses of your mind, that you have anything to do with the One Power, or the dreaded Aes Sedai." Amusement flitted across Moiraine's face. "But I can tell you how it began."

"I don't want to hear any more of your lies," she said, but the Aes Sedai went right on.

"Perhaps as much as eight or ten years ago—the age varies, but always comes young—there was something you wanted more than anything else in the world, something you needed. And you got it. A branch suddenly falling where you could pull yourself out of a pond instead of drowning. A friend, or a pet, getting well when everyone thought they would die.

"You felt nothing special at the time, but a week or ten days later you had your first reaction to touching the True Source. Perhaps fever and chills that came on suddenly and put you to bed, then disappeared after only a few hours. None of the reactions, and they vary, lasts more than a few hours. Headaches and numbness and exhilaration all mixed together, and you taking foolish chances or acting giddy. A spell of dizziness, when you tripped and stumbled whenever you tried to move, when you could not say a sentence without your tongue mangling half the words. There are others. Do you remember?"

Nynaeve sat down hard on the ground; her legs would not hold her up. She remembered, but she shook her head anyway. It had to be coincidence. Or else Moiraine had asked more questions in Emond's Field than she had thought. The Aes Sedai had asked a great many questions. It had to be that. Lan offered a hand, but she did not even see it.

"I will go further," Moiraine said when Nynaeve kept silent. "You used the Power to Heal either Perrin or Egwene at some time. An affinity develops. You can sense the presence of someone you have Healed. In Baerlon you came straight to the Stag and Lion, though it was not the nearest inn to any gate by which you could have entered. Of the people from Emond's Field, only Perrin and Egwene were at the inn when you arrived. Was it Perrin, or Egwene? Or both?"

"Egwene," Nynaeve mumbled. She had always taken it for granted that she could sometimes tell who was approaching her even when she could not see them; not until now had she realized that it was always someone on whom her cures had worked almost miraculously well. And she had always known when the medicine would work beyond expectations, always felt the certainty when she said the crops would be especially good, or that the rains would come early or late. That was the way she thought it was supposed to be. Not all Wisdoms could listen to the wind, but the best could. That was what Mistress Barran always said, just as she said Nynaeve would be one of the best.

"She had breakbone fever." She kept her head down and spoke to the ground. "I was still apprentice to Mistress Barran, and she set me to watch Egwene. I was young, and I didn't know the Wisdom had everything well in hand. It's terrible to watch, breakbone fever. The child was soaked with sweat, groaning and twisting until I could not understand why I didn't hear her bones snapping. Mistress Barran had told me the fever would break in another day, two at the most, but I thought she was doing me a kindness. I thought Egwene was dying. I used to look after her sometimes when she was a toddler—when her mother was busy—and I started crying because I was going to have to watch her die. When Mistress Barran came back an hour later, the fever had broken. She was surprised, but she made over me more than Egwene. I always thought she believed I had given the child something and was too frightened to admit it. I always thought she was trying to comfort me, to make sure I knew I hadn't hurt Egwene. A week later I fell on the floor in her sitting room, shaking and burning up by turns. She bundled me into bed, but by suppertime it was gone."

She dropped her head in her hands as she finished speaking. *The Aes Sedai chose a good example,* she thought, *Light burn her! Using the Power like an Aes Sedai. A filthy, Darkfriend Aes Sedai!*

"You were very lucky," Moiraine said, and Nynaeve sat erect. Lan stepped back as if what they talked about was none of his business, and busied himself with Mandarb's saddle, not even glancing at them.

"Lucky!"

"You have managed a crude control over the Power, even if touching the True Source still comes at random. If you had not, it would have killed you eventually. As it will, in all probability, kill Egwene if you manage to stop her from going to Tar Valon."

"If I learned to control it. . . ." Nynaeve swallowed hard. It was like admitting all over again that she could do what the Aes Sedai said. "If I learned to control it, so can she. There is no need for her to go to Tar Valon, and get mixed up in your intrigues."

Moiraine shook her head slowly. "Aes Sedai search for girls who can touch the True Source unguided just as assiduously as we search for men who can do so. It is not a desire to increase our numbers—or at least, not only that—nor is it a fear that those women will misuse the Power. The rough control of the Power they may gain, if the Light shines on them, is rarely enough to do any great damage, especially since the actual touching of the Source is beyond their control without a teacher, and comes only randomly. And, of course, they do not suffer the madness that drives men to evil or twisted things. We want to save their lives. The lives of those who never do manage any control at all."

"The fever and chills I had couldn't kill anyone," Nynaeve insisted. "Not in three or four hours. I had the other things, too, and they couldn't kill anybody, either. And they stopped after a few months. What about that?"

"Those were only reactions," Moiraine said patiently. "Each time, the reaction comes closer to the actual touching of the Source, until the two happen almost together. After that there are no more reactions that can be seen, but it is as if a clock has begun ticking. A year. Two years. I know one woman who lasted five years. Of four who have the inborn ability that you and Egwene have, three die if we do not find them and train them. It is not as horrible a death as the men die, but neither is it pretty, if any death can be called so. Convulsions. Screaming. It takes days, and once it begins there is nothing that can be done to stop it, not by all the Aes Sedai in Tar Valon together."

"You're lying. All those questions you asked in Emond's Field. You found out about Egwene's fever breaking, about my fever and chills, all of it. You made all of this up."

"You know I did not," Moiraine said gently.

Reluctantly, more reluctantly than she had ever done anything in her life, Nynaeve nodded. It had been a last stubborn effort to deny what was plain, and there was never any good in that, however unpleasant it might be. Mistress Barran's first apprentice had died the way the Aes Sedai said when Nynaeve was still playing with dolls, and there had been a young woman in Deven Ride only a few years ago. She had been a Wisdom's apprentice, too, one who could listen to the wind.

"You have great potential, I think," Moiraine continued. "With training you might become even more powerful than Egwene, and I believe she can become one of the most powerful Aes Sedai we have seen in centuries."

Nynaeve pushed herself back from the Aes Sedai as she would have from a viper. "No! I'll have nothing to do with—" *With what? Myself?* She slumped, and her voice became hesitant. "I would ask you not to tell anyone about this. Please?" The word nearly stuck in her throat. She would rather Trollocs had appeared than she had been forced to say please to this woman. But Moiraine only nodded assent, and some of her spirit returned. "None of this explains what you want with Rand, and Mat, and Perrin."

"The Dark One wants them," Moiraine replied. "If the Dark One wants a thing, I oppose it. Can there be a simpler reason, or a better?" She finished her tea, watching Nynaeve over the rim of her cup. "Lan, we must be going. South, I think. I fear the Wisdom will not be accompanying us."

Nynaeve's mouth tightened at the way the Aes Sedai said "Wisdom"; it seemed to suggest she was turning her back on great things in favor of something petty. *She doesn't want me along. She's trying to put my back up so I'll go back home and leave them alone with her.* "Oh, yes, I will be going with you. You cannot keep me from it."

"No one will try to keep you from it," Lan said as he rejoined them. He emptied the tea kettle over the fire and stirred the ashes with a stick. "A part of the Pattern?" he said to Moiraine.

"Perhaps so," she replied thoughtfully. "I should have spoken to Min again."

"You see, Nynaeve, you are welcome to come." There was a hesitation in the way Lan said her name, a hint of an unspoken "Sedai" after it.

Nynaeve bristled, taking it for mockery, and bristled, too, at the way they spoke of things in front of her—things she knew nothing about—without the courtesy of an explanation, but she would not give them the satisfaction of asking.

The Warder went on preparing for departure, his economical motions so sure and swift that he was quickly done, saddlebags, blankets, and all fastened behind the saddles of Mandarb and Aldieb.

"I will fetch your horse," he told Nynaevé as he finished with the last saddle tie.

He started up the riverbank, and she allowed herself a small smile. After the way she had watched him undiscovered, he was going to try to find her horse unaided. He would learn that she left little in the way of tracks when she was stalking. It would be a pleasure when he came back empty-handed.

"Why south?" she asked Moiraine. "I heard you say one of
the boys is across the river. And how do you know?"

"I gave each of the boys a token. It created a bond of sorts
between them and me. So long as they are alive and have those
coins in their possession, I will be able to find them."
Nynaeve's eyes turned in the direction the Warder had gone,
and Moiraine shook her head. "Not like that. It only allows me
to discover if they still live, and find them should we become
separated. Prudent, do you not think, under the circumstances?"

"I don't like anything that connects you with anyone from
Emond's Field," Nynaeve said stubbornly. "But if it will help
us find them. . . ."

"It will. I would gather the young man across the river first,
if I could." For a moment frustration tinged the Aes Sedai's
voice. "He is only a few miles from us. But I cannot afford to
take the time. He should make his way down to Whitebridge
safely now that the Trollocs have gone. The two who went
downriver may need me more. They have lost their coins, and
Myrddraal are either pursuing them or else trying to intercept
us all at Whitebridge." She sighed. "I must take care of the
greatest need first."

"The Myrddraal could have . . . could have killed them,"
Nynaeve said.

Moiraine shook her head slightly, denying the suggestion as
if it were too trivial to be considered. Nynaeve's mouth tightened. "Where is Egwene, then? You haven't even mentioned
her."

"I do not know," Moiraine admitted, "but I hope that she is
safe."

"You don't know? You hope? All that talk about saving her
life by taking her to Tar Valon, and she could be dead for all
you know!"

"I could look for her and allow the Myrddraal more time
before I arrive to help the two young men who went south. It is
them the Dark One wants, not her. They would not bother
with Egwene, so long as their true quarry remains uncaught."

Nynaeve remembered her own encounter, but she refused to
admit the sense of what Moiraine said. "So the best you have

to offer is that she may be alive, if she was lucky. Alive, maybe alone, frightened, even hurt, days from the nearest village or help except for us. And you intend to leave her."

"She may just as easily be safe with the boy across the river. Or on her way to Whitebridge with the other two. In any case, there are no longer Trollocs here to threaten her, and she is strong, intelligent, and quite capable of finding her way to Whitebridge alone, if need be. Would you rather stay on the chance that she may need help, or do you want to try to help those we know are in need? Would you have me search for her and let the boys—and the Myrddraal who are surely pursuing them—go? As much as I hope for Egwene's safety, Nynaeve, I fight against the Dark One, and for now that sets my path."

Moiraine's calm never slipped while she laid out the horrible alternatives; Nynaeve wanted to scream at her. Blinking back tears, she turned her face so the Aes Sedai could not see. *Light, a Wisdom is supposed to look after* all *of her people. Why do I have to choose like this?*

"Here is Lan," Moiraine said, rising and settling her cloak about her shoulders.

To Nynaeve it was only a tiny blow as the Warder led her horse out of the trees. Still, her lips thinned when he handed her the reins. It would have been a small boost to her spirits if there had been even a trace of gloating on his face instead of that insufferable stony calm. His eyes widened when he saw her face, and she turned her back on him to wipe tears from her cheeks. *How dare he mock my crying!*

"Are you coming, Wisdom?" Moiraine asked coolly.

She took one last, slow look at the forest, wondering if Egwene was out there, before sadly mounting her horse. Lan and Moiraine were already in their saddles, turning their horses south. She followed, stiff-backed, refusing to let herself look back; instead she kept her eyes on Moiraine. The Aes Sedai was so confident in her power and her plans, she thought, but if they did not find Egwene and the boys, all of them, alive and unharmed, not all of her power would protect her. Not all her Power. *I can use it, woman! You told me so yourself. I can use it against you!*

CHAPTER
22

A Path Chosen

In a small copse of trees, beneath a pile of cedar branches roughly cut in the dark, Perrin slept long after sunrise. It was the cedar needles, pricking him through his still-damp clothes, that finally pricked through his exhaustion as well. Deep in a dream of Emond's Field, of working at Master Luhhan's forge, he opened his eyes and stared, uncomprehending, at the sweet-smelling branches interwoven over his face, sunlight trickling through.

Most of the branches fell away as he sat up in surprise, but some hung haphazardly from his shoulders, and even his head, making him appear something like a tree himself. Emond's Field faded as memory rushed back, so vivid that for a moment the night before seemed more real than anything around him now.

Panting, frantic, he scrabbled his axe out of the pile. He clutched it in both hands and peered around cautiously, holding his breath. Nothing moved. The morning was cold and still. If there were Trollocs on the east bank of the Arinelle, they were not moving, at least not close to him. Taking a deep, calming breath, he lowered the axe to his knees, and waited a moment for his heart to stop pounding.

The small stand of evergreens surrounding him was the first shelter he had found last night. It was sparse enough to give little protection against watching eyes if he stood up. Plucking branches from his head and shoulders, he pushed aside the rest of his prickly blanket, then crawled on hands and knees to the edge of the copse. There he lày studying the riverbank and scratching where the needles had stabbed him.

The cutting wind of the night before had faded to a silent breeze that barely rippled the surface of the water. The river ran by, calm and empty. And wide. Surely too wide and too deep for Fades to cross. The far bank appeared a solid mass of trees as far as he could see upriver and down. Certainly nothing moved in his view over there.

He was not sure how he felt about that. Fades and Trollocs he could do without quite easily, even on the other side of the river, but a whole list of worries would have vanished with the appearance of the Aes Sedai, or the Warder, or, even better, any of his friends. *If wishes were wings, sheep would fly.* That was what Mistress Luhhan always said.

He had not seen a sign of his horse since riding over the bluff—he hoped it had swum out of the river safely—but he was more used to walking than riding anyway, and his boots were stout and well soled. He had nothing to eat, but his sling was still wrapped around his waist, and that or the snarelines in his pocket ought to yield a rabbit in a little time. Everything for making a fire was gone with his saddlebags, but the cedar trees would yield tinder and a firebow with a bit of work.

He shivered as the breeze gusted into his hiding place. His cloak was somewhere in the river, and his coat and everything else he wore were still clammy cold from the soaking in the river. He had been too tired for the cold and damp to bother him last night, but now he was wide awake to every chill. Just the same, he decided against hanging his clothes on the branches to dry. If the day was not precisely cold, it was not even close to warm.

Time was the problem, he thought with a sigh. Dry clothes, with a little time. A rabbit to roast and a fire to roast it over, with a little time. His stomach rumbled, and he tried to forget about eating altogether. There were more important uses for that time. One thing at a time, and the most important first. That was his way.

His eyes followed the strong flow of the Arinelle downriver. He was a stronger swimmer than Egwene. If she had made it across. . . . No, not *if.* The place where she *had* made it across would be downriver. He drummed on the ground with his fingers, weighing, considering.

His decision made, he wasted no time in picking up his axe and setting off down the river.

This side of the Arinelle lacked the thick forest of the west bank. Clumps of trees spotted across what would be grassland if spring ever came. Some were big enough to be called thickets, with swathes of evergreens among the barren ash and alder and hardgum. Down by the river the stands were smaller and not so tight. They gave poor cover, but they were all the cover there was.

He dashed from growth to growth in a crouch, throwing himself down when he was among the trees to study the riverbanks, the far side as well as his. The Warder said the river would be a barrier to Fades and Trollocs, but would it? Seeing him might be enough to overcome their reluctance to cross deep water. So he watched carefully from behind the trees and ran from one hiding place to the next, fast and low.

He covered several miles that way, in spurts, until suddenly, halfway to the beckoning shelter of a growth of willows, he grunted and stopped dead, staring at the ground. Patches of bare earth spotted the matted brown of last year's grass, and in the middle of one of those patches, right under his nose, was a clear hoofprint. A slow smile spread across his face. Some Trollocs had hooves, but he doubted if any wore horseshoes, especially horseshoes with the double crossbar Master Luhhan added for strength.

Forgetting possible eyes on the other side of the river, he cast about for more tracks. The plaited carpet of dead grass did not take impressions well, but his sharp eyes found them anyway. The scanty trail led him straight away from the river to a dense stand of trees, thick with leatherleaf and cedar that made a wall against wind or prying eyes. The spreading branches of a lone hemlock towered in the middle of it all.

Still grinning, he pushed his way through the interwoven branches, not caring how much noise he made. Abruptly he stepped into a little clearing under the hemlock—and stopped. Behind a small fire, Egwene crouched, her face grim, with a thick branch held like a club and her back against Bela's flank.

"I guess I should have called out," he said with an abashed shrug.

Tossing her club down, she ran to throw her arms around him. "I thought you had drowned. You're still wet. Here, sit by the fire and warm yourself. You lost your horse, didn't you?"

He let her push him to a place by the fire and rubbed his hands over the flames, grateful for the warmth. She produced an oiled paper packet from her saddlebags and gave him some bread and cheese. The package had been so tightly wrapped that even after its dunking the food was dry. *Here you were worrying about her, and she's done better than you did.*

"Bela got me across," Egwene said, patting the shaggy mare. "She headed away from the Trollocs and just towed me along." She paused. "I haven't seen anybody else, Perrin."

He heard the unspoken question. Regretfully eyeing the packet that she was rewrapping, he licked the last crumbs from his fingers before speaking. "I've seen no one but you since last night. No Fades or Trollocs, either; there's that."

"Rand has to be all right," Egwene said, quickly adding, "they all do. They have to. They're probably looking for us right now. They might find us anytime now. Moiraine is an Aes Sedai, after all."

"I keep being reminded of that," he said. "Burn me, I wish I could forget."

"I did not hear you complaining when she stopped the Trollocs from catching us," Egwene said tartly.

"I just wish we could do without her." He shrugged uncomfortably under her steady gaze. "I suppose we can't, though. I've been thinking." Her eyebrows rose, but he was used to surprise whenever he claimed an idea. Even when his ideas were as good as theirs, they always remembered how deliberate he was in thinking of them. "We can wait for Lan and Moiraine to find us."

"Of course," she cut in. "Moiraine Sedai said she would find us if we were separated."

He let her finish, then went on. "Or the Trollocs could find us, first. Moiraine could be dead, too. All of them could be. No, Egwene. I'm sorry, but they could be. I hope they are all safe. I hope they'll walk up to this fire any minute. But hope is like a piece of string when you're drowning; it just isn't enough to get you out by itself."

Egwene closed her mouth and stared at him with her jaw set. Finally, she said, "You want to go downriver to Whitebridge? If Moiraine Sedai doesn't find us here, that's where she will look next."

"I suppose," he said slowly, "that Whitebridge is where we *should* go. But the Fades probably know that, too. That's where they'll be looking, and this time we don't have an Aes Sedai or a Warder to protect us."

"I suppose you're going to suggest running off somewhere, the way Mat wanted to? Hiding somewhere the Fades and Trollocs won't find us? Or Moiraine Sedai, either?"

"Don't think I haven't considered it," he said quietly. "But every time we think we are free, Fades and Trollocs find us again. I don't know if there *is* anyplace we could hide from them. I don't like it much, but we need Moiraine."

"I don't understand then, Perrin. Where do we go?"

He blinked in surprise. She was waiting for his answer. Waiting for *him* to tell her what to do. It had never occurred to him that she would look to him to take the lead. Egwene never liked doing what someone else had planned out, and she never let anybody tell her what to do. Except maybe the Wisdom, and he thought sometimes she balked at that. He smoothed the dirt in front of him with his hand and cleared his throat roughly.

"If this is where we are now, and that is Whitebridge," he stabbed the ground twice with his finger, "then Caemlyn should be somewhere around here." He made a third mark, off to the side.

He paused, looking at the three dots in the dirt. His entire plan was based on what he remembered of her father's old map. Master al'Vere said it was not too accurate, and, anyway, he had never mooned over it as much as Rand and Mat. But Egwene said nothing. When he looked up, she was still watching him with her hands in her lap.

"Caemlyn?" She sounded stunned.

"Caemlyn." He drew a line in the dirt between two of the dots. "Away from the river, and straight across. Nobody would expect that. We'll wait for them in Caemlyn." He dusted his hands and waited. He thought it was a good plan, but surely she would have objections now. He expected she would take charge—she was always bullying him into something—and that was all right with him.

To his surprise, she nodded. "There must be villages. We can ask directions."

"What worries me," Perrin said, "is what we do if the Aes Sedai *doesn't* find us there. Light, who'd ever have thought I'd worry about something like that? What if she doesn't come to Caemlyn? Maybe she thinks we're dead. Maybe she'll take Rand and Mat straight to Tar Valon."

"Moiraine Sedai said she could find us," Egwene said firmly. "If she can find us here, she can find us in Caemlyn, and she will."

Perrin nodded slowly. "If you say so, but if she doesn't appear in Caemlyn in a few days, we go on to Tar Valon and put our case before the Amyrlin Seat." He took a deep breath. *Two weeks ago you'd never even seen an Aes Sedai, and now you're talking about the Amyrlin Seat. Light!* "According to Lan, there's a good road from Caemlyn." He looked at the oiled paper packet beside Egwene and cleared his throat. "What chance of a little more bread and cheese?"

"This might have to last a long time," she said, "unless you have better luck with snares than I did last night. At least the fire was easy." She laughed softly as if she had made a joke, tucking the packet back into her saddlebags.

Apparently there were limits to how much leadership she was willing to accept. His stomach rumbled. "In that case," he said, standing, "we might as well start now."

"But you're still wet," she protested.

"I'll walk myself dry," he said firmly, and began kicking dirt over the fire. If he was the leader, it was time to start leading. The wind from the river was picking up.

CHAPTER
23

Wolfbrother

From the start Perrin knew the journey to Caemlyn was going to be far from comfortable, beginning with Egwene's insistence that they take turns riding Bela. They did not know how far it was, she said, but it was too far for her to be the only one who rode. Her jaw firmed, and her eyes stared at him unblinking.

"I'm too big to ride Bela," he said. "I'm used to walking, and I'd rather."

"And I am not used to walking?" Egwene said sharply.

"That isn't what I—"

"I'm the only one who's supposed to get saddlesore, is that it? And when you walk till your feet are ready to fall off, you'll expect me to look after you."

"Let it be," he breathed when she looked like going on. "Anyway, you'll take the first turn." Her face turned even more stubborn, but he refused to let her get a word in edgewise. "If you won't get in the saddle by yourself, I'll put you there."

She gave him a startled look, and a small smile curved her lips. "In that case. . . ." She sounded as if she were about to laugh, but she climbed up.

He grumbled to himself as he turned away from the river. Leaders in stories never had to put up with this sort of thing.

Egwene did insist on him taking his turns, and whenever he tried to avoid it, she bullied him into the saddle. Blacksmithing did not lend itself to a slender build, and Bela was not very large as horses went. Every time he put his foot in the stirrup the shaggy mare looked at him with what he was sure was reproach. Small things, perhaps, but they irritated. Soon he flinched whenever Egwene announced, "It's your turn, Perrin."

In stories leaders seldom flinched, and they were never bullied. But, he reflected, they never had to deal with Egwene, either.

There were only short rations of bread and cheese to begin with, and what there was gave out by the end of the first day. Perrin set snares along likely rabbit runs—they looked old, but it was worth a chance—while Egwene began laying a fire. When he was done, he decided to try his hand with his sling before the light failed altogether. They had not seen a sign of anything at all alive, but. . . . To his surprise, he jumped a scrawny rabbit almost at once. He was so surprised when it burst from under a bush right beneath his feet that it almost got away, but he fetched it at forty paces, just as it was darting around a tree.

When he came back to the camp with the rabbit, Egwene had broken limbs all laid for the fire, but she was kneeling beside the pile with her eyes closed. "What are you doing? You can't wish a fire."

Egwene gave a jump at his first words, and twisted around to stare at him with a hand to her throat. "You . . . you startled me."

"I was lucky," he said, holding up the rabbit. "Get your flint and steel. We eat well tonight, at least."

"I don't have a flint," she said slowly. "It was in my pocket, and I lost it in the river."

"Then how . . . ?"

"It was so easy back there on the riverbank, Perrin. Just the way Moiraine Sedai showed me. I just reached out, and. . . ." She gestured as if grasping for something, then let her hand fall with a sigh. "I can't find it, now."

Perrin licked his lips uneasily. "The . . . the Power?" She nodded, and he stared at her. "Are you crazy? I mean . . . the One Power! You can't just play around with something like that."

"It was so easy, Perrin. I can do it. I can channel the Power."

He took a deep breath. "I'll make a firebow, Egwene. Promise you won't try this . . . this . . . *thing* again."

"I will not." Her jaw firmed in a way that made him sigh. "Would you give up that axe of yours, Perrin Aybara? Would you walk around with one hand tied behind your back? I won't do it!"

"I'll make the firebow," he said wearily. "At least, don't try it again tonight? Please?"

She acquiesced grudgingly, and even after the rabbit was roasting on a spit over the flames, he had the feeling she felt she could have done it better. She would not give up trying, either, every night, though the best she ever did was a trickle of smoke that vanished almost immediately. Her eyes dared him to say a word, and he wisely kept his mouth shut.

After that one hot meal, they subsisted on coarse wild tubers and a few young shoots. With still no sign of spring, none of it was plentiful, and none of it tasty, either. Neither complained, but not a meal passed without one or the other sighing regretfully, and they both knew it was for the tang of a bit of cheese, or even the smell of bread. A find of mushrooms—Queen's Crowns, the best—one afternoon in a shady part of the forest was enough to seem a great treat. They gobbled them down, laughing and telling stories from back in Emond's Field, stories that began, "Do you remember when—" but the mushrooms did not last long, and neither did the laughter. There was little mirth in hunger.

Whichever was walking carried a sling, ready to let fly at the sight of a rabbit or squirrel, but the only time either hurled a stone was in frustration. The snares they set so carefully each evening yielded nothing at dawn, and they did not dare stay a day in one place to leave the snares out. Neither of them knew how far it was to Caemlyn, and neither would feel safe until they got there, if then. Perrin began to wonder if his stomach could shrink enough to make a hole all the way through his middle.

They made good time, as he saw it, but as they got farther and farther from the Arinelle without seeing a village, or even a farmhouse where they could ask directions, his doubts about his own plan grew. Egwene continued to appear outwardly as confident as when they set out, but he was sure that sooner or later she would say it would have been better to risk the Trollocs than to wander around lost for the rest of their lives. She never did, but he kept expecting it.

Two days from the river the land changed to thickly forested hills, as gripped by the tail end of winter as everywhere else, and a day after that the hills flattened out again, the dense forest broken by glades, often a mile or more across. Snow still lay in hidden hollows, and the air was brisk of a morning, and the wind cold always. Nowhere did they see a road, or a plowed field, or chimney smoke in the distance, or any other sign of human habitation—at least, none where men still dwelt.

Once the remains of tall stone ramparts encircled a hilltop. Parts of roofless stone houses stood inside the fallen circle. The forest had long swallowed it; trees grew right through everything, and spiderwebs of old creeper enveloped the big stone blocks. Another time they came on a stone tower, broken-topped and brown with old moss, leaning on the huge oak whose thick roots were slowly toppling it. But they found no place where men had breathed in living remembrance. Memories of Shadar Logoth kept them away from the ruins and hurried their footsteps until they were once more deep in places that seemed never to have known a human footstep.

Dreams plagued Perrin's sleep, fearful dreams. Ba'alzamon was in them, chasing him through mazes, hunting him, but Perrin never met him face-to-face, so far as he remembered. And their journey had been enough to bring a few bad dreams. Egwene complained of nightmares about Shadar Logoth, especially the two nights after they found the ruined fort and the abandoned tower. Perrin kept his own counsel even when he woke sweating and shaking in the dark. She was looking to him to lead them safely to Caemlyn, not share worries about which they could do nothing.

He was walking at Bela's head, wondering if they would find anything to eat this evening, when he first caught the smell. The mare flared her nostrils and swung her head in the next moment. He seized her bridle before she could whicker.

"That's smoke," Egwene said excitedly. She leaned forward

in the saddle, drew a deep breath. "A cookfire. Somebody is roasting dinner. Rabbit."

"Maybe," Perrin said cautiously, and her eager smile faded. He exchanged his sling for the wicked half-moon of the axe. His hands opened and closed uncertainly on the thick haft. It was a weapon, but neither his hidden practice behind the forge nor Lan's teachings had really prepared him to use it as one. Even the battle before Shadar Logoth was too vague in his mind to give him any confidence. He could never quite manage that void that Rand and the Warder talked about, either.

Sunlight slanted through the trees behind them, and the forest was a still mass of dappled shadows. The faint smell of woodsmoke drifted around them, tinged with the aroma of cooking meat. *It could be rabbit,* he thought, and his stomach grumbled. And it could be something else, he reminded himself. He looked at Egwene; she was watching him. There were responsibilities to being leader.

"Wait here," he said softly. She frowned, but he cut her off as she opened her mouth. "And be quiet! We don't know who it is, yet." She nodded. Reluctantly, but she did it. Perrin wondered why that did not work when he was trying to make her take his turn riding. Drawing a deep breath, he started for the source of the smoke.

He had not spent as much time in the forests around Emond's Field as Rand or Mat, but still he had done his share of hunting rabbits. He crept from tree to tree without so much as snapping a twig. It was not long before he was peering around the bole of a tall oak with spreading, serpentine limbs that bent to touch the ground then rose again. Beyond lay a campfire, and a lean, sun-browned man was leaning against one of the limbs not far from the flames.

At least he was not a Trolloc, but he was the strangest fellow Perrin had ever seen. For one thing, his clothes all seemed to be made from animal skins, with the fur still on, even his boots and the odd, flat-topped round cap on his head. His cloak was a crazy quilt of rabbit and squirrel; his trousers appeared to be made from the long-haired hide of a brown and white goat. Gathered at the back of his neck with a cord, his graying brown hair hung to his waist. A thick beard fanned across half his chest. A long knife hung at his belt, almost a sword, and a bow and quiver stood propped against a limb close to hand.

The man leaned back with his eyes closed, apparently asleep, but Perrin did not stir from his concealment. Six sticks slanted over the fellow's fire, and on each stick a rabbit was skewered, roasted brown and now and then dripping juice that hissed in the flames. The smell of them, so close, made his mouth water.

"You done drooling?" The man opened one eye and cocked it at Perrin's hiding place. "You and your friend might as well sit and have a bite. I haven't seen you eat much the last couple of days."

Perrin hesitated, then stood slowly, still gripping his axe tightly. "You've been watching me for two days?"

The man chuckled deep in his throat. "Yes, I been watching you. And that pretty girl. Pushes you around like a bantam rooster, doesn't she? Heard you, mostly. The horse is the only one of you doesn't trample around loud enough to be heard five miles off. You going to ask her in, or are you intending to eat all the rabbit yourself?"

Perrin bristled; he knew he did not make much noise. You could not get close enough to a rabbit in the Waterwood to fetch it with a sling if you made noise. But the smell of rabbit made him remember that Egwene was hungry, too, not to mention waiting to discover if it was a Trolloc fire they had smelled.

He slipped the haft of his axe through the belt loop and raised his voice. "Egwene! It's all right! It *is* rabbit!" Offering his hand, he added in a more normal tone, "My name is Perrin. Perrin Aybara."

The man considered his hand before taking it awkwardly, as if unused to shaking hands. "I'm called Elyas," he said, looking up. "Elyas Machera."

Perrin gasped, and nearly dropped Elyas's hand. The man's eyes were yellow, like bright, polished gold. Some memory tickled at the back of Perrin's mind, then fled. All he could think of right then was that all of the Trollocs' eyes he had seen had been almost black.

Egwene appeared, cautiously leading Bela. She tied the mare's reins to one of the smaller branches of the oak, and made polite sounds when Perrin introduced her to Elyas, but her eyes kept drifting to the rabbits. She did not seem to notice the man's eyes. When Elyas motioned them to the food, she fell to with a will. Perrin hesitated only a minute longer before joining her.

Elyas waited silently while they ate. Perrin was so hungry he tore off pieces of meat so hot he had to juggle them from hand to hand before he could hold them in his mouth. Even Egwene showed little of her usual neatness; greasy juice ran down her chin. Day faded into twilight before they began to slow down, moonless darkness closing in around the fire, and then Elyas spoke.

"What are you doing out here? There isn't a house inside fifty miles in any direction."

"We're going to Caemlyn," Egwene said. "Perhaps you could—" Her eyebrows lifted coolly as Elyas threw back his head and roared with laughter. Perrin stared at him, a rabbit leg half raised to his mouth.

"Caemlyn?" Elyas wheezed when he could talk again. "The path you're following, the line you've taken the last two days, you'll pass a hundred miles or more north of Caemlyn."

"We were going to ask directions," Egwene said defensively. "We just haven't found any villages or farms, yet."

"And none you will," Elyas said, chuckling. "The way you're going, you can travel all the way to the Spine of the World without seeing another human. Of course, if you managed to climb the Spine—it can be done, some places—you could find people in the Aiel Waste, but you wouldn't like it there. You'd broil by day, and freeze by night, and die of thirst anytime. It takes an Aielman to find water in the Waste, and they don't like strangers much. No, not much, I'd say." He set off into another, more furious, burst of laughter, this time actually rolling on the ground. "Not much at all," he managed.

Perrin shifted uneasily. *Are we eating with a madman?*

Egwene frowned, but she waited until Elyas's mirth faded a little, then said, "Perhaps you could show us the way. You seem to know a good deal more about where places are than we do."

Elyas stopped laughing. Raising his head, he replaced his round fur cap, which had fallen off while he was rolling about, and stared at her from under lowered brows. "I don't much like people," he said in a flat voice. "Cities are full of people. I don't go near villages, or even farms, very often. Villagers, farmers, they don't like my friends. I wouldn't even have helped you if you hadn't been stumbling around as helpless and innocent as newborn cubs."

"But at least you can tell us which way to go," she insisted. "If you direct us to the nearest village, even if it's fifty miles away, surely they'll give us directions to Caemlyn."

"Be still," Elyas said. "My friends are coming."

Bela suddenly whinnied in fear, and began jerking to pull her reins free. Perrin half rose as shapes appeared all around them in the darkening forest. Bela reared and twisted, screaming.

"Quiet the mare," Elyas said. "They won't hurt her. Or you, if you're still."

Four wolves stepped into the firelight, shaggy, waist-high forms with jaws that could break a man's leg. As if the people were not there they walked up to the fire and lay down between the humans. In the darkness among the trees firelight reflected off the eyes of more wolves, on all sides.

Yellow eyes, Perrin thought. Like Elyas's eyes. That was what he had been trying to remember. Carefully watching the wolves among them, he reached for his axe.

"I would not do that," Elyas said. "If they think you mean harm, they'll stop being friendly."

They were staring at him, those four wolves, Perrin saw. He had the feeling that all the wolves, those in the trees, as well, were staring at him. It made his skin itch. Cautiously he moved his hands away from the axe. He imagined he could feel the tension ease among the wolves. Slowly he sat back down; his hands shook until he gripped his knees to stop them. Egwene was so stiff she almost quivered. One wolf, close to black with a lighter gray patch on his face, lay nearly touching her.

Bela had ceased her screaming and rearing. Instead she stood trembling and shifting in an attempt to keep all of the wolves in view, kicking occasionally to show the wolves that she could, intending to sell her life dearly. The wolves seemed to ignore her and everyone else. Tongues lolling out of their mouths, they waited at their ease.

"There," Elyas said. "That's better."

"Are they tame?" Egwene asked faintly, and hopefully, too. "They're . . . pets?"

Elyas snorted. "Wolves don't tame, girl, not even as well as men. They're my friends. We keep each other company, hunt together, converse, after a fashion. Just like any friends. Isn't that right, Dapple?" A wolf with fur that faded through a dozen shades of gray, dark and light, turned her head to look at him.

"You talk to them?" Perrin marveled.

"It isn't exactly talking," Elyas replied slowly. "The words don't matter, and they aren't exactly right, either. Her name isn't Dapple. It's something that means the way shadows play on a forest pool at a midwinter dawn, with the breeze rippling the surface, and the tang of ice when the water touches the tongue, and a hint of snow before nightfall in the air. But that isn't quite it, either. You can't say it in words. It's more of a feeling. That's the way wolves talk. The others are Burn, Hopper, and Wind." Burn had an old scar on his shoulder that might explain his name, but there was nothing about the other two wolves to give any indication of what their names might mean.

For all the man's gruffness, Perrin thought Elyas was pleased to have the chance to talk to another human. He seemed eager enough to do it, at least. Perrin eyed the wolves' teeth glistening in the firelight and thought it might be a good idea to keep him talking. "How . . . how did you learn to talk to wolves, Elyas?"

"They found out," Elyas replied, "I didn't. Not at first. That's always the way of it, I understand. The wolves find you, not you them. Some people thought me touched by the Dark One, because wolves started appearing wherever I went. I suppose I thought so, too, sometimes. Most decent folk began to avoid me, and the ones who sought me out weren't the kind I wanted to know, one way or another. Then I noticed there were times when the wolves seemed to know what I was thinking, to respond to what was in my head. That was the real beginning. They were curious about me. Wolves can sense people, usually, but not like this. They were glad to find me. They say it's been a long time since they hunted with men, and when they say a long time, the feeling I get is like a cold wind howling all the way down from the First Day."

"I never heard of men hunting with wolves," Egwene said.

Her voice was not entirely steady, but the fact that the wolves were just lying there seemed to give her heart.

If Elyas heard her, he gave no sign. "Wolves remember things differently from the way people do," he said. His strange eyes took on a faraway look, as if he were drifting off on the flow of memory himself. "Every wolf remembers the history of all wolves, or at least the shape of it. Like I said, it can't be put into words very well. They remember running down prey side-by-side with men, but it was so long ago that it's more like the shadow of a shadow than a memory."

"That's very interesting," Egwene said, and Elyas looked at her sharply. "No, I mean it. It is." She wet her lips. "Could . . . ah . . . could you teach us to talk to them?"

Elyas snorted again. "It can't be taught. Some can do it, some can't. They say he can." He pointed at Perrin.

Perrin looked at Elyas's finger as if it were a knife. *He really is a madman.* The wolves were staring at him again. He shifted uncomfortably.

"You say you're going to Caemlyn," Elyas said, "but that still doesn't explain what you're doing out here, days from anywhere." He tossed back his fur-patch cloak and lay down on his side, propped on one elbow and waiting expectantly.

Perrin glanced at Egwene. Early on they had concocted a story for when they found people, to explain where they were going without bringing them any trouble. Without letting anyone know where they were really from, or where they were really going, eventually. Who knew what careless word might reach a Fade's ear? They had worked on it every day, patching it together, honing out flaws. And they had decided Egwene was the one to tell it. She was better with words than he was, and she claimed she could always tell when he was lying by his face.

Egwene began at once, smoothly. They were from the north, from Saldaea, from farms outside a tiny village. Neither of them had been more than twenty miles from home in their whole lives before this. But they had heard gleemen's stories, and merchants' tales, and they wanted to see some of the world. Caemlyn, and Illian. The Sea of Storms, and maybe even the fabled islands of the Sea Folk.

Perrin listened with satisfaction. Not even Thom Merrilin

could have made a better tale from the little they knew of the world outside the Two Rivers, or one better suited to their needs.

"From Saldaea, eh?" Elyas said when she was done.

Perrin nodded. "That's right. We thought about seeing Maradon first. I'd surely like to see the King. But the capital city would be the first place our fathers would look."

That was his part of it, to make it plain they had never been to Maradon. That way no one would expect them to know anything about the city, just in case they ran into someone who really had been there. It was all a long way from Emond's Field and the events of Winternight. Nobody hearing the tale would have any reason to think of Tar Valon, or Aes Sedai.

"Quite a story." Elyas nodded. "Yes, quite a story. There's a few things wrong with it, but the main thing is Dapple says it's all a lump of lies. Every last word."

"Lies!" Egwene exclaimed. "Why would we lie?"

The four wolves had not moved, but they no longer seemed to be just lying there around the fire; they crouched, instead, and their yellow eyes watched the Emond's Fielders without blinking.

Perrin did not say anything, but his hand strayed to the axe at his waist. The four wolves rose to their feet in one quick movement, and his hand froze. They made no sound, but the thick hackles on their necks stood erect. One of the wolves back under the trees raised a growling howl into the night. Others answered, five, ten, twenty, till the darkness rippled with them. Abruptly they, too, were still. Cold sweat trickled down Perrin's face.

"If you think. . . ." Egwene stopped to swallow. Despite the chill in the air there was sweat on her face, too. "If you think we are lying, then you'll probably prefer that we make our own camp for the night, away from yours."

"Ordinarily I would, girl. But right now I want to know about the Trollocs. And the Halfmen." Perrin struggled to keep his face impassive, and hoped he was doing better at it than Egwene. Elyas went on in a conversational tone. "Dapple says she smelled Halfmen and Trollocs in your minds while you were telling that fool story. They all did. You're mixed up with

Trollocs, somehow, and the Eyeless. Wolves hate Trollocs and Halfmen worse than wildfire, worse than anything, and so do I.

"Burn wants to be done with you. It was Trollocs gave him that mark when he was a yearling. He says game is scarce, and you're fatter than any deer he's seen in months, and we should be done with you. But Burn is always impatient. Why don't you tell me about it? I hope you're not Darkfriends. I don't like killing people after I've fed them. Just remember, they'll know if you lie, and even Dapple is already near as upset as Burn." His eyes, as yellow as the wolves' eyes, blinked no more than theirs did. *They are a wolf's eyes,* Perrin thought.

Egwene was looking at him, he realized, waiting for him to decide what they should do. *Light, suddenly I'm the leader again.* They had decided from the first that they could not risk telling the real story to anyone, but he saw no chance for them to get away even if he managed to get his axe out before. . . .

Dapple growled deep in her throat, and the sound was taken up by the other three around the fire, then by the wolves in the darkness. The menacing rumble filled the night.

"All right," Perrin said quickly. "All right!" The growling cut off, sharp and sudden. Egwene unclenched her hands and nodded. "It all started a few days before Winternight," Perrin began, "when our friend Mat saw a man in a black cloak. . . ."

Elyas never changed his expression or the way he lay on his side, but there was something about the tilt of his head that spoke of ears pricking up. The four wolves sat down as Perrin went on; he had the impression they were listening, too. The story was a long one, and he told almost all of it. The dream he and the others had had in Baerlon, though, he kept to himself. He waited for the wolves to make some sign they had caught the omission, but they only watched. Dapple seemed friendly, Burn angry. He was hoarse by the time he finished.

". . . and if she doesn't find us in Caemlyn, we'll go on to Tar Valon. We don't have any choice except to get help from the Aes Sedai."

"Trollocs and Halfmen this far south," Elyas mused. "Now that's something to consider." He rooted behind him and tossed Perrin a hide waterbag, not really looking at him. He appeared to be thinking. He waited until Perrin had drunk and replaced the plug before he spoke again. "I don't hold with Aes

Sedai. The Red Ajah, those that like hunting for men who mess with the One Power, they wanted to gentle me, once. I told them to their faces they were Black Ajah; served the Dark One, I said, and they didn't like that at all. They couldn't catch me, though, once I got into the forest, but they did try. Yes, they did. Come to that, I doubt any Aes Sedai would take kindly to me, after that. I had to kill a couple of Warders. Bad business, that, killing Warders. Don't like it."

"This talking to wolves," Perrin said uneasily. "It . . . it has to do with the Power?"

"Of course not," Elyas growled. "Wouldn't have worked on me, gentling, but it made me mad, them wanting to try. This is an old thing, boy. Older than Aes Sedai. Older than anybody using the One Power. Old as humankind. Old as wolves. They don't like that either, Aes Sedai. Old things coming again. I'm not the only one. There are other things, other folk. Makes Aes Sedai nervous, makes them mutter about ancient barriers weakening. Things are breaking apart, they say. They're afraid the Dark One will get loose, is what. You'd think I was to blame, the way some of them looked at me. Red Ajah, anyway, but some others, too. The Amyrlin Seat. . ŧ . Aaaah! I keep clear of them, mostly, and clear of friends of Aes Sedai, as well. You will, too, if you're smart."

"I'd like nothing better than to stay away from Aes Sedai," Perrin said.

Egwene gave him a sharp look. He hoped she would not burst out that she wanted to be an Aes Sedai. But she said nothing, though her mouth tightened, and Perrin went on.

"It isn't as if we have a choice. We've had Trollocs chasing us, and Fades, and Draghkar. Everything but Darkfriends. We can't hide, and we can't fight back alone. So who is going to help us? Who else is strong enough, except Aes Sedai?"

Elyas was silent for a time, looking at the wolves, most often at Dapple or Burn. Perrin shifted nervously and tried not to watch. When he watched he had the feeling that he could almost hear what Elyas and the wolves were saying to one another. Even if it had nothing to do with the Power, he wanted no part of it. *He had to be making some crazy joke. I can't talk to wolves.* One of the wolves—Hopper, he thought—looked at him and seemed to grin. He wondered how he had put a name to him.

"You could stay with me," Elyas said finally. "With us." Egwene's eyebrows shot up, and Perrin's mouth dropped open. "Well, what could be safer?" Elyas challenged. "Trollocs will take any chance they get to kill a wolf by itself, but they'll go miles out of their way to avoid a pack. And you won't have to worry about Aes Sedai, either. They don't often come into these woods."

"I don't know." Perrin avoided looking at the wolves to either side of him. One was Dapple, and he could feel her eyes on him. "For one thing, it isn't just the Trollocs."

Elyas chuckled coldly. "I've seen a pack pull down one of the Eyeless, too. Lost half the pack, but they wouldn't give up once they had its scent. Trollocs, Myrddraal, it's all one to the wolves. It's you they really want, boy. They've heard of other men who can talk to wolves, but you're the first they've ever met besides me. They'll accept your friend, too, though, and you'll all be safer here than in any city. There's Darkfriends in cities."

"Listen," Perrin said urgently, "I wish you'd stop saying that. I can't—do that . . . what you do, what you're saying."

"As you wish, boy. Play the goat, if you've a mind to. Don't you want to be safe?"

"I'm not deceiving myself. There's nothing to deceive myself about. All we want—"

"We are going to Caemlyn," Egwene spoke up firmly. "And then to Tar Valon."

Closing his mouth, Perrin met her angry look with one of his own. He knew that she followed his lead when she wanted to and not when she did not, but she could at least let him answer for himself. "What about you, Perrin?" he said, and answered himself. "Me? Well, let me think. Yes. Yes, I think I'll go on." He turned a mild smile on her. "Well, Egwene, that makes both of us. I guess I'm going with you, at that. Good to talk these things out before making a decision, isn't it?" She blushed, but the set of her jaw never lessened.

Elyas grunted. "Dapple said that's what you'd decide. She said the girl's planted firmly in the human world, while you"—he nodded at Perrin—"stand halfway between. Under the circumstances, I suppose we'd better go south with you. Otherwise, you'll probably starve to death, or get lost, or—"

Abruptly Burn stood up, and Elyas turned his head to regard the big wolf. After a moment Dapple rose, too. She moved closer to Elyas, so that she also was meeting Burn's stare. The tableau was frozen for long minutes, then Burn whirled and vanished into the night. Dapple shook herself, then resumed her place, flopping down as if nothing had happened.

Elyas met Perrin's questioning eyes. "Dapple runs this pack," he explained. "Some of the males could best her if they challenged, but she's smarter than any of them, and they all know it. She's saved the pack more than once. But Burn thinks the pack is wasting time with you three. Hating Trollocs is about all there is to him, and if there are Trollocs this far south he wants to be off killing them."

"We quite understand," Egwene said, sounding relieved. "We really can find our own way . . . with some directions, of course, if you'll give them."

Elyas waved a hand. "I said Dapple leads this pack, didn't I? In the morning, I'll start south with you, and so will they." Egwene looked as if that was not the best news she could have heard.

Perrin sat wrapped in his own silence. He could *feel* Burn leaving. And the scarred male was not the only one; a dozen others, all young males, loped after him. He wanted to believe it was all Elyas playing on his imagination, but he could not. Just before the departing wolves faded from his mind, he felt a thought he knew came from Burn, as sharp and clear as if it were his own thought. Hatred. Hatred and the taste of blood.

GLOSSARY

A NOTE ON DATES IN THIS GLOSSARY. The Toman Calendar (devised by Toma dur Ahmid) was adopted approximately two centuries after the death of the last male Aes Sedai, recording years After the Breaking of the World (AB). So many records were destroyed in the Trolloc Wars that at their end there was argument about the exact year under the old system. A new calendar, proposed by Tiam of Gazar, celebrated freedom from the Trolloc threat and recorded each year as a Free Year (FY). The Gazaran Calendar gained wide acceptance within twenty years after the Wars' end. Artur Hawkwing attempted to establish a new calendar based on the founding of his empire (FF, From the Founding), but only historians now refer to it. After the death and destruction of the War of the Hundred Years, a third calendar was devised by Uren din Jubai Soaring Gull, a scholar of the Sea Folk, and promulgated by the Panarch Farede of Tarabon. The Farede Calendar, dating from the arbitrarily decided end of the War of the Hundred Years and recording years of the New Era (NE), is currently in use.

Adan, Heran *(ay-DAN, HEH-ran):* Governor of Baerlon.
Aes Sedai *(EYEZ seh-DEYE):* Wielders of the One Power. Since the Time of Madness, all are women. Widely distrusted and feared, even hated. Blamed by many for the Breaking of the

World, and thought to meddle in the affairs of nations. At the same time, few rulers will be without an Aes Sedai advisor, even in lands where the existence of such a connection must be secret. Used as an honorific, so: Sheriam Sedai, and as a high honorific, so: Sheriam Aes Sedai.

Age Lace: *see* Pattern of an Age.

Age of Legends: The Age ended by the War of the Shadow and the Breaking of the World. A time when Aes Sedai performed wonders now only dreamed of. *See also* Wheel of Time.

Al Ellisande! *(ahl ehl-lih-SAHN-dah):* In the Old Tongue, "For the Rose of the Sun!

Aldieb *(ahl-DEEB):* In the Old Tongue, "West Wind," the wind that brings the spring rains.

al'Meara, Nynaeve *(ahl-MEER-ah, NIGH-neev):* The Wisdom of Emond's Field.

al'Thor, Rand *(ahl-THOR, RAND):* A young farmer and sheepherder from the Two Rivers.

al'Vere, Egwene *(ahl-VEER, eh-GWAIN):* Youngest daughter of the innkeeper in Emond's Field.

Amyrlin Seat *(AHM-ehr-lin):* (1) The title of the leader of the Aes Sedai. Elected for life by the Hall of the Tower, the highest council of the Aes Sedai, which consists of three representatives from each of the seven Ajahs. The Amyrlin Seat has, theoretically at least, almost supreme authority among the Aes Sedai. She ranks as the equal of a king or queen. (2) The throne upon which the leader of the Aes Sedai sits.

angreal *(ahn-gree-AHL):* A very rare object which allows anyone capable of channeling the One Power to handle a greater amount of the Power than would be safely possible unaided. Remnants of the Age of Legends, the means of their making is no longer known.

Aptarigine Cycle, the: a famous cycle of stories, which numbers in the hundreds, following the intrigues, loves and romances, both happy and doomed, that join and divide two dozen noble families over fifty generations. The stories of the *Aptarigine Cycle* are usually told by bards, and few gleemen know more than a handful of the stories.

Avendesora *(Ah-vehn-deh-SO-rah):* In the Old Tongue, "the Tree of Life." Mentioned in many stories and legends.

Aybara, Perrin *(ay-BAHR-ah, PEHR-rihn):* A young blacksmith's apprentice from Emond's Field.

Ba'alzamon *(bah-AHL-zah-mon):* In the Trolloc tongue, "Heart of the Dark." Believed to be the Trolloc name for the Dark One.

Baerlon *(BAYR-lon):* A city in Andor on the road from Caemlyn to the mines in the Mountains of Mist.

Barran, Doral *(BAHR-rahn, DOOR-ahl):* The Wisdom in Emond's Field prior to Nynaeve al'Meara.

Bel Tine *(BEHL TINE):* Spring festival in the Two Rivers.

biteme *(BITE-me):* A small, almost invisible biting insect. Its bite is very sharp, like the stab of a needle.

Breaking of the World, the: When Lews Therin Telamon and the Hundred Companions resealed the Dark One's prison, the counterstroke tainted *saidin.* Eventually every male Aes Sedai went horribly insane. In their madness these men, who could wield the One Power to a degree now unknown, changed the face of the earth. They caused great earthquakes, leveled mountain ranges, raised new mountains, lifted dry land where seas had been, made the ocean rush in where dry land had been. Many parts of the world were completely depopulated, and the survivors were scattered like dust on the wind. This destruction is remembered in stories, legends and history as the Breaking of the World. *See also* Hundred Companions, the.

Carai an Caldazar! *(cah-REYE ahn cahl-dah-ZAHR):* In the Old Tongue, "For the honor of the Red Eagle!" the ancient battle cry of Manetheren.

Carai an Ellisande!: In the Old Tongue, "For the honor of the Rose of the Sun!" The battlecry of the last king of Manetheren.

Cauthon, Matrim *(CAW-thon, MAT-rihm):* a young farmer from the Two Rivers.

channel: (1) (verb) To control the flow of the One Power. (2) (noun) The act of controlling the flow of the One Power.

Covenant of the Ten Nations: A union formed in the centuries after the Breaking of the World (circa 200 AB) which was dedicated to the defeat of the Dark One. The nations that made the Covenant were Jaramide, Aramaelle, Almoren, Aridhol, Safer, Manetheren, Coremanda, Essenia, Eharon, and

Aelgar. Few of the nations of the Covenant survived the Trolloc Wars, and none for long; all were replaced by new nations formed from the ruins of the old nations. *See* Trolloc Wars.

Dark One: Most common name, used in every land, for Shai'tan: the source of evil, antithesis of the Creator. Imprisoned by the Creator at the moment of Creation in a prison at Shayol Ghul; an attempt to free him from that prison brought about the War of the Shadow, the tainting of *saidin*, the Breaking of the World, and the end of the Age of Legends.

Dark One, naming the: Saying the true name of the Dark One (Shai'tan) draws his attention, inevitably bringing ill-fortune at best, disaster at worst. For that reason many euphemisms are used, among them the Dark One, Father of Lies, Sightblinder, Lord of the Grave, Shepherd of the Night, Heartsbane, Heartfang, Grassburner, and Leafblighter. Someone who seems to be inviting ill fortune is often said to be "naming the Dark One."

Darkfriends: Those who follow the Dark One and believe they will gain great power and rewards when he is freed from his prison. Some even believe he will reward them by making them live forever. For that, they are willing to commit any crime and to murder even members of their families. Darkfriends are organized in a number of highly secretive groups which cooperate with one another at times but also compete with one another for power. Among Darkfriends, only rank within the Darkfriends is important. A beggar who is a Darkfriend and gave the proper signs would expect to be obeyed even by a king who is a Darkfriend.

Domon, Bayle *(DOH-mon, BAIL):* The captain of the *Spray.*

Dragon, the: The name by which Lews Therin Telamon was known during the War of the Shadow. In the madness which overtook all male Aes Sedai, Lews Therin killed every living person who carried any of his blood, as well as everyone he loved, thus earning the name Kinslayer. A saying is now used, "taken by the Dragon," or "possessed of the Dragon," to indicate that someone is endangering those around him or threatening them, especially if without cause. *See also* Dragon Reborn.

Dragon, false: Occasionally men claim to be the Dragon Reborn, and sometimes one of them gains following enough to require an army to put it down. Some have begun wars that involved many nations. Over the centuries most have been men unable to channel the One Power, but a few could. All, however, either disappeared, or were captured or killed, without fulfilling any of the Prophecies concerning the Rebirth of the Dragon. These men are called false Dragons. *See also* Dragon Reborn.

Dragon Reborn: According to prophecy and legend the Dragon will be born again at mankind's greatest hour of need to save the world. This is not something people look forward to, both because the prophecies say the Dragon Reborn will bring a new Breaking to the world, and because Les Therin Kinslayer, the Dragon, is a name to make men shudder, even more than three thousand years after his death. *See also* Dragon, the; Dragon, false.

Dragon's Fang, the: A stylized mark, usually black, in the shape of a teardrop balanced on its point. Scrawled on the door of a house, it is an accusation of evil against the people inside.

Dragonwall, the: another name for the Spine of the World. *See also* Spine of the World, the.

Dreadlords: Those men and women who, able to channel the One Power, went over to the Shadow during the Trolloc Wars, acting as commanders of the Trolloc forces.

Eyeless, the: *See* Myrddraal.

Fade: *See* Myrddraal

Fain, Padan (FAIN, PAHD-ahn): A peddler who arrives in Emond's Field just before Winternight.

Farstrider, Jain (JAY-ihn): A hero of the northern lands who journeyed to many lands and had many adventures; the author of several books, as well as being the subject of books and stories. He vanished in 981 NE, after returning from a trip into the Great Blight which some say had taken him all the way to Shayol Ghul.

fist: The basic military unit of the Trollocs, varying in number; always more than one hundred, but never more than two hundred. A fist is usually, but not always, commanded by a Myrddraal.

Five Powers, the: There are threads to the One Power, and each person who can channel the One Power can usually grasp some threads better than others. These threads are named according to the sorts of things that can be done using them —Earth, Air (sometimes called Wind), Fire, Water, and Spirit —and are called the Five Powers. Any wielder of the One Power will have a greater degree of strength with one, or possibly two, of these, and lesser strength in the others. Some few may have great strength with three, but since the Age of Legends no one has had great strength with all five. Even then this was extremely rare. The degree of strength can vary greatly between individuals, so that some who can channel are much stronger than others. Performing certain acts with the One Power requires ability in one of more of the Five Powers. For example, starting or controlling a fire requires Fire, and affecting the weather requires Air and Water, while Healing requires Water and Spirit. While Spirit was found equally in men and in women, great ability with Earth and/or Fire was found much more often among men, with Water and/or Air among women. There were exceptions, but it was so often so that Earth and Fire came to be regarded as male Powers, Air and Water as female. Generally, no ability is considered stronger than any other, though there is a saying among Aes Sedai: "There is no rock so strong that water and wind cannot wear it away, no fire so fierce that water cannot quench it or wind snuff it out." It should be noted this saying came into use long after the last male Aes Sedai was dead. Any equivalent saying among male Aes Sedai is long lost.

Foolday: a festival celebrated in the fall where people wear masks and play pranks, and everyone exchanges sweets and small pastries. Everyone's role is changed about, so that servants give orders and those whom the servants work for must themselves serve. The silliest and most foolish man and woman are crowned as King Fool and Queen Fool, and for that day everyone must do as they say.

Forsaken, the: Name given to thirteen of the most powerful Aes Sedai ever known, who went over to the Dark One during the War of the Shadow in return for the promise of immortality. According to both legend and fragmentary records, they were imprisoned along with the Dark One when his prison was resealed. Their names are still used to frighten children.

gentling: The act, performed by Aes Sedai, of shutting off a male who can channel from the One Power forever. This is necessary because any man who learns to channel will go insane from the taint upon *saidin* and will almost certainly do horrible things with the Power in his madness. A man who has been gentled can still sense the True Source, but he cannot touch it. Whatever madness has come before gentling is arrested by the act of gentling, but not cured by it, and if it is done soon enough death can be averted. Men who are gentled seldom want to live, though, and they seldom live long.

gleeman: A traveling storyteller, musician, juggler, tumbler and all-around entertainer. Known by their trademark cloaks of many-colored patches, they perform mainly in the villages and smaller towns, since larger towns and cities have other entertainments available.

Great Hunt of the Horn, the: A cycle of stories concerning the legendary search for the Horn of Valere, in the years between the end of the Trolloc Wars and the beginning of the War of the Hundred Years. If told in their entirety, the cycle would take many days.

Great Lord of the Dark: The name by which Darkfriends refer to the Dark One, claiming that to use his true name would be blasphemous.

Great Pattern, the: The Wheel of Time weaves the Patterns of the Ages into the Great Pattern, which is the whole of existence and reality, past, present and future. Also known as the Lace of Ages. *See also* Pattern of an Age; Wheel of Time.

Great Serpent: A symbol for time and eternity, believed to have been ancient before the Age of Legends began, consisting of a serpent eating its own tail. A gold finger-ring made in the form of the Great Serpent is the sign of a woman who has trained in the White Tower.

Halfman: *See* Myrddraal.

Hawkwing, Artur: A legendary king who united all the lands west of the Spine of the World. He even sent armies across the Aryth Ocean, but all contact with these was lost at his death, which set off the War of the Hundred Years. His sign was a golden hawk in flight. *See also* War of the Hundred Years.

Heartfang; Heartsbane: *See* Dark One.

Horn of Valere *(vah-LEER):* The legendary object of the Great Hunt of the Horn. The Horn supposedly can call back dead heroes from the grave to fight against the Shadow.

Hundred Companions, the: According to legend, the hundred male Aes Sedai, among the most powerful of the Age of Legends, who, led by Lews Therin Telamon, launched the final stroke that ended the War of the Shadow by sealing the Dark One back into his prison. The Dark One's counterstroke tainted *saidin*; the Hundred Companions went mad and began the Breaking of the World.

Illian *(IHL-lee-ahn):* A great port on the Sea of Storms, capital city of the nation of the same name. The sign of the nation of Illian is nine golden bees on a field of dark green.

Lace of Ages: *See* Great Pattern, the.

Lan; al'Lan Mandragoran *(AHL-LAN man-DRAG-or-an):* A warrior from the north; Moiraine's companion.

league: A measure of distance equal to four miles. *See also* mile.

Lurk *(LUHRK): See* Myrddraal.

Malkier *(mal-KEER):* A nation, once one of the Borderlands, now consumed by the Blight. The sign of Malkier was a golden crane in flight.

Mandarb *(MAHN-dahrb):* In the Old Tongue, "Blade."

Manetheren *(mahn-EHTH-ehr-ehn):* One of the Ten Nations that made the Second Covenant, and also the capital city of that nation. Both city and nation were utterly destroyed in the Trolloc Wars.

Maradon *(MAH-rah-don):* The capital city of Saldaea.

Merrilin, Thom *(MER-rih-lihn, TOM):* A gleeman who comes to Emond's Field to perform at Bel Tine.

mile: A measure of distance equal to one thousand spans. Four miles make one league. *See also* span.

Min *(MIN):* A young woman encountered at the Stag and Lion in Baerlon.

Moiraine *(mwah-RAIN):* A visitor to Emond's Field who arrives just before Winternight.

Mordeth *(MOOR-death):* Councilor who turned the city of Aridhol to use Darkfriends' ways against the Darkfriends, thus bringing its destruction, and earning it a new name, Shadar Logoth. Only one thing survives in Shadar Logoth beside the hate that killed it, and that is Mordeth himself, bound in the ruins for two thousand years, waiting for someone to come whose soul he can consume and so take on new flesh.

Myrddraal (MUHRD-draal): Creatures of the Dark One, commanders of the Trollocs. Twisted offspring of Trollocs in which the human stock used to create the Trollocs has resurfaced, but tainted by the evil that made the Trollocs. Physically they are like men except that they have no eyes, but can see like eagles in light or dark. They have certain powers stemming from the Dark One, including the ability to cause paralyzing fear with a look and the ability to vanish wherever there are shadows. One of their few known weaknesses is that they are reluctant to cross running water. In different lands they are known by many names, among them Halfmen, the Eyeless, Shadowman, Lurk and Fade.

One Power, the: The power drawn from the True Source. The vast majority of people are completely unable to learn to channel the One Power. A very small number can be taught to channel, and an even tinier number have the ability inborn. For these few there is no need to be taught; they will touch the True Source and channel the Power whether they want to or not, perhaps without even realizing what they are doing. This inborn ability usually manifests itself in late adolescence or early adulthood. If control is not taught, or self-learned (extremely difficult, with a success rate of only one in four), death is certain. Since the Time of Madness, no man has been able to channel the Power without eventually going completely, horribly mad; and then, even if he has learned some control, dying from a wasting sickness which causes the sufferer to rot alive, a sickness caused, as is the madness, by the Dark One's taint on *saidin*. For a woman the death that comes without control if the Power is less horrible, but it is death just the same. Aes Sedai search for girls with the inborn ability as much to save their lives as to increase Aes Sedai numbers, and for men with it in order to stop the terrible things they inevitably do with the Power in their madness. *See also* channel; Time of Madness; True Source.

Pattern of an Age: The Wheel of Time weaves the threads of human lives into the Pattern of an Age, which forms the substance of reality for that Age; also known as Age Lace.

saidar; saidin *(sah-ih-DAHR; sah-ih-DEEN): See* True Source.

Second Covenant: *See* Covenant of the Ten Nations.

Shadar Logoth *(SHAH-dahr LOH-goth):* In the Old Tongue, "the Place Where the Shadow Waits." A city abandoned and shunned since the Trolloc Wars. Also called "Shadow's Waiting."

Shadowman: *See* Myrddraal.

Shai'tan *(SHAH-ih-TAN): See* Dark One.

Shepherd of the Night: *See* Dark One.

Sightburner: *See* Dark One.

Span: A measure of distance equal to two paces. A thousand spans make a mile.

Spine of the World, the: A towering mountain range, with only a few passes, which separates the Aiel Waste from the lands to the west. Also called the Dragonwall.

Sunday: A feast day and festival in midsummer, widely celebrated.

tabac *(tah-BAHK):* A noxious weed, widely cultivated. The leaves of it, when dried and cured, are burned in wooden holders called *pipes*, the fumes being inhaled. A nasty habit.

Ta'maral'ailen *(tah-MAHR-ahl-EYE-lehn):* in the Old Tongue, "Web of Destiny."

Tanreall, Artur Paendrag *(tahn-REE-ahl, AHR-tuhr PAY-ehn-DRAG): See* Hawkwing, Artur.

Tar Valon *(TAHR VAH-lon):* A city on an island in the River Erinin. The center of Aes Sedai power, and location of the Amyrlin Seat.

Telamon, Lews Therin *(TEHL-ah-mon, LOOZ THEH-rihn): See* Dragon, the.

Thakan'dar *(thah-kahn-DAHR):* An eternally fog-shrouded valley below the slopes of Shayol Ghul.

Time of Madness: *See* Breaking of the World, the.

Trolloc Wars: A series of wars, beginning about 1000 AB and lasting more than three hundred years, during which Trolloc armies ravaged the world. Eventually the Trollocs were slain or driven back into the Great Blight, but some nations ceased to exist, while others were almost depopulated. All records of the time are fragmentary. *See also* Covenant of the Ten Nations.

Trollocs *(TRAHL-lohks):* Creatures of the Dark One, created during the War of the Shadow. Huge in stature, vicious in the extreme, they are a twisted blend of animal and human stock, and kill for the pure pleasure of killing. Sly, deceitful and treacherous, they can be trusted only by those they fear. They are omnivorous and will eat any kind of meat, including human flesh and the flesh of other Trollocs. Largely of human origin, they are able to interbreed with humankind, but the offspring are usually stillborn, and those which are not often fail to survive. They are divided into tribe-like bands, chief among them being the Ahf'frait, Al'ghol, Bhan'sheen, Dha'vol, Dhai'mon, Dhjin'nen, Ghar'ghael, Ghob'lhin, Gho'hlem, Ghraem'lan, Ko'bal and the Kno'mon.

True Source: The driving force of the universe, which turns the Wheel of Time. It is divided into a male half (*saidin*) and a female half (*saidar*), which work at the same time with and against each other. Only a man can draw on *saidin*, only a woman on *saidar*. Since the beginning of the Time of Madness, *saidin* has been tainted by the Dark One's touch. *See also* One Power.

Village Council: In most villages a group of men, elected by the townsmen and headed by a Mayor, who are responsible for making decisions which affect the village as a whole and for negotiating with the Councils of other villages over matters which affect the villages jointly. They are at odds with the Women's Circle in so many villages that this conflict is seen as almost traditional. *See also* Women's Circle.

War of the Hundred Years: A series of overlapping wars among constantly shifting alliances, precipitated by the death of Artur Hawkwing and the resulting struggle for his empire. It lasted from roughly FY 994 to FY 1117. The dates are uncertain. The war depopulated large parts of the lands between the Aryth Ocean and the Aiel Waste, from the Sea of Storms to the Great Blight. So great was the destruction that only fragmentary records of the time remain. The empire of Artur Hawkwing was pulled apart, and the nations of the present day were formed.

War of the Shadow: Also known as the War of Power, it ended the Age of Legends. It began shortly after the attempt to free the Dark One, and soon involved the whole world. In a world where even the memory of war had been forgotten, every facet of war was rediscovered, often twisted by the Dark One's touch on the World, and the One Power was used as a weapon. The war was ended by the resealing of the Dark One into his prison.

Warder: A warrior bonded to an Aes Sedai. The bonding is a thing of the One Power, and by it he gains such gifts as quick healing, the ability to go long periods without food, water or rest, and the ability to sense the taint of the Dark One at a distance. So long as a Warder lives, the Aes Sedai to whom he is bonded knows he is alive and in what direction from her he is however far away, and when he dies she will know the moment and manner of his death. The bond creates a certain awareness in both Aes Sedai and Warder of the physical and emotional condition of the other. While Most Ajahs believe an Aes Sedai may have one Warder bonded to her at a time, the Red Ajah refuses to bond any Warders at all, while the Green Ajah believes an Aes Sedai may bond as many Warders as she wishes. Ethically the Warder must accede to the bonding, but it has been known to be done involuntarily. What the Aes Sedai gain from the bonding is a closely-held secret. *See also* Aes Sedai.

Wheel of Time, the: Time is a wheel with seven spokes, each spoke an Age. As the Wheel turns, the Ages come and go, each leaving memories that fade to legend, then to myth, and are forgotten by the time that Age comes again. The Pattern of an Age is slightly different each time an Age comes, and each time it is subject to greater change, but each time it is the same Age.

White Tower: The palace of the Amyrlin Seat in Tar Valon.

Wisdom: In villages of Andor, a woman chosen by the Women's Circle to sit in the Circle for her knowledge of such things as healing and foretelling the weather, as well as for common good sense. Usually a position of great responsibility and authority, both actual and implied. She is generally considered the equal of the Mayor, and in some villages his superior, and almost always is considered the leader of the Women's Circle. Unlike the Mayor, she is chosen for life, and it is very rare for a Wisdom to be removed from office before her death. Almost traditionally in conflict with the Mayor, to the extent that such conflicts often appear in humorous stories. In lands other than Andor, Wisdoms are known by other names, such as Wise Woman or Adviser or Reader, but in one form or another, they exist everywhere. *See also* Women's Circle.

Women's Circle: In Andor, a group of women elected by the women of a village, responsible for deciding such matters as are considered solely women's responsibility (for example, when to plant the crops and when to harvest). Equal in authority to the Village council, with clearly delineated lines and areas of responsibility. Frequently at odds with the Village Council; this conflict is often at the heart of humorous stories. In lands other than Andor, the Women's Circle is often known by another name, such as the Ring or the Gathering, but in one form or another, they exist everywhere. *See also* Village Council.

Book Five: *The Fires of Heaven*

0-812-55030-7 • $7.99 ($9.99 CAN) / in hardcover: 0-312-85427-7 • $25.95 ($29.95 CAN)

"This volume, indeed the whole saga, surpasses all but a few of its peers." —*Booklist*

Book Six: *Lord of Chaos*

0-812-51375-4 • $7.99 ($9.99 CAN) / in hardcover: 0-312-85428-5 • $27.95 ($39.95 CAN)

"A great read....Some surprising new developments....I can't recommend starting anywhere but at the beginning, but the volumes only get richer as they go along." —*Locus*

Book Seven: *A Crown of Swords*

0-812-55028-5 • $7.99 ($9.99 CAN) / in hardcover: 0-312-85767-5 • $27.95 ($34.95 CAN)

"Jordan's preeminent saga [has] remained remarkably rich....Will not disappoint." —*Booklist*

Book Eight: *The Path of Daggers*

0-812-55029-3 • $7.99 ($9.99 CAN) / in hardcover: 0-312-85769-1 • $27.95 ($38.95 CAN)

"For sheer imagination and storytelling skill . . . *The Wheel of Time* rivals Tolkien's *The Lord of the Rings*."
—*Publishers Weekly* (starred review)

Book Nine: *Winter's Heart*

0-812-57558-X • $7.99 ($9.99 CAN) / in hardcover: 0-312-86425-6 • $29.95 ($41.95 CAN)

"The plot continues to thicken and intrigue, as always, runs rampant." —*Booklist*

All these books are available in both hardcover and paperback. If you do not see them on display, ask your bookseller to order them for you.